# THIS BROKEN MEMORY

# THIS BROKEN MEMORY

## THE COLD AS IRON TRILOGY
### BOOK ONE

## KAYLA MCGRATH

This book includes content that may be disturbing to some readers, discretion is advised. Content includes graphic violence (blood, gore, body mutilation, decapitation, murder, death, child death), fire/arson, sexually explicit scenes, vague mentions of sexual assault, and mild substance abuse (alcohol). Content will shift to slightly darker themes throughout the trilogy, future warnings will be outlined in each installment.

*To Michael, for believing in me and supporting me, even
when I couldn't.*

# CHAPTER

1

There are monsters in the north and one is dead at my feet.

I didn't kill it. I'm not sure I'm capable but given the circumstances and opportunity I would. I absolutely would. The iridescent wings allow a false sense of whimsy, but I know their jagged edges are a more reliable indicator of their nature. What I know is that they hunt for pleasure, and they kill for more.

Whatever got to this one was no gentle beast, rounds of torment haunt this corpse, varying levels of healing wounds scatter its form. Missing nails and teeth, gashes in delicate flesh, burns upon limbs. Its face is a ruin, its eyes flat and white. It's as if it were tortured.

This is the second one I've found.

It had been only three days ago and I'd mistaken the last one for human. It was after a closer look I noticed its pupils were cat eye slits and patches of its skin were lilac-scaled, glimmering in the catching light like a fish.

With a start, I notice the soundlessness of the air. There's the easy quiet of almost silence—of breath and birdsong—and then there's the eerie silence before their arrival. It twists up and out, blanketing the world beneath a heavy cloak, as if even the river cowers in its bed.

I pause in my investigating, listening. Springy boughs of the evergreens above sway in the wind, whistling through. The permafrost layering the vast Yukon muffles sound and bites into my knees through the leather, nipping into my toes. My eyes survey the silvery sky, noting the likelihood of snow on the horizon—another sound dampener. Snow, in this northernmost hell can be the difference between life and death. It's the difference between exposure from the elements and exposure to them.

Dread sinks low in my gut, an oppressive haze of malicious sick. The foul aura scrapes at the edges of my consciousness, the malevolent presence closing in. Dark. Wrong. Sinister. Deadly.

Finally, there's a definitive rustle and I'm on my feet, alert.

It isn't one of them, but they're coming.

Palming a blade I'd stolen years ago, I shoulder my backpack encumbered by venison and a strapped compound bow, and begin hastily backing up. Keeping my eyes trained upon the direction of the sound, I feel behind me for the rough bark of a climbable tree, sweat beading upon my brow. Through the thicket and beyond the bushes, the sharp, steady crunch of twigs sets my fight or flight alive.

A creature launches forth from the woods and my heart lunges in my chest. I curse and stumble, realizing with an exhalation that the beast is not a bear with salivating black jaws or worse, but a terrified deer. It's hardly a blink before it's gone. Fear-induced adrenaline sets my heart thundering only for reality to strike it still. The stag is scared, and the apex predator it's outrunning is drawing straight for me.

I turn and climb. Despite the plenty of handholds I claw into, I do not find myself grateful. My hitched breathing is marred by frequent swearing as I haul myself and my bag up the tree, each branch becoming more and more precarious. It's when a rotted branch snaps, where I slip down the trunk, that my mortality hits me. A fall will kill me just as easily as they can.

The bark rips into my palms as I scrabble and gasp, but with bleeding fingers I manage a last reach and find myself blessedly on a sturdy branch. My feet are supple and sure upon the last couple limbs, the final ascension to moderate safety. Seconds later I lean back against the evergreen, chest heaving and sweat burning my eyes. Gazing down through the needles, I spot the dead monster below—which might be a shining beacon on my location. I pray that they pass me over, that they stumble across the body without searching for foul play. Or even, that they find a new thrill before that ominous and ever creeping presence discovers me.

I pray it goes away.

I breathe.

The sickness crawls over me, telling me that they're here, and then there's a vibrant spot of color in the clearing. I clasp a bloody hand over my mouth, knowing exactly what the bright bit of blue and ill sensation means.

*Them.*

White flesh melds with a shock of cobalt blue scales upon forearms to razor-tipped claws that spread down forelegs into the talons of a dragon. It's humanoid, with a beautiful face and midnight eyes. Long silver hair flows like a banner, a crown of antlers settling on its brow. It is garbed in little more than a draped sheet, dingy and dirty but once white.

Unsheathing the blade I'd managed to wedge into my boot during the climb, I grip it in a fist like a talisman and hold my breath. My heart crashes in its cage, frantic as a bird.

The creatures have a wicked presence about them. It is an aura, penetrating like smoke and darkness, a sticky haze that becomes progressively more oppressive until you feel as if you'll never take a breath again. I've had this sixth sense of detection as far back as I can remember. Ever since I became trapped in this wasteland and waking without a flicker of memories.

I watch in horror as the creature stands next to the slain beast. The monster stops and ponders, prodding the corpse with a toe. A second figure, small horns coiling from its brow, a lion-like tail swishing from the base of its spine, steps from the shadows uttering a chiming, masculine chuckle, while the first lets out a snort of disdain. As nausea threatens to lodge in my throat, the horned-and-tailed figure hauls off the butchered thing without a word. I hold my breath, an anxiety-riddled scream threatening to burst as they depart, moving with animal grace and the surety of being completely unrivalled.

I wait, watching the evening light fade fast and burn into the deep purple of night. I wait, clutching the knife. I wait longer than I must. I wait until the anxiety quells and my heart slows to a natural rhythm.

When I eventually deem it safe to descend, I wince from my stiff neck and aching muscles. Rubbing my pains away, I search the vicinity, probing with that innate sense and finding no creatures roaming or lingering.

Returning my weapon to my boot, I clamber down from the tree, stewing in resentment. Try as I might, I cannot escape the forest. I have no long-term means to defend myself and I have little to show for my extended survival here. I don't even know who I am. I have no idea where I'm supposed to be or what to do. Was I truly the only survivor of the crash with Jacob? I've only been able to bring myself to venture that way once, unable to stomach the massacre that Jacob had painted before me. I've never investigated for evidence of survivors, but the frenetic energy of the creatures surrounding the site has been enough to keep me at bay.

Halfway down the tree an explosion rings out and I jump in surprise, nearly plummeting the remaining distance. Far to the east is a large fire, orange and yellow flames licking up the sides of something considerable, smoke pluming into the air aggressively like a locomotive train. It isn't so unusual for the monsters to create unnecessary destruction.

Exhausted from day's events, I drop the remaining feet and pull out a small flashlight, anxious to navigate the long stretch of forest to my cabin. My home base used to be a cabin for a well-off—if not particularly wealthy—family, but aside from my stay, has remained vacant. The building is entirely self-sufficient with solar panels, generators, personal well, and every system required to manage a household. There's a semblance of safety to it, a presence of protection in addition to its natural warmth. There's something about the place that naturally deters the monsters—something about it so repellent that they refuse to come near.

Within hours the sky permeates into solid ebony—midnight—and only the thin beam of my light cuts the dark. It's when I find myself at home, I can breathe a sigh of relief.

The cabin stands sturdy and grand, from the preciously chosen logs, to the immaculately maintained tin roof. It welcomes me with a solid door made from cedar and iron, its black shutters hammered into the same metal that flank the windows. The structure spans an acceptable two floors, boasting a single furnished bedroom and another smaller bedroom, sans mattress, as well as a lavish but entirely unused study. The slate steps leading up to the porch before the front door are comfortably worn with age and unknown footsteps.

I know this place's secrets like an old friend. I know that the shutters on the bathroom window have rusted out and now rattle in the wind, that the second step on the inside staircase creaks, and that the kettle on the kitchen stove has a heart-shaped dent in the bottom edge.

As I begin up the stone path, watching my feet on the uneven pavers, a sense of something wrong bleeds into my awareness. I pause. It isn't them, but I take in the home. It takes exactly seven seconds before I realize.

The lights are on and smoke is curling out of the chimney.

# CHAPTER

## 2

I instantly draw my bow, yanking back the string and loading an arrow before I burst into the home without a second thought. My bloodied hands sting upon the weapon, but I ignore the pain; use it to fuel me. As soon as I break through the threshold, I'm met with a wash of heat and golden light upon the wool rug and dancing off the polished entry table. I dare not lower my arrow as I kick the door closed behind me and proceed to enter further. Anxiety hums a stately alarm, keeping me hyper-aware. I take a left into the living room to find the fire in the hearth glowing strong, and stained glass lamps cutting out shadows with their jewel-toned brilliance on the two side tables.

Where a pair of sunglasses I've never seen before lay.

Upon the brown leather sofa, its back facing me, a figure lies across the cushions. I step carefully as to avoid one of the creaky floorboards, and manage to find myself in front of the couch, looking down on what I've discovered is someone distinctly human. Someone male. Shock alights my bones as I meet the first person I've seen since Jacob's death.

He's East Asian and in his late twenties or early thirties. His hair is rich and dark, and his skin is a smooth, caramel hue. He has visible shadows cast upon his high cheekbones from long lashes, and in unconsciousness there is a vulnerable frown pulling on his full lips and softening his brow. Sleeping, the man inhales serenely and I watch his bare, sculpted chest rise and fall with an open book on his abdomen. There's something familiar about him, something about his face—have I seen him before? Do I know him from my life when I remembered? Regardless of that, I can't help but note how breathtakingly handsome he is, and a thrill goes through me at that realization.

I blink in surprise as lustful thoughts invade my mind, and I berate myself for noticing anything other than the fact that there's a stranger in my sanctuary.

Clearing my mind, I aim my weapon and obnoxiously clear my throat.

His almond-shaped eyes spring open and their stunning amber shade startles me. As he takes me in, he leaps to a standing position. In his waking hours he appears much less innocent and much more like someone you might easily take to bed.

"What the hell? Who are you?"

"Evelyn," I introduce dismissively, "what are you doing here?" I ask coolly, keeping my bow trained on his chest—exactly where his heart lies.

"Whoa! Okay hang on a moment," he begins gently, brandishing his palms. "This is my family's hunting cabin; I came here to get inspiration."

"Why have you never been here before?"

"My dad had a stroke five years ago and since then he hasn't been able to hunt, but he couldn't bring himself to sell it. So, it sat." He pauses. "Evidently, it didn't sit unused."

"I didn't have much choice," I allow, lowering the bow infinitesimally. I only do so because I realize why he was familiar; he matches the boy in the broken photo frame on the mantle—albeit much older now—the glass spider-webbing across what would be his father's face. A flash of disappointment courses through me.

"No judgement," he whispers, eyes still wary, hands still raised.

"How did you even get here?"

"I drove so far on the road then hiked the rest, why?"

I let out an oath and toss my bow—technically his bow—and the backpack onto the floor beside us. He raises a brow and lowers his hands, watching me carefully as I cast my coat aside.

That road—which is truly a poor excuse of one, and should really be called a trail—is patrolled by those creatures at all times. Two years ago, I'd discovered it and decided to travel the length of it to see if it would lead out. I never got to the end of it because I caught flashes of monstrous creatures and pings on my internal alarm at regular intervals. They won't let the humans out of this cage so it doesn't take a genius to figure out that the road is a death trap.

"They blew up your vehicle," I tell him, laughing defeatedly as I move to the liquor cabinet that I know is still well-stocked despite my years of heartily drinking. I select a bottle of scotch that I'd prepped earlier in a decanter and pour it straight, right into a crystal glass.

"Who? How do you know?" he asks, astonished, walking over to me and snatching the decanter from my hand. I debate stealing it back for a moment but then decide against it. I have my drink.

I laugh. "Why the monsters did. I saw the explosion." I pause and scrutinize his face. "And what is *your* name, anyway?"

"Gideon," he informs me, following me to the couch, carrying the decanter. I greatly dislike that he trails after me—it feels cagey. I dislike the fact more that it excites me.

"In simple terms, Gideon, you're stuck here."

Feigning coolness I lounge in the corner like a cat, languorous and outwardly unworried. I need a moment of mindlessness after my brush with the monsters. The creatures won't touch the cabin and he won't hurt me—unless I want him to. Even if I'm wrong, there is a knife in my boot.

I swirl my glass lazily, looking at him from beneath my dark lashes.

He swallows a mouthful straight from the decanter, sighing. "Well fuck me."

"I know, we're quite fucked. Not all is lost, though. You've stumbled into territory filled with monsters yes, but you're looking at your best chance of survival here." I take a swig from the crystal glass, indolently pondering his name and deciding it suits him.

"Am I to be your damsel, then?"

A smirk quirks my lips. "Damsel, Knight-in-Shining-Armor, Dragon-to-Slay…either way, whatever archetype, I think we can figure something out."

He appraises me skeptically, eyes roving up and down my slender frame and long legs. Delicate bones and muscles of steel. I watch him take me in and I watch the casual observation turn to liquid heat, lingering on my breasts and hips, on the curve of my knee and the slope of my shoulders. Feeling an unfamiliar surge of boldness, I slowly unzip my stolen vest. His eyes zero in as I shrug it off lightly, amber darkening as the apex of my thighs aches.

"I know I don't have wealth to bring to the table and I don't have much to show in the department of goods," I murmur, gesturing to my chest airily, more gray shirt than anything. I lean forward. "But what I can assure you is that I am *very* skilled in a *physical* fight." I wink at him to humor myself and watch his face flare scarlet from the tips of his ears to the broad width of his chest.

"I promise you I am also quite *skilled* and I bring a variety of scholarly knowledge myself. Maybe I could teach you a thing or two? Maybe *hands* on." His eyes wander me pointedly and I realize he's playing my game. Not only that, but his playful manner and reciprocation has coaxed that feeling in my core further.

"You've piqued my curiosity," I tell him, sipping my drink. "Continue."

He falters. "I have to be honest, I'm not sure what we're doing here. Are we actually making a plan or are you hitting on me?"

Like a bucket of ice my desire is doused and I sigh. "Don't worry," I laugh, knocking back the rest of my drink. My throat burns and my belly warms. "I'm more concerned about finally escaping this hellhole than entertaining sexual antics with someone I've just met."

Gideon purses his lips in amusement or frustration I can't tell and rests his elbows on his knees. I assess him critically. There's an off feeling about him, something irking me. He has a peculiar energy that I can't decipher. I can't fathom what it may be, or if I'm actually just imaging things from being alone for so long.

"Okay, what if I told you I already knew this was fae territory? Unseelie faerie territory to be exact."

I nearly drop my empty glass as Gideon reveals a question and statement all in one.

Recoiling from the revelation, I stare at him with eyes like saucers. "Faerie?" I demand, mulling the word and coming up with vague references to Celtic and Welsh mythos. I place the empty glass on the table in front of us to better hide the shake of my nerves.

"Yes, faeries. They are not the lovely, shy creatures of children's fantasy; they're bloodthirsty killers who will tear you to shreds. Killers who will rip a human apart with their bare hands and laugh while doing it. Creatures that can be immensely beautiful or hideous, even like nothing you've ever seen before. They're blessed with cruelty and immortality. Hindered only by their weakness for iron and their compulsion to the truth."

I close my eyes against the undeniable truth that Gideon bestows upon me. It makes sense. All of it. The tearing of shreds, the laughing, the exquisiteness, the wrongness, the malice. Jacob was a first-hand witness to all that Gideon has described before me. What also makes perfect sense is their aversion to iron. The cabin is chock full of iron, that's why they never come near it.

"And how would you know any of this?" I'm beyond denying his claims, I know they're true. I've seen them myself.

"My dad is an occult scholar, specializing in mythology, and a long time ago he stumbled too close to the truth and the Seelie Court intervened—they're considered the Light Court and govern in less hostile terms. They extended an invitation for him to be a sort of ambassador to protect their world from ours. Anyhow, there's an infamous missing person's case and potential murder investigation that is leading straight to the Unseelie Court—also known as the Dark Court—as a prime suspect. If evidence can properly lay blame on the Unseelies it could lead to a war between the courts," he tells me, taking my empty glass and filling it with the decanter.

I allow him a moment as I take a drink to calm my nerves. I want to call him a liar but I know that's just denial. Even more so, there is something so frank and genuine about him that begs me to trust him.

"I thought you came here for inspiration?" I accuse, narrowing my gaze.

"And what better sort than what the fae can provide?"

I can't decide if he's ignorant or stupid or playing me.

Pondering back, I clarify his story. "So, a murder you say? And which of their many victims was lucky enough to attract your interest?" I use a coy tone to hide my worries. During my prison sentence here, I've come upon three humans. Three corpses—five if the mutilated faeries count.

Shredded and torn apart.

Stabbed by briars and antlers.

Swollen, black lips from poisoning.

It should be a joke that I'd never figured out the monsters were faeries in the first place. Many of them had *wings* for fuck's sake.

"The Harbinger," Gideon informs me, tapping his fingers on his chin, drawing me back to my body. "They say he's been missing for a while, and now sources are coming forward with details because someone decided to start interrogating and killing the fae. All of them Unseelie. I want to know why."

Were the deceased faeries I'd discovered results of this someone's investigation? I decide not to mention it and instead question down a different avenue.

"Who's the Harbinger?"

"The Seelie Queen's personal guard and her most trusted advisor. Allegedly, he is the most lethal of the fae to exist and not a soul has crossed him and lived. He's absolutely unbeatable in combat and has killed hundreds of his queen's enemies." Gideon's words are smooth, almost conditioned, but I can't quite tell if that is skepticism in his jeweled eyes.

"And where do you come into this picture?" I question, pulling myself into a standing position of authority. He's a human, how can he compare to faeries? He already puzzles me.

"Can't a guy have some secrets?" He feigns hurt and I brush it off, turning my back to him as I collect my thoughts.

A man whom radiates peculiar energy, teases, and bears knowledge of the fae while being holed up in the only sanctuary in the bloody territory is either recipe for disaster of my life or my heart.

Motherfucker.

I waltz around the room hiding my trepidation, surveying my new living companion with an air of incredulity. The banked fire behind my back is overly warm, heating the living space to sweltering degrees. I kick off my boots carelessly and toss my gray over-shirt onto the spot I've recently vacated. Truthfully, the lesser clothing is as equally because of the heat as much as for an unfamiliar reaction to

Gideon. It's unsettling, but I quell the unease and tilt my chin up.

One of Gideon's dark brows quirks as he also watches me. "I see you have a bad habit of stripping in front of me, is this some show of dominance?" His voice takes on a deep tone that strikes a nerve.

"I see you have a bad habit of deflecting with teasing." I cock my head, allowing my long, pale hair to fall from my bare shoulders. "But it doesn't hurt to make our situations fair from here," I tell him, plucking at the straps of the top I wear, thanking the racerback for a very bare shoulder I trail my fingers down. "Does it bother you?" I smile mischievously, ignoring my irregularly beating heart.

"Or, you're just trying to fluster me," he counters, easily avoiding my question and clearly displayed chest. "Hoping I'll reveal something I don't mean? I hate to disappoint you, but I truly don't have any relevant secrets for you."

"Touché," I agree, realizing that I'm losing ground. "But let's make this clear." I slam my palms down on the coffee table in front of him and I'm pissed that he doesn't startle. "I don't give a shit about who owns this place, I make the rules and you are not to disobey them. Otherwise, I'm shooting an arrow straight through your skull and not thinking twice about it."

Internally, I flinch at my own words, the savage nature of it flickering familiarly, but not enough to grasp. The thought is fleeting, distorted as if beneath a wave. Disbelief floods my nerves and the intangible memory sinks away from my focus.

"Duly noted," Gideon accepts, knocking me back into the matter at hand and pulling on his discarded tee shirt. Despite the fact that he refused me, his eyes traitorously admire the swell of my breasts. He shakes his head and averts his gaze before he meets my storm-gray ones with some evident strain. "But may I just say that I doubt you've actually killed anyone."

I hide my insecurity with a giggle. "Oh, don't be so sure, I have my secrets too, Gideon." I instantly regret using his name as the sound rolls off my tongue pleasantly. The effect jolts me and heats an anger in my chest.

"So, how do you suggest we escape here?" Gideon poses, gesturing around the room. "It doesn't look like you've made much progress."

My lip curls in irritation. He has no idea what I've suffered here these last two years, and such knowledge is none of his business. "I've been told south of here is a Canadian province free of these faeries, starting there would be a good bet."

"Well, you're not exactly wrong. British Columbia borders the Yukon, though we're fairly deep north." His eyes suddenly light in surprise. "How'd you end up here anyhow?"

Suddenly nervous, I rub my upper arms and turn my face away angrily. "Plane crash," I mutter darkly.

He arches a dark brow, discreetly eyeing me up. "When?"

I realize then that I want to relent, to tell *someone* the truth. It's an immediate hypocrisy to my prior thoughts. "Two years ago." Regret swells and I bite it off. "But that's not what we need to talk about." My dismissal is nonchalant as I wave a hand, but Gideon nearly staggers from my revelation. "What bright ideas do *you* have to get us out of here?"

"You what?" I wave him off and he continues in a different direction after a moment. "I was hoping to find the Harbinger. The Seelie Queen promises anything you can desire for his safe return. I initially thought to come here and kill two birds with one stone, that maybe I could help my dad and find,

I don't know a magical cure for his stroke. But I think our escape has become much more pressing."

*Anything you can desire.* Could that include my memory loss? Is there a way for the Seelie Queen to restore my memories? A pang of fear and a spike of excitement flare within me, what if I could return to who I am? To who I was before this nightmare?

"Find the Harbinger," I repeat, now intrigued. I could have a stake in this. "This legendary, unbeatable warrior. You plan to capture him?" My voice is high with disbelief.

He shrugs. "Or earn his trust. Whatever it takes."

The idea is ludicrous, but I decide to cross that bridge when we get to it. Finding him is the first hurdle. What I can't help but fear is, what if the Harbinger is the one hunting down and killing the fae? What is stopping him from doing to us what he did to them?

"You mentioned the Unseelie Court being a prime suspect, are they offering a reward for him too?" I ask, wondering at what could be an advantage. Perhaps the other queen can offer the same thing I am searching for. Myself.

"The Unseelie Queen is offering a prestigious position in her court and a bounty of wealth. Everything from riches, people, wine, jewels, luxury, anything of materialistic quality she can buy," Gideon informs me, leaning back against the couch and I find my eyes traitorously watching the muscles of his abdomen flex with the movement through his white shirt.

I forcibly tear my gaze away, taking a swig of my refilled glass, gritting my teeth at the potency. Materialism doesn't feel helpful. "I didn't think people were considered material."

"To most of the fae, humans are simply fodder. So, to them, yes, we are material," Gideon proclaims wretchedly, running a hand through his wavy hair. "Not to mention capitalism in all its forms."

I had lamented earlier about my loneliness so it seems the universe has taken pity on me and blessed me with this mysterious stranger. A stranger that my survival and escape of the Yukon now rely on as a best hope.

"Oh, irony, you sweet bitch," I mutter distastefully to myself, knocking back the rest of my drink. Gideon shoots me a confused look, drawing his brows together in a scowl. "Does anyone know you're here?"

Gideon hesitates. "No."

Stupid man, who doesn't let anyone know when they take a trip?

"There's only one room, care to share?" I inquire suggestively, slowly licking the bottom of my teeth. An internal war wages inside me, equal parts pleading and begging two very different things. One stark and plain for his refusal, the other a velvety darkness crooning for him to accept.

"I'll take the couch," Gideon decides, refusing the invitation outright.

A surge of relief and dejection rips through me.

Pushing out my full bottom lip, I give Gideon an exaggerated pout. "Pity."

"Get some sleep," he sighs, grabbing a blanket off the back of the couch. "We have a big day ahead of us tomorrow."

Taking the hint and the note of finality in his tone, I extricate myself from our tension plagued conversation and deposit the deer meat that I'd hunted earlier into the freezer—powered via an expensive generator and many solar panels.

Upon opening the freezer, I discover that Gideon didn't come to the Yukon unprepared and the once scarce container is now nearly overflowing with goods. My eyes light up at the sight, imagining a winter, if we're still here, where I won't have to ration and hunt at every slim opportunity. A time where I can gorge myself on carrots and green-beans glazed in garlic butter, or a salmon roasted with lemon and thyme.

A swell of emotions catches in my throat and I slam it down with the lid of the freezer, delighting in the sound that makes Gideon jump.

Taking my leave to the single bedroom upstairs, I gather my clothes from the couch and leave every door open, discarding articles of clothing as I go. Stripping down to nothing, I crawl into the king-sized bed dressed in a down duvet, cotton sheets and a heavy quilt.

Grudgingly, I internally thank Gideon for lighting a fire and saving me from the chore of doing so while I search for slumber. As sleep captures me in its embrace of night terrors, whispered nothings and sweet lies, I realize for the first time that it's promising a better tomorrow.

# CHAPTER

## 3

*TWO YEARS AGO*

Everything is a haze.

Smoke, thick and suffocating masks my vision as flames devour the tree line and lay waste to the world. The acrid scent torrents down my throat, clawing its way through my lungs as I lie face-down on the ground, coming to consciousness. My back screams in agony with every wracking cough as a muffled voice urges at me, insistent and detached.

With measurable concentration and bleary eyes, I push up from the earth and gasp. Pain lances my spine and blood streams onto the forest floor. I manage to get myself to my hands and knees, grinding my teeth to keep from crying out. Stars rattle and nausea swims with my movements, threatening to upheave the contents of my stomach.

The once muffled voice is now shrieking as I come up onto my knees, pushing from the one foot I've managed to plant on the earth. A violent grip on my bicep latches on, and suddenly I'm met with the face of a man screaming at me. With absolute terror searing his eyes, he drags me upright in the middle of a forest fire.

"Evelyn, get up we have to go!" he yells, yanking my disjointed body along with him.

I choke and splutter, my muscles crying out in protest. The back of my shirt is soaked with a heavy mixture of sweat and blood, while my light hair hangs tangled around my face, stained scarlet. My ears ring and my mind moves sluggishly as I realize that I surely have a concussion.

Sparks rain down, casting us into an orange glow, while trees groan as we avoid falling branches. Black night drowns our voices in its void, our escape lit by Hell itself. Roots and rocks reach up to trip us, flaming shrubbery grasps with fingers and tongues to stroke and taste.

"Who are you?" I cough, clutching my throat with fingers slippery with more red.

The man looks at me with confusion, still dragging me along, away from the hypnotic embers twirling behind us. Moments pass, that expression still plastered upon his features until he finally responds.

"I'm your brother, Jacob," he responds with a raspy breath, his blue eyes fevered by fear.

The world spins and falls as I begin to fold, tripping over my own two feet. Dizziness surges and I forcibly fight back bile. A few involuntary words escape me as the blackness descends on me, extinguishing the fires from my vision.

A palm-cracking slap burns across my cheek and my eyes fly wide at the contact.

"You don't *know*? You don't know *what*?" Jacob demands angrily, shaking me viciously.

"Anything," I whisper, my voice dry as sandpaper. I grit my teeth, fighting my weakness and lack of memory. A memory of nothing. I don't know anything. Nothing personal, nothing associated with my history, nothing indicating my sense of self. Who am I? Jacob said a name—Evelyn—which must be mine, but what else?

There's nothing. A gaping, black hole of nothing.

"You're Evelyn, you're twenty-one. I'm your brother, we were in a plane crash with our parents and we're the only survivors. There's shrapnel all in your back, there are *things* after us, and we need to *go!*" he screeches at me, breaking through the film on my mind.

Gathering everything that I am now, I pull myself together. I ignore my wounds, forcing away the mist on my mind. I imagine that the sickness isn't taking over, and stagger on my feet, supported by Jacob. We take off as fast as my injuries will withstand while the cloying scent of smoke disappears behind us. The woods become progressively darker, the boughs more oppressive under the towering trees and lush foliage. The sparks no longer filtering down upon us, the fire burning itself out on wet woods.

After what could be hours of running, I finally collapse against a tree, believing myself to be on death's door, submitting myself to the cosmic abyss of whatever becomes of a person after life. Jacob's yelling fails to make sense, instead its fuzzy as if underwater. I begin to slip until another scorching slap lands on my cheek. Anger flares with my newfound awareness.

"You need to stay awake, you hit your head and you probably have a concussion," Jacob snaps, brows furrowed. "Let me see your back."

A small rebellious part of me wants to refuse, to be defiant and deny his demand. But fear of another blow cows me into submission and I begin to wonder if he'd always been such a hostile sibling. Though I don't doubt the possibility of it being the product of a survival dependent environment that brings out his less than favorable qualities.

Painstakingly, I turn and allow my brother to see the damage that the plane crash has inflicted. He sucks in a harsh breath and I catch an array of emotions wheel across his face.

"That bad?" I whisper, carefully quirking a brow.

He grimaces. "I need to remove the shrapnel and bandage you up," he tells me as he searches the small clearing. "There," he says, pointing to a fallen log. "I need you to lay down on that."

Refusal tempts me but grudgingly, I do as he says and I'm startled to find the wood damp with dew. When I lay, true fear skitters through my veins while he hands me a branch, telling me that it's a bit for me to bite down on. A cold sweat breaks out across my dirty flesh and denial washes through me. With no words of mercy, he sets to work upon my shredded flesh. The first pull of the foreign material elicits white-hot, branding pain and for a moment I believe it has killed me. I gasp and whimper as each piece is dragged from my back, cursing the sound of metal clinking against plastic on an ever-growing pile. Sweat leaks down my face as I hiss against the branch.

An eternity of torment where I'm forever soaked through with various liquids later, Jacob pulls out a singed first aid kit. Retrieving a bagged roll of gauze and alcohol, he begins sanitization prep. But fortuitously, before he can touch me, the relief of sleep, sweet and torturous finally graces me. Jacob doesn't get the chance to slap me again because I fall to peace beneath Lady Fate's hand.

Hours later, still deep into the night, I wake to a small campfire and Jacob crouched before it. He's considerably older than I, perhaps a decade or so and already a man grown. Distantly, I wonder about what our parents thought about that age gap. Was I an accident? Was he? Were we both planned? A pang beats in my chest over the fact that I have no idea. That I can't even recall them to miss them. Can't cry because there is no pain. There's no memory to associate with the loss. I'm just confused.

Slowly, I get my bearings, adjusting to the tight bands across my torso. Jacob's gaze flickers over and I meet his eyes, finding a desolation there that I'd not expected. He pokes the crackling fire with a stick and a shower of sparks shoot upward like a majestic bloom in the ebony sky. Elbows on his knees, he appraises me with those blue eyes, eyes that remind me of the sea, despite sincerely lacking a personal memory of one.

Jacob runs a hand through his short brown hair, small specks of blood freckling his wrist. "There are *things* in these woods, Evelyn. Monstrous things," he breathes, haunted eyes trained on the embers. "Things that will kill us. I saw them. I saw them kill people."

"What? What do they look like? What are we going to do?" I ask timidly, fear lacing my words. I try to appear strong, perching on the edge of my log, but anxiety thrums a vicious beat.

The air is cold and nips at my exposed skin, an ironic accompaniment to the desperate atmosphere that Jacob is projecting. He stabs the stick into the flames again, a spurt of sparks dance into the ether.

"I don't know. They all look different. I just know that we're not safe." Leaning forward, the flames shadow his face starkly, cutting angular planes in his face out of a soft jawline and high cheekbones. "But we'll figure out a plan."

"Where are we?" I inquire, searching the framing woods around us. The sights are unfathomably black and silent. Around us, not even a bird sings or a rodent chitters.

Jacob shrugs, a nervousness to the gesture. "If I'd have to guess?"

"I'll accept speculation."

"Probably in one of the northern territories of Canada."

I freeze, realizing the legitimate dangers of not getting out of here. Of escaping this wilderness. The cold, sub-zero temperatures, exposure, dehydration, starvation, infection, illness.

A distinct snap in the woods east of us sounds and Jacob springs to his feet. He clutches the charred stick so tightly his knuckles surely turn white and his posture shoots rigid. With his other hand, he ushers me behind him. A sense of wrongness washes over me and my heart thumps unevenly with the first trills of panic.

"Stay back and if I say run, you goddamn run," he whispers quickly and fervently, his expression hardening as he flickers about our little clearing.

From the east, directly where the snap was heard appears a creature, a woman like I've never seen before. Her orange-amber eyes are luminous in the firelight, framed by lashes of white petals. She is unblinking as she focuses on Jacob. A pair of moth-like wings extend behind her and brilliant copper hair cascades over her breasts, breaking over her pointed ears. Her complexion is fair and beautiful, yet *wrong*. As if perpetually gilded by an artist's hand. She smiles with lips painted hazelnut brown, but it doesn't reach her eyes as a second figure steps forward.

This one is several inches taller than the woman who is already nearing a good six feet. It—because its features are entirely androgynous and inhuman—appears to nearly float over the ground while the woman moves quick and stuttering, almost in an insectile fashion. Its face is long and narrow, hair dark as ink falls straight over its shoulders with eyes, a void of black that bury themselves beneath an arched brow. In its fingers is a snapped twig that twirls over the top of its periwinkle knuckles.

"You have something quite dear to us," the moth-like one murmurs, her voice gentle and smooth as velvet. "And you are unfortunate enough to become trapped within our land, many weeks journey to what would be a southern haven."

Jacob nudges me back with a bit more strength.

"Yes," the blue-skinned, androgynous one agrees in a cool voice that leads to no hints to gender identity. It smiles, several of its teeth ending in translucent points.

"I must say," the woman begins, "you were quite the easy find, what with you thrashing those sparks in the sky—it was as if you were beckoning us..." She smiles again and although there is nothing inhuman about her teeth, there is raw malice there.

Jacob meets my eyes quickly and I can see the meaning behind them. He mouths one word to me:

*Run.*

I don't hesitate.

Snatching up the bag that Jacob had packed for me, I sprint away from our camp to the west. I'm blindingly crashing through the bushes and ignoring the abrasions of the pack against my bandaged wounds with a single thought in mind. *Escape.* Behind me, an attack instantly breaks out and I hear a scream I know is Jacob's. A sinister giggle ensues from there and then I stop listening to everything.

Bracken rips at my exposed arms and tears through my thin tee shirt as I leap over roots and fallen trees. Yet I still run. My back cries out as my ruin of flesh weeps again. Yet I still push on. My breath is ragged and laborious. Yet I don't stop.

The night is dark, but I don't care, all I care about is escape. I'm panting from the exertion and injuries I've sustained, pushing past my breaking point. I ignore the foolish urge to look over my shoulder and instead race on. I leap, and on that one careless motion my boot snags on the branch of an old log and I fly forward, crashing onto my forearms into squelching mud stinking of old leaves. The impact jars me and I fight against the surge of agony rocketing up my spine. Nausea from the concussion and pain surges up my throat.

Biting my lip to keep silent, I gather myself up behind the log and breathe in through my nose when I hear a soul-stripping scream. *Jacob.* It sounds again and I shudder at the noise. My heart constricts as I batter away at prickly ferns around me and burrow into the hollow log. Burying my terror deep within me, I pray that no wild creatures have claimed this rotting corpse of a tree as their home.

Horror claws up my throat. It's my fault and I don't even regret my decision. I only did as I was told and I don't remember loving him, so the worst part is that it doesn't hurt me. All I feel is guilt *because* I don't feel anything but distant remorse. This guilt boils inside me like some sickly poison, racing to my heart and staining it black, dyeing my insides the insidious color of evil. Everything twists inside me, clamoring with hatred and fear, spiraling wholly out of control. It becomes too much as it drags its talons through my heart and I make a split-second decision.

I steel myself and seal everything off completely. My priority is survival and survival only. I build an impenetrable wall around my emotional state, ignoring the wrongness of it and pull myself together. I disassociate so that I can exist.

An hour later, Jacob's final scream tears apart the night, the finality of the sound branded into my mind. The rasp from ruined vocal cords, the desperation of the noise, the abrupt ending of the note.

Nearby, a sense of unease works through my nerves. Holding my breath, a chittering laugh drifts overhead and the distinct sound of sucking assaults my ears. Peeking through a rotted knot, I find the two monsters taking a northern path. The androgynous one licks blood from its fingers, shuttering its eyes in pleasure. The moth-woman passes next, twirling in ecstasy on graceful toes as her wings tremble. They pass innocuously, untroubled by me and my hiding spot. I remain rooted, breath held, long after they disappear, and wait for the sound of their return.

But they never do.

Reaching out of the log, I push myself up and out of the mud, grab my bag and immediately set off to my former camp. The trip back is reckless and dangerous, but I persist, an innate sense of navigation leading me in the right direction. Trampling over my panic-traversed steps, I come upon the clearing with our once innocent campfire still crackling with embers.

Revulsion encompasses me as I discover Jacob. He's left by the fire, the skin from his arms and torso flayed, exposing sinew and muscle, and blood that pumps heedlessly into the already darkened earth. The soft, organic mess of pink and red and white sends my already upset stomach into somersaults. Viscera of that sort isn't supposed to be revealed to northern nights or sights like mine.

A broken sound threatens to escape me, but I squelch it as I make my way over to my brother, kneeling next to him. Blue eyes flicker open, heavy-lidded and glazed with anguish. A weak smile graces his lips, bloodied teeth revealed.

"Evelyn?"

"I'm here, Jacob."

"Of course, you're still alive," he rasps, his voice destroyed.

"You told me to run," I deadpan, imprisoning all my roiling emotions.

"I did, but I led you on a fool's errand." He drags in a labored breath and tries to chuckle, only releasing a flood of crimson. "No one gets out of here." A sardonic smile graces his torn lips, fading almost as soon as it arrives into existence.

I nearly question him, but without a further word, a sigh drags from his chest as the life drains from him. With parted lips and stark blue eyes staring vacantly, Jacob escapes this hellhole of monsters, leaving me utterly alone.

# CHAPTER

4

"You never quit, do you?" Gideon accuses, leaning against the doorframe of the master bedroom as I leap into a set of burpees on the cedar plank floor.

Dropping to my hands into a plank position, I blink away the sweat dripping from my brow. "Seducing or surviving? Because you missed the former by an hour," I heave out as I launch to my feet and jump, mock reaching for the exposed beams of the twelve-foot ceilings. "I had that bed all to myself and not a scrap of clothing to be found." I grin, meeting his eyes as I come back down to position again.

Gideon tilts his head back, staring beseechingly at the skylight above him. "Lord, help me."

He's silent for a few moments, the only sounds being a mixture of my hands and feet hitting the hard-wood floor and heavy breaths as I force my crying muscles to obey every jump and resistance.

When I'm not obviously looking, I watch him. His gaze is trained on me, appreciating what I know is my well-formed backside, taut stomach, and small, but full breasts. I grin in spite of it and he catches my smile, suddenly understanding. A flush burning magenta upon his cheeks displays his guilt at being caught in the act better than a verbal accusation could.

"If this is another tactic of yours—" Gideon begins as I transition into push-ups, somewhat embarrassed.

"It's not," I interrupt, launching into a set of fifty, face reddening with exertion. "When my survival is dependent upon being in shape, I have little choice."

I catch Gideon's shame-faced flush burn redder upon his cheeks, underestimating me at a face value. Despite the unwarranted and strange confidence, as well as the desire to display around him, I'm not an idiot. I still need to keep my wits and body about me. I can't let my heart rule my brain. That's a simple spell for disaster.

"I'm sorry," he says, a genuine concern lacing his words. "I shouldn't have said that or acted the way I did last night. I'd had a few drinks and I behaved inappropriately. Even so that's not an excuse. I promise I won't hit on you like that again."

Startled, I pause at thirty-seven and push back onto my knees, sitting back on my feet. I quirk a dark brow.

"I shouldn't have thought so shallow of you."

I shrug trying to brush off the pang of hurt, lifting an arm to run my wrist across my forehead, finding the hot slickness of sweat there. I grimace, suddenly aware of my overly disheveled appearance. Red-faced and likely splotchy, dripping in sweat, with a straggly ponytail. Meanwhile, he stands in casual confidence and put togetherness. Dark hair, shorter on the sides, styled with an act of effortlessness that can only come from years of practice.

"You don't know me, it's fine. Besides, I don't get much socialization here; the lack of a norm is routine at this point." To avoid what I feel is awkwardness rising in my nerves, I switch into crunches, making up for my missing thirteen push-ups by changing my current set into seventy-five. "I'm going to be a while, no sense in waiting unless you're enjoying the view."

Gideon releases a heavy sigh, rolling his eyes upward as he vacates the doorway and the sound of his steps recedes down the stairs. The clanking of pots and pans follows as I finish my set, continuing on with a hundred squats.

He's a curious one. Mind-boggling too, all things considered. His outward attitude has been relatively pleasant, the only negative aspects being the peculiar feeling I pick up and his recent snap-judgment. Though that isn't fair because I haven't been projecting the most virtuous of my qualities. If I even possess any.

I distantly wonder if perhaps I jumped in with both feet. I hadn't hesitated when I'd found a literal stranger in my house and I never questioned if he had ill intents towards me. Of course, I'm confident in my defensive skills and a gut-instinct told me I could trust him, but even still…Mayhap, I should be a little more aware.

Finishing my workout off with some lunges, I mop my face with the hem of my baggy tee shirt. Making my way barefoot downstairs, I find Gideon sliding a frying pan off the stove and its contents onto a plate.

"What is that?" I call in surprise, nearing the granite-topped island counter.

Wordlessly, Gideon pushes a rust orange plate toward me, loaded with an array of fruit, toast, and an omelet. Cautiously, I step closer, clutching the back of a black leather stool. I breathe in the scents and instantly begin salivating.

"I made breakfast," he announces, digging into his own plate across the island, leaning against the counter. When I make no move, he urges me with a nod and his fork-clad hand.

"Do we have enough supplies for this?" I question, hesitation clear in my tone and the clipping of my words.

Gideon stops chewing for a moment, critically assessing me before realization dawns. "You've had to ration everything, haven't you?" His voice is softened with sympathy. It raises my hackles.

"Yes, and if we end up being stuck here, you will too."

"Well, for now we are fine. I brought several totes of groceries with me—you probably noticed when you put whatever you hunted in the freezer," he replies easily, indicating the direction of the fully stocked icebox. "I was planning on camping out here for a while."

I cross my arms, debating if this is an argument worth the energy. Taking a few measured breaths and calculating the likely scenarios, I decide against fighting and instead dig in. As soon as the first bite passes my lips I have to keep from moaning.

I haven't had food this good in…well as far back as I can remember. I can't recall if I've ever tasted anything so fresh and well prepared. Most of my meals have consisted of bland stews or hastily cooked fish. Seasoned eggs and sautéed vegetables were never on the menu with my lackluster skills.

"We need to trap some faeries," Gideon informs me, smearing peanut butter on his toast. "Figure out any information they may have, any rumors they might've heard."

I halt cutting my eggs with the side of the fork, bringing up my gaze to meet the man before me. "I'm not even going to get into the semantics of that insane plan, but how, pray tell, will we know whether they're telling the truth?"

"Easy. Faeries can't lie," he tells me inelegantly, making a circling gesture with his hand, toast poised in it. "Of course, they can twist words to their liking, but they are unable to tell a bald lie. Though they can pass off a lie if they believe it to be a truth, that's where things can get messy."

"And here I thought that the trapping part would be the messy bit."

Gideon cocks a brow. "Do you have anything to add to my plan? Or, perhaps, do you have a better one?"

I think for a moment, mulling over my thoughts while I finish off the omelet. "We should talk to the humans." I don't add, *if we can find them alive*.

Abruptly, choking erupts from Gideon's throat. "*There are other people here?*"

"Yes…" I trail off, my voice hitching oddly. "There have been…trapped. Like me."

Gideon settles his face into his hands, muttering a stream of obscenities.

"If we can find any, then yes, we will speak to them. And help them."

"Thank you," I murmur, suddenly insecure.

"It appears I came severely unprepared for this trip."

Laughter barks from me, dark humor striking around us, off of the pendant lights, bouncing off the ebony counters and reverberating through the cherry wood cabinets. Cupping a hand over my mouth, I'm shocked by my inflated reaction. "I apologize, it's just that, that is such an understatement you can't appreciate."

His brows draw together and I'm taken by how attractive he is, even perturbed as he is.

*Stop*, I scold myself, *you're being absolutely ridiculous.*

Even so, I notice the sharp line of his jaw, the luscious swell of his lips, the cleverness in his eyes. At this moment in time these are not things I should be noticing. Especially with someone who has made it distinctly clear that he's not interested.

With humiliation I comprehend my own thoughts. He's not interested. I'm making a fool of myself. Somehow in the duration of our acquaintance and meeting, my wall of apathy has fallen. *That*, or something more unsettling.

That Gideon broke it.

Simply overnight? Am I truly so weak-willed?

Walling myself back up, I shove all thoughts of attraction, rejection, and distraction out of my mind. Slamming down over my features, the façade becomes an impenetrable mask floating over every emotion, boiling just beneath the surface. I've spent two years alone and strong, I can't allow a flummoxing man unravel me.

"Eat," Gideon says with finality, somehow able to detect the change in my demeanor. "I'll start looking for ways to build traps."

Leaving me at the island alone, I watch his retreating back as he turns to a closet, pulling out chains and anything else possibly made out of iron.

The array of traps that Gideon is able to concoct suddenly makes me question my safety. And the idea that he may be a serial killer. Or seriously into some seriously freaky BDSM.

With an ease that can only come from practice, he strings up a fishing net webbed with an assortment of iron links: chains, utensils, broken electronics, and a few unfamiliar items added to the collection. He'd even dismantled the desk in the study to gather the iron adornments. Set aside for said net, are iron tent spikes, hooked to trap the lines of netting once our prey has been struck.

Nearby, an empty coffee tin is chock full of screws and nails, and a small part of me worries what Gideon might plan to do with them. Old plumbing pipes and rusted tools promising tetanus lean against a tree, tucked behind some brush.

He's innovative, I'll give him that. And clearly clever. And good with his hands.

The air is mild today, offering a slight breeze that ruffles my unbound hair, tucked beneath a generic, black toque. Thankfully though, the sun is reaching its zenith, its rays filtering through the boughs, casting our poor excuse of a clearing into a silvery suffused glen.

Despite the month of March, the climates are not forgiving in the north, although preferable to the sub-zero temperatures of the deep winter. Not to mention the summertime midnight sun is a lovely reprieve from the oppressive eternal night of the winter months.

Propping myself against a tree, I alternate between watching Gideon work, his fingers proficient, and staring at the laces on my boots—which are in desperate need of replacement. I can't help but find a guilty pleasure in observing him. For years I've been deprived of human interaction.

With startling clarity, I grasp how socially inept I must be and how my advances last night were likely interpreted. As desperate. Then again, must I be judged so? I've no idea whether the impulses I felt were the effects of my personality prior to my memory loss, or something I've developed through my own isolated upbringing these last couple years. Or even more unsettling, just my reaction to *him*.

He sets me at unease in more ways than one. I've always had a stable, constant understanding of myself in regards to my environment—regardless of the fact that it's likely an unhealthy reality. That is, until Gideon came around and screwed up everything in my already screwed up world.

"So, your scholar daddy taught you all he knows?" I begin, turning over a tent spike in my hand, the metal cool to the touch.

Gideon looks up, watching me turn the spike in my grasp, a strange glimmer gracing his eyes before he returns to adjusting a chain link in the trap. "He taught me lots, yes."

"Including how to capture faeries," I respond, tossing the spike back into the pile, suddenly bored. "I can't imagine that's a skill many people possess."

"On the contrary, they teach Faerie Trapping 101 now, I'm actually quite behind."

I stop, caught off guard. Watching his body language, I begin processing. "That's a joke, isn't it?"

Gideon grins, tossing a rope over a thick branch. "Yes. Not my best one, though."

I neglect to answer as I make my way over, fingering Gideon's elaborate—yet atrocious—web. The once plain, wheat-colored fishing net is now speckled with arrays of shining gray, the silver tones of silverware to the darker of

"I'm sorry, is that a frying pan?" I ask incredulous.

Gideon grins impishly as he hoists his strange contraption up into the ceiling of evergreens, instantly part of the canopy above us. "Sure is," he tells me, leveraging the rope around a snapped branch within our immediate reach. "Cast iron, couldn't pass it up. Who knows, maybe we'll knock a faerie out with it?"

"What's so special about iron anyway? You said faeries don't like it?"

"It's not that they don't like it. It's toxic. Iron burns them and ingesting enough of it is a fatal poison."

"Faeries are weird. And you're sure they're going to want this dead deer?" I indicate the hunting bag several meters away, bundling my kill from yesterday inside it.

"It's the scent of something dead so it'll lend to simulated chaos" he tells me, a teasing cocking of his brow accompanying it. "Lesser fae will be driven mad by it while others will be curious about what killed it."

I haul the meat over with ease across the pine needle-strewn ground. Once the sack is in position beneath the net, I dump the contents on the forest floor, the sour scent of it assaults my nostrils and sets my heart panging at the needless loss. "Now what?"

"That's the bait, now we attract them. Unseelie faeries have one significant difference over their Seelie counterparts. They essentially have a chaos detector built into their nervous system and they can smell the scent of a battle."

"They can *smell* that? Are you sure this isn't a ploy to get physical with me?" I wink.

"*Evelyn*," he says my name and it drips scorn.

"Fine, fine!" I toss up my hands. "How does it work?"

He nods sagely. "It's pheromones or something. Sense or scent, I don't know. It could be vibrations in the air or energy and hormones. What I do know is the more vicious and life-threatening the fight is, the more it draws them out and can send them into a frenzy."

"Wouldn't that be a disadvantage?" I counter. Considering frenzies are generally a blinding rage or bloodlust, that would then mean that their attention is otherwise preoccupied.

Gideon points a dirty finger at me. "Correct, which is where we have the upper hand. More frenetic, less aware. Less aware, more likely to become prey, especially since this net isn't exactly hidden. However, they will know exactly where we are due to this."

"Do Seelies have an advantage over Unseelies?"

Gideon twists his full lips. "Yes, but…it's not relevant."

"So, we're fighting and hoping we'll attract them while risking injury to each other? Do I have that right?"

His expression this time is disarming, the way the innocuous tilt of his mouth changes his face and morphs that confidence into insecurity. "It's not the most ideal plan, but it's the only one I've got."

Heaving a nervous sigh, I scan the perimeter, assessing where every root and rock is to avoid unnecessary injury to either myself or partner. Just because we're trying to elicit feelings of peril and ferocity, doesn't mean that we're wanting to instill those feelings for real.

"Okay," I breathe, an unhinged nervousness coating my words. "Let's do this."

# CHAPTER

Once my hair is braided back and my hat stowed away, Gideon and I face off holding awkward stances. He's limned in the shafts of sunlight breaking through the canopy above us, casting shadows of evergreen boughs across his body. Meanwhile, I'm shrouded in the nearby gloom, eyes hooded and darkened by both the foreboding nature of our fight and general lack of good weather.

We unanimously agree no cheap shots—no strikes to the face or below the belt, no choking and absolutely no weapons. Rather than a true fight, we'll be simulating one and mocking a struggle.

"If you feel like it's going too far, please say so," Gideon implores of me, tracking the nervous energy emanating off of my frame and revealing itself through my causal fidgeting.

Empathy glows in his eyes and he easily reaches for my hand to reassure me. His palm is calloused but not uncomfortably so, as he takes in my much smaller palm, mine too calloused. When he squeezes, I startle.

Sparks dance at the contact and make me gasp, setting my heart hammering. I haven't been touched in years. Human contact has been so impossible that I'd forgotten what it was like to crave it so. Gideon must feel it too, because his brows rise and he quickly detaches himself from my grasp. My heart plummets, but I push it away from the surface, burying it deep in the blackness hidden behind my wall.

I smirk to break the atmosphere, the movement steeped in deliberation. "Reserve those words for yourself."

Gideon chuckles softly, the sound threaded with a tinge of anxiety. "Just make sure you're projecting your emotions; we can spare more energy that way."

I nod, not trusting my voice as adrenaline begins pouring into my veins. I can feel the chemical mixing in my blood, can imagine it as if it were turning into mercury. Transforming it anew. Into something dangerous.

Gideon holds his feet at the breadth of his hips, staggering them for balance with hands poised in an upraised position beside him. I mimic the stance and find that my body settles into it comfortably, reassuring me that I'm not making an utter fool of myself.

"Ready?"

I nod again.

Rushing me, Gideon takes off making the first move. He's preparing for a tackle and I'm surprised by his speed and immediacy. I let the spark of shock flow and curse myself for giving him the advantage of striking first.

Throwing myself to the left, I narrowly dodge him, striking out with a blow to the ribs. Clutching the soon to form bruise, he spins around and drops to a crouch, knocking my feet out from under me. Luckily, I catch myself on a branch and go down only a moment before I regain my footing, managing to avoid a blow to the abdomen. His fist meets the rough bark upon the tree, scraping the flesh from his knuckles while I twirl around him. He reaches for a hasty lock that I scarcely avoid, my energy already dogging with it.

Hurling himself at me again, he overshoots and I leap upon his back. Gideon twists but his momentum and upset center of balance ruin him as he crashes to the ground with me still latched atop him. He hits the loamy floor with a thud, a small oath of air escapes his wind-knocked lungs before he flips himself over and tosses me aside.

Astonishment lights my bones and excitement suddenly replaces the nerves that thrummed only moments before. My heart thunders in my chest, eager and racing, my fingers twitching with an unmet urge. Liquid heat flares at my core, between my thighs suddenly aching. Impatient.

*My body craves this*, I understand abruptly, *my body wants this outlet of venting and frustration. One way or another.*

Rolling through the shrubberies and muck, I come up on my knees and find Gideon coming up to his feet. Hastily, I meet his stance, both of us disheveled with dirt streaks and crowns of leaves upon our brows. With such detritus mixed into his dark waves, it makes it easier to picture him as one of those wild and feral fae. One of the monsters that so easily and laughingly slaughtered my brother.

With resolve thrumming in my blood, I draw up all the longing for vengeance, for justice upon the faeries for Jacob and vent them through this perfect outlet that Gideon has supplied. Rage erupts with a fury untold as I watch Gideon, picturing his bronzed eyes as the too-orange shade of the moth-faerie, his dark hair the oily tendrils of the iridescently-scaled faerie who unwillingly gifted her blade.

Furiously, I launch myself at Gideon. Surprise brightens in his eyes before he rockets to the ground as I land straddling him, my knees braced on either side of his hips. His hands lie flat upon the soil on which he is pinned, my own hands manacles to his wrists strained above his head. To achieve such a position, I must stretch, my abdomen resting upon his which heaves with every startled breath he draws.

For a moment, time halts. The earth ceases to rotate, the birds neglect to sing, the nearby river quiets. My breath becomes stuck in my throat, a hitching in my inhales evident as my body becomes painfully aware of every press of my body against his. Especially the miniscule space between our chests as we both struggle for air, coming up for oxygen like we're drowning. Electricity zings between the contact of our flesh, a hum vibrating up my arms and surging into my heart, stronger than the contact of our hands. I can feel the desire growing at his groin, the hardness beginning to press against my all too sensitive center. The urge to grind myself closer is all-consuming. My nerves become all too aware of everything my body suddenly craves, the instinctual thoughts racing rampantly through my mind. The want to tear his clothes off and take him on the forest floor. A craving so sudden and abrupt tears through me, my adulterated thoughts reflected just as clearly back at me in Gideon's own desire-glazed eyes.

Hypnotized, Gideon swallows hard and brings a hand to my face, and upon instinct, I lash out and catch the offending limb, not realizing he meant to caress. Blushing with humiliation and anger over my own poor social skills, I shove off of him as the fire that burns his eyes is doused to a whisper of coals.

Releasing his wrist that burns in my palm. I circle the perimeter and search for an opening in Gideon's fairly adept stance. At the same time, the two of us attack, either oddly in tune or horrifically out of tune—depending on your viewpoint—and immediately countermove the other's mistakes. I dance aside as Gideon hastily pulls back, yanking his elbow with him, which causes him to inadvertently clip me in the nose.

There's a spark of pain and my eyes water of their own accord, while wetness begins to leak out in earnest, spotting my gray tee shirt and the damp forest floor. Spluttering out an obscene curse, I clutch my suddenly bleeding nose, cupping the hot liquid that flows over my fingers. Gideon instantly freezes, horror shrouding his features with a transformation that feels anamorphous and at war in a singular instant.

"Shit!" Gideon curses, turning to me and tilting my chin up with two gentle fingers. "I'm so sorry, I swear that was an accident." His voice is contrite, controlled with knowledge, but somewhat overruled by emotion.

I laugh awkwardly, the metallic taste of blood dripping down my throat, immediately choking the sound. "I didn't think you would take such extreme measures to damage my pretty face," I joke deprecatingly as I pinch my tender nostrils.

His other hand comes to cup my jaw, those fingers sending delectable tingles across my skin, his lips twisted into a wry grimace. "Your face will still be pretty, Evelyn." My name rolls off his tongue and makes my stomach spiral pleasingly. Though, my reaction could be from the injury. My mind continues to loop upon his compliment like an eagle circling its prey. He thinks I'm pretty. "I didn't hear a crack," he continues, unaware of my eddying response to him. "Did you?"

"No," I inform him, voice thick from the clotting blood and nasally from the pressure on my sinuses. *My nose isn't broken, but it sure hurts like a bitch*, I grumble internally.

With startling clarity, I become markedly aware of the fact that we're the same height. I've measured myself countless times desperate for something consistent and I know that I've maxed out at 5'9". It appears he has halted here too. Gideon's shoulders are in line with my own, though he's significantly broader with hips tantalizingly distanced with mine. His brow would rest upon mine if only he leant forward. If only I weren't a disgusting, bleeding mess.

"I think this should be enough to draw out the Fair Folk from their burrows and courts, let's just hope they have enough information for us to go on."

I'm about to contradict him when a signal laps at the edges of my perception, the sure-fire alarm bells of an approaching faerie. The sensation becomes increasingly pungent as the creature nears.

I nod, the blood crusting dry on my nostrils finally. Gideon hesitatingly releases my jaw from his grasp and I feel the loss of the contact like a physical blow. Urging me to get into position, the two of us duck into a den we'd fashioned earlier. The den itself is made from moss-draped across two boulders resting at the base of the tree where our net is strung. Here, we wait.

It takes only minutes of anxiety-wrought silence for a faerie to arrive and undulating terror fills me. They truly can sense battle. Or at least hear the chaos that surrounds our relatively botched fight, if anything.

The faerie that arrives is shockingly familiar. Her oil-slick hair is a hue of gasoline green and violet, toxically changing colors under the slender shafts of sunlight, while her scales glitter ominously. She is the faerie who'd tried to kill me two years ago. The faerie whose knife resides inside my boot right now.

Stiffening, I hold my breath as Gideon senses my apprehension, but returns his stare to our prey. Waiting for her to get into position, Gideon draws his ax, ready to chop. Nearby, the tin of iron screws and nails sits within reach, my job to weaponize them, should the net fail. Gideon assures me this is just a precautionary measure.

The faerie woman flares her snake-like nostrils, flattening as she slits her reptilian eyes and surveys the land and dead deer meat. Two more steps puts her in our desired position. She pauses, flicking that black tongue, sensually extending it and brushing across her top lip. With a clawed hand, she extends it slowly, curious about my wasted bounty.

Anticipation hums like a bassline from Gideon, his muscles stilled into preparation and anxiety. His eyes glisten with a predatory expectation, a watchfulness that eliminates all traces of the innocent man of slumber. No, now Gideon has become something of daunting nature, a force not to be quarreled with, unless one desires a death wish.

I shiver in apprehension just as the faerie takes two tentative steps, poking the once frozen meat.

With a speed I am unprepared for, Gideon leaps to his feet and swings the iron ax at the tree. The rope is severed and in seconds, the net descends before she can react. The clattering of metal smashing together accompanies the faerie screeching. Unfortunately, the pan doesn't knock her out, but it sure bashes her head and the sound rings out across our glen accompanied by her yowls of fury.

# CHAPTER

*TWO YEARS AGO*
*Jacob is dead.*

I repeat this to myself as I journey through the wilds, now carrying Jacob's extra pack. My newly dead brother's pack. The forest has grown quiet in my presence, unaccustomed to a human tramping down the carpet of loam as I travel through the night, a flashlight dimmed between my fingers. I refuse to sleep in this darkness, I need to put as much distance between them and myself as physically possible.

Daylight began to break from the east, a gray filtering beginning through the vast evergreens towering above me, threatening the uppermost limbs. A few birds begin to sing, chirping away the sound of the night, inviting the coming morning. I loathe their cheer.

The cold is a permanent fixture here, I decide, as my whining boots and frozen toes make contact with another merciless puddle. Inwardly I sigh, but outwardly, I maintain a façade of coolness. A lack of empathy, a lack of anything but self-preservation, even if I am doing it alone for no one to see.

Just as I begin to slow, sheets of rain pour down from the sky in relentless panes. Overhead, thunder rumbles and I stare up into the heavens, realizing how terribly my hopes have dived. I immediately pick up my pace and search for shelter in earnest.

Within minutes I come upon a miracle. A generously sized outcropping appears through the encroaching dawn. It's easily the best happening I've received upon my newfound memory loss. The rock is stately and proud, the overhang shielded with a natural curtain of moss. Inside promises safety and dry lodging, protection from the harsher elements, albeit not all the cold.

Slipping into the structure, I find the area spacious and blessedly dry—even if the stone will leach my warmth. Huddling into myself and my wet, sticking clothing, I dig into one of the bags and find a thick red flannel. Eagerly, I put it on, wrapping it over my ruined tee shirt. A deeper delve into the pack displays the singed first aid kit, empty containers for food storage, a half-full metal water bottle, a tiny pocket knife, twine, fishing line, iodine, a lighter, flint, and—oddly enough—tablets of toothpaste. The other holds a couple shirts, another flannel, socks, and a bunch of useless clutter.

I pause, noticing the contents of what should have been my only bag. Why would Jacob have given me such a lackluster survival kit? Was it because it's lighter? Was he concerned about my injuries, but didn't want to insult? Was I the sort of person that demanded equality and chose independence from men? I suppose my answers died with him.

Discarding those thoughts, I curl up with the clothing pack beneath my head, my limbs pulled in close. I stare out at the overhang and the waking sunlight just beyond. Despite the daylight, the air is still cold and unforgiving, but I won't make a fire. I won't make Jacob's mistake.

*I'll get out of here.*

*I have to.*

The sun is near to setting when I wake. Peachy pink and dusky lavender are streaked through with brilliant orange. Orange that reminds me much too soon of the moth-woman. The monster. My brother's murderer.

Pulling my knees to my chest, I stare down the skyline, noticing that the rain died while I slept, and admire the shadowy trees to the distance as I begin to plan. One of the monsters hinted at safety towards the south, and even though it is allegedly weeks away, it is the only lead I have. If my basic knowledge of geography serves me correct, if I head south, I should hit one of the Canadian provinces. That is, if Jacob's presumption is correct.

Deciding to travel by dark, I begin to prepare. I have no idea if these monsters can see well in the dark—because I certainly can't—but it's a chance I have to take. Broad daylight calls too much notice and from my apparent white hair so I'll be a beacon no matter what. Braiding my long hair into a rope, I pile it atop my head and wrap a dark shirt around it, obscuring the color in almost all of its entirety.

At nightfall I leave the safety of my temporary camp and head south, flashlight in hand. Ensuring I don't leave a transparent path through the forest and trample the ground, I place each footfall upon rocks or dry earth. Gently, I push away branches, careful not to break any, and I'm suddenly grateful my hair is tucked away as to not get snagged.

Coming upon a clearing, I pause, taking in the vacant area. In an instant my body turns to stone. A sense crawls over me, a darkness, a cold hatred slithering down my spine. A thing is near. A monster lurking in the woods. I shut off the light.

Scanning the perimeter, my eyes land on one particular spot beside an old fir tree. There is draw, something foreign, and I know that's where it is. A preternatural sense screeches at me about the danger, a surety of what is there.

I instantly avoid the source of the alarm, making a detour about a third of a kilometer around the clearing heading west to arc away from the thing. After a cautious hike through dense vegetation with my flashlight on the lowest setting, I make my trip around and find myself several dozen meters from where I sensed the monster was.

The alarm is silent. The feeling is gone.

Dread drops in my stomach like lead and I spin in the forest, trying to detect where it went, searching not just with my eyes, but my developing sixth sense. Soapberry bushes, fir trees, evergreens, fireweed, everything blends together in a greenish blur.

Then it flares, racing toward me and she appears.

Stepping out from my left, three meters off, the creature stands, smirking with feral anticipation. Her eyes are the green of spring grass, inhuman and tilted too high. Her hair is twisted into oily tendrils that seem to have a spirit of their own and her inimitable skin is covered in iridescent scales that mesmerize and blind. Long fingers, each double-jointed and tipped with curling claws, dark and slick, threaten to rip my flesh away.

Just like Jacob's.

"Where are you going, child?" she asks, her forked tongue reaching out and licking quirked, onyx lips, hissing as she does so.

I compose my face, turning my façade into a smirk of my own. "None of your concern."

She tsks immediately in response. "Now, now, I don't believe that's any way to speak to your elders." She laughs and the sound is like a chime. "No, see on the contrary, you are not going anywhere."

Her face hardens and in half a second, she lunges for me. My reaction is delayed but I manage to spin from her claws but feel them lightly graze my shoulder. She catches a few strands of hair that has escaped my binding and a white-hot bolt of distress strikes me while death begins knocking on my door. She spits in anger over her miss and leaps again, this time I am more prepared, and my body listens to instruction as I allow myself to fall back from her attack. She overshoots her goal but just barely catches my throat. As she tumbles over my head, I push to the ground, rolling to my right, the beam of the flashlight tangling in the darkness. There, where I was only moments before, a dagger slams into the earth. I steal it immediately.

In the distance, a male voice yells and fear skitters down my spine. Regaining my footing, I stand tall, heaving breaths, and brace myself for her next attack. Except that she is gone and I am left with blood pouring from my wound.

Anxiety rises and my brain frets from the risk of exsanguination. *No, no, it's superficial. The blood is from my forehead. When I rolled, my skin scraped a pointed rock and that's where my forehead wound came from. I am not going to die.*

Not pausing to look this gift-horse in the mouth, I race away from the clearing and wind through trails and wilderness to once again return to my cave. Blood leaks into my vision, obscuring the world into a red-cloaked horror story that burns and sticks my lashes together.

Taking time to be ultra-careful with my steps near the shelter, I verify that I haven't left blood or a trampled trail for the thing to follow. I finally find myself at the curtain of moss that calls out my sanctuary and relief leaves me light headed.

Inside, I tear strips from my ruined shirt and tie one around my slashed throat and another around my forehead. Securing the two with uncomfortable knots, I settle against the cave wall and stare out beyond to the stars and moon.

Hours pass as dread snarls through my heart, the dark and adrenaline playing tricks on my mind. At one point, during fitful bouts of sleep, I swear through the midnight veil I see ruby eyes staring out at me. Before I let panic take me in its grasp, I blink and they're gone.

Trying to calm, I stare at the stone ceiling above me and contemplate how utterly fucked I am as another northern downpour begins. There's a reason why no one gets out of here.

It's that they can't.

# CHAPTER

7

Gideon exits our hidey-hole, myself following in awe. The shining faerie thrashes in our presence, the iron burning her at every contact upon her flesh and scales. I find that I cannot dredge up any sympathy—she did try to kill me, once upon a time.

"We want to talk," Gideon begins, clutching the ax with both hands, displayed clear as day before him. "Are you up for that?"

The faerie hisses, a sound distinctly serpentine.

Anger fuels me and I push past Gideon, unsheathing my stolen blade and stabbing the iron tent spikes into the ground. Every interval, I slam one into the forest floor and I stare at the void in her eyes. Poison green irises and pupils of black, soulless depths.

"He asked you a question," I snarl, pointing the knife at her.

She stills despite the welts forming upon her body and the faint hissing from the iron on flesh. "I know you, human-girl." Her voice has yet to change, though her eyes zero in on my stolen blade.

"We met two years ago," I inform dryly.

"Yes, I remember those gray eyes. So stormy, so ominous." She cackles, the sound broken, malformed. "You evaded a killing blow, if I hadn't been called away I would have finished the job."

"I seem to recall that." My voice is bland, revealing not a shred of my discomfort. Gideon meanwhile, shoots me a startled look, brows raised and eyes widened. That man's emotions read like an open book. "Though we aren't here to discuss that matter, we're here on another." I crouch down, shrouding so-called ominous gray eyes, as I draw indistinct shapes in the leaf and needle-strewn floor.

"What is your name?" Gideon demands, stepping forward, his knees become level with my shoulders.

"What do I get in exchange for revealing such information?"

Gideon shrugs. "Nothing, I just want to address you appropriately."

The faerie lifts a hairless brow, her scales fracturing colors like a diamond as the lights hit every angle. "If you hope to glean my name, I wish for something in return. I'm certain you've heard the legends of the significant power names hold?"

"You may not be able to lie, but you sure are evading," I murmur towards the ground. "Name."

"You want secrets of the Fair Folk, do you not?"

"Those who know the truth of the fae, know that names hold no control over the bearer. You are making an empty bargain," Gideon says bored, but there is a wicked gleam of delight in his eyes. He's outfoxed her in that regard.

Our identical glares of impatience seem to penetrate the faerie, her eyes shrewd and half obscured by the old net. She lets out a sound crossed between a hiss and groan. "My name is Tegwyn of the Unseelie Court."

"Tegwyn," Gideon starts, voice velvety. "I require you to answer my questions, and before I'm able to release you, I need to know what you want. What the want is of your heart, so that I may ask of you one command."

The faerie—Tegwyn—caterwauls in her cage of net and iron, refusal written in every line of her frame. Still, I cannot bring myself to feel anything but contempt and cool satisfaction. A predator who has met their match. It is a delicious twist of fate.

Mayhap names do not bear sway, but desires do.

I'm suddenly more than thankful for Gideon's knowledge of faeries. I would not have known to question Tegwyn's statement and hollow offer. I'd have continued into her trap, believing that names are the key. I'd have failed. At best I'd make a fool of myself, at worse, I'd meet Lady Fate.

"You know the ways of the Folk," she snarls, baring ebony teeth.

"I've studied."

"How do I know that you won't use your one command to ensnare me for eternity?"

"I give you my word."

She spits at the ground. "Mortals are no more bound by oath than a maggot can rule a kingdom."

"It's your only offer."

We're at an impasse, the three of us refusing to break the staring match of the century. The birds are silent, sensing the predators, the only sound is the sizzling of iron against fae.

"Freedom," she spits, eyes hard and furious as a spoon melts the scales of her forearm. She clenches her teeth against a scream of pain.

"No, not like that. I need you to say: *'the desire of my heart is…'* and you must be specific," Gideon explains crossly, his demeanor clear that this is not his first encounter with the Fair Folk.

Tegwyn scoffs, irritated with the forced wording, disparaging at the intricacies he'll no doubt weave, should she evade answering again. She rolls those lizard-like eyes, alighting upon me before roving them to Gideon. "The desire of my heart is freedom from this net woven with iron."

Gideon accepts the confession under the guarantee that faeries can't lie. Despite the folklores surrounding compulsion or control bearing from a true name, it seems that it is false, though the reality is akin to the myth. The command stems from a heart's desire, the want of the faerie, not their identity.

But what is a desire undefined by an identity?

I don't wonder if it had been a faerie to thread the lore of true names and their command. To unsuspecting or uneducated sorts, they'd show a vulnerability in order to lull a mortal into a false sense of security, to lead them into a bargain of one-sided nature. Then, when a dishonest deal is made, they'd strike with their bladed truth, revealing the falsehood for what it is, and the fatal mistake a human made.

"What do you know of the missing Harbinger?" he asks, crossing his arms, tucking the ax beneath one.

Tegwyn seems startled. "You do not wish for the secrets of immortality?"

"That doesn't interest me, the Harbinger does." His voice has taken on an edge of petulance. I don't blame him; she seems to be a particularly trying faerie.

On the other hand, wouldn't immortality be exactly what he'd need for his father's cure? To be impervious to illness and harm? It's almost like dangling bait, and a trill of nerves twists in me at the prospect, but he doesn't take it. He hardens his gaze and waits.

"The Harbinger is an unparalleled warrior belonging to the Seelie Queen." Gideon stares Tegwyn down, she averts her gaze. "He is missing, allegedly having been spotted in this territory. Aneira Gwyndolyn mourns for him."

"The Seelie Queen," Gideon intones, voice breathless.

"Yes. Rumors speak he was akin to a child of hers, some whisper as lovers. Perhaps we shall never know of such a tryst."

"How long has the Harbinger been missing?"

"I have been told seven months," she responds coldly, examining claws that could slice through the net with half a thought, for if she weren't drained by instruments of iron.

"What other information have you heard of him?"

"Nothing more. He was a secretive one, even for fae, such as I."

"Did you ever see him? What does he look like?" I demand, blade still brandished and prepared in my palm.

She laughs, throwing back her head, the sound grating and high-pitched. "Few have seen the Harbinger's face. He wears a suit of golden armor. Folk know that it is likely that the Seelie Queen is the sole witness to his identity."

My heart plummets. Even should we find a lead on the Harbinger, we have no appearance to go on to substantiate the information. Perhaps he doesn't want to be found, particularly by two insignificant mortals.

After a few more unsatisfactory questions with just as many disappointing answers, Tegwyn provides to be no more of value.

"Tegwyn, I command you to never touch, harm, maim, or kill me or Evelyn and to never speak of this capture to any living creature." Gideon's words are carefully phrased, but I still, noticing small gaps.

Tegwyn scoffs. "As if I would mention this trap to anyone, this humiliation is torture enough."

Releasing her proves tricky, dragging out the iron stakes and judiciously peeling back the net that has now melded to her flesh. The fibers of the rope have fused to the scales of her form and pull away with a gag-inducing sucking sound. Iridescent scales decorated with the bright red of her blood are revealed once she is unveiled.

With as much dignity as she can muster, she draws herself up, penetrating us with a scathing glower. As she leaps for the forest beyond, the rustling of the shrubbery her only farewell, I desperately heave a sigh of relief.

"Well, she was a bit of a bust," I mutter, beginning to gather up all our supplies and call it a day from here.

Gideon reluctantly agrees. "At least we know she'll spread the word. Faeries love a challenge, especially since we expressly forbid her from doing so without much restriction."

Enlightenment prods me. "You never said she couldn't write."

"That was deliberate."

Despite his cleverness, his spirits are darkened as he begins hauling more equipment with us. I silence the urge to reassure him. Cautious to avoid leaving anything behind as evidence, we trudge back to the cabin in a hushed manner, processing Tegwyn's words.

The next day arrives without a second captured faerie. I would have preferred one who knows nothing, rather than actually nothing. I deflate under the lackluster responses of our fight. Discouraged, I create a modified plan, discarding the fouling deer.

Gideon still strings up the same net, woven with the same iron riggings. Only this time we fetch lengths of chains tucked into the basement, the same one that holds the generator and copious containers of fuel. Likely most of it has gone stale, but that won't stop me from attempting to use it. This time, we implement a new routine to bind the captive to a tree trunk and fashion a crude gauntlet of busted sheets of steel and a mechanic's glove.

"You really think this is a good idea?" Gideon quizzes me as he finishes hoisting the net above us.

"How much more information do you think we could've gotten from Tegwyn? How much more, had we applied just a bit more pressure?" I ask, brandishing our macabre invention upon my fist. After several hours tossing that night, I balked at all the plot holes we'd left and realizing what we could've gleaned if only we'd detoured down a different avenue. In the morning I'd accosted Gideon and modified his more practical plan. But I'm not about practicality when I can taste escape upon the tip of my tongue.

Gideon shifts uncomfortably, the set of his jaw working against what he knows could be a massive success under the sacrifice of moral ambiguity. He purses his full lips, the soft flesh yielding to pressure as I'm caught, captivated momentarily by his involuntary response. I rip my gaze away.

He is an enigma. Readily willing to trap and ensconce a faerie in the brutal torture of *bearing* iron, but wavers when it comes to physical force accentuated by *more* iron. I have no such qualms. They are monsters. Creatures of the night.

"Likely a lot," he finally answers, having used needing to tie a shortening rope on the tree again as an excuse. "But I need you to not take it too far."

I smile coyly, admiring the instrument of torment applied to my person. "I don't think it was me who took it too far last time."

My brow is quirked as Gideon flushes at the insinuation of his accidental blow to my nose two days prior. "Just promise me."

I sigh dramatically. "I promise not to let it get too far, all right? I'm not going to kill something right now."

He sends me a sidelong glare at my implicit use of *something* rather than *someone*.

Depositing the glove in the damp, moss-curtained den, I return to Gideon readying for our baiting struggle. It rained last night and during this early morning so a mist rises around us, winding like a snake, as coiled as our nerves. I take note of the bladed grass with droplets poised upon them, adjusting my tactics to accommodate slippery ground. He sighs softly, but matches my stance and the two of us engage in a scuffle worthy of drawing attention.

After learning each other's favored strikes and countermoves from yesterday and the day before, the quarrel is more controlled. Our squabble is deliberate and singing in unison as our bodies instinctively recognize the other, morphing into a newfound dance. I slink around Gideon, but he's quicker, whirling on me and preventing my attack on his exposed spine. Suddenly, he presses up on me and pushes me against a tree. Heat unfurls in my core and desire tears through me, hurtling me into an engulfing inferno. The bark is rough on my back, his wrists twin manacles to the ones I'd latched him with only forty-eight hours past.

Ripping away from the yearning both in my heart and his eyes, and ripping from his clutches, I manage to squirrel myself into the tree behind me, using broken branches to aid me. Several feet up, I use momentum and launch myself at him, sending us rolling to the forest floor. Mud streaks our limbs, faces, and clothes, bracken and twigs decorate our forms like rustic jewelry.

Blood blooms upon a wound new to Gideon's forearm, a scrape from an exposed shard of rock. Ruby droplets descend upon the ground, spraying like shattering ice. He comes up on one knee as I freeze, the awareness of a fae presence pinging in my consciousness.

# CHAPTER

# 8

Sending a panicked look and decisive nod to Gideon, I indicate the den and lurch for it. Gideon does not question me, probably thinking I'd heard something he didn't. He listens despite me not revealing my sixth sense of fae detection. We both arrive in our hiding spot, concealed just in time for a faerie to approach the area with a deliberate air, contrary to Tegwyn's more predatory gait.

The faerie is male with curly black hair and dual-pupiled, Prussian blue eyes, a shade owned by the night sky.

His features are sharp and angular, stretched thin over bones that jut inhumanly. His sloped nose twitches and he twists his bow-shaped lips into a frown, seemingly disappointed by the lack of human presence or altercation.

Three more steps puts him in danger's path, but he's still. He makes no more move and stress begins to eat me inside. The faerie stands statue-still, queer eyes devouring the landscape of densely forested woods and feeble glimpses of sunlight.

I realize he needs a little assistance. Dragging a twig from the dank undergrowth that Gideon and I are pressed up in, I take the dry wood in my grasp. Recalling the periwinkle-faerie, I press the stick in-between my two fingers until it gives.

The snap is like a gunshot and both Gideon and the faerie react. Gideon whips towards me, betrayal written across every line of his face. The faerie lurches for the sound, to us, lips pulling back over teeth forged of midnight steel. My heart becomes lodged in my throat.

Fortunately, the faerie's step was enough to put him in the way I have chosen and snatching the ax from Gideon, I swing with an unmatched ferocity and separate every thread in the rope. The net clatters and jingles dauntingly and the faerie does not miss the foreboding sound.

Throwing himself from the path of the net, my terror grips me, but a shard of electronic equipment pierces his calf. The rest of the net gathers around his legs. He erupts with an ear-piercing howl as I desperately clutch the tow chains to my chest. Bracing myself against the fear of the near incapacitated faerie, I heave my anxiety leaded feet into a sprint. Every thought of the faerie escaping is incomprehensible. I force every alternate version of reality where I don't succeed from my mind. Anything but victory will not exist here in this world.

Yanking the faerie up by his hair, I whip one length of chain beneath his shoulders, throwing him back down and mercilessly binding his arms to his torso as the iron takes effect. The metal begins weakening and burning his pale flesh, screeches of torment lashing from his throat whose vocal cords will be ruined, should he continue as such.

Dragging the furious faerie behind me, I lug him to the base of a generous sized tree and retrieve the lock from my jacket pocket. Locking the chains into place with the steel padlock, I meet the faerie with a level stare. "What is your name and status?"

"Tadhg," he wheezes hoarsely, "Messenger of the Unseelie Court."

"We require information from you," I inform him, my gaze haughty as I don the gauntlet.

"I'll tell you anything," he cries desperately, his pale flesh welts in earnest from iron burns. It peels back like curling paper and I wrinkle my nose at the sight and stench.

"What are your heart's desires?" This time I request not one, but at least two as I use the plural wording rather than singular. Gideon had briefed me on how heart's desires and the corresponding command works. The wielder of the command is the one who earned the faerie's truth.

He howls for freedom from the iron—as Tegwyn did— as well as something more. "The desire of my heart is to regain the love of my lost lover, from he who has scorned me, yet still possesses my thoughts."

"What do you know of a missing member of the Seelie Court?" I demand and decide to change the narrative. Skirting the straightforward questions sitting on my tongue.

"I know of one, perhaps two," he whimpers, "the Harbinger and the *Ceidwad Cudd.*"

"The *Kaydwa*-What?"

"*Ceidwad Cudd*. It's Welsh."

My interest piques at the faerie's revelation. "Who are they and what of them?"

"The *Ceidwad Cudd* is a masterful spy who crossed the wrong monarch, which queen, I am unsure because she works separate from each court. The Harbinger is the Seelie Queen's warrior. He was sent to dispatch the *Ceidwad Cudd* and never returned. Following that, my queen sent someone after the Harbinger, hoping to catch him unaware." Tadgh's voice quavers and I pity him because he needed no prodding to spill his heart and knowledge, gauntlet unneeded. Pathetic for a faerie. "There is also a small rumor that claims that the Harbinger is not fae, though I doubt the merit of it, especially if certain physical attributes had to be replicated. The Seelie Queen herself denied the claims. The *Ceidwad Cudd* though, she is most definitely one of the Fair Folk. I have met her myself."

The Harbinger not a faerie? How could that be such a thing? Why would the Seelie Queen employ a personal guard who may not be universally loyal? I immediately dismiss it as nonsense and just an empty rumor as Tadgh claimed.

"What does the *Ceidwad Cudd* look like?" I inquire, fingering the metal plates of my gauntlet. Tadgh's eyes grow, the four pupils blowing wide.

"I do not know, she remained hooded and clad in silk armor."

"Then how do you know she was fae?"

"She could not lie when she was asked to, she admitted she was Folk in my presence." She could have lied if she weren't, though. "She showed me iron burning her." Perhaps not, then.

"All I know about the *Ceidwad Cudd* is that she refuses to kill but she has no qualms about coercion, extortion, manipulation, or seduction. She has blackmailed with her body and controlled royalty with her secrets."

"She sounds like a force to be reckoned with. Could the Harbinger and *Ceidwad Cudd* be lovers, then?"

He shakes his head. "I do not know."

"Well, what else *do* you know?" Gideon inserts.

Tadgh then continues a stream of information *we* already know, and I realize grudgingly that my brutal methods were unrequired, and Tadgh did more than his part. Upon releasing the pitiful faerie, I command him the same thing that Gideon had of Tegwyn, but save the last command for myself. Who knows when you'll need to call in a faerie debt?

With a startling escape from Tadhg, I realize he is the poorest excuse of a faerie I've ever met. How can he be of the same species as the moth-faerie, or the androgynous one, or even Tegwyn? Could there be less dangerous faeries? More disgraceful sorts in their own type?

Gideon and I share a look of understanding, coming to the same conclusion; the fact that we both see Tadhg and the fae in a new light.

"What do you mean, you don't think you've ever had pizza?" Gideon asks incredulous, his dark brows arched well above their usual height.

Upon returning to the warmth of the cabin, Gideon suggested a meal and apparently the first choice for a man is pizza. A food I cannot recall ever having eaten, courtesy of my memory loss. No doubt, I know what pizza is, I have memories of its general structure and composition, but its taste evades me.

I shrug, face heating in mild embarrassment. "I just can't remember ever having it, I've always had a limited diet."

"Ah, health fanatic parents, I get it. Harsh. Well—" he turns, his face beaming, "I have a treat for you, we're making it. From scratch."

I give him a wavering smile but nod as he hollows the cupboards of their ingredients. Plying the island counter with flour, salt, yeast, sugar, oil, and warm water, Gideon explains the process as he scours for a mixing bowl and rolling pin. Walking me through the motions and explaining how the yeast reacts with the warm water, and how the sugar activates it. Everything is painstakingly measured, and I watch his devotion to the craft with enrapture, admiring the effort and ease with which he works.

Recently bathed and dressed in a cream-colored, cable-knit sweater, my wet, white hair hangs over my shoulders as I brace my forearms on the counter. I thank myself for having the long hair for a curtain to hide behind as I watch Gideon's deft fingers knead the dough, to watch his forearm muscles flex. Drawn back to his fingers and begin imaginings.

"What kind of toppings do you think you'll like? Do you have any allergies?" Gideon inquires and it knocks me from my thoughts. He looks at me with a flour dusted face and somehow the lightly disheveled nature is more becoming of him.

"You pick, I don't have any allergies that I know of," I tell him shyly, distinctly out of my element. It would be easy to just tell him that I don't know what anything tastes like because I have no memory prior to these two years past. I could tell him that my parents could have been health fanatics, but I wouldn't be able to confirm for certain because the recollection of them is nonexistent. But something stops me. For some odd reason, I don't *want* him to know. Don't want him to pity me more than he already likely does.

Gideon makes a pleased sound of affirmation and continues working the dough. I swirl a finger through the layer of flour on the dark granite, sketching a crescent moon and a poor excuse of a flower before erasing it with a brush of my hand.

"You were smart to draw out Tadgh the way you did," Gideon begins, lifting his shining amber eyes to mine. "Had you not snapped the branch and encouraged him to take that step…well, we may never have found out about the *Ceidwad Cudd*, or why the Harbinger went missing. So, thank you."

My face heats upon the compliment and I avert my face to stare at the stone hearth of the fireplace. "You're welcome," I mumble, eyes still trained on the living room through the open-concept space.

A pause fills the room and I find curiosity drawing me out, tempting me with thoughts and words to learn more about Gideon. "You said you came here for inspiration," I start heedlessly, "what are you working on?"

He blushes furiously as he greases a bowl with oil. "I'm writing a novel."

I lean forward, propping my chin on my palm. "Well, that is fascinating, what kind?"

His ears turn garnet red from my attention and questions. "I wanted to write fiction versions of my dad's work and maybe add some dragons. You can never go wrong with a few of those. But I'm mostly intrigued by the Harbinger. I met him briefly years ago with dad, but it was only from a distance and he wore armor. Like the faeries have already said."

I begin to wonder if the mystery of the Harbinger alone would have been enough to bring him to Yukon. There's a passion stirring in his eyes when he speaks of the warrior, a reverence that is generally reserved for celebrities.

"Anyhow, dad wrote about the fae and such, some of his books and those he admires are here," he tells me, gesturing with an arm toward the floor-to-ceiling bookcase that lines one wall of the cabin's living room.

I turn to view the works Gideon indicates and recognize the tomes and books I've never once picked up because time and survival had never permitted me to do so. Dusting off my flour-sprinkled fingers, I make my way to the shelf and admire the titles and authors.

"My mom has two shelves on it, they're second and third from the top," Gideon explains while divvying up ingredients across the kitchen, a bowl of shredded mozzarella already before him.

I find myself drawn to that section then, titles of varying dramatic interest and intrigue. Some display love stories, others epic adventures. All of them supernatural in nature, mainly dominated by magic, vampires and the fae.

"You're welcome to read any of them," Gideon offers, his face returned to his richer hue, stray waves hanging upon his forehead.

I pause and twirl with my hand upon the spine of a book, caught off guard. "I am?" I don't know if I was much of a reader before, and despite my living in the cabin there was some inexplicable line that felt crossed by using non-necessary possessions. So, I refrained, even when the longest and snowiest of days kept me indoors. Perhaps it was me feeling like a fraud, as if I were trying to force myself into this family by relating or enjoying their pastimes. I didn't want to feel like I could lose something I didn't actually have.

"Absolutely, you can even start right now, and I'll finish making dinner."

Warmth swells in my chest, a sincerity and generosity that my stone-cold heart has never known. Near giddy with excitement, I curl before the fireplace with a blanket and dive in.

Pizza turns out to be delicious.

Late into the evening we talk and share pizza, one Gideon topped with pepperoni and green peppers, mostly formulating plans of capture for the following day. We sprawl before the fireplace, watching the flames dance, with a quickly disappearing pizza between us. Eventually, Gideon selects a bottle from the cabinet and pours us two small glasses, declaring cheers for a job well done.

"How old are you?" I ask, my voice—normally quite husky—has taken on a trilling tone and I cringe at the direct question.

"Twenty-seven," he replies cheekily, toasting before swallowing the last contents of his glass. "You?"

"Twenty-three," I reveal softly, also finishing my glass.

"Did you ever drink when you were underage?"

"Not that I can remember."

"I did, a lot. I was a little rebellious in my youth, broke a few laws. But after a stint of breaking and entering with my stupid friends, I smartened up."

"Ah yes, I have also broken into a home," I tell him, gesturing around the cabin.

"Well, I'm thankful you did," Gideon informs me, a smile upon his face as he refills our cups again. "Also, I believe that kidnapping, holding someone hostage, and torture are all illegal as well."

I chuckle behind my glass. "Then here's to our wicked ways of delinquency. May we be as cold as iron."

My grin spreads from ear to ear and Gideon picks up the infectious nature, sharing a mirror image to my own. "To our wicked ways of delinquency."

So, we drink, and dine, and laugh, the fire warm and the company warmer. All the while my coldness begins to melt. My wall has begun to truly crumble with my mask of apathy shredding.

I don't think I'll ever have the skill to repair it.

I don't think I'll want to, for that matter.

# CHAPTER

"I think it's safe to say you can use your glove on this one."

The following day, Gideon and I are poised in the clearing, a snarling and angry faerie having been caught in our net. Countless attempts to get her to talk beyond supplying her name have been for naught and her refusal has finally pushed us to harsher methods.

I sigh as I take in the plant-like faerie, her features wide and flat. Her skin is the sage green of foliage, delicate vines like arteries are imbedded along her arms and legs. There are small white flowers peppering her limbs with a few small patches covering her groin that wrap like a belt and stem from sheer sheets of fabric. Her hair is a thick fall of ivy, crowned by deep, heart-red roses, her eyes glowing a fierce amethyst.

The faerie—Róisín—screeches against the bindings that have her against the tree. She was not an easy one to trap and I display a slash of nails across my bicep by her ferocious reach. She throws herself against the iron, the flowers living on her wilting at the contact of the toxic substance.

"I will peel the flesh from your bones and drink your marrow," she howls, teeth made from rose thorns lining her ruby lips. "Your lives shall be forfeit."

"She's quite dramatic," I tell Gideon conspiratorially, glancing at him sidelong. "And I thought I was bad."

Gideon chuckles. "You have competition."

She screeches at our casual conversation, furious at not being taken seriously. I ignore her, gazing skyward. The day is overcast, promising rainfall that our rain barrels sorely need. Clouds gather like a shroud of smoke, no sunlight piercing the veil of pine needles and branches today.

"I will slaughter you first, bitch," she snarls, her thorn-teeth shredding through her bottom lip. "And I will make your lover watch."

Erupting into laughter spikes her wrath. "Gideon, are we lovers now? You should have told me," I tease, sending Róisín into a battering rage.

"Your death will be painful," she spits venomously.

"Okay, that's enough of that." Donning my ghastly gauntlet-like glove, I slam a blow into her jaw without hesitation. There's a shock that reverberates up my arm and it is a powerful surge of pleasure.

*Oh, that felt good.*

Two thorns fly from Róisín's mouth, deep red blood pumping from a nasty split in her green flesh. She screams. I grin. Gideon is bewildered.

"Maybe that has given you some incentive to answer our questions and follow some orders," I suggest dryly, admiring the crimson fluid spattered across my metal knuckles.

"My heart's desire is to kill you!" she finally screeches, pricking at my eardrums. I don't let it show. Rather, I blink sweetly, innocently against her wrath.

"And what do you know about the Harbinger?"

"Nothing you don't already know. Word gets around, faeries tell of two mortals trapping, interrogating, and killing the Fair Folk."

"We have not been killing the fae."

"Well, someone has been," she says witheringly.

"Yes, I suppose someone has." I think back to the dead faeries I found the days past, the one I'd ignored and the one that its fellows took away, presumably to their queen. Who really was killing the fae? The Harbinger? Is he laying waste to the Unseelies that hunt him? Will he do the same to us?

Gideon sidles close to me. "There's been dead fae here and you didn't think to tell me?" His voice is low with a slight tinge of irritation.

"We had a lot going on, it didn't feel as important." I return my attention to our captured faerie. "Continue."

"They say you search for the bounty that the discovery of the Harbinger can bring." She leans forward for effect, the iron sizzling on her skin, ivory flowers turning to dust. "I can broker you a sweeter deal, for my freedom of these chains I will take you to the Unseelie Queen for an audience. I promise, no harm shall befall you there."

She seems to say the last part with difficulty, clearly dreaming of all the harm she could inflict and judging from her earlier threats, such acts would not be her first attempt.

"You have the power to do that?" I ask skeptically.

I sense, rather than see Gideon come to stand silently behind me. Flanking me protectively against the suggestion the faerie puts forth. I can read the refusal upon his frame, yet I am curious as to what she may say.

"Of course." She lifts her chin regally. "I am a Lady of the Unseelie Court, I am within the queen's confidence."

Shock ripples through me at our newfound discovery. We have ensnared faerie *royalty* with our backyard junk. Such possibilities had never crossed my mind. Briefly, I consider ransoming her, but I dismiss the idea. Too many outcomes, too much danger.

"Swear it," I prompt her without using my sacred command. "Swear that you will not harm either of us here, on the way to, or at the Unseelie Court, and ensure that no one else does either."

She snarls realizing I've clarified the language and making a distinct lack of loopholes, ensuring not just the safety from release, to travel, to audience, but also extended it to both Gideon and I, and past her. Surely, she'd been planning on twisting the words to find an opening to attack, or to cover only one of us. Faeries enjoy the precision of words considering untruths are not in their capacity.

"Swear it!" I repeat, anger rising like a tidal wave.

She stares me down hard, the gemstone eyes darkening to pure stone. Sighing, I pull back my fist and let it fly, the movement oddly soothing as I launch it into Róisín's sage cheekbone. Upon contact my arm hums with energy and adrenaline, the sound following is a dull thump as Róisín's chlorophyll flesh splits and blooms forth a blossom of scarlet.

"I swear it!"

"Specify it, Róisín."

"I swear that no harm will come to you or the mortal man here, on the way to, or at the Unseelie Court, should you release me." Her voice is venom, the tone dripping with poison; and the promise to break the vow despite the constraints that she is unable to.

Somewhat satisfied, I accept her oath and release her from her bonds. She brings herself up to her full height, nearly a full head taller than Gideon and I. Immediately, she saunters up to me, reaching out a slender, amethyst-tipped finger. As weightless as a feather, she brushes her unnaturally long index finger down the length of my jaw. I stiffen, but refuse to pull away. She can't hurt me.

"You are quite lovely for a mortal, a cunning, clever thing too."

Irked by her audacious behavior, I reach up with my gloved hand and ensnare the offending appendage. She squawks, undignified as the metal eats away at her skin, devouring quicker by the pressure I exert.

"Don't touch me," I warn dangerously.

She pulls away, ribbons of sage shredding with the movement as she cradles her mutilated wrist. "Bitch."

"Unseelie Court," I demand, a nervous hollowing to my tone, I attempt to squash it into oblivion. "Now."

She smirks despite herself.

Gideon and I meet each other's gaze across the clearing, twin expressions of fear mingling with anticipation and the potential of looming demise. Regardless, we push on, knowing this could be our only—and best—bet. If we manage to offer the Harbinger for our freedom, we won't have to fight our way out of here.

Arming ourselves with tent spikes, we tuck away our net and remaining weapons beneath the moss curtain. We set off as I send a backwards glance to our most vital tool, now blanketed by the same moss that obscured us to safety so that we may make this possibly fatal journey.

Róisín leads us to the edge of the clearing and then pauses, her translucent skirts swishing about her ankles. Her purple eyes meet mine, glowing with a mix of pain and something unidentifiable. "To take the Faerie Roads, we must be touching." Her eyes flicker like candlelight. "A chain of sorts if you will. It shall work if you hold my hand or touch my shoulder."

She extends her hand and I draw in a cautious breath as I entwine my own grip in hers. Her skin is cool to the touch, slicked with her blood from my various battering of her person. Behind me, Gideon wraps his comfortingly warm hand in mine, his nearly hot in comparison, with his other clamped to Róisín's shoulder.

"The Faerie Roads are accessed through in-between's, once we pass the threshold of this tree line, you will find yourself transported. Do not fear it." Her voice rasps ever so slightly, the sound of leaves brushing against each other. It still drips with venomous scorn, though.

Gideon leans in. "For clarity, in-betweens are anything between two things. A doorway, the line of light and shadow, whatever an individual fae believes to be an in-between can activate their inherent magic and gain access to the Roads."

"So convenient you have a scholar daddy for moments like this."

Gideon laughs and it is harsh under the current ambience.

The three of us linked together take the last remaining steps through the clearing. After the third step the world wavers and suddenly the gray light fades behind us and we're plunged into an earthy darkness.

I gasp as I take in my newfound surroundings.

The Faerie Roads are cavernous, underground tunnels, the height extending a dozen feet from the floor, perhaps twice that many times across. Flecked with bioluminescent mushrooms to guide the path, the fair blue light glows and highlights the roots that dangle from the ceiling. They reach with concern and curiosity, eager to caress and poke from above. Heady, upturned earth is the primal scent here, evoking the sensation of safety—a womb-like atmosphere.

My breath is taken.

"So, the courts are underground?" I inquire, gazing about.

"No, the courts reside in pocket realms that are parallel with their claimed territory," Róisín explains in a clipped tone. "Us Unseelies reside in the north, the Seelies in the south. To access the courts we use the Faerie Roads. They are bridges between the two realms, but act as pathways to many other places—if you know where to look."

"Good to know."

Róisín guides us down the Roads and a shiver trembles around me, the air turning electric. I glance at Gideon, wondering if he feels this too.

"*Come to us*," hypnotic voices whisper, so breathy I have to wonder if I didn't imagine it. Gideon's answering jolt seems to cement the idea that it was in fact real, though.

"What is that voice?" I demand of Róisín, her back still to us, where I notice an iridescent set of wings. Markedly modelled like a dragonfly's and painfully damaged by burns. Eerily similar to the dead fae I found.

"'Tis the Wild Hunt, they seduce and coax with their voices. Should you follow, you become a member or victim.

You want to be neither." Seeming to consider further, she smiles softly, dangerously. "They call to the Fair Folk just as much as to a mortal. It's simple knowledge that keeps such mistakes at bay."

"Fascinating," I whisper in return. Seems they are not so invulnerable as I'd thought. I file that away for later use. So far, weaknesses consist of burning by iron, inability to lie, and now the Wild Hunt.

She sniffs disdainfully, but I sense a note of pride in the set of her shoulders. Continuing on, Róisín walks with the straight-backed posture of regality as she seemingly navigates the labyrinth-like Road with ease.

Within minutes, we take a left-handed turn and come upon a wide stone expanse of an open foyer and I realize we've hit the end of the Faerie Roads. Overhead, a jagged crystal chandelier threatens, glimmering with shards of purple. Several yards before us is a grand flight of stone stairs, the black rock's polish winking with the eyes of a thousand stars. By some innate knowledge, I determine the stone is gabbro—and I wonder if I'd once been enamored by geology.

Flanked on either side of the flight of steps are two statues, both depicted in black marble. To the right is a tall and proud figure, dressed in what appears to be a fitted tunic and leggings with a full-moon insignia upon his breast. He is battle-ready with two daggers in each hand and a horrifically spiked sword sheathed behind him. He embodies a ferocity that plucks a nerve. Hooded by a cloak, his features are shrouded, and the stone-carved fabric billows out, reaching to the heels of elaborate boots. On the opposite side is another tall and proud statue, clad in full armor with great leathery wings proudly extending from his back. A simple sword is pressed between his two palms, held with the blade bisecting his helmed face.

A trill of fear ignites in me at their sight.

Ascending the glamourous staircase that is hugged by glittering and dangerously spiked crystals, we make our way to the top where I freeze in a balking mix of horrified and mesmerized.

The last step reveals an expanse of a plateau that spans a generous berth. The walls are glass and the same refined crystal that arc towards a dome, sharpening to a deadly point, boasting an impressive height taller than the evergreens surrounding my cabin. Sharp, silvery soldering melds the glass sheets together, scattering fractures of lustrous limned light across the diamond panes. Beyond, the night sky enchants with constellations that challenge and defy all laws of the universe, eliciting their fiery glow in a cadence that composes an orchestra to deaf ears.

My internal alarm screams in terror at the presence of so many faeries. Faeries of every appearance imaginable mill about, some stopping to gawk, others continue to titter in their musical voices, laughing with relish and melancholy. Delighting next to vases of crystal-formed, skeletal trees, a group of too-bright fae sparkle and giggle, both sight and sound almost too painful to bear. The cruelty winds a dreamscape-like tune across and within the captured space. Claws, wings, tails, eerie eyes, or every sort of nightmare bedeck every single one of the fae.

Róisín hurries us along. Gideon and I have since re-linked hands in solidarity, fearful of the new environment whose maw threatens to swallow us whole as our footsteps echo across the translucent quartz floor.

In the center of the elegant and extravagant space is a dominating throne, carved of pure diamond and framed with silver. The design of anemones and fawns borders the arms and cascades behind the growing visage of bucks and more flora.

Culminating in a high point above the bearer of the chair's head is an elaborately detailed sigil, worked onto a perfect glass ball.

Terror seizes me as I meet the fathomless black eyes of the woman seated upon the throne. Horror rips through me as I comprehend that Róisín has taken us straight to the Unseelie Queen's throne room.

"Welcome to the Unseelie Court, mortals," the queen declares with an air of false benevolence. Benevolence laced with the promising thread of death.

*We're not going to be swallowed whole*, I realize with panic, *we are going to be devoured.*

# CHAPTER 10

The Unseelie Queen is beautiful in a haunting and eerie way. Her moon-white hair streams down her back in an ivory sheet, falling to her waist. The black eyes that forgive no light swallow hope where no whites are to be found. Crowned above her head are a pair of hoary antlers with pale jewels and silk cobwebs strung between the prongs. With a diadem perched upon her brow with a teardrop-shaped diamond dipping to the bridge of her pretty, pert nose, she is the epitome of otherworldly beauty.

Flanked behind her are six guards, three to a side, each as distinguished as the last, bearing marks of the fae. Beyond them is what I had assumed to be a fourth wall to this cavern, but in reality, it is a complete lack thereof. A cool breeze rips off of the mountaintops around us from the massive opening, while the sheer white curtains flutter in the wind.

I realize the absolute drop and the accompanying death sentence of it.

From my peripheral vision, I notice one of the guards to the queen's right stiffen at the sight of our presence, yet immediately evoke a calm and controlled exterior. I don't bother to check anything beyond that as a strange energy weaves through the room and the queen commands attention.

"I fear I'm not in the mood to parade under the pretense of politeness and court semantics," the queen announces frostily, her voice ethereal. "I shall ask this once, and once only." The queen leans forward, perching a dainty elbow on one of her crossed knees and leaning forward so that a panel of her hair slips forward. With a jolt, I notice the nails that trace her full lips are long, sleek claws that mimic obsidian. "What use are you to me?"

I'm caught in a moment of illusion—a moment of our path where the world can go one of two ways. One being we answer correctly and are allowed to continue this audience to the next obstacle. Or two, we meet Lady Fate.

The queen's sclera-less, obsidian eyes are unblinking as she keeps her eyes trained upon both Gideon and I. Suddenly, I feel grubbier than ever and more inferior than my existence has yet to allow. My clothes are worn and dingy, completely casual in attire and my hair is capped under a knitted toque, a low ponytail hanging limply down my back. Gideon, however—also dressed in casual attire of a wool sweater and jeans—seems more put together, his back ramrod straight, similar to a soldier's stance. There is pride there, a confidence too, and my heart is sucked into my throat.

"The Harbinger is here. In the Yukon, hiding. I can find him."

It takes several moments for me to deduce that the voice spewing nonsense is Gideon's. His voice is even and carefully articulated, and I'm suddenly glad all attention is trained on him because I need more than a moment to compose myself. I close my mouth that gapes like a fish, stifle the sound of shock, and attempt to shutter my surprise-wide eyes. One of the queen's guards, a golden-eyed faerie, catches my expression, and I quickly rip my guilt-laden features away.

The queen arches a perfectly sculpted brow beneath the artful band of jewels, full lips pulling up in a captivated smile. She is intrigued and beautiful. So utterly beautiful and bewildering that I can't help my heart from racing.

It doesn't help that my heart is already racing from Gideon's blatant lie.

"You have aroused my curiosity, mortal," she purrs, voice velvet.

"Gideon Zhao, Your Majesty," he corrects and my face blanches as a shot of icy fear spears through me.

He corrected her. He corrected a monarch. He corrected the queen.

*Dear world, save us.*

I also realize with a pang of surprise that I hadn't known his surname.

"And this is Evelyn."

Dread drops an anvil in my stomach as the queen meets my eyes, boring deep and demanding. Fear spirals in my stomach, an intense surge of anxiety thrumming a staccato rhythm throughout my being. Luckily, the queen chooses to avert her glance askance to Gideon, a coy narrowing to her eyes.

The queen presses the tips of her fingers together, the claws clicking ominously throughout the room. Standing in one graceful movement, she comes to her feet and I take in her elegant height, her luxuriously long legs displayed by a generously curve-hugging diaphanous gown. I catch myself gawking and have to forcefully pull my gaze from the daring neckline that nearly grazes her navel.

"Gideon," she purrs, the gauzy gown trailing behind her as she approaches. "You have ensorcelled my attention. If what you say shall be proven true, I grant you my word that you will want for nothing, should you deliver the Harbinger to me in a fortnight. Should you fail, I will have no mercy upon you and Evelyn, as you have committed several unprovoked attacks upon my people. Do you accept my terms?"

The golden-eyed faerie catches my attention again, his eyes are intense, as if he can see right through me. A primal panic in my eyes that registers on his face. He cocks his head ever so slightly to the side in curiosity, his dark, blood-red hair swinging as he does so. Meaningfully, his eyes flicker to Gideon, a question in them. Irritated by his faerie trickery, I tear my gaze away again to settle on the queen and Gideon.

Gideon nods sagely with the radiant queen only inches away from his face, in the proximity of a lover and I find a jab of envy striking me. I imagine shoving the queen away from him and clutching him possessively. Horrified, I squelch the thoughts and allow my jealousy to burn as she sketches a line across his throat, tapping the pulse. Though, to my surprise, she pulls away somewhat miffed when he doesn't react.

"We agree to your terms," Gideon announces, a tone of settlement in his voice.

The queen smirks joylessly and sweeps a moon-white arm across the throne room, a swath of gossamer fabric draping from her waist and connecting to a ring on her middle finger swinging with it. "I am so pleased. Now, I insist you join us for a toast of our newfound alliance." She makes a motion with her hand and a servant scurries over with a silver tray laden with crystal goblets. She plucks one from the tray and gestures for Gideon and I both to do the same.

When the servant makes her way over to us, her pink skin is flushed by the cold, yet she performs her job even if she shivers as she does so. Carefully, I select a goblet and Gideon mimics the motion. With the crystal in hand, a deep, instinctual sensation crawls over me and screams.

*Do not drink that.*

The words are repeated over and over, spiraling out of control with its panicked speed and warp it into a mutilated jumble. Fear strikes me as I peer into the scarlet liquid and in terror, I whip my gaze to Gideon just as he begins raising the cup to his lips.

Without my own accord, my body is locked into place and my mind screeches at Gideon, desperately calling out to him without making a scene. Suddenly, he pauses, and the cup descends from his mouth without having made contact with his lips.

"Your Majesty," Gideon asserts, addressing the queen with a brusque tone. "What is in this glass?"

A breath of relief floods me as the queen quirks an innocent brow. "Wine, Mr. Zhao," she replies, grinning with red-stained teeth.

Gideon's brows draw together. "And what else?"

The smile falls from the queen's face, her lips twisting into a snarl and her brows lower over her terrifying eyes. "I think you've overstayed your welcome. Lady Róisín, please escort our guests out of my court. Mr. Zhao, you have a fortnight." With that, she takes her leave, spinning away with a swirl of her silver skirts, and disappearing down a quartz-lined hallway.

Róisín, having slipped away and melded into the court life upon arrival, returns now and takes Gideon's hand, effortlessly guiding us to those gabbro stairs again. A smile lines her face, but it is a tight smile, no doubt having expected a much different outcome for this visit.

We pass a cluster of faeries near the exit, one with eyes apple-red and coiling horns spiraling from her temples titters to her companion. "I do wonder how long it will take the Harbinger to annihilate them. I once watched him cut down three faeries in a single fell swoop—my sister had been one he beheaded." She sighs. "Such prowess and wasted on Seelie scum."

I shudder as Róisín leads us through the Faerie Roads once again and deposits us on the threshold of our clearing. It's there I make a revelation with startling clarity.

The queen had been expecting us. Which means that Róisín had meant to get caught all along. Which means we'd been led into a trap we just scarcely avoided. I don't wonder that the *wine* that was offered was part of it.

Standing in the clearing with the same dappled gray sunlight filtering in from earlier, I realize that we'd nearly been out-plotted, had it not been for Gideon's startling revelation. The worst part was, we didn't realize we'd nearly been outsmarted until after the fact.

I suddenly feel as if there are spiders crawling up my spine.

"Enjoy your search of the Harbinger," she cackles, "he'll probably kill you both the second he sees you hunting."

Once Róisín is well and truly gone, I wheel on Gideon and immediately shove him. Gideon is taken aback and stumbles, a look of complete surprise obscuring his features.

"What the hell was that for?" he exclaims aghast.

"Why didn't you tell me your plan?" I shout at him, a snarl creeping onto my face. My muscles tremble with adrenaline and anger.

"Because I didn't have one," he says befuddled, his dark brows raised in innocence.

"So, you just pulled that whole '*I know where the Harbinger is*', bullshit out of thin air? How could you lie to the *Unseelie Queen*?"

"I didn't—" he breaks off, drawing a scowl. "What did you expect me to say in there?" he demands, a furious flush traveling over his caramel complexion. "You think I'm going to grovel in front of the Unseelie Queen and the Revenant? They would luxuriate in torturing us for that. So no, I brokered a deal. Is that so bad?"

I halt in my wrath and suddenly feel very stupid. He was smart. What did I expect? Faeries have a trickster nature and love a challenge. What better challenge than two mortals forced to hunt down a legendary fae warrior with only two weeks to do so? It's a task with odds stacked against us, and it is exactly the sort the queen would like to see play out just to fail.

A gust of cool forest air rushes over me, bringing a calming atmosphere with it. It's unseasonably warm, but I'm grateful for the rise in temperature to keep us out of sub-zero levels. Another breeze kicks up and my anger evaporates with it, carried off on the wind. Suddenly I am drained, deflated of the fuel that had straightened my spine. Finally, I can think rationally and realize that Gideon likely saved our lives back there—despite the queen's deal being our biggest hope.

"Who is the Revenant?" I ask, surprised and processing Gideon's explanation.

Gideon jolts, realizing a slip-up, but takes in a deep breath anyway. "The Revenant is the Harbinger's counterpart; they were formally trained together for a century. Whereas the Harbinger is the Seelie Queen's personal guard, the Revenant is the Unseelie's."

"And he was there?" I ask, brow quirking up.

"Yes, the Unseelie Queen keeps multiple guards at a time though, so no one truly knows which one is the Revenant. But he is without a doubt one of the six always with her."

Abruptly, the image of the ruby-haired, topaz-eyed faerie who'd kept stealing glances at me floods my mind. The idea is sinister but sticking nonetheless, and I instantly decide with an intuition I've always trusted that, that faerie is the Revenant. Why else would he assess us so? And why would he look at me with that question in his eyes? The question he indicates in association with Gideon.

A staggering comprehension begins to fill me, and my mind rejects it the minute my brain settles on it as concrete truth. My world teeters precariously on its axis, nausea swims in my stomach.

I watch as Gideon turns away and moves to the moss curtain, only to shout out a scream of obscenities. I crane my neck, momentarily distracted, as I notice the empty burrow. The faeries took our net and all our weapons. Including my glove, garbage gauntlet that it was.

Yet another ploy from the Unseelie Court to steal our tools and leave us vulnerable to all of their attacks. I shouldn't be surprised at their audacity, but I am. The only bit of solace I can take in it is that they likely burned and injured themselves in the removal process.

"Fuck!"

Kicking the remains of our trap, a chip of electronic equipment and some scattered utensils, Gideon fumes while my fleeting distraction wanes. Luckily though, they didn't manage to take away the chains I'd tucked deeper into the hollow beneath the roots of the supporting tree.

I inhale sharply, thinking about our failing prospects when a terrible question strikes me. "Gideon?" He lifts his face to me. "How do you know about the Revenant?" I inquire, my voice hard.

Gideon winces and I know this is the question he'd been praying I wouldn't ask. "Due to my dad's work, I've met a few members of both courts. The Revenant was one of them."

"You saw him?"

"I spoke to him."

"On more than one occasion?"

"Yes."

Fear thrums in my chest as I meet Gideon's amber eyes in a new light. For the first time, I feel truly frightened of him. Time slows to a standstill as anxiety upends my world.

I think Gideon is the Harbinger.

# CHAPTER 11

Tumultuous thoughts rampage in my mind all day even once we return to the cabin. I cannot absolve the issue in my mind and instead, I run through every scenario that my brain can construct. Everything from concrete proof that Gideon is the Harbinger, and undeniable evidence as to why he's not.

If Gideon is the Harbinger, then Tadgh's rumor that the Harbinger isn't fae would be accurate. So, to add to that, what would his true reasoning be to travel to the Yukon? Perhaps he was searching for the *Ceidwad Cudd* that Tadgh had mentioned. He'd claimed that the Harbinger was sent to dispatch her. What if he never returned to his queen because he never found the *Ceidwad Cudd*? What if the *Ceidwad Cudd* had become trapped here? Gideon said he knew that the Harbinger was here, he wouldn't be lying if he was in fact him. People don't know the identity of the Revenant or the Harbinger; would it be a stretch that, aside from Tadgh, they don't know the appearance of the *Ceidwad Cudd* either?

Dawning realization strikes me.

He did cut himself off when I accused him of lying. He said *he didn't*. Because he *didn't* lie to the queen.

Then again, Gideon said that the Harbinger and the Revenant trained together for a century. So, unless my eyes are deceiving me, or I'm horribly blind, then I don't think that Gideon is a one-hundred-year-old, elderly man. But he *can* lie.

Unsettled, I cannot quell the torrent of emotions and thoughts barraging me. Deciding to shut down my mind this afternoon—at least for a few hours—I retire to the lonely bedroom upstairs. Cocooned in the sheets, I find myself staring at the ceiling, wondering in equal parts if I'd like to be alone or have Gideon assuage all my doubts. But what remains is a bigger question.

If Gideon is the Harbinger, what am I going to do about it?

Later, after bathing and sloughing off the stale feeling of sleep, I nest in one of the outdoor lounge chairs on the front deck. The nighttime spring air is crisp and cool, a perfect balance from my scalding shower and thick blanket on my lap. Beside me, a porch light emanates a golden glow over the small text of the book I read, a glass of brandy next to me.

There's a difference between enjoying the peacefulness of your own company, and being lonely, I realize. The most notable deviation is knowing of Gideon's presence in the house, and that, should I want it, his company is there. Before, such a luxury had never been available.

"Care for some company?"

Gideon arrives, carrying his own glass of brandy in hand, and a rolled-up flannel under his arm.

"Make yourself comfortable," I respond softly, gesturing to the chair adjacent to mine, connected by a small table between them.

Easily, he slides into the wooden, royal-blue chair, tossing his blanket on his lap. Turning to me, he rests his hand on his chin, his elbow on the table. His face is adulterously endearing. The sudden energy prickles, the knowledge of his attention trained on me sends my nerves misfiring. My heart races its traitorous rhythm and I attempt to control my breathing.

Eager to break the tension wrought silence, I say, "I don't know what I'd do if vampires were real too." I brandish the novel I hold for effect—a smutty book about a human falling in love with a vampire.

Gideon smiles, but it doesn't reach is eyes. "Funny." He shifts his weight uncomfortably. "But I need to be honest, I didn't come out here to talk about your book."

"Oh?" I say with mock disappointment. "I could have done with some scintillating conversation on the topic." Yet I slide the marker in place—a thin sheet of iron shaped like a leaf.

"I wanted to talk about everything that happened today, at and after the Unseelie Court."

"You have my attention, Mr. Zhao," I mock the queen, a strained teasing note ringing in my voice. I'm hyperaware of his presence and I stare at him, trying to find an inhuman aspect about him. He is unfairly handsome, but that hardly qualifies exclusively as a faerie characteristic.

"I'm sorry I haven't been entirely forthcoming with my knowledge of the fae, I just don't want to overwhelm you. Or scare you rather."

I laugh and scoff. "I've survived in the wild for two years with these assholes, I think I'm beyond scaring."

"Mostly thanks to this place," he chides with a nervous smile. "You know this cabin has wards? And a fuck-ton of iron. It's why faeries won't come near here."

"I figured the iron, but I didn't know about the wards."

"They start there—" he says, indicating a tree stump a dozen feet from the stairs, "and then circle around the same circumference. A Seelie associate of my dad's warded this place against Unseelie fae, but Seelies are exempt. Even then though, Seelies don't come around for one of two reasons. One, this is Unseelie territory, and two, yet again, the iron."

"You talk about your dad a lot. Can you tell me more about him?"

Gideon smiles sadly, looking fondly into his glass. "I've always looked up to him. Dad is my role model, everything I aspire to be. He is honorable, intelligent, driven…he's my best friend." He fiddles with the glass in his hand, turning it over before sighing and taking a swig.

"What happened when he had his stroke?" My voice is breathy, tentative as to not offend or intrude.

"It was Christmas Eve, and he'd just been feeling *off* the whole day, getting ready for our dinner party and such. Anyhow, he put on a show for us, we had a great time and all, and when it came time for all the guests to go, we noticed he couldn't say '*apam balik*.'" He cracks a wry smile. "For context, that's a Malaysian dessert like a pancake. Dad liked it with ice cream. Anyhow, it was a huge red flag.

"My mom—who is a nurse—was in the middle of her program and had just learned the warning signs. So, she went through a checklist of instructions and immediately told us to call 911. The ambulance came, and it was absolute chaos. I remember the stupidest things about it too. How those seats were so stiff, the ride was bumpy as all hell, and even the paramedic who kept trying to lighten the mood.

"We managed to save him, but he lost all ability to the function in the left side of his body. Since then, I've always wondered if I'd just told him to sit down, or to take his blood pressure, or have done *something*, how it could have been different."

"Gideon," I whisper softly, my hand itching to reach out to him. "You didn't know. You couldn't have prevented that."

He shrugs nonchalantly, swigging the glass. I don't miss the vulnerability in the movement. "It would make me feel better if you told me about you," he finally whispers, averting his eyes, protecting himself in case I reject his request.

This time it's my turn to fiddle with the glass and I too, take a long pull from my drink. "There's not much to know. There's not much *I* know."

"What do you mean?"

I draw in a deep breath, terrified to bare my soul to him, but there's a broken piece of me that needs to tell him. To confide in someone, to unleash all the unknown inside me. "I have no memory prior to the last two years."

I drop the bomb on him, waiting for it to explode in his waiting arms. I watch as he processes the information, and I watch as his face warps into a film of horror. His eyes widen, his mouth drops open.

"You remember nothing? No family? Friends? Relationships?"

I shake my head to every question. "Nothing."

"But you remember your name, right?" His voice is a mix of apprehension and empathy.

I laugh darkly. "That's the worst part. I didn't. My brother, Jacob, told me. Worse so, is that I don't know my last name."

"And where is your brother, now?"

It doesn't matter that for the brief time that I knew and remembered Jacob that he was a jerk. Slapping me into consciousness and such, but he was my brother. He was all I had.

I duck down into my glass. "Dead. Faeries killed him the night we survived the plane crash that our parents didn't."

Gideon is silent. His revulsion is palpable in the air, the silence thick with it. The emotions play out on his face, a range of terror, befuddlement, concern, anger, pity, finally coming to a rest upon a damaged version of understanding.

He blows out a breath. "Well fuck me, I'm sure glad that I brought this with me," he announces, pulling from beside him the rest of the bottle of brandy.

I laugh and reach for it, and as I do so, our hands connect. A sudden surge of electricity floods through me and I'm shocked by the vibrant connection I feel between us. This isn't the first time we've touched or rather even held hands—Róisín had seen to that—but this is most definitely the first time that I'd felt the connection with the accompanying jolt.

No, that's not quite right either. I'd felt this electricity the first time we touched before our faux fight. The first time

I'd been touched by another human in two years or more. I've been so lonely, I realize.

Gideon stills, his eyes flittering from our joining hands upon the bottle to my steel gray eyes. He lets the bottle slip harmlessly from our grasp to his lap, and links our fingers together. Our hands are both calloused and battered, both of us have broken and short nails, we both feel the vibration of the connection. My lips part in surprise as we simply watch each other, our eyes flicker across each other's faces taking in high cheekbones and full mouths. I caress his jaw with my eyes, the sharp line of it and think of him stroking mine, the more rounded line of it, coming to a petite chin, his fingers trailing along…

Energy hums with a rising power, a thrumming sensation that stirs in my heart, pounding a matching beat to Gideon's. Sensing the same things I do, Gideon reaches forward with the hand I yearn for, praying for the caress of my fantasy. His fingers come to rest on my collarbone and I watch his lashes lower as he observes his exploring fingers, sliding from my collarbone, across the racing pulse of my throat, and to twine in the locks at the nape of my neck.

Ever so slightly, I lean forward as Gideon pulls me towards him, his lashes shuttering closed as my own flutter shut. Just a breath away.

Suddenly, there's a boisterous crash in the bushes and our moment is broken.

Both of us break apart, whipping our gazes to the sound, hands torn from each other. Hearts racing for another reason altogether.

There, near the clearing that empties to accommodate the cabin is a rustle that produces a battered and wobbling faerie and a tremor of alarm. The faerie appears young enough, perhaps my age at most, her face almost familiar, but unplaceable. She is a beauty, with a thick fall of onyx hair and shimmering obsidian eyes. She struggles a few steps and bewilderingly, we watch her cross the invisible threshold that bars any Unseelie from trespassing. Which only means one thing.

She's a Seelie.

The two of us toss our blankets and rush the faerie who crashes to the ground within our sanctuary. Gideon turns her over gently, careful not to damage her leathery, bat-like wings as he shifts her to me to cradle. She stares up at the sky beyond, her eyes belonging to the stars, her broken body already pulling to the universe. Scarlet blood covers her, obscuring the lace front of her shirt almost entirely, her leather leggings torn, caked with mud.

"I thought I'd never find you," she rasps, her eyes roving over the two of us, seeing us but not truly so. She mumbles incoherently. "...so grateful."

With that, a small smile graces her lips and the faerie exhales a final shuddering breath. Dying in my arms. Her stare wide as the light in them fades out, forming a blessed union of a spirit that has joined the stars.

# CHAPTER

The Seelie's death leaves us reeling and wondering if her dying words weren't just rambling nonsense of a brain expiring but the confirmation needed to reveal Gideon as the Harbinger.

I don't get my answer right now as we dig a shallow grave for a faerie we'd hardly met, whose name will go unmarked. The two of us heave iron shovels, sending piles of cold earth over our shoulders. Nearby the deceased faerie lies wrapped in a white sheet, her dragonesque wings carefully tucked behind her, night-sky eyes closed.

I can't bear to look at her cold white face any longer, it reminds me far too much of a fate I face here daily. For a moment I almost believe I see my face reflected in hers. Watching the black bleed out and leave my pale shell. Immediately, I rip my anxiety-filled mind from her and instead settle on another complication.

My mind whirls with so many revelations, always circling back to *Gideon is the Harbinger*. But other's make themselves known:

There are Seelies here.

There are faeries searching for the Harbinger.

We can be found here.

After the unmarked grave has been dug, Gideon and I carefully carry the Seelie by the sheet we've bound her in and lower her as graciously as we can manage into the sad excuse of a hole. Silently, we begin shoveling the earth back onto her, not knowing any funeral rites of the Fair Folk, and not knowing her long enough to give her a proper eulogy.

The grave is patted level by the flat of our shovels, all that's left is the scent of upturned earth and the disturbed dirt to make her presence. Without that, this unknown faerie has faded out of existence, not a soul to know.

Gideon and I return to the cabin in a traumatized silence, our hands linked in solidarity as we leave our blankets, book, and booze on the porch, reluctant to expend the energy required to bring them inside.

"You take the first shower, I'll make some tea," he tells me, voice deadened to a monotone, eyes haunted. There's a bleakness in him as his eyes flitter to me and down, continually watching.

I nod, not able to draw upon my voice.

Gideon slips into the bathroom, turning on the hot water for me. He returns to the bathroom again and has deposited a set of clothes for me on the bathroom vanity, along with a stack of fresh towels.

I try to crack a smile as I pass by him, I'm not sure I succeed, and then I slip into the bathroom, hoping to unthaw from the icy emptiness.

The shower is scalding when I step in. I don't mind the burn as I let the sweat and dirt run off of me, turning the water dark. I stand there, distantly aware, until the water runs clear and I lather with the mint-lime scented soap.

It could be twenty minutes or two hours later when I get out, of that I have yet to decipher. For a moment, I stand there, steam wafting off my pinkened, naked, body, finding a pair of eyes as hollowed as Gideon's. The gray has turned oppressive, the utter lack of color more deadening than the dulled amber of Gideon's.

On the vanity counter is the thick, cream sweater I'd worn when we'd made pizza together and a pair of gray sweatpants. A sad smile breaks across my face and I quickly dry off and proceed to dress, brushing aside the fact that I've yet to wear pajamas upon living here.

I exit the bathroom, bare feet padding on the wooden floors to find Gideon in the kitchen, pouring us two cups of spearmint tea from the kettle on the stove. The kettle with the heart-shaped dent. Softly, I cross the threshold and come upon the island. Gideon looks up and wordlessly pushes a steaming cup towards me. I wrap my palms around it, desperate for some sort of feeling.

"I'm going to take a quick shower, I'll be back," he tells me tenderly, briefly touching my hand upon the cup, a small electrical zing penetrating my fog.

I don't answer, but I must make some note of affirmation because Gideon disappears to the bathroom. I stand there, lost to the world, peering into the spearmint tea as if it has all the answers in the universe.

There's a hollowness to me, a strange un-uniform ache as realities and morals shift. The Seelie carved an odd hole in my foundation, leaving behind the rubble as a puzzle.

Gideon returns some time later, his hair wet, but fluffed by towel drying. Distantly, I'm aware that it appears cute. He urges me to drink the tea in front of me, and I do, startled to find that it has cooled significantly. By the time mine has emptied, Gideon has already washed his mug and put it away.

"Let's get you to bed."

He guides me up the stairs and I follow along docilely, grateful for his assistance. In the room, Gideon pulls back the covers and helps me slip inside them, tucking me in. As he turns to go, an animalistic instinct strikes me. I latch onto his wrist and meet his confused gaze, my own pleading.

"Stay," I whisper. "Please. I don't want to be alone tonight."

I fear that the nightmares will return. Nights of smoke and blood, of death and Seelies, of teeth and Unseelies. Most of all I fear the fire that flickered behind my lids for two long years, I fear admitting I'm afraid of such an element. I'm afraid to admit that I need Gideon tonight.

Gideon seems to ponder for a moment and I'm worried he'll refuse on grounds of honor because of my past advances. But he doesn't, and gingerly he comes to the other side of the bed, peeling back the covers.

With him slipped into the sheets beside me, I'm hyperaware of his presence. Turning to face him, I find his gaze trained on me. Reaching out to him, needing to feel the realness of another human, I grasp at his chest and tangle my fingers in the fabric of his shirt. Wordlessly, he draws me close and holds me, slowly melting away the trauma induced fog.

As the fog evaporates, a sweeping emotion takes its place, something tender but all consuming. Something that craves more of *this*. Of him holding me. Of his presence. Slowly, I come back to myself, feeling the sensation of *feeling* return to my fingertips and then my toes, gradually drawing towards my core.

Minutes pass in silence once I've returned to being Evelyn, and minutes more pass before I speak. "You know, I usually sleep naked."

Gideon's answering chuckle vibrates in my chest, the sound sending warm and fuzzy sensations throughout my being. "I may have been informed of that once."

"What do you want out of life?" I suddenly ask, eager to hear his tender voice. "Once we get out of here," I add hastily.

"You mean, what is my heart's desire?" He chuckles.

"I suppose."

"I want to be a writer. I want to share the stories that my father discovered. I want him to be proud of me. I suppose I also want someone I can spend my life with, someone who is also my best friend. And hopefully she can put up with my bouts of inspiration that make me lose sense of all else." He pauses, taking in my features. "What about you?"

"Well, I've recently discovered I'm quite fond of reading, but I don't think writing is in the cards for me. I can't tell a story to save my life. But something that I want? My heart's desire? Just like those faeries, above all I want freedom. I want to know a true home. But more painfully, the real desire of my heart is to get my memory back."

Gideon sighs. "You keep one-upping me on the tragedy front. Here I am; woe is me, I want to be an author, and here you are; just wanting a home. I sound like a privileged fool."

"The little things are important. Life is nothing if you're only surviving."

"How'd you get so wise?" he teases.

"I had a stranger burst into my sanctuary and show me the way of enlightenment."

"Well, I should thank him."

"As should I." I pause, swallowing. "Thank you, Gideon. For everything. I never realized how much I needed you."

Gideon tenses with surprise, his eyes sparkling for a moment. "You're welcome."

For a moment we are silent, and then he speaks. "You know, when we find the Harbinger we could probably ask for your memories as well as the way out in exchange for him."

I twist my fingers. "That's what I was hoping for."

He tightens his grip on me and again quiet descends.

"Gideon?"

"Yes?"

I bite my lip. "Please don't leave me."

He dips my head down to come to rest at his throat—despite our identical height—and his warm and clean scent soothes me. "I won't leave you," he promises.

There's nothing sexual in our embrace. There is comfort and support, both of which we require after such a trying time. There is warmth and safety, something I'd never achieve sleep tonight without. We are two people simply needing not to be alone, and needing the proof of it in the physical contact.

I don't let go of Gideon and he doesn't let go of me as we cease speaking, relaxing into the veiled world between waking and sleeping. Internally, I thank him again, wishing everything of those dreams he desires to come true.

It doesn't take long for sleep to claim me, Gideon's embrace lulling me deeper than any drink ever could. Though, just as I'm about to slip into the realm of dreamers, I hear Gideon's velvety voice speak and I realize it was not something I was meant to hear.

"Evelyn, what have you done?"

The next morning our grayed world fills with color and all remnants of fear fade away. As if nothing had ever happened, and that Seelie's death had never occurred. Aside from the memories, and waking wrapped inside Gideon's arms, we continue about our day avoiding the grave outside the tree line.

"I think we should head south," Gideon voices over breakfast.

I quirk a brow and pause with the fork halfway to my mouth. "To look for the Harbinger?"

"No, to find more Seelies. Maybe one of them is the *Ceidwad Cudd.*"

My brows pull together in confusion. "We're looking for the *Ceidwad Cudd,* now?"

Gideon shrugs and lifts a spoonful of cereal to his mouth. "The Harbinger was sent to eliminate the *Ceidwad Cudd,* it makes sense if we find her, we then find him."

With Gideon's suggestion, my spine straightens in uneasiness. Why would he want to switch the search from the Harbinger, unless he *is* him? To cover my anxiety though, I shovel a forkful of melon in my mouth. The one bright point though, is that I cannot be so upset by using a faerie for our own personal gain—they are sociopathic killers.

"Unless that was her."

"Unless, yes."

"So, you want to use her as bait?" I ask tightly, though I try to lend an unconcerned air to my voice. Excitement and anger surprisingly linger on my tongue.

Gideon seems to catch it, his face registering the inflection before he seems to brush it off. "If we can, absolutely. The *Ceidwad Cudd* is allegedly one of the most dangerous members of either court, despite of never killing. She knows the darkest depths of each queen's reach without a formal alliance, but I strongly believe she's Seelie."

"How do you suggest we catch her then?"

"Tadgh said she was fae, so I think you'll have an excuse to make a new glove."

I smirk to Gideon. "Count me in."

We spend the entire day planning and packing, Gideon revealing a set of tent stakes warded against the Unseelie fae. He explains if we create a perimeter with them around our camp each night, it creates a warded boundary and we'll be safe from their threat. I realize with that, that we'll be leaving the cabin behind. The dwelling that has become my sanctuary for the last two years. We end up forfeiting most of our weapons, having had our macabre net stolen, but bring the iron chains I'd favored. Even so, we probably wouldn't have been able to carry such a cumbersome device. Trying to pack light, yet effectively seems to be a more daunting task than I'd been prepared to admit.

When all is said and done, all essential survival equipment packed by the front door, Gideon and I lounge on the couch together. Sharing cups of tea rather than cognac—we need our wits about us tomorrow—and discussing our mutual distaste of the Unseelie Queen.

"She is beautiful, I'll give her that—in an absolutely creepy way," I remark, sipping the herby concoction Gideon had brewed.

"You say that now, but you weren't the one she was feeling up. It was revolting."

"Faeries don't get you going?" I joke casually, a glimmer of humor in my eyes.

"I have equal amounts of crippling fear and morbid curiosity for faeries. I don't think those are promising feelings for the beginning of a relationship. Besides, faeries generally enjoy mortals only for playthings, long-term is impossible with their immortality in mind. It's never something I could compromise."

"You hopeless romantic, you."

"Is that so bad?" he asks timidly, and suddenly, the tone shifts. My heart quivers in my chest, my breath tight. I suddenly burn hot beneath the blanket draped over the two of us, all too aware of the fine layers between us. Knowing I only wear jeans and a thin sweater, no undergarments to be found. Knowing Gideon only has one extra layer over me. Knowing how quickly those things could likely be shed.

"I bet your girlfriend back home would be thrilled to hear that," I breathe out raggedly, averting my gaze to the hearth that burns as hot as my ears.

"I don't have a girlfriend."

"Boyfriend, then."

"There's no one."

Gideon's very warm hand suddenly catches mine, reassuring and real. My eyes whip to him, surprise and excitement trilling through me. My head swims with the genuine attention he fixes on me, his eyes filled with sincerity.

Reaching with his other hand, he strokes my jaw and my eyes shutter in response. His fingers are tentative, but sure, ensuring the touch is welcomed and reciprocated.

I reach out with my free hand and wrap it around our other clasped hand as I lean my cheek into his experimental touch. My storm gray eyes open to lock onto his bronze ones, finding a question in them. Involuntarily, I blush.

"Gideon, I don't know if I've ever…"

"I know, and if there's one thing I could change, it would be to bring back your memories."

My heart swells with emotion, a mix of gratitude and respect. Surprise at his concern and care, shock at his tenderness and understanding. Tingles race through my blood upon every place he touches, his fingers tracing a trail of electrified flesh in their wake.

"Gideon," I breathe, leaning toward him, allowing him to pull me in closer.

The scream of the kettle on the stove shocks me out of the trance. Suddenly, I find myself fumbling backwards, clumsily pushing Gideon away, our moment shattered. Immediately I berate myself for the action, for squirming away and likely sending a wash of rejection Gideon's way. To cover up my embarrassment, I lurch to the stove and remove the kettle, staring loathingly at the heart-shaped dent and cursing it for its irony.

"I think we should call it a night," Gideon announces awkwardly as he collects our abandoned mugs and deposits them in the sink. There's shame on his face while an internal battle wages war across his features, gleaming in his eyes. The conflict is unmistakable.

Humiliation burns in my cheeks and prevents me from speaking so I simply nod and slip away upstairs, shame lighting my bones. Each step is heavy like cinderblocks weighing me down, every stair a protest in my limbs.

I long to return to Gideon, to throw myself at him and kiss him. To dissolve into his embrace and tangle on the woven carpet in front of the fire.

*Stupid. You stupid girl. Isn't this what you want? Why are you letting it slip away? Do you enjoy torturing yourself? Are you a masochist?*

The relentless thoughts savage my mind as I undress and find myself imagining a different reality where I'm not shedding these clothes alone. Where Gideon's hands are sure on my exposed skin, skimming my ribs and caressing my thighs. Where his lips press upon the throb of my pulse in my throat, evoking a gasp and his velvet laugh responds with satisfaction. But the thoughts shatter and I come to my senses, grieving for the fact that those fantasies are not of this world.

Not my world.

So, I slip into the bed, alone and disappointed.

# CHAPTER 13

It could be midnight and it could be near morning when I wake, parched. Judging from the deep night bleeding into my room, I believe it to be the former. I wish I could admire the stars that peek from the curtains for the beauty that they are, but once again it reminds me unnervingly of that deceased Seelie.

With my head pillowed, hair spread around me like a tangled spider's web, I stare up at the ceiling, knowing that I'm wide awake and sleep will not find me anytime soon. I spend a good few minutes debating whether it's worth it to traverse down the steps to sate my thirst. If it's worth the risk of seeing Gideon and feel shame light me up like fireworks.

*Stupid, you* stupid *girl.*

It takes a few more minutes for me to decide that my thirst isn't going to disappear on its own and that sleep refuses to claim me. Sighing, I roll from the sheets and pull on the sweatpants and white sweater.

Padding carefully down the steps, I ensure my strict avoidance of the second stair—the one that creaks—and slip through the empty space between the living room and scarcely used dining room. From there, I pause and briefly watch Gideon asleep on the couch, snoring lightly, blankets piled atop him, and an arm thrown over his eyes. I sigh again and tip-toe to the fridge, silently retrieving the pitcher of purified water.

I pray that I'm quiet enough not to wake him as I pour the water and escape up the stairs. A loud creak suffuses the ground floor of the house as I misstep. My heart stops. In my effort of haste, I neglected to remember the *bloody stair.*

I freeze like a startled rabbit, my gaze whipping to the sleeping man on the couch across the way. Gideon doesn't stir. I exhale in relief and scamper up the stairs, finally returning to the safety of my sleeping area.

Careful not to spill, I take a drink and return to my bed. As I pull the glass from my lips, I suddenly have the foreboding sense that something is innately wrong. Glancing down at my last drops of water, I catch sight of fire.

Dropping the crystal, it shatters across the hardwood floor just as my window is obliterated by a flaming container of gasoline. Diving to the far side of the bed, I narrowly dodge a second shattering window and more flaming, flammable substances. The piercing scent of gas fills the room as the containers spill and begin to leak across the floor, climbing towards my bedding.

Huddling against the wall, my breaths come short and quick as I stare at the orange and red that licks up the room, at the purply smoke billowing from what it devours. Memories begin flashing, and I remain transfixed, frozen by fear. The night I woke to nothing and Hell. The night that claimed Jacob's life to Lady Fate's knife.

A third smash forces me out of my anxiety as a downstairs window is destroyed. Panic erupts within me, spreading through my veins as I realize that Gideon is downstairs, hopelessly unaware. Oblivious to the fact that the flames of have come to earth, eating at the dwelling we'd believe to be a haven in this unforgiving purgatory.

More and more crashes sound and my breathing has become slightly unhinged. But everything is so much worse when I realize, as white-hot fear strangles me, that I haven't heard Gideon call out in shock or fear. My own terror multiplies tenfold as my nightmares become realized and that Gideon could already be dead downstairs.

My traitorous mind strays to images of fire eating Gideon's black waves. Of blood pouring from his amber eyes. Of his heart impaled. Continually, they skitter through my brain, looping in an endless stream.

Could Seelies have found their way inside? Did the Unseelie Court decide to get us moving? Are other humans trying to take over our lodging?

"*Gideon?*" I scream at the night, coughing and spluttering.

No response. His lack of answer only fuels all my worries into a monster amalgamation of true panic.

Pushing off from the wall I've backed into, I lunge for the door, slamming it and closing the smoke out of the rest of the house. I half tumble down the stairs, not giving a damn about that creaking step as I come to the bottom floor. In horror and spasming lungs, I cover my airways with the collar of my sweater, eyes leaking and burning.

Closing the door was naught for anything.

Hell awaits. Fire climbs up the curtains of the living room, eating all the precious books on Gideon's mother's and father's shelves. The room is alight with flame, dark smoke pillowing the ceiling in a foreboding cloudscape. Glass skitters across the wooden floor as rocks soar through the room, knocking over plants and destroying lamps.

Our home has become a funeral pyre.

*"Gideon!"*

Through the film of smoke, I find my way around the broken glass, to the couch, grasping the back of it like it's a life preserver and I'm drowning. But what I wouldn't give for an ocean right now. A tidal wave to douse this inferno into a sad, smoldering disaster.

There is not a single chance of this blaze going out.

With bleary and leaking eyes, I peer over the edge of the couch, finding Gideon collapsed upon the rug. A bloodied mess upon his forehead glares at me and an offending rock sits scarlet beside him.

"Gideon?" I call again, my vocal cords raw with smoke damage. Heartbreakingly, he does not reply and I begin to fear the worst.

Uttering a vicious curse, I vault the couch and stand over him, reaching beneath his arms and hauling him bodily to the door. He is not light and I strain with the effort of hauling the deadweight of someone generously muscled. Dragging him, I near the front door where I can just make out our packed bags.

Every extension and strain of my muscles burns through as hot as the fire I'm trying so desperately to escape from. My back aches from the poor mechanics of yanking him, muttering expletives all the while. Sweat douses my brow, both from heat and looming exhaustion.

Lancing agony shoots through my foot and I yelp, dropping Gideon. Luckily, I have adequate enough reflexes to catch his head with a hand and extended calf. Turning to the pain, an embarrassing whimper leaks out of me. A shard of broken glass protrudes from the arch of my foot, slender and three inches long. Beside my foot lies Gideon's shattered family portrait, his own face now spiderwebbed across the photo.

Nausea roils in my stomach and a new, cold sweat breaks over my face. Drawing in a breath, I yank the glass out with all the ferocity and hate for the Unseelies. I gasp at the bolt of pain that radiates up my leg, clutching my suddenly profusely bleeding foot.

Gritting my teeth, I limp back over to Gideon and once again yank him to the front door as the fire consumes the kitchen in its entirety, swallowing everything in its maw. As I haul Gideon, his head lolling, I curse him out, cursing his unconsciousness. As a bookcase collapses, desperation and adrenaline spike in full force as I realize this place could come down very soon. Letting that fuel me, I become frantic and pull harder, sliding dangerously on the bloody footprints I leave behind me. I slip to the floor onto my ass and suddenly time slows.

I mourn the home that is being utterly destroyed before my eyes. The sanctuary threatens to become a cage and I watch everything crumble. Holes begin to burrow through the hardwood, beams char and groan, ash flutters, all metal reddens, and plastic décor melts. Memories turn to ash, opportunities become smoke, chances burn.

Time resumes and with it, clarity as I realize that sparks are beginning to rain down into the basement. A basement filled with gasoline and a generator.

"*Fuck!*" I hiss, "Fuck, fuck, fuck. Gideon, please wake up."

Finally, I make it to the door with sweat sliding down my back and I pause only to turn the handle, throw a pair of Gideon's shoes into the night, and yank on my own boots before I toss two of our three bags onto Gideon's lap. I'm hoping that they don't tumble off into a fiery demise. Taking the third, I strap it quickly to my back and finally exit into the deep, Yukon night.

I am not gentle, I am frantic, and panicked, so I don't waste breath on apologies as we trip from the stairs and I fall with a still unconscious Gideon atop me. The ground is wet and blessedly cool and I could weep from relief. The air is clean and clear, and like a high in my lungs. The euphoria is exquisite, spinning my mind and sweeping my vision with vertigo.

"*Evelyn…?*" Gideon suddenly coughs, his bronze eyes opening just enough to see the fire reflected back in them.

"We have to move," I urge, pulling him to his feet and carrying his arm over my shoulder. He listens, hauling the bags to his shoulders and pressing a palm to his head. Together, we stumble to the tree line, him leaning on me more than he likely realizes and stop. Gideon halts seconds after me due to the glassiness of his gaze and potential concussion as I help him into his shoes.

At the edge of the cabin clearing is a silver-limned figure.

The Unseelie Queen stands just outside the shadows. Her white and silver frame is calm and collected, a wicked smile carves her face. Fury alights in my soul when I catch sight of what unspools from her claws. A twirling lighter in one and in the other, dangling from a thin silver chain is a stopwatch.

Her message is clear.

Time is ticking.

Flicking the clock and lighter to the brush, the queen turns on her heels and disappears into the night with a lingering, malevolent smile.

Gideon and I manage to escape the inferno, braving the risk of the fae in exchange for abandoning the flames. A look of confusion crosses Gideon's features as I lead him to the cave I had recalled from my first nights stranded here. The only guide I have is whatever I recollect from memory led by the beam of a flashlight.

Placing warded tent stakes at the entrance of the cave prevents any Unseelie from entering, but won't stop any more fires if the queen wishes for it. I set the flashlight down, aiming it to illuminate most of the cave and return to my survival partner, easing Gideon against the wall as his eyes shutter with exhaustion. But I can't allow that, not when he potentially has a concussion.

"Gideon," I say sternly, cupping his cheeks. "You need to stay awake."

His eyes flutter, revealing glassy amber. He cracks a smile. "You saved my life."

I tentatively smile back. "I did."

"I like the sound of your voice. It's rough and husky, but lovely," he tells me dazedly, reaching forward and gripping my fingers. "Talk to me more."

"About?"

"Anything."

I bite my lip, but begin, resting my hands on his shoulders, looking away.

I don't tell him that my foot is injured. I don't tell him that my lungs spasm with every breath. I don't tell him that my eyes burn.

"I wish I could tell you who I am, not just because it would give me something to tell you, but I want you to know me. No one has ever known me, and I wasn't sure I wanted anyone to. Until you. I wish I could tell you stories of my childhood, tell you all my favorite things." I pause. "But I don't know who that is. I don't know who I am when I'm not surviving. I don't know an Evelyn who lives and thrives." My eyes burn and this time it isn't from the smoke. "But I'd like to meet her."

Returning my attention to Gideon, I find his eyes closed and his lips parted.

"Gideon?" A shrill tone leaks into my voice. Shaking him, he doesn't wake, so I immediately take his vitals and I deflate with relief to find a steady pulse.

Sinking beside him, I hold his hand, wrapping my fingers to his wrist, monitoring his pulse. I survey our bags and hesitate upon his, finding a brown, leather-bound notebook, filled with his scrawling handwriting, seeing the word *Harbinger* jump out. My eyes flicker to his face, and I hold the book in my lap. I stay resolute with a bleeding foot and smoke-choked skin, checking his vitals every fifteen minutes and fingering the pages of his book. We stay like that and I remain awake long enough to watch the stars sink below the horizon before the first rays of sunlight replace the night's horrors.

I'm awake long enough to hear the cabin's explosion.

# CHAPTER 14

GIDEON'S NOTES

*His fathomless soul is as black as his mercy. His dark heart is as cold as the abyss. His cruel mind is as sharp as a blade. If one dares thwart his queen, they soon find their end, upon that golden blade is Hell's own gate.*

*Unparalleled to any, feared by all, no one knows the nightmare they call Harbinger.*

*Tales of lore are no story; every rumor is truth of his dealings. Ripe with glory, with a reputation which precedes* him. *All would tell of his power, if their neck had not met his hand.*

*The beheaded assassin would have told of how her clever ploy crumbled in his presence and turned to ash in her hands. But the dead do not speak.*

*The eviscerated creature would have blamed his folly upon the alignment of the stars and moon and predetermination. But the dead do not speak.*

*The starving prisoner would scream for an untruth, swearing fealty to his new false queen. But the dead do not speak.*

*He was singled out by six and he was one, count down from ten and they were done. None stood before him, but the corpses he slew, flaunting the dangers of which he can do.*

*Feats of victory are blessed by Lady Fate, by her hand and blade, he is unstoppable. His inception began with the earning of his name and the first battle of the legendary warriors.*

*A century of training eclipsed the lives of two fae; one of gold, one of silver. It was a fateful night when the two warriors ceremoniously concluded their arduous training and were ambushed. With a contingency of thirty against two, Silver and Gold threatened to be swallowed whole. Equipped with dagger and sword, the ground was soon soaked with blood.*

*The first insurgent broke from the lines to be impaled by one. The second, obliterated by the other. Wave after wave crested over the two, diminishing with every tide break upon the shores of their swords.*

*Clashes of steel sang songs in chorus, moans of the dead beat the rhythm to the night. Oath-Sworn drank its fill. When the water turned red, Gold saw Silver fall, calling out for his comrade in arms. Crimson ran rivers, scarlet flooded the plain. Upon sixteen bodies stood Gold. Upon fourteen bodies lay Silver.*

*Gold demanded of Lady Fate to bring Silver back. Gold demanded that his equal be returned. Gold demanded nothing less. It was then, when Silver returned to the land of the living, having passed the veil and earned his name. It was then the Revenant was born from the blood of Silver. And there, by the warrior's threats to the goddess, did Gold earn his name, having been gifted and spoken by Lady Fate herself.*

*Harbinger.*

*So, begins, the legend of two. Harbinger and Revenant, forever remembered, never truly known.*

# CHAPTER 15

The afternoon dawns and Gideon wakes, clear and nursing only a mild headache and some nausea. Myself, surprisingly enough, retains only a shallow foot injury, a wound which only seemed more severe from adrenaline.

I explain our last night's situation to a still groggy Gideon as I take stock of our inventory, relieved that our packed bags made it out—albeit smelling potently of smoke. I tell him about the destroyed cabin, the arson organized by the Unseelie Queen herself, his blunt force injury, and grudgingly inform him about my foot in case I drop dead of gangrene. However, I neglect to mention how much I'd dragged him out. I also refrain from admitting that I'd read his notebook.

It startles me when I'm disappointed Gideon doesn't remember my confession from last night. Instead, he remains somewhat distant and detached, conversing when necessary but drawing into himself and resting his energy when not.

We decide to rest for the day, safely in our cave before we journey out. It is suggested that we don't uphold the Unseelie Queen's request of searching for the Harbinger for her—at least for now—but rather attempt to escape to the south. Finding him may be one of our only ways out, but if Róisín's quip was anything to go by, then he may be the most lethal option. With the plan tentatively laid, I reluctantly agree and in moments my sleep-deprived brain takes over.

After years of traversing the Yukon, the trek never becomes any more pleasant. The two of us clamber over fallen, moss-eaten logs, and duck beneath dipping tree limbs, while tramping down lichen littered earth. The permafrost is unforgiving and only the most resilient of flora prosper and thrive within it, lending a pronounced set of obstacles to tackle. Above, the sun filters through evergreen boughs, limning shafts of sunlight with speckled shadows.

Only hours into our journey south and I'm starting to feel the weight of the pack on my back, sweat sliding down my neck. I refuse to say anything though, to open up to weakness, especially when I'm unprepared for any unsympathetic air Gideon might display.

I'd inadvertently rejected him the night before last, and despite my not meaning to, he'd felt it and I'd fractured, if not severed, something between us. I scold myself still, especially when the fantasies of Gideon taking me to bed run rampant through my mind, each one becoming more elaborate than the last, his hands on my breasts, his mouth on my neck, his cock between my legs...

Anger lights my bones and fuels my steps onward as I push the thoughts down with every stomp of my boot. How could my concerns and rejection over lovesickness have occurred the same night our safe haven burned to the ground?

Hours more pass in silence, the only sounds are of the wood around us. Noises from the trickling of a stream, to the tittering of birds, to the tromp of our feet upon the forest's carpet. Occasionally, there's a snap of a twig from a poorly placed foot, but thankfully, faeries have yet to bother us. Even so, we remain armed.

Gideon hacks away at a swath of thorns blocking the narrow deer trail we've discovered, swinging with an ax imbued with that faerie's hated iron. Shallow scratches line his hands from the swipe of blackberry thorns, cursing the foliage all the while.

The next day, the stubbornness in both of us is evident by an unbroken quietude that strains in my chest, producing a palpable aura of tension. The tension itself is a fog so thick its near physical. A knife could cut through it and even meet resistance. Setting up camp at night is awkward, both of us unwilling to take the first step forward and it speaks legions of our will power—and frankly needless self-restraint. But I refuse to be the failure. The one who gives in first.

So, we don't speak.

There are small grunts and sighs in each other's general vicinity while camp is set, though. The placement of the warded tent spikes surrounding our camp with the tent assembly had been achieved through such noises, but beyond that is asking for more than either of us are willing to give. Though I do nearly break during the night, during the darkest hours. From the cold that is bone deep and penetrating, and though we slept side by side in the canvas tent, we did not touch. It was only the fact that the temperatures were too high for snow that allowed us this pettiness. We knew the other was awake, yet we were both too pig-headed to change. Or perhaps I was too embarrassed and he was too.

Sleep did not come for us last night.

We trudge through the morning at first light, bleary-eyed and grumpier than all hell. By then the soundlessness is piercing and awkward.

By midday, the silence is deafening, and the tension is further wrought between us. We stop by an easily defendable lake, a small oval body of water frozen with the last grips of winter. Generous sized boulders frame one side of it. I perch on one of them while Gideon breaks through the ice and refills his canteen while I swig from my own, distantly grateful for the Yukon's low temperatures. For once.

Though, I won't be singing the same tune should we be stuck here after September—or rather, another night stuck like this together.

The sun is more golden here, beaming down on us, and chased with the scent of fresh mountainous air and pine. Across the lake a small deer sips from the water and nestled high in an evergreen tree is an eagle's nest. This slice of paradise is a caustic twist on the serenity that could be offered. Had this not been Unseelie territory, this could be admirable, picturesque even.

I try to imagine a world I'd lived in once before. A world where I'd come upon a sight such as this and sat down to sketch or photograph the world around me. Or perhaps I'd been more accustomed to city life, where concrete and steel were a constant way of life, where there could be any sort of person I might come across. Maybe even I'd existed in a world revolving upon music and parties, of burning liquor and kisses just as fierce.

But I don't know. Try as I might, anything before waking up to the forest burning around me is a yawning chasm of nothingness. An abyss where my memories fall to their deaths.

"Should we talk?" I finally ask, breaking the stillness around us. I keep my eyes averted to my backpack and sweater by my feet.

Gideon lifts his head, his forehead wound healing quickly, and I'm startled to see a smile painted there. "There is nothing to talk about, Evelyn. I understand."

"No, I don't think you do," I correct him, raising my hands helplessly.

"It's okay, really you don't need to explain yourself. I read the signs wrong, I won't make the same mistake again."

"Gideon, that's not—you didn't—I," I falter for words as he turns away, a mask sliding down over his features. I deflate and sink into a cowed position, wishing to just become part of the boulder that I'm seated upon.

My own form of pitying rejection swims over me and I bite my lip, realizing just how unreachable the depths to this fissure have formed. But what should I care in regards to my feelings if Gideon's the Harbinger? Perhaps he is the key to getting out, but does that have any bearing on my desires? Should I even care what the Seelie Queen's pet thinks of me? Should I even care about him? Care if he cares for me?

I shouldn't.

But regardless of it all, I do.

Strengthening my resolve, I storm over to him and force him to face me. He looks up startled to see me in all my glorious irritation, the lines of the anger tracing the shape of my frame and emanating from my very core. My teeth ache from the forcible urge to grind them and a throb begins in my forehead.

"If you don't like me, Gideon, that's fine. But if you're avoiding me like this because you think that *I* don't care for *you*, then think again." My voice is borderline hostile, taking on an edge of urgency.

"That's not why." He pinches the bridge of his nose, shutting his eyes against the emotion I catch tearing through them. "I shouldn't be involved with anyone; I've gotten carried away with you and I'm sorry. I'm angrier at myself."

"Is it because you *do* have someone waiting for you at home?"

"No, I already told you I don't, I—" Suddenly he breaks off and his eyes fill with terror. *"Get down!"*

Heedlessly, Gideon tackles me to the ground just as a bite of metal slices across the right side of my exposed back. I shout a curse and fumble to my hands and knees, discovering a faerie advancing on us.

Not just any faerie, but Róisín. I realize with dawning horror that I'd never commanded her not to harm us, all I did was ask her to swear on the journey involving the Unseelie Court. I'd never amended the statement.

Shit.

I'd also been so wrapped up in my Gideon drama that I didn't feel her approaching.

Fuck.

Gideon and I both make it to our feet, standing side by side, facing Róisín head on.

"Isn't this sweet," she preens, twirling a dirk with a rose-patterned handle. "I've interrupted the lovebird's reconciliation. Perhaps the star-crossed lovers' fate shall suit you better."

I crouch slowly to the ground, scavenging for Róisín's discarded knife, the twin to the one she spins now. My fingers touch the wet blade and I find the handle in my grip immediately. Coming up to my full height, I brandish the weapon, feeling its balanced weight and finding it remarkably comfortable in my palm.

"Róisín, I command you to not harm—" Róisín's second blade flies past me as I lean back from the line of fire. "—or kill," I continue, advancing slowly on my newfound prey.

Róisín hisses and launches herself at me with a hand upraised and clutching a third knife. We meet, her arm descending just as I slam my own rose-hilted blade into her heart.

In the same moment, Gideon throws her second knife into her trachea.

Startled, I spin to find Gideon unfurling himself from a leaning downward position, having used his upper torso for momentum. He draws his dominant hand back, pulling it back to his side. His eyes are hard and burning, and with a certainty, I know mine are not.

Whipping back to Róisín, I find her spluttering and choking, each hand reaching for each knife as she stumbles back. Crimson blood pumps from her fatal wounds as she crashes to her knees, her sage pallor graying with descending death. Her rose-red lips open, her thorn teeth stained dark as more blood pours forth, spilling down her chin. She falls to her side, arms loose around her as her amethyst eyes dull and go flat with the sleep of death.

Slowly, I turn to Gideon, finding him stock still. He appraises me carefully, his lips blanched into a thin line.

Thoughts run rampant as I realize our mutual kill has occurred. That this event did not feel foreign to me, and I realize from the coolness in his eyes that this event was not foreign to him either.

We've both killed before.

Whatever I was before, it involved death. Whatever Gideon is now, it involves death.

*Harbinger...*

The word is whispered with sinister intent, darkening to its namesake, the title stained with another layer of blood. The idea is insidious and parasitic, latching onto my brain and forcing its religion down my throat. It chants Gideon's new title.

Gideon's precision with the blade was not luck. I'd been mere inches from where the blade sunk and only someone with the confidence and training could have achieved such a feat. He doesn't pitch forward with apologies. He doesn't lurch to ensure my safety. He doesn't even flinch to ask if the blade nicked me. He knew.

*Are you the Harbinger?*

It's on the tip of my tongue, the urge to say it, to ask those four enormous words. But I can't. I can't bring myself to somehow draw them from my vocal cords. To elicit them from my throat.

"No, I'm not," Gideon whispers, and I realize the question must be painted across my face with bold color.

"Then how?" I return, coming toward him, bloodied hand outstretched.

He takes a few steps closer to me, watching me carefully as I do to him. "I was trained. All my life. You don't negotiate with faeries and not know how to defend yourself."

I swallow carefully as I truly take him in, as if for the first time. He'd been soft at times. So soft in every way that counted. His voice, his eyes, his mouth, even his mannerisms, his wordplay and movements. They were sweet, tender, mild. But of course, I should've seen the strength in his battle. The moments of his harshness and hardness. The trap he'd laid, the way we fought to bait the faeries, the way he swung the ax against the rope, the way he killed Róisín.

The way *we* killed Róisín.

How could this man, with the bright amber eyes and silky locks be capable of the sweetness and ferocity held in the capacity he has displayed?

"That makes sense enough," I breathe heavily.

He quirks a slight smile. It doesn't reach his eyes. "Can I see your back? I think she got a good slice in there."

I nod, turning my back to Gideon, and crossing my arms over my chest. He tries to pull up the material, but it sticks and I suck in a hiss of a breath.

"Sorry," he says softly, gently plucking the fabric from the wound and easing it onto my shoulder. I feel his fingers pause and realize that he's seeing my back for the first time. All the scars. All the ruination of it. My entire back is a map of destruction, with scars lacing the entirety of it, most silvery, some red and angry. I still, tensing for the revulsion.

But it doesn't come.

Instead, I feel his calloused fingertips tracing the raised welts that create a labyrinth across my spine. Instead, I feel his concern and empathy.

Eventually, His fingers find the space at my spine that I prayed he would miss. Between my shoulders, at a particularly mauled bit of flesh, is something distinctly solid beneath the skin.

"It's a bone deformity," I answer before he can voice the inevitable question.

"No, it's not," he tells me. Surprising me.

I stiffen, ready to rebuke his claim but he senses it and stops me. "Feel," he says, tracing the shape. "That's too round, too perfect to be a deformity. There's something there."

"Maybe Jacob forgot to remove some of the shrapnel from the plane crash."

"If he did, that's one odd piece of shrapnel." He stops, his fingers pressing down on the spot. "Evelyn, I think we should remove it."

I draw in a breath, apprehension gripping me tight. I don't want to be seen as weak, and if I'm honest with myself, I'm curious. Pointing to the first aid kit in my backpack, I attempt to quell my fear. Gideon guides me to the boulder I'd been sitting on prior to this mess, and I perch upon it, and wait.

Memories replay in my mind. Scenes of Jacob forcing me to bite down on a bit as he carved out my flesh, as he worked away the metal and plastic imbedded inside. Memories of his skewed graciousness, how he kept me awake with cracks across the face. How slumber found me and guided me to rest, so that I could heal and recover from the torture he'd inflicted. My instincts warn me, reminding me of what I've been through, but I know Gideon. I know he's not Jacob.

I pull the shirt completely off of my person and cover my chest, leaning forward while Gideon sets out all our supplies. He turns his eyes that are darkened with reluctance, and I meet his concern from my curled position with my head resting atop my knees. A small smile traces my lips. "I trust you," I tell him breathily.

He swallows, but nods in affirmation.

"Then let's do this."

# CHAPTER 16

Minor surgery in the middle of the woods probably isn't anyone's idea of a practical task, yet here we are.

Gideon proceeds to hammer the warded tent stakes into the ground around us before sanitizing his equipment—that being his hands and one of Róisín's dirks. Having handed me a flannel to put on backwards, I slide my arms into the sleeves, and let the buttons rest against my ribs as if they're meant to do up my spine.

As we both get our bearings, we don't speak, but it's a different sort of silence. An assessing and processing quiet rather than the tension bound one we'd been forced into only minutes before. When I indicate for him to begin, his hands don't shake, and the prospect reassures me as I wrap my arms around my knees.

The first prick of the knife is a starburst of pain. A blinding white star burning across my vision as he neatly slices an incision. Gritting my teeth together, my muscles tensing, I curse to myself and curse Jacob's half-assed job. Or perhaps even Gideon's mistake. Regardless, with the deeper cut, I hiss an expletive, and I sense, rather than hear Gideon's accompanying apology.

Suddenly, I feel Gideon's fingers dig into the wound and my vision momentarily blacks from the pain and discomfiting pressure. Revulsion roils in my gut at the wrongness of someone's hands beneath my flesh, but I breathe through it and reassure myself of the necessity.

I remind myself that it's Gideon and he won't hurt me. I trust him.

An abrupt pressure lifts from my back as Gideon withdraws his hand with an item clutched in it. I chance a look at him and find him staring dumbfounded at his scarlet gloved hand. His almond-shaped eyes are widened in shock and his mouth has dropped open.

"What is it?" I ask, my husky voice made rougher by pain.

"It's a coin."

"A *coin*?" I repeat, certain I'd misheard, but something in his tone indicates that it's not as simple as that and not just any coin.

"Do you recognize this pattern?" He wipes away the blood coating the silver coin, and I find myself staring at a sigil I've seen once before.

"Is that—?"

"The Unseelie Court sigil," Gideon completes for me, expression still dumbstruck.

The design is simple and elegant, a full buck-moon cupped by a pair of antlers with three anemones adorning the crest like a crown. The same design I'd seen etched onto the glass globe above the Unseelie Queen's head.

"Why would I have an Unseelie coin under my skin? And what is it covered in?" I ask, astonished, eyeing the syrupy substance leaking from the coin. It's a thick moving liquid the color of tar.

Before Gideon can answer, a sudden, unmistakable urge rises up, and I have only moments to avert my face before all the contents of my stomach come spewing out. The bile burns my throat and the wracking dry heaves tear my trachea apart. An upsurge of sweat pours off of me, like a cresting of a wave, bringing with it a tingling sensation like the patter of raindrops.

And just as soon as it came, it leaves, carrying with it a breeze of fresh air.

Wiping my mouth with the ruined and blood-soaked shirt on my lap, I discard the tee, only to turn and find Gideon's horror-struck expression. Rejection washes through me mixed with humiliation and frustration.

I just vomited in front of him, of course he's going to be disgusted.

With that same expression pasted across his face, he stumbles back, dropping the dirk from his grip. It plummets and lodges in the ground, glinting in the dappled sunlight.

"Evelyn...?" His voice is suddenly thin, meek, and terrified.

"What's wrong?" A hot flush burns in my cheeks. What *isn't* wrong right now?

"Evelyn, you need to go look at your reflection *now*." His tone leaves no room for questions, and with drawn brows I do as he says and carefully cross the threshold of our wards and make my way to the lake.

When I kneel down to look at myself, I see what Gideon realized.

I almost collapse with repulsion.

"What the *hell*?"

Staring back at me is a creature of wondrous and ethereal creation. My previously ordinary gray eyes shimmer like frozen silver starlight, glittering with the night sky. Once lank and dull hair now shines a brilliant silver-white, a perfect shade of platinum that falls in sleek panels around my face. A new complexion of smooth alabaster replaces what used to be washed out and plain. High cheekbones, pointed chin, and a rounded jaw have shifted infinitesimally, taking on a set of trademark characteristics.

But what truly shocks me are the ears that break from the sheets of my long hair that are ever so slightly peaked, pointed with the distinct marker of the Fair Folk.

I realize with uncomprehending horror that I am a faerie.

I am fae.

Turning in abject terror, I face Gideon, emotions clear as day streaming across my face. "Gideon...I didn't know. I *swear* I didn't know."

"I know," he whispers, hardly breathing.

"You believe me?"

"Of course. You're fae, you can't lie."

The truth of that fact hits me like a punch to the gut. The fact that he only trusts my word because I can't lie. Not because he trusts *me*. The world threatens to suffocate me with my new reality, the upended lies I'd been fed, the untruths right in front of my face.

"How did we never figure this out?" Gideon asks, and I notice that he distinctly stays within the perimeter of the wards. I don't bother to tell him that I'd crossed them before without a single problem.

"I don't know, but this doesn't make any sense. I've been touching iron with no issues this entire time." I reach for the iron ax we've been using for the past week, clearly wrapping my palm around the blade head. Not even a tingle of pain follows. No welt forms. No nausea surges. "You're the expert, how can this work?"

Gideon considers, watching me reproachfully as he stares at my hand wrapped around the ax. "Try to lie. Maybe you're only part fae."

"And say what?"

"Anything. Anything that's obviously a lie."

I pause, thinking, and a niggling thought strikes me. "I have red h—" The word gets lodged in my throat, a force blocking my tongue from moving. From saying the word *hair*. I realize without a shadow of a doubt that I have the inability to lie.

"*What the fuck*," we whisper in unison.

I fall to the ground, clutching my head in my hands, careful to avoid touching my offending ears and feel the world fall out from under me. Feeling my sanity slip into a yawning pit below my feet. Blackness croons beneath me, chuckling at my utter misfortune. The void luxuriates in my misery and thirsts for my feeble lucidity.

"Why would your own turn on you, Evelyn? Obviously, someone wanted to shut you up or keep you hidden. Why else would you get dumped in the Yukon?" Gideon implores, uneasily edging out of his protective square.

I lift my head slowly; my unnaturally silver eyes meeting his warm amber ones, and connect the dots. Slowly translating.

*Hidden.*

Tadhg said she was fae. He said she was missing.

"Gideon. I think you've found the *Ceidwad Cudd.*"

Gideon sucks in a quick breath, brows rising comically high, the whites of his eyes showing all around. Beside him, his hands hang uselessly, for the first time utterly at a loss as to what to do. We'd planned to use the *Ceidwad Cudd* as bait to draw out the Harbinger, but now that we think that I could be her, is he still willing to use me so?

A pang of sorrow reverberates in my chest as I remember our conversation from only days before, how we'd unabashedly relished the idea of torturing and using the *Ceidwad Cudd* for our personal gain. How I'd grinned at the prospect of beating her senseless with my garish glove. How he'd coolly explained how we'd catch her.

She was just fae after all.

But now we know that I am too.

Now, we know that I might be her.

Now, there is a perfectly Evelyn-sized wrench in our plan and we have ten days to figure a way out of it before the Unseelie Queen comes for our heads. The Unseelie Queen who likely organized for the *Ceidwad Cudd's* silence and anonymity arranged by the coin we'd extracted.

"Obviously we have a severe change in plans," Gideon finally announces. "I'm sure anything you can remember will be helpful."

I draw in a breath that catches in my throat, but more than anything I want to be held. To be reassured. For Gideon to do those things. But I can see very clearly in his apprehensive body language that the likeliness of that scenario being successful is a snowball's chance in Hell. I avert my eyes to hide the pain blooming in them.

"I know we do," I whisper. "But I don't know what to do. I don't know *what* I know."

"What about your brother? He must've known something?"

"Jacob?" I realize I haven't once taken him into consideration, and what my identity means for him.

As I bring his image into my attention, a hazy picture fills my mind and I startle at the memory surging upon me. As it unfurls, I fall into it and find myself transported.

I lean against a nondescript stone wall, my shoulder pressed to the cool rock, my arms over my chest. Before me is Jacob as I had remembered him, only this time his blue eyes are sly, his mouth quirked into a seductive smile. He reaches for me, trailing his index finger from my collarbone and through my long, silvery hair. I laugh, a delicate chiming sound, threaded with a husky tone that sends my hair rising. My own disloyal hand comes to his chest and places it over a racing heart. As I lean into the touch, my lips graze his ear as I whisper into it.

"I hear you have news of the queen."

He chuckles, his lips brushing my lobe. "Now what would give you that impression? Are you perhaps spying on me?"

"Oh, you mustn't play a fool. You know who I am. By now you're aware I trade in confidences."

"You work with me only because I discovered you're the *Ceid*—"

The memory evaporates and with it, the conclusion I draw solidifies.

Grounding myself with the forest floor beneath me, my nails burrowing into the earth, I heave deep, staggering breaths. An absolute truth hits me, a daunting discovery that I *know* without a shadow of a doubt.

"Jacob was certainly *not* my brother," I reveal, nausea roiling in my belly.

"How do you know?"

"Because a memory just came back to me, and that is absolutely *not* the way you interact with siblings."

Gideon's face reddens. "So, you two were together." The sentence is worded as a statement, yet his tone lends to the fact that he wishes it were a question.

I purse my lips together. "I don't think it was like that." His face flushes deeper. He must be thinking to what Tadgh said about the *Ceidwad Cudd's*—my—use of seduction. "That being said, I think it was flirty banter and selling secrets. I think we were using each other." I hesitate. "And in my memory…he began to call me the *Ceidwad Cudd*."

All the air floods from Gideon's lungs. "Fuck." He paces as he contemplates, his voice made gravelly by stress.

"I know."

"Well, on a different topic. I think I know what that black stuff was," Gideon informs me, toying with the coin. "It's a faerie tonic, causes specific amnesia. On faeries it's temporary, on everyone else, it's permanent. It makes you forget the *other* world and generally used as a punishment."

"So, how long do you think it'll take for me to get my memories back?"

He shrugs a muscled shoulder. "Maybe weeks. That shit was in you for two years, it could be longer. Maybe something can trigger them back. And this—" he lifts the coin to eye-level, "is an amulet for glamours, it was how you looked human all this time."

"Dammit," I mutter, getting to my feet and pacing the lake in my worn-out boots. "Regardless, none of this explains me being able to touch iron."

"You've got me there," Gideon sighs, pocketing the amulet and packing up our equipment. "But I don't think we should stick around here. The sooner we leave here, the sooner we can get south and get you to your court."

I realize with a start that I must be Seelie, that I'd belonged to the Seelie Queen. Otherwise, the warded stakes would have prevented both my entry and exit to them, including those surrounding the cabin.

The *Ceidwad Cudd* was loyal to the Light Court. But to what extent?

One mystery solved. Millions more to go. Though I've proven something to myself about my own identity.

The *Ceidwad Cudd* is not pacifist, nor adverse to killing.

# CHAPTER 17

That night, Gideon takes the first watch at camp while I doze fitfully in the tent, anxieties and questions whirling in my mind. I stare up at the low ceiling of the canvas tent, wishing for all the answers and solutions. Wishing even for sleep to claim me in a deep embrace, but all I'm graced with are brushes of slumber.

"For how malicious you can be, Evelyn, you are quite the prude," a girl's celestial contralto whispers in memory, her black hair fanned across a peach-colored pillow.

The room is doused in a faint copper light, red satin sheets lie rumpled beneath us, the two of us are twined beneath a coral bed cover. Alabaster and ivory skin are marked with fingerprints and love-bites. Eyes that are pale and icy, like gray chips from a glacial lake meet those that glitter with decadent intentions of melted chocolate. Pale pink lips dance with rose-red ones.

My husky laugh is muffled by the warmth of soft flesh, my lips pressed against a slender throat, her scarlet locks smelling of orchid and cherry. Her pulse hammers as my mouth descends. "As much as I enjoy kissing you, I'd prefer to lick you," I proclaim before I slowly trail my fingers and lips below her navel.

As I reach her apex a low moan is elicited by the girl and I wake with a start.

Flying to an upright position, I clutch the blankets to my chest and pant heart-racing breaths, sweat beading upon my brow. I search around the tent, finding an empty bed, and an even emptier chest.

Who was that faerie? Clearly there was something going on there. How many lovers have I had and forgotten? How many heartbreaks had I faced that vanished? Did I love her? Do I still? Is she searching for me? Grieving for me? Is there anyone else?

What does this mean for Gideon? Clearly there is *something* going on here—or at least, was. The electricity is unmistakable. The connection deep and ingrained by trust and reliance for survival. Perhaps that is also past tense. The attraction is certainly there, having been displayed clear as day as soon as I met him. But what of those moments? Sharing our hopes and fears, the history we remember, the near kisses? Those weren't nothing. So, what does that mean for the faerie with the contralto and eyes of warmth?

Nothing?

Everything?

Betrayal?

Frustration gets the best of me, so I whip off the blankets, and climb outside the tent. The first thing I see is the sky. The Northern Lights dance in shades of green and turquoise, flashing like the gemstone and acid. As if the gases were waving in a breeze, the lights flicker in and out of existence on ribbons of magic, beautiful and ethereal in the sky.

There, Gideon sits alone staring out into the night, searching the trees for any signs of movement, of danger—though, those things aren't mutually exclusive. His black hair shows signs of having run his hands through it, his amber eyes—a peculiar shade of orange-brown—have darkened with the heavy burden of our new truth.

"Couldn't sleep?" he asks distantly without looking at me, staring at the small fire before him. Not even bothering to wonder at the majesty of the Aurora Borealis above him.

I wrap the red flannel around me tighter, coming up next to him and taking a seat beside him on the cold earth. "Had a bit of a nightmare."

He snorts lightly. "A creature of the night having a nightmare."

A jolt of hurt spears me in the chest at his ruthless delivery and feel my heart crush ever so slightly, like an anvil pressing down. Gideon turns to me, wincing.

"That was supposed to come out a little more light-hearted. It was supposed to be a joke."

"It didn't feel like one," I mutter to the dirt.

"Evelyn." Gideon turns to face me, both of us in the safety of the Seelie wards, as he reaches for my hand, the one that had been digging into my jean-clad leg. "I'm sorry, it's just— this is not how I envisioned my plan going. You being fae has thrown everything I've known out the window."

"What do you mean?"

He drags in a sigh that throws his shoulders back. "Everything was black and white before. Faeries were bad, we were good. Now, you and Tadgh, and that dead Seelie have shown that not all faeries are horrid, and that we may not be so virtuous when we torture, kidnap, and threaten creatures like that. I can only imagine it being worse for you because they're your kind."

I wrap my arms around my knees staring at the glowing green auroras high above, twirling with the stars that beckon so far out of reach. I watch Gideon, his face so close, but so far away. I think of the faerie from my memories, of her full, red lips and fierce, creaseless eyes, unfathomably distant. I remember Jacob and the flirty smile he'd sent me, forever gone.

"Do you see me differently now?" I ask, my voice guarded. I refuse to meet his gaze and instead stare headlong into the trees.

Gideon stays silent and I can sense him thinking, wanting to lie, but not being able to. His kind heart shines through and he inhales. "Yes, you know I do. I told you how I felt about faeries."

*I have equal amounts of crippling fear and morbid curiosity for faeries.*

And darker even, I recall what he'd further said.

*I don't think those are promising feelings for the beginning of a relationship.*

I bite my lip, hurt blooming in my chest, but I keep it from my face.

"But I think there's more gray in the world, and I don't think fear and curiosity are the only things I feel for a certain one of the fae."

Hope spans in my chest, fanning wings wide and proud around my heart. My lungs fill and my heart races in its cage. And suddenly I become all too aware of my attraction and feelings for Gideon.

Suddenly, everything in this moment is the black and white that Gideon has claimed he doesn't know anymore. I realize the sweetness that drew me in without my accord, the strength that keeps me on my toes, the empathy that cornered my heart, and the ruthlessness that is a match to my own. I discover with a harsh slap of reality that my heart swells with the thought of him. Whether it be the adulterous desires of my fantasy, or the genuine comfort and safety of his arms that simply hold me through the night.

With a confidence bolstering me, I come up on my knees, and as Gideon turns, I place my forearms on his shoulders, taking him in carefully. Slowly, I bring myself over him straddling him as I fist my hands in his hair. Gideon gazes at me, startled, yet facing me, nonetheless. His features are traced with golden lines from the fire, his tilted eyes limned with the embers, his black hair highlighted orange. Those waves of his remain tousled and swallow the night, even as my fingers twine through those silken locks, pulling him closer. His breath hitches slightly in his throat, his lips parting in response. Upon my hip his palm burns, searing me with the same desire that simmers in his fiery eyes.

"Do you want me to stop?" I ask gently.

This moment with the auroras in the sky, casting magic onto us feels unbelievably perfect. Electricity zings between us, a connection humming with a rightness that feels ultimately new and thrilling. Tantalizing tingles race from the fingertips pressed to me, on the slight curve there and on every spot his eyes trace. I feel our matched longing, the other half to my own.

"No," he nearly growls.

His full lips brush my throat, on my pulse that races as he gently nips the sweet spot, and I gasp from the flash of pleasure that rips through me. I dig my fingertips into his hair and the defined muscle of his shoulders, inhaling the scent of him. Pulling him into me, luxuriating in the smell of pine and woodsmoke, and that lime soap from the cabin. A smell of *home*. A smell like coming home.

Curiously, his fingers graze the edge of the flannel I wear unbuttoned, and I allow him to reach beneath. To explore as he spans his palm on my flat abdomen, raising goosebumps in his wake. I trace the shape of his jaw, tangling my fingers in his waves. I let him push the flannel from my shoulders and underneath all that remains is a thin and worn tank top. He pushes the shirt up to my ribs, exposing my toned stomach. His fingers skim the flesh there and I lean back my head, a soft sound escaping my throat. Gideon presses his lips to the edge of my jaw, nipping up and down my throat. He plucks the strap of the top, guiding it down my shoulder, his thumb grazing my peaked nipple. I groan and grind against him, finding his erection straining at his jeans.

"Evelyn," he moans softly, biting below my ear.

I reach down and palm him through his pants, feeling him throb for me. He clutches me tighter and his breaths come faster, his thumb stroking and brushing that nipple over and over again. His desire for me is evidenced by the thick member I feel between us and the idea of it inside me has me aching and wet for him.

As if he knows exactly where my thoughts went, his hand slides down to my jeans, popping open the button with a flick of his fingers. Underneath I wear nothing and as his fingers skim just beyond the zipper. I rock against him, eager to feel those fingers deeper. He acquiesces and I can feel the heat of his fingertips exploring, almost where I want it. A second later and he finds my slickness and swirls his finger around it. I moan and grind myself against that tantalizing finger. He meets the pressure and the friction increases, I palm him rougher and he growls, fisting a hand in my hair and crushing his mouth to mine.

His lips are rough and demanding, his tongue slipping into my mouth and dancing with mine. My lips move against his wanting more, needing more. His fingers don't stop their lavish swirling, until a finger slips further and dips into my core, taking the wetness and bringing it back to my apex. He kisses harder as I begin to moan in earnest, approaching a cliff that I want to throw myself from. My hand scrambles for the button on his jeans, begging to free him and feel the hot length of him.

Breaking from the kiss for breath, he palms my breast in his other hand. He brings his mouth to it, licking it through the thin material, nipping the tight bud. Sending thrills of pleasure racing through me.

I want to come undone.

"Tell me…" he whispers softly.

"Tell you what?" I ask roughly, yearning allowing my words to have the effect of strokes or caresses, my eyes heavy lidded and liquid with thirst.

He shutters his eyes.

"Tell me why we shouldn't be together."

"I don't want to."

"I need you to. I don't think this should go further unless we talk. Right now."

Surprise is a bucket of ice water. It loosens my grasp, my heart freezing in its cavity as frost begins crawling through my chest. I pull back, removing my hand from his still hard cock, my desire cooling. He withdraws his hand from my pants.

I search him beseechingly, confused with his line of thought. He keeps his eyes closed.

Embarrassment floods through me.

"You could have just said you didn't want…w-why should I tell you why not?"

"Think about it, Evelyn. You can't lie to me."

I shrug inelegantly, my arms awkwardly at his shoulders. Yet they are tensed this time and I'm unsure whether we'll slide into chaos or climb to heaven despite hesitations. All it depends on are my words and his response.

"I suppose there is the issue of me being the *Ceidwad Cudd*, of me being fae and you mortal. Of you wanting to be a writer and me relatively wanted as a criminal. Of us being stuck here, losing resources…" I realize with disdain that Gideon is wanting me to convince myself of these reasons.

I loosen my arms entirely around his neck. "You…you don't want me?"

Shame or humiliation burns in his cheeks and with a savage suddenness, I extricate myself from our embrace. Feeling stupidity and rejection flare through me, I shove away from Gideon, his eyes lower with some emotion that I miss.

"I think you should go get some sleep," I inform him brusquely readjusting my clothes. "I'll wake you when we need to leave."

Gideon opens his mouth to say something, but my vicious glare silences him and he closes his mouth, nodding and slipping into the tent alone. The whine of the zipper closing behind him is the only sound that penetrates the night. I ensure that no sobs reach his ears, I ensure it because I force them down and refuse to cry.

He will not see me weak, because I am *not* weak.

Is it because I'm fae? Would everything have been different had I not been a faerie? Had Gideon not discovered and removed that amulet? Would he have taken it further? Taken me to bed?

Leaning against a young tree, I sit there, under the goddamned perfect night sky with my lonely thoughts and dreams of everything that could have been. Of everything that I was ultimately wrong about. As I do so, a new memory intrudes upon me.

A tall, dark figure spars with me, clad in the same black that I wear. We wield staves and learn footwork from an imposing figure several paces off. He pushes me up against the wall, his body flush with mine. I can feel the memory of his hard muscles pressing into me. A delight suffusing me. The figure watching us is lithe with long, tiny braids, and dark skin with a russet tone of earthen clay. His emerald eyes watch the two of us, nodding in approval, or scolding and reprimanding us with the claws of his left hand.

The room is a broken and overgrown church-like space, dappled sunlight filters in, limned by the ivy that reaches over the giant hole in the stone ceiling. Moss crawls up the walls and thrives in the moist shadows of the arches, decorating the statues that adorn the space with their yellowed greenery. Scarlet lichen hides in corners and bleeds outward, mingling with petite white flowers. In the center is a wide-based fountain with seven faces, each of them with the Fair Folk's trademark pointed ears.

"I will not have my name sullied by your failure. Be better!" he yells, the ferocity of it pulling taut the scar that bisects the right side of his face.

In response, the two of us pick up a frenzy, now battling with fervor, the male across from me gritting his white teeth as I bare my own. We are fast, frenetic, in sync. It's clear that we are familiar with each other, if only in combat styles. A heavy burden weighs on me, my back aching with it. I notice with each swipe and blow that the body I wield is young and scarred, pink and red healing welts and slices lining my arms.

The memory dissipates with the disfigured faerie's pleased smile.

Immediately, I examine my forearms in the firelight and the faint tracery of those harsher wounds are on full display. With that new memory, I sink into myself and I'm left with my thoughts and scars, and wonders and fears.

Who was the male I battled with and why did he feel so familiar? And who was the man who watched us?

For a moment I sit in my desolation. Rejected, alone, and clueless. Anger suffuses me and I get to my feet. I am fae, I should be able to access the Roads. Gathering my nerves, I give a small shake before I cross the wards—an in-between— and picture myself stepping into the Faerie Roads.

It doesn't work.

I huff a sound of frustration and return to the safety of the tent stakes, seating myself before the fire and stare up at the stunning Northern Lights. The moon does not reveal itself to shed any of its wise light upon this dark, dancing night, and sadly, I feel it's fitting. When dawn breaks over the eastern tree line, I know that neither of us slept through the night.

# CHAPTER

18

Early in the morning Gideon tries to pretend that the night before never happened. That we hadn't been held in an intimate embrace. That we hadn't felt each other's arousals. That I hadn't been ready to lay my soul bare to him. And that he hadn't rejected me.

*What an idiot I was.*

I ignore him in response, refusing to meet his false cheer and eager smile. I refuse to allow myself to be fooled, or to be tricked into thinking I'd imagined everything. I know that

I didn't. I refuse to be patronized and that's exactly what he's trying. I'm having none of it.

So, he's getting none of me.

We'd packed in silence, the coin heavy at the bottom of my bag. The March sunlight is gray and never quite warm, hardly reaching sixteen degrees Celsius at best when it hits peak temperature. The red-checkered flannel is buttoned over a gray shirt that I wear with a ripped, down vest overtop. We'd refilled our canteens and picked some berries last night in a nearby stream before everything had gone to shit. Mint had grown on the bank, so I'd snatched up some, recognizing another plant nearby. The warded stakes went very distinctly into my pack and I found pleasure in Gideon's nervous flinch.

I wonder what his fears about a faerie who can wield and withstand iron are.

Despite it all though, he attempts a forced stream of steady conversation that I never once answer. He talks for nearly two hours before I finally break his ramblings with one single, cold sentence.

"I'm starting to remember things."

This gives him pause but I refuse to elaborate further as I stalk from him, a crooked smile on my face. I hide it as I pop a leaf into my mouth and chew. Behind me, he runs to catch up, begging me to wait. I don't, and continue with my long-legged strides, delighted by the fact that we're the same height.

With the preternatural fae grace that I've always possessed unknowingly, I side-step roots and rocks with ease, traveling with the innate navigation I have ingrained. The sooner we're in Seelie territory, the better. Ferns and branches, and bushes and thicket are no obstacle as I hack away, dodge, leap over, or duck beneath each and every one of them. Gideon, however, seems to falter every now and then, judging from his curses and I begin to wonder if it's due to a distracted mental state.

By afternoon, Gideon has finally given up his incessant talking or coaxing me to speak. The two of us now traverse in the quietude that had once plagued me, this time, I find glee in it. Satisfaction in it.

"Talk to me," Gideon begs out of the blue.

I turn slowly to face him, a dark brow quirked. Wordlessly, I begin trekking more. Gideon's anger behind me hits me like a cinderblock and I nearly stutter-step, but catch myself before I give myself away.

"*Evelyn.*" His voice is harsh and demanding. Like the scolding of a child.

I twirl with a serenity that I muster from deep within me, using a savage twist from instinct. My eyes are near feral and they flicker like mercury, a sinister smile baring my teeth from my lips as they peel away. Fury lights my bones and I stalk the missing steps between us, closing the gap and facing him. His eyes are level with mine, our wraths matched like our desires once were.

"Let's talk then. Let's talk about your double standard. Why'd you touch me only to make me refuse you?" I confront, blazing like an inferno that has no hopes to be doused. "You don't have to put the blame and responsibility on me, if you didn't want to continue all you had to do was say. I would never force you. If you think so little of me then I have nothing left to say to you."

"*Evelyn,* it's because I want you. What if you remember everything you were and suddenly, I mean nothing? That I'm not to your standards? You're a faerie, the *Ceidwad Cudd,* what would you want with a human?" The dark anger fades from his eyes, a glint of something like guilt sweeping it before it's replaced by a chill of hollowness. Then he continues, "I don't think I could handle having you—no, you're not a possession, I can't '*have*' you. I couldn't imagine being with you and then have you leave me in the end. Call it self-preservation if you will."

I soften. For a moment, all the fury dissipates, melting away to nothing. I lift an unsteady hand, a hand that shakes with the upsurge of emotion that I desperately attempt to quell. Swarming through my chest is longing and desire, and wish and want. Fear and anxiety thrum in tandem, rushing through my blood and choking me with it.

Pressing that shaking hand to his cheek—lightly roughened with a few days without a shave—and feel the warmth seep through. The electricity in his skin is a match to my own, it surges through me, while yearning strains in his bold eyes.

"How could you ever mean nothing to me?" I ask breathily.

And suddenly his lips are upon mine.

His kiss is rough, passionate. Heady with desire and everything that has been pent up between us. In response, I kiss back, fierce and intoxicating. The hand that had been upon his cheek curves under his jaw, clutching the sharp, squared line of it, while the other reaches around to twine through his ebony hair. I part my lips, a small sound escaping me as he flicks his tongue to trace my lower lip. His arms wind around me, tightly crushing me to him, my waist wound by his strong arms, our chests pressed together. Our tongues dance, a tantalizing war of teasing and submitting, of dominating and pleasing.

With a force I hadn't expected of him, he pushes us back until I'm pressed against the trunk of a sturdy tree, never breaking the kiss. I feel his hands roam down my sides, caressing the slender curves I possess, confidently gripping my rear as he hitches my thigh upon his hip.

I gasp, and he slips from my mouth, his own eager for my throat as his teeth graze at the pulse there, hammering. He trails his kisses higher until he reaches my lobe and his gentle nip unleashes something else within me. I force his mouth back to mine, kissing with a newfound ecstasy, my arms weaving around him. My nails dig into his shoulders, wanting more, and *more*.

A sudden sound gives us pause. A distinct trampling of the forest floor sounds and we break from each other with lips swollen, eyes glazed, and nerves trembling. Armed with iron tent stakes, we wait, appraising and searching before a figure steps out.

I still. Frozen, shock freezing me to the ground.

He's human.

A real, *living* human. Not a corpse.

Rich, warm brown eyes, a tousled mess of auburn hair, tanned—nearly olive skin—and dressed in a mud-speckled and torn outfit. He appears to be mid-twenties, perhaps a bit younger or older depending on lifestyle. There is fear emanating from him as well as confusion and near hysteria.

Until he catches sight of us.

The expression across his face becomes awed, as if he'd discovered salvation. He's beaming, an elation splitting the devasted mask that once owned him. It's the face of a man finding an oasis in the desert. He races over to us, joy and desperation, and even foolishly enough, hope.

As he approaches, he pauses a few meters off and skids to a stop. He's staring at me. At my ears that now poke from my hair. At the undeniable marker of the fae.

"You're one of them…" he chokes out, stumbling backwards over his brown hiking boots. His movements made clumsy by panic.

I pause, unsure whether I should assuage his fears, but Gideon steps in for me. Taking a confident and welcoming step forward, Gideon harmlessly outstretches his hands and fixes a benevolent smile on his face.

"She's not like them, she's here to help us," Gideon says placatingly.

The human eyes us nervously, his tension wavering ever so slightly.

I attempt to soften my husky voice into a more tender tone. "What's your name?"

The human startles, and for the first time I notice a set of scratches raking down through the collar of his shirt. I cringe, realizing that an Unseelie must've gotten too close. He's likely imagining that I was the one to have done it. I wouldn't blame him for thinking so. I'd once thought all faeries were the same too.

"My name is Callahan," he finally responds. His eyes continually flitter to Gideon, preferring the other human over me. Yet again, I don't blame him.

"I'm Gideon," he introduces, then indicates me. "And this is Evelyn."

Callahan's mouth twitches in the first betrayal of a smile, the first sign that his fear is easing. I wonder how long he's been subjected to the savage wilderness of the Yukon. I wonder if he knows that this is his fate.

With Callahan's sudden presence I'm reminded of Jacob's dying words.

*No one gets out of here.*

He'd known. He'd known they weren't just *things*, he knew that we were in Unseelie territory. Which combined with my most recent memory leads me to believe that he was likely the one to ultimately betray me and leave me for dead in the Yukon here. The only question now, is why?

The most obvious reason is my being the *Ceidwad Cudd*, but I feel as if there's more to it. What specifically had I done? Was I sent after the Harbinger? If so, what does that mean if Gideon is him after all? And had anyone else suffered as a result of my actions and Jacob's rebuttal to them?

I know for a certainty there was a plane crash, I'd seen the wreckage of the remains for myself, but hadn't gotten much closer than being able to identify it. Beyond that, I'd refused, fearing the bodies and carnage I'd find. My parents, I'd thought. Though now I know that my parents had definitely not been onboard that plane.

"Do you guys have any idea what's going on here?" Callahan asks, breaking me from my reverie. I blink quickly to refocus myself and find Callahan with his arms wrapped around himself. As if he's holding himself together.

"It's a bit of a long story," Gideon starts, rubbing his jaw.

"I think you'll find that I have the time."

"Then I'll explain as we go. We shouldn't stay in one place out in the open too long." And so, Gideon draws in a deep breath and begins with our tale, and by some unspoken agreement, excluding the fact that I'm the *Ceidwad Cudd*. We start to make our way towards British Columbia once again and he tells Callahan about my crash, two-year survival, us meeting, capturing the faeries, being taken to the Unseelie Court, and my recent discovery of being fae.

"And I thought that I was fucked," Callahan mutters darkly, his awestruck expression trained on the ground. Hours later into the late afternoon, the three of us have reached solidarity, with Callahan not so terrified of me anymore after Gideon humanized me. Still, I can't imagine he'd want to be alone with me.

But being alone with *Gideon* is something I certainly want. The memory of our kiss and touches replays in my mind, the heat still stirring my core, my lips still tingling. The thought is unbelievable, a fantasy I'd concocted and only half hoped would come to fruition.

"How long have you been here?" I ask Callahan, forcing myself out of my thoughts before they lead themselves into explicit territory.

"A week, I think. I'm a journalist and I was doing a piece on northern countries and the impact that climate change has on them. My guides and assistant…they didn't make it. One of those *faeries*—which I'm just beginning to wrap my head around the fact that they exist—killed two of them and dragged the other off. I just ran for it. That's when one of them clawed me," he tells us haltingly, absently touching the gouges in his chest. "The thing is, they looked so different, but they had those *ears*." His eyes treacherously flit to my own for emphasis. "The one that took my assistant was like…you've ever seen a picture of a shaved bear? Like that, but its face was wrong, like a snake. And those eyes…all red. It freaked me the hell out."

Chills crawl up my spine. I can't remember ever having encountered a faerie that isn't at least somewhat humanoid, but also, I have still so few memories. Would a faerie of that sort be able to communicate? Or would they just be feral beasts? I find my feet suddenly moving significantly faster.

"The thing is…if I hadn't been faced with this sort of thing, I wouldn't have realized."

"Realized what?" I inquire, the two of them catching up to my long-legged strides.

"I had an…epiphany. What I wanted, all I needed crystallized in that moment," he stops, blushing, but continues on. "I finally figured out what life meant to me. What I want to do with it." Callahan breathes in a long draw of air, his eyes closing against the fading sunlight. "I want to see the world and its moments. I want to watch the sun set in Santorini, or drink Thai iced tea by some elephants, or even go skiing in the Swiss Alps. I want to do things simply because I *want* to. I'd decided that life is made up of all these moments and every moment you don't take is a moment wasted. So, I'll eat the cake, kiss the girl, take the risk. I don't want to live life regretting all my *'what if's?'* that I've left behind."

His epiphany resonates with me. I've never had the forethought to ponder much what I want after this place. It's unsettling…but also inspiring. I also worry dreadfully. Such a bright light cannot survive here, that sort of hope will get you killed, if only by wanting. I wonder if I'd thought in a similar manner before I'd lost my memories. Was I an entirely different person?

A dark lurch of certainty tells me that I was.

And I don't know if I liked her.

# CHAPTER 19

It's just after nightfall when I figure out that we should have made camp an hour before. Dark is descending quickly and Gideon has already commented on the state of light, so while I grudgingly agree, I also want to put as much space between us and whatever took Callahan's entourage—not mattering how long ago that was. Additionally, Callahan's visible distress feeding off the commencing night is less than helpful.

All the wicked things come out to play in the dark.

Around us, the towering trees are oppressive, the uneven ground bumpy at best and treacherous at worst. Currently, we've had the fortuitous occurrence of trekking across a mossy swath of open ground, but sooner or later we'll be forced back into weaving between trunks. The three of us hike through the dimming rays of daylight, hoping to stave out the light and bare warmth just a bit longer.

Just as the first specks of stars erupt over the horizon, a growling hiss in the bush freezes us all. Becoming stock still, Gideon and I send panicked looks between us, attempting to quell the energy from reaching Callahan's more sensitive anxiety.

Bears can growl.

Snakes can hiss.

But that combination…faeries can make that noise. Bears and snakes cannot. And my internal alarm spiking is undeniable proof of their presence.

My heart hammers and not communicating further than eye contact, Gideon and I leap into position around Callahan, herding him behind us. Closing Callahan in formation, Gideon and I reach for our weapons to protect the only one of our ranks utterly defenseless.

I don't know where Gideon learned any of his skills and techniques, I don't know how he learned to fight as he does. For that matter, I don't know how I did either. My training is clearly further than a basic concept and I have no memory to lend possibilities besides the single recollection of a training session. Other than that, my only hint is my fae status.

Another growling hiss shreds our chaotic calm and I immediately take out two of the warded tent stakes I carry, flinging them out the same time Gideon does to create a wobbly square. Both Gideon and I relax slightly, our shoulders losing their tenseness as we settle into the truth that we are safe from the Unseelies. For now.

Seconds after deploying the stakes, a young-woman—perhaps still a girl—stumbles from the trees and my heart speeds into a gallop when I catch sight of her. The faerie is surprisingly human-looking—aside from ruby red eyes. She searches about in panic, those red eyes wide with fear, her long dark hair a tangled mess of leaves and other foliage with golden skin streaked with dirt. Her tiny feet are bare and filthy, and I become abruptly aware of how short and waifish this Unseelie is.

Immediately brandishing a stolen blade from Tegwyn in my left and Róisín's thieved rose dirk in the other, I urge Callahan back. Directly beside me, Gideon wields an iron tent stake and an ax, both dangerous in his capable hands.

The faerie steps further from the deeper forest and closer to us, stepping with near twitchy movements. I tense as does Gideon. But then, when she steps closer, I get a second shock.

What I had thought was water on her clothes is blood. Blood cakes her black clothing and furrows of scarlet mar her throat. Seeming disoriented, she blunders more, tripping over to us and holding her head.

"They're coming, please, save yourselves," she calls out hoarsely in a vaguely accented voice.

And then we hear the chuckle.

The faerie stiffens and staggers to a tree.

Suddenly, two more red-eyed faeries appear, both beautiful creatures, one with bright, red hair, the other curly brown and with both possessing curvaceous, womanly physiques. These three are the most humanoid faeries I've encountered, especially in one group.

The redheaded faerie twirls a silver chain between fast fingers, a tiny symbol flashing on it—I can only imagine it's the Unseelie sigil. Next to her, the brunette faerie wears blood on her fingers, taunting the scared one as she points an index finger at her before licking a trail of crimson from her wrist.

The first faerie shrinks back, clutching at her neck and I put the pieces together, realizing that the glove of red matches the gouges on her throat. But what is further peculiar is that they're preying on her.

Unseelies don't often prey on each other, but rather torment unsuspecting and unfortunate humans that wander into their territory together—and judging from the Seelie who'd died in my arms, us too. But I suppose when options are limited, choices are made and it happens, as natural selection does. Regardless, the hunting of one's own is unnerving.

The dirty faerie backs away from her hunters, my alarm system pinging strangely with every step closer. I straighten my spine further, Callahan's anxiety thrums a nervous wreckage behind me, meanwhile Gideon's eyes flicker with predatory light.

With another step back, the other two progress forward in their pursuit of their prey. Every footfall they gain on us is another footfall that kicks our fear higher and higher. Then the redhead changes things.

Spinning that silver chain still through her fingers, she takes the length of it between her two hands before giving it one forceful tug, tearing both link and clasp from the necklace. The small symbol goes flying. The redheaded faerie tosses it aside while the preyed-upon fae makes a broken noise of distress.

Taking the pained sound as weakness, the two hunters attack, streaking for the faerie that is much too close to our fragile safety. In that moment, I make a split-second decision, and cursing myself all the while, I break from the group and act.

Bolting from the wards, I leap into the fray, a cry of fear echoing behind me as Callahan sidles up to Gideon. The tiny faerie scarcely dodges a clawed hand from the brunette and grasping fingers from the redhead. Using no time to take stock, I quickly assess the area and charge the brunette coming out of her failed maneuver.

Adjusting my grip on the rose blade, I come upon the brunette faerie the same moment she spins to me. With a brutality that distresses me, I impale her eye upon the point and shove upward into her brain, scraping the bone and effectively lobotomizing her. She drops with a lifeless thud. Not a successful lobotomy in terms of psychological practices, but for my uses of one, a victory.

The other faerie snarls in fury, her lovely jaw suddenly unhinging, opening wider than any should be capable of, displaying two long sets of fangs and too sharp teeth. In the horrific process, all the veins surrounding her eyes swell purple-black, becoming a truly realized monster.

Fear skitters true and potent down my spine. My mind blanks, my breath locks in my throat, my heart stutters. Suddenly in that moment death seems very much possible and the idea that I'm not as invincible as I'd felt upon leaving Gideon and Callahan in the wards.

I falter, stumbling back a step while she advances on me. In that same moment, Gideon shouts and Callahan breaks from the wards and tosses a rock with all his might at the advancing faerie, knocking against the back of her head. The redhead spins and hisses a bone-chilling sound. I make no mistake in using the opportunity to utilize Tegwyn's old blade and plunge it straight into the faerie's heart.

The faerie whips around, yowling before her mouth floods over and she drops to the forest floor beside her fellow tormentor. I stare down for a moment, watching the light fade from those demonic eyes and the dull gray sheen of death take over.

I finally get a moment to look up from my kills and find Callahan standing with a second arsenal of stones in his shaking grasp, the dirty faerie holding a rock of her own. She's perhaps sixteen in appearance at the most, her crimson eyes ringed with night-dark shadows, her dark hair purple-brown beneath the dusk. The faerie trembles, her entire frame a vibrating mess as her breaths heave from her chest.

"Callahan, get back to the wards," I command and the human doesn't hesitate, scurrying with the rock still in his hand. Gideon, having followed Callahan out of the protective square now stands at the edge, an ax in his grasp.

Carefully, I crouch down, catching sight of silver. I gather the broken necklace, putting together the three pieces and gently make my way towards her. "Why did they attack you?" I ask softly, extending the jewelry towards her.

"I don't know."

"How did you get here?" Could she have been dumped here like me? Could she be a Seelie too? Is she something to be hidden too?

Carefully, she creeps forward and eyes me warily, snatching the necklace from my open palm. She's quick as a snake and as suddenly as I saw the silver in my hand, it's just as soon gone. Cupping the necklace gratefully, she skitters back, covering her partially open mouth.

"Do you know why you're here?" I ask, adjusting the repeated question.

She fidgets, clearly not preparing to answer. She pulls away slightly and her eyes flicker about like she's afraid something else will come for her. Here, you never know, because that is entirely within the realm of possibility.

For a moment I consider and weigh the options. We could help her, she could be on our side. Or we could abandon her to an Unseelie fate. I debate resources and practicality. We're low on food, lower even on objects of comfort. Water thankfully is prevalent and we have easy methods to purify it. Rationing, while not ideal is possible. In the end, morality wins despite the logistics of it not being all that suitable.

"We can help you," I inform, taking a step towards her.

"No!" she yelps, leaping away. "I might hurt you, too."

"It's okay," I tell her placatingly, trying to embody Gideon's gentle tones. "I'm like you, I can help you." I don't know why I'm offering to help a potential Unseelie, but maybe it's because there's a chance she's Seelie. Maybe it's because she seems so truly helpless, so sincerely frightened for her life. Clearly, she's not as big of a threat here if her own turned on and hunted her as such.

"No! Stay away from me!" She instantly backs away more, her feet sure on their destination away from us. "I'm sorry, thank you for saving me, but I can't risk hurting anyone else."

Tears begin welling in those ruby eyes and suddenly she tears off into the night, vanishing through the trees.

"Wait!" I shout after her, stumbling into the woods, cresting the tree line she disappeared through. But she's gone. Not a sound, sight, or internal alarm to be found.

I return to the small massacre I'd created, stunned and in a haze. Outside the wards, Gideon stands before me and cups my chin in his strong and fierce hands, his bronze eyes boring into me.

"You were incredibly courageous and considerate and compassionate, but dear lord, you scared the fuck out of me."

And suddenly, he yanks me closer to him and wraps me in a crushing embrace.

For a moment, I cling to him, not caring about Callahan watching, and dig my nails into his back, just to be certain he's real. Gideon presses his cheek to mine, his hand cupping the back of my head, tangling in the messy silvery strands of it. My breath comes in and out shuddering, tasting of mint-lime and deep Yukon woods, and *Gideon*. His muscles are warm and comforting around me, giving me a deep sense of safety and something queerer still, but *home*.

Not home, like the cabin that went up in flames, but a deep longing sense of the word. The thing you crave when all seems hopeless and meaningless. When all you want is a bath and a book, or a drink and pizza. A soul-searching *want* of the word.

When Gideon and I disentangle, I make my way over to Callahan and don't hesitate as I wrap him in a crushing hug. A human, utterly defenseless in the face of Unseelie fae potentially saved my life. "Thank you," I tell him, adrenaline still thrumming through me. "But don't ever try to save me again."

He laughs against my shoulder. "I'll do my best."

With that, I break from the human and trek over to the bodies, plucking the blades from their orbital and thoracic cavities, and clean them off in the moss. It's too dark and too dangerous to deal with the bodies, so we leave them behind as we set off again, holding the tent spikes in our shaking grasps.

It's twenty minutes later when Callahan finally speaks again.

"I want to know everything you guys know about these things."

That night, the three of us camp under the shade of a large oak tree and use the cover of the leaf foliage to allow a campfire. We dine on a meager dinner of beef jerky and canned pineapple, sparingly sipping from our canteens and trying to forget the attack only hours before. I very much miss my liquor from the cabin.

"Do you think faeries can eat things with iron in it?" Callahan poses after we describe to him the semantics of the Fair Folk's vulnerability to iron and my distinct immunity to it.

I tear into a strip of jerky, deliberating. "I don't know, they seem to eat humans just fine," I respond slowly, thinking back to the brunette faerie and the androgynous one from two years ago sucking Jacob's blood from its fingers. "I'm not much help there." I twirl one of the tent stakes and eyeball the chain I've hung around my neck like a scarf, waiting to see if a delayed reaction will occur. Over an hour and no such luck. "Though, it's likely that cold iron is the true weakness."

Beside me, Gideon nudges my thigh with his knee. His fingers tentatively trail up my arm and slip over my shoulder to lift one of the chain links from resting against my throat. He whistles softly through his decadently full lips before setting the iron back down.

"Not even red," he comments gently, his fingers still resting against my collarbone, my pulse thrumming an eager rhythm.

"What kind of faeries were those? Are there different types? Subtypes?" Callahan voices and Gideon straightens his shoulders and inhales. Myself, mildly taken off guard, I consider. Though my lack of memory seems to stunt my thought process.

"There are different types within Seelie and Unseelie fae, but mostly it's relegated to gentry, common, and beast. Evelyn would be considered gentry because she's nearly human in appearance," Gideon explains, planting a comfortably warm hand on my thigh, as if grounding himself. Despite the fact that we have shared kisses and a little more, it doesn't erase the fact that fear and curiosity are two of the main reactions he has to the fae. I suppose I may elicit those sorts of emotions too, regardless of if others follow in their wake.

"So, what are you two?" Callahan demurely chews a spoonful of pineapple through his interruption. "Like, to each other."

My face heats and I don't look over to Gideon to see if we wear matching shades of red. I train my eyes to Callahan's left, catching his curiously watchful expression from my periphery.

"I suppose we're friends," Gideon voices tentatively, his words uncertain.

"Friends who make out in the woods?"

My neck flushes a deeper magenta and Callahan's brow quirks, a smile pinning his lips upward. "How could you have seen that? You weren't even into the clearing yet."

Callahan blinks once. Twice. "Oh. I was just joking, but that makes sense why your hair was so messed up when I saw you…and that hickey on your neck." His own cheeks turn red as my hand flies guiltily to my throat. "I guess I sort of interrupted you, sorry."

I shrug nonchalantly, brushing away the embarrassment. "Better you than a faeric."

Callahan laughs boisterously at this, whether from nerves or true humor, I'm unsure, but soon Gideon joins in and

I'm left blushing with a wry smile. I don't think I've ever been funny; never had the opportunity, I suppose. I don't even know if that *was* funny, or just relief.

Gideon quietly slips his fingers into my palm, carefully gracing them—asking if it's okay—before he twines them in mine. So, the three of us sit there, warm from the campfire, laughing and telling stories. Reminiscing about life. Gideon squeezes my fingers every so often, as if asking if I'm real. I squeeze back for an unbelievable yes.

Reassured by the Unseelie wards, the three of us curl up in our bedrolls within the canvas tent, for once feeling safe and hopeful for a better future.

# CHAPTER 20

"How'd you manage to survive here all this time?" Callahan asks me the next morning. His questions have been incessant and insatiable, everything we know about the fae, he wants to know. Everything we theorize about the fae, he wants to speculate on.

I smile softly, pondering back to my meagre cave upon waking in a forest fire and then a couple of days later stumbling upon the cabin not a half a kilometer off. Lady Fate blessed me in that regard I suppose, though she cursed me when I became stuck in this hellhole.

I tell Callahan the unbelievable story of Gideon's family's hunting cabin, of the recent torching of it and our narrow escape.

Callahan's brown eyes grow wide and he cusses colorfully. Ducking his head down, watching his steps, he continues contemplating, assessing and grilling us for information. Both Gideon and I share a secretive smile, comforted by the small mercy of satiating Callahan's curiosity. It's a small benediction, but we have to savor the little things.

"Have you noticed more extreme weather conditions these last couple years? Blizzards and wildfires?"

And so, the questions continue and both Gideon and I answer where we can, probing Callahan for information while we're at it. By noon, we need to take a water break and I decide to use the moment to express common courtesy.

"Do you have anyone back home in Toronto, Callahan?" I ask, swigging from my canteen, remembering his mention of the city. "I thought since you pried into our romantic life, we're privy to enquire into yours, no?"

Callahan ducks down shyly. "Yeah, my girlfriend, Amari."

"What's she like?"

"Stubborn, passionate," he chuckles fondly. "She has a no-bullshit kind of attitude. We met in California of all places. I was at a Climate Change convention and she was at a Black Lives Matter rally, and I dunno…our paths just crossed and it was like magic. We got talking and we found we had the same ideals, and as fate may have it, it turned out we both lived in the same city. Her in North York and myself downtown.

"I know it's silly but we felt like we were transcending boundaries, fighting for our causes, ya know? We joined the other's fight and I didn't realize how much harder hers was. I'm a white man, born into privilege—which I try to use for good. Amari is a Black woman, forced into oppression because of the color of her skin, and yet she works ten times harder I do for the things I hardly have to think twice about. She is so strong and inspiring; it makes me want to share her views with everyone."

"You sound like you love her."

"I do. I was planning to propose when I got back, but…" He shrugs, a non-committal movement, but it doesn't fool me. He's hurting and it shows in his dark eyes. It's only a glimmer of pain, but leaking into the set of his jaw.

I look away shamefully, staring out at the small ripples across the pond, the shifting breeze through the pines, the gray, overcast sky. I look at everything and anything to avoid Callahan's gaze as my realization takes hold. I wish I could reassure him, but I realize with a pang of shame that I can't. I can't lie to him and say that he can do just that when he gets home. I can't form the words because they refuse to roll from my tongue. I can't, because deep down?

I don't believe we're getting out of here.

"You're quiet."

I turn in surprise to find Gideon leaning against a tree trunk, half his face cast in shadow, the other in stark contrast as sunlight limns him in heavenly light. One eye glints weakly like an old bronze coin, the other brilliant amber like a gem. His face is painted in soft lines, concern etched there, but there's an openness to the set of his frame, telling me I can trust him.

Ducking my head in shame, I return to my water gathering. It's midday, perhaps late afternoon, and after depleting a fair amount of our water, we'd decided to rest near a spring and set camp for a few hours. At a visible distance, our canvas tent is pitched, surrounded by Unseelie warding stakes, cradling a peacefully snoring Callahan within. Unlike us, he isn't quite used to trekking or physical activity that survival is reliant upon.

Reluctantly, though, I have to admit that Gideon is right and too perceptive for his own good. "Not much gets by you, hmm?" I ask darkly, but then my tone sours. "Do you ever feel like you're a bad person? That perhaps there's no redemption and you're not worthy of saving?"

Gideon comes beside me, crouching and brushing a curtain of hair behind my too-pointed, fae ears. My face reddens. "Evelyn, you're quite the enigma, and I see you struggling but I need you to know that there is a goodness in you. I see it. I see *you*. You will always be worth saving."

My face burns hotter, wondering if I've ever been noticed by anyone in the way that Gideon Zhao has seen me. Been seen as he sees me. It's an utterly new feeling, one that I selfishly wish I could surround myself with, to imagine living in a cocoon of his attentions.

"I can't lie."

"I know."

"I wish I could."

"I know." He pauses. "You wanted to lie to Callahan." It's not a question, but rather a statement as the gears turn and he puts it together. Gideon's lips thin with a pensive expression and he twirls a lock of silver around his finger—such stubborn hair, straighter than a blade, shining like one polished against a whetstone.

"I was ready to, I didn't realize it was a lie until I tried to say it."

"And what was the lie?"

I draw in a breath and shutter my eyes. "That he could propose to Amari *when* he gets home."

"That's not your fault."

I sigh, abandoning my task of acquiring water. "Isn't that part of human nature though? White lies? What sort of reassuring can I offer when comfort can't come in a time of need? If these—" I point treacherously to my ears, "—weren't enough of a divide between our kind, then my coldness into the truth is."

Gideon's hand comes up under my jaw, gently probing the sharp line of it, guiding my face to his. I allow my cheek to turn as his calloused fingers grace the edges, holding me there. "Someone cold does not risk their life without asking anything in return. Someone cold does not return an object of comfort to another when they could turn just as fast. Someone cold does not willingly offer dwindling resources because it's the *right thing to do*."

"What if I had ulterior motives?"

"You didn't," he responds simply.

I bite my lip, unable to lie again. I didn't have ulterior motives. My sole instinct had been to protect, whether that protection extended only to Gideon and Callahan, I'm unsure. I could've felt the surge of guardianship to the preyed-upon faerie too, but it certainly is a mystery. Looking back, perhaps I could convince myself that there was reasoning to it. Perhaps we could glean some information from her about sightings of the Harbinger. Perhaps we could discover a way to subvert the Unseelie Queen's expectations of us. Perhaps she knew a way out.

But that isn't what I thought. It still isn't.

Still chewing on my lip, still comforted by Gideon's palm upon my jaw, I realize he's watching my mouth. I realize an ache that burns in my chest. A want that sears my soul. A desire I see reflected back at me.

"What if I were selfish?" I ask breathily, bringing my hand up to rest upon his chest, feeling his heart kick up like a startled rabbit. "What if all I did was just a ploy to earn your favor? What if it was all to lure you in?"

Gideon smiles, noticing my careful wording, still keeping in mind that I cannot lie, and so formatting as such is a question of what if. "Then I would consider that a mission well accomplished."

Pulling me close, Gideon hides his smile before he presses his full lips to mine, the kiss exquisite in its chaste nature, curious and tender rather than hungry and wild. My mind blooms with color and bliss, luxuriating in the feel of his silky mouth, taut muscles, and overwhelmingly satisfying heat. Beneath my hand that begins to roam, his heart beats a staccato rhythm that matches the excited nervousness of my own.

Winding my arms around his neck, I pull him closer, tugging him atop me as I fall to the ground. His excitement perks up, suddenly opening and touching my tongue with his as he deepens the kiss, still gentle. Extending a hand over my head to balance, he palms the ground, his other hand poised on my hip, clutching the curve and pressing us together. Heat floods me as he lowers himself, the same moment I hear a tinny noise and a slosh.

Gideon curses and pulls away from me just as my hair begins to dampen. I chuckle darkly and adjust myself into a sitting position. "Are you knocking over the water to get away from me? Have you reverted back to your old ways?" I tease, my lips still tingling from his kiss.

How does one get enough of this? This feeling? This longing? The sensation of Gideon's mouth, hands, chest…how much more can I handle?

"I think that was the most sobering thing we could ask for. We would've given poor Callahan quite the heart attack." Gideon rushes a hand through his hair, color high on his cheeks. Something squirms inside me at his comment, a sense of unfulfillment that still begs to be sated.

"A pity that a cardiac arrest is so troublesome."

Gideon cracks a smile but bends to collect the upturned canteen without response. As he fills the container, he checks back towards Callahan's dutifully sleeping form. "I think we should wake him up, get a few more kilometers in before dark."

And so, we do just that, collecting our sleeping comrade, packing up the tent and carrying the tent stakes in grips still tingling from the other. Callahan, luckily is ignorant to the thread of tension between Gideon and I, even luckier is that he is utterly oblivious to the explicit thoughts rampaging my mind.

Finally, hours later with aching feet and heavy eyes, we retire at sundown, camping in the center of a bowl-shaped valley. The valley hosts a flat plain and a wide circle of lush trees. Moments after eating a scarce meal, I crash to my bedroll, exhausted in so many ways. It doesn't take long for my tired eyes to close and drop me into oblivion.

When I wake, it's to my internal alarm screaming at me. Extricating myself from Gideon's arm thrown over my chest, I scramble from the covers and slip out of the tent into the light blue of early dawn air. There, circling the entirety of our perimeter are faeries.

"Fuck."

# CHAPTER 21

"Gideon! Callahan!" I call out loudly, panicked. Within moments I hear scrambling and two bleary-eyed males exit the tent, immediately waking and wearing matching sets of fear.

One of the faeries cocks its bulbous head to the side and nausea crawls up my throat. This can only be the faerie that Callahan described. Dried blood lines its slit mouth, rusty and flaking. Its thin nostrils flare flat against its globular face, with garnet eyes glowing malevolently. It stands on all four legs, its frame thin, with loose skin hanging from it, gray in pallor and slick with some sort of wetness. A whip-like tail trails behind it, brushing the pine needles from the forest floor and distinctly the ears are there. Pointed and prominent against its serpent skull.

It's not a regular faerie, it's a fae beast. More animal than human, more unpredictable than trainable. Rare, but the most vicious and bloodthirsty of the fae to exist.

Another faerie steps forward, her obsidian palm pressed flat against an invisible wall, her tight, lavender curls hang around her beautiful lilac eyes like a halo. She watches us, her movements graceful, her face content and curious. She removes her hand from the shield and joins it with her other one, pressed against the blanched folds of her shift's abdomen. Still content. I think I catch a glimpse of hooves beneath the hem.

"What do you want?" I demand, my voice strong despite the tremor that lies beneath the surface of it.

The monstrous faerie beast steps towards the dark one and she lifts a hand to its skull to stroke it. As if it were a *pet*. She smiles a lovely smile, pulled lovingly from her full, painted lips. "Why the red-haired human of course. My lovely here never got to taste him. Though, I've heard his friends were quite delicious." She giggles musically. A fine-furred, lavender tail flicking behind her.

A third faerie prowls the perimeter, a flash of white there, a swath of blanched fabric here, a glint of gold. My eyes flash to him, the human aspects and calculate methods in which to apprehend.

Both Callahan and Gideon tense behind me and in response I widen my stance and pluck a knife from my boot, twirling it in my deft fingers. The glint of the rose-handled blade catches the faint spring sunlight at the same time the faerie's eyes are fully enraptured by me.

"You are fae," the woman breathes, somewhat startled.

"I am."

"You are not Unseelie?"

"I am not."

"And they let you into their protective circle?"

I smile a cunning smile. "They need not let me in." Driving home my words, I take a spare tent stake, the stench of iron emanating from it. The faerie's eyes blow wide, her tail stills as she scents the air and understands how unnatural the sight is.

Gideon, with a predatory grace, comes up beside me, he himself displaying the ax we'd used with our faerie trapping net and a tent stake peeking from his back pocket. Had his modified bat not burned in the inferno of the cabin, he'd likely be using that. His eyes flicker back to Callahan who stands behind, guarded by us, by two who have slain before. Callahan's eyes are rounded by terror, but he holds his composure.

"It is such a shame, young fair one, that you should be so impetuous."

I clutch the tent stake and knife in my hands, unsettled by her words and the mischievous glint in her eyes. Her face is stony, trained upon mine, all lovely curves masquerading over cruel intent. I assess the area, searching each of the offending faeries for weaknesses as I slip a second stake into my boot – this one unwarded but stinking of iron.

She shakes her head and *tsks*, an emotion almost solemn crossing her face. "The wards you possess are quite brazen, but they are flawed. Impervious to all of the Dark Court, yet utterly defenseless against the Light Court." She grins wickedly, and a surge of genuine fear slides up my spine as she gives a nod. "I am quite blessed to keep a Seelie in my entourage."

A wet gasp sounds behind me, accompanied by the sucking plunge of a knife. I spin in horror and find the painfully pale faerie clutching Callahan from behind, the faerie's hand wrapped around his throat while his other brandishes a scarlet-slick saber. Upon Callahan's abdomen is a spreading stain, as red as the eyes of the one who'd killed his guide. Blood burbles from his mouth, dripping down his chin.

I come to a realization stupidly; that a faerie born faithful to the Seelie Court can choose to change loyalties. But until that treasonous decision is made by an act of such nature against the Court or Crown, these anti-Unseelie wards do nothing against them. It takes a bold move for the universe to understand the switch in allegiance. The same for switching sides is as equally true for an Unseelie turning to the Light Court. It is extremely rare, but it has happened.

This is the defining moment the pale one chose to betray the Seelie Court.

This is his proof.

In the span of seconds, I've taken in the chilling scene, and without thinking, have flung the tent stake with unrelenting force at the ivory-skinned faerie. The stake sinks into his forehead, pinning his golden-blond hair within the wound. A look of utter shock is branded into his icy eyes, bewilderment on his face before the iron begins to eat away and blacken his flesh. A yellow curl turns to charcoal and crumbles under the deadly toxin. He drops to the ground, falling backward as Callahan totters forward.

The pale faerie is dead.

The lavender-obsidian one gives a screech of devastation.

The beast roars.

I lunge from the protective circle and roll forward, carrying my momentum from the tuck and pulling out the stake. I approach the beastly faerie by sliding across the ground, grass and moss tearing beneath me. An unforgiving strike of the unwarded tent stake is no competition for the soft underside I've seen of the creature's jaw. With the upward jerk, the blade penetrates the faerie's brain, the iron that is imbued into the stake poisoning the organ further. It wails with multiple tones, the sound reptilian and avian and lupine all at once. I imagine the fatal wound blooming like a macabre rose just as the creature uncontrollably tosses its head and falls to its side. Dead.

I do not pause to watch any further as the cruel beauty still remains. She has advanced, albeit unsurely, the faerie taken off guard by my speed and efficiency. Her floral-toned irises are stewed in anguish, and though I could fetch the stake from the still cooling corpse of her companion—or trade it for Róisín's blade now in my boot—it is not the method I crave. Slowly and deliberating, I march on the remaining faerie, paying no heed to anything but my prize.

She throws the first punch and I duck it swiftly, coming up to her side and planting my boot onto her ribs. Stumbling into a tree, she uses the leverage to throw herself in my direction, shining onyx hooves stamping the ground. Yet again, I twirl out of the way, tugging her tail to taunt her. She snarls angrily and comes at me, claws-out, driving for my eyes. I smile before tucking-and-rolling beneath her reach. Taking my favored position of attack, I leap onto her back and latch on with my powerful calves and trained thighs. Her jaw is clasped in my hands and I whisper into her ear:

"This is for Callahan."

And snap her neck.

She crashes to the earth, her knees cracking against the solid surface as her eyes roll back into their whites while she tumbles to the ground. I stand over her, staring at the carnage I've inflicted, the death that I've reveled in. Purple curls lie in the dirt, strewn with pine needles. A creature not of this world bleeds and decays for the earth. And a bleached imitation of life remains crumpled in a protective boundary.

Remembering that I'm not alone and that Gideon and Callahan still remain with me, I spin away from the waste I've laid and find Gideon cradling the redhead in his lap. He wipes blood away from Callahan's lips as more leaks out. He has suffered a gut wound, and the faerie had no mercy when he dragged the blade up through his belly. I know there's no saving him and it's a terrible way to die. It is painful and long.

I race over to them and come skidding to my knees through the barrier. A plume of dirt rises between us, almost acting like the veil between life and death. A pang strikes my heart at the pain that has been cursed upon him, the pain that I pray is fleeting now, though I cannot be sure.

Gideon meets my gaze, a grim look in his eyes. It won't be long for Callahan now. Callahan himself lies with his head of ginger waves pillowed, a weak smile stippled with blood graces his mouth. His fingers move limply, and I recognize what he indicates as I gently take his hand in mine, applying a soothing amount of pressure. I do not comment about his and the faerie's blood mingling in my palm.

"You were pretty badass," he wheezes.

"That wasn't the core of my intentions."

"Doesn't matter." His tone shifts. "Evelyn…Gideon, don-don't leave me, okay?"

I grip his hand tighter. "I'm right here."

"We're not going anywhere," Gideon reassures instantly, his hand, I realize is pressing a wadded piece of fabric to Callahan's wound.

"I'm so scared. I don't want to die. This isn't what I—" He sounds desperate as he chokes on blood, gurgling. "I wanted to do more. I didn't get to do enough. Please, please fix this."

Tears burn in my eyes. "I can't. I'm sorry." My voice is thick.

Emotion burns in Callahan's glassy eyes. "If you ever find her, tell-tell Amari I love her, okay? And I'm sorry about leaving the shoes in the hallway. Tell her I wish I'd married her."

"I will," Gideon replies, knowing I can't lie.

He smiles at our reassuring, his teeth pinkened by blood. "Do me a favor," he breathes hoarsely. "*Live*."

"Yes," Gideon accepts.

"Of course," I whisper back, throat thick. "We will honor you in every way we can. I swear it."

His smile melts into a smaller, closed lip one, his eyes shuttering. "Good, save the world if you have to…just *live*."

And with that, he exhales one breath and then no more.

Callahan grows slack in our hands, an uneasy sense of lightness to the air. His faintly freckled face loses any rigidity, his muscles loosen, the slits of his eyes already go flat. We place his cooling hands upon his chest, folding them delicately while Gideon hangs his head.

Muttering something about washing away blood, Gideon slips from our circle to find a stream. Luckily, I don't have to remind him to be aware, he's already got a tent stake in his pocket. I just hope he remains cautious.

Alone with Callahan's body, I release a silent prayer to his spirit, wishing him safe passage to the afterlife and whatever he may believe in. I wish him a silent thanks for opening my eyes to what the world propositions, and reminding me how cruel it can be. How it can snatch away the opportunities it offers so graciously. I thank him for his presence and the work he'd tried to convey to the world. I thank him forever more for saving my life with his act of dangerous distraction. And I apologize to those that never discovered the words he wished to share in his articles and the sights that his eyes will never meet.

As I bow my head over Callahan's corpse, I hear snapping twigs and a muffled shout from beyond the foliage. I straighten, my heart already racing, worrying for my survival partner. I'm about to clamber to my feet when Gideon returns covered in more blood than what he left with.

A slash of red splatters across his finely shaped nose, crossing his arched brow, and tugging near the corner of his full mouth. There is a smear across his lips, as if he'd wiped more of it away. A glove of scarlet drips down his arm, the tent stake glinting like a morbid ruby. I start with surprise.

"There was another one," Gideon informs me clinically. "I took care of it. Stay alert." And he turns away again to hopefully wash off for real.

Kneeling vigil over Callahan's body, I don't shift away when Gideon approaches again. He comes up beside me, resting a hand upon my shoulder. I draw in a breath and lean into him. Slight pangs of guilt are battering my frame, squandered hope is writhing in my chest, and wisps of solemnity begin coloring my breath. I do not cry, do not feel the urge to, yet the sadness still lingers, nonetheless.

"We need to take care of his body," Gideon announces despondently, his grip tightening on my collar.

"I know."

"We should burn him. I don't think he'd want his body laid to rest here."

I pinch my eyes closed. "You're right."

Hours later, the flames from Callahan's funeral pyre dance in the air, the tongues of flame reaching for the blue-gray sky where he dreamt of everywhere it could take him. The sickly-sweet scent fills the air and out of respect I refrain from covering my nose—though I do stand a reverential distance away. Instead, I stand and watch the conflagration before us, the heat transforming the vessel that once held him into ash.

Beside me, Gideon stands in the clearing, his hands by his sides, his head ducked low. He'd watched Callahan die longer than I did. He held that dying man in his arms and comforted him while I enacted vengeance. It is a different sort of deference to Callahan and his memory.

I reach over and slowly intertwine our fingers together, watching our companion burn. Standing unified against our enemies that once sought to destroy us. They were near successful.

We leave the remains of the Unseelies on the battlefield, a warning to those who threaten to cross us. A reminder that we can be quarreled with, though coming out alive is not an option. A signal of our united force and what we are to contend with.

So, the bodies lie disgraced and fallen without honor behind us, Callahan's pyre burning to embers. We turn south together, unified, and encounter the first shred of hope we can believe.

# CHAPTER

## 22

As the daylight begins to fade and twilight has beyond creeped in, Gideon and I crest a hill freeze. If Gideon had not seen what I do, I would've thought myself hallucinating. The two of us come upon a small town by the name of Aberth, boasting a miniscule population of 297. Despite the fact of its minute population, it brags a curious amount of bustling nightlife.

The town is immaculately maintained, it flows from the forest, into a lush field before us. The entire area seems to have been dropped into existence by magic. Breaking from the fringes of the meadow, I spit out chewed leaves, and find ourselves on a main road, a brightly lit strip of storefronts decorates each side of the paved asphalt. Neon lights beckon, and pumping bass reverberates in ribcages from every direction. People mill about casting us curious, if not speculative glances.

Midway down the road, we come to the town's center, a town square that is a large expanse that can comfortably fit three-hundred people for attendance. Lampposts are vintage and charcoal in fashion, dotted with baskets of white, purple, and blue flowers while benches in much the same style perch nearby. The square divides into a fork in the road and from there, the fork diverges, two of the prongs to residential addresses—where I can see solar panels adhered to each roof—then the straight tine leads towards more of the intriguing shops. As far as the eye can see, the road ends with a two-floor building of antiqued design in ash gray, stretching from end to end, banking the edge of the forest and beyond it.

I can't help but feel that this town is out of place. That the exciting and bold lights that accompany the gyrating music stick out like a sore thumb. Like it shouldn't be here. Unnervingly, I feel like Hansel and Gretel coming upon the witch's house made out of candy.

With a flash of no small amount of surprise, I realize that we've garnered much more attention now that we've approached the main fork. Glancing over at Gideon, I see apprehension written across the planes of his face, his discomfiture vibrating off of him in waves. His readiness—should it be required—is evident in his stance. As if he's prepared to grab his tent stake and ax and take on the town.

"Maybe we should go in," I propose, indicating the venue next to us. "Then we can figure out a place to stay."

Worst case scenario, this place is run by a deranged— yet human—cult, and since taking on multiple Unseelies, I'm very much confident with my abilities. Best case, this is just a peculiar and remote town in the Yukon. Such places surely exist? Even so, I'm much too tempted by relief and the seduction of sanctuary to really question this gift-horse and retreat back into the woods.

Gideon nods, despite his anxiety thrumming a staccato beat. I don't bother to tell him that I don't sense any of the fae around. Rather, he wouldn't know if I could anyhow as I've neglected to inform him about that particular ability of mine. Something of a gut instinct prevents me from doing so, and despite the want in my chest that wishes he knew me, that isn't a part I think he needs to know. Not yet.

Turning to the building I'd pointed out, I find us faced with a façade bathed in violet neon light. A building I determine to be black or slate gray stretches a generous distance, double the amount of many of the others, with blacked-out windows overworked with filigree embellishments even spaced upon its front. An awning yawns overhead, displaying the extravagantly lit sign of The Anemone in shades of electric purple and shimmering white, its namesake flower blooming above it.

A spark of knowledge hints at me. But it is elusive as smoke and the fleeting thought is gone.

Nearing the building, music throbs from within, pounding beneath my feet. A black-clad man stands outside the door, giving us a single, curt nod. He ignores our bags weighed down with weapons and resources entirely. Slipping through the frosted-glass double-doors, Gideon and I find ourselves in what can only be described as a foyer of a nightclub.

The room we enter is cast in more shades of purple than imaginable with every surface graced with tones of amethyst or plum or lilac. Descending a grand staircase below is a polished concrete floor, segregated into four quadrants. Leather booths line each wall, a massive dancefloor is centered, made with glossy plexiglass, and beyond, backing the far wall is a luxurious glass bar.

Regardless of the early hour, the club is already packed, bodies writhing in the rhythm of the night around them, sweat-slick skin glittering under the lavender atmosphere. Patrons dress scantily in lace, leather, net, and costume, more than one dancer twirling in little more than glitter. Around us, electronic music blasts from speakers, squeals of delight pierce the chaos of the party, and shouted voices become coated in a blanket of intoxication.

Gideon and I trade bewildered glances. Still, I sense none of the Fair Folk.

Slipping over to the front door, Gideon tucks his ax behind a serendipitously placed leafy plant, and returns once again, shrugging. I suppose carrying a particularly sharp ax into a nightclub isn't the wisest of ideas. The two of us creep down the staircase, oddly bedecked in grubby traveling clothes and dirty backpacks. We don't draw attention from anyone's ecstasy.

Slinking along the fringes of the dancers, Gideon follows me, hands linked, avoiding more than one thrown elbow or obnoxiously shaken hips. We come upon the edge of the bar, attempting to signal the busy bartender's notice when we're approached.

"You two are not from here," an ordinary female voice begins beside us.

Turning our attention from the hopeless bartender, we find a curvaceous, young woman, perhaps a handful of years older than I with a rich fall of chestnut hair and twinkling brown eyes. Her smile is wide and genuine, albeit a bit drunk, as she takes us in. We must look something miserable, especially compared to her casual—yet clean attire—a black tank top tucked into a pair of dark jeans and a flannel shirt tied around her waist. I find it humorous that she's wearing a polished aesthetic version of my own outfit.

"No," Gideon responds, all fake cheer, a white smile to match hers. "Do you know a place we can stay? We had some car trouble." Not a lie, per se.

She waves dismissively, that smile still painted on her face. "Let me buy you a drink at least before you get settled in."

"Oh, that's really not necessary."

"Don't worry about it, I'll get one for your girlfriend, too." She winks and turns to flag a drink. "I'm Rachel by the way." She waves once, and the bartender comes running over.

"I'm Gideon, this is Evelyn," he says, introducing us succinctly.

The man comes over, with a silver hoop glinting in his ear, and a circular tattoo on his neck that I can't make out. Rachel signs for three cocktails—her voice having been swallowed by the crowd—and he hurries off, his short brown hair slipping below the bar. She turns toward us, back against the ledge of the bar and appraises us.

"You two look like shit."

My scoff turns into a bark of a laugh at her dispassionate appraisal of us.

"That's probably an understatement," Gideon supplies.

She laughs, a pleasant, ordinary laugh, unlike the beautiful and dangerous tones of the fae before they attack.

"How long have you guys been out and about?" she inquires innocently, though it sends my nerves to life, the hair on the back of my neck standing on end.

Is that a true drunkenness I see in her eyes? Or an act?

"A while," I inform smoothly, slapping a false smile on my face.

She nods appropriately—too carefully?

I push away a curtain of my hair to turn to Gideon, as if to rest my head against his shoulder. In actuality it's to voice my concerns discreetly, but I stop when Rachel gasps and fails to cover it. Meeting her gaze, I find her eyes widened, trained upon my ears that poke from the fine panels of my messy hair.

I really need to cover them better.

Gideon notices immediately and swoops in to save my would-be-lying-ass. "Oh, her ears, hey? They're weirdly cool, right? She got them done at a body mods place a few years ago. The healing process was a bitch, you couldn't bump them at all or she'd scream bloody murder."

I send Gideon the most thankful look I can muster without falling to my knees.

Rachel composes herself and shakes out her long locks. "People won't take well to those around here. You should get going." All pretense of the drunken young woman gone, a clear warning heeding her words.

I'm startled by her distress. Surely, people here don't know about the fae? Surely, they aren't worried that I could be one? It would be ludicrous to think a whole town has the awareness of the Fair Folk. Right?

A sinking sensation spreads in my gut at the naïveté of that thought.

I don't trust this girl in the slightest. Regardless though, we have the tent stakes to protect us from Unseelies and Gideon and I have more than proven we can hold our own against whatever comes at us.

"Go where?" I laugh harshly. "Where can we stay for the night?" What I wouldn't give for a shower.

Rachel bites her plump lower lip, eyes flickering in conflict. "There's an inn at the end of the road, it's a big gray building. Lorelai works the desk there, tell her I sent you."

Gideon and I nod, taking Rachel's information with a whole handful of salt before departing without the drinks she ordered. We weave through the throng of vigorously swaying bodies, drunk on substance and youth in the heart of The Anemone.

Something about the color and name tickles a note of apprehension. Something I seem to be forgetting, though can't place a finger on it.

An uncomfortably warm body launches itself at me and I stumble in shock. A girl with green hair and sparkles upon her heavy-lidded eyes throws her arms around my neck, attempting to drag me into the swallowing crowd. A flare of panic erupts through me before I duck from her intoxicated grip and back towards Gideon.

Only he is not where I left him.

Genuine and ultimate fear sink into my veins, battling against the synthetic beat that rattles against my nerves. Ice plunges through my blood as I frantically spin around the crowd, every face morphing sickeningly into something malevolent.

Anguished, I determine we truly were Hansel and Gretel stumbling into the witch's house. Too late, we've realized our mistake. Now she has us and plans to devour us.

Bassline. Heartbeat.

Hot and stuffy air assaults my lungs, constricting them painfully. Dancers reach for me, ill-intent lined in their ravenous eyes. All four walls begin closing in, the sticky floor holding me prisoner.

Bassline. Heartbeat.

Anxiety trills through me, ripping at the fibers of my being. Frustration mows over my mind, shredding reason and rationale. Fear poisons my muscles, paralyzing them to atrophy.

Bassline. Heartbeat.

Taking control of myself, I center my thoughts and open my eyes that have shuttered to the world. Assessing the crowd, I scan the faces and breaks in the masses, finally finding Gideon's distinct facial features, made even more exotic by the predominantly Caucasian demographic.

His eyes are filled with distress over the three girls that cling to him, latched to his muscular arms, pawing at his chest. A flash of unrecognizable fury erupts through me, figuratively flattening me against the press of emotions. Shoving through the crowd, I make my way to the would-be kidnappers and tear Gideon bodily from them, baring a flash of malicious white teeth.

"Hands off, he's spoken for," I snarl, my fingers denting the taut muscle of Gideon's forearm.

The girls before me grin lazy, drunken smiles, and titter between the three of them before prowling off for a new, more willing victim. I efficiently straighten out Gideon's clothing, ensuring nothing has been torn or removed. Fortunately, we're in luck. Though with my skimming hands, Gideon's face deepens in color.

"Let's get the hell out of here," I call to him over the steadily increasing noise.

He nods, not bothering to try to shout, we're near a large set of speakers, speakers which are pumping out the crescendo to a bass drop. Weaving past the throb of the crowd and navigating our way back to the stairs, we climb and the pressure of the atmosphere lifts its suffocating nature. Heedlessly, I bowl through the foyer and fling open the double doors, bathing in the cool night air.

I inhale deeply once outside, the floral scent of numerous flower pots rising to my senses. Night has fully descended now, a starless night with a sliver of a moon and I'm suddenly lost as to how much time had passed within the chaotic nightclub. Twenty minutes? An hour? More?

Tugging Gideon along, we cross the fork in the road, sparing a single glance both ways to determine each is much of the same. A main residential road with branching side streets that I can only assume are more homes. We quicken our pace and come to a near jog as we approach the building Rachel had directed us to, the same one I'd noticed before entering The Anemone.

The exterior is elegant, akin to a set of row houses trimmed with Victorian friezes and spandrels lining the wrap-around porches, filigree brackets painted in a fresh coat of white glow against the night. Five row houses, each connected to the other by their outer walls frame in the center building, one whose sign proclaims Aberth Inn, and below that *OFFICE* in large, almost western type.

Ascending the few stairs to the porch, we enter the inn carefully, a tinkling brass bell on the door announces our presence overhead. We step into a warmly lit room with a modestly renovated interior, a wide space spanning a good third of the house's diameter to make up the front office. The walls are papered with a pastel floral pattern, original hardwood flooring shines below our feet, and an intricate rug is laid before us. A large, dark wood desk curves around a slight woman, owl-eye glasses magnifying her glimmering pair of brown eyes.

Without having been told, I know this woman is Lorelai, Rachel's sister. If the matching brown eyes didn't give her away, then the identical mane of wavy hair would have. She doesn't retain her sister's more voluptuous body, but she is nonetheless just as pretty.

"Hi, you must be Lorelai."

"I am," she confirms, her eyes wary despite the warmth within them. "Can I help you?"

"Rachel sent us, we need a room for the night." I realize as the words leave my mouth that we have no method in which to pay for such lodgings. Stress turns my face white.

"I'm quite certain I can assist you in that matter." Her voice is just as ordinary and content as her sister's. Just as wary too.

Do they know about the fae? Do they fear them? Is that why Rachel had such an adverse reaction to my ears? Even so, if they feared or were aware of faeries, I'm not so sure they'd dress up as them and go clubbing.

Human nature is troubling at best and incomprehensible at worst.

For the second time tonight, I notice a circular tattoo on her neck, though I can't quite decipher it due to being done in silver ink. Perhaps it's a match to the bartender, they could be a couple. Which could be why he responded to Rachel rather than us.

I remain on high alert, hoping she doesn't require us to abandon our bags someplace. Though, I still find it odd that neither she, Rachel—nor anyone else—have commented on our belongings. Who carries around a figurative arsenal of impromptu weapons? I pray that we've cleaned away all traces of blood effectively.

Lorelai nods politely and taps at the very expensive and modern computer before her, scanning the pages that come up to greet her. Her lips twist in concentration and just like her sister, the lower is fuller. Light sparks in her eyes as she discovers what was necessary for our request.

I begin to concoct a plan for us to use the room without having paid for it, perhaps we could ask to pay tomorrow morning and just sneak out a window? Or maybe we could just give her an effective knock on the head and send her into a pleasant nap while we take our leave?

But my straying thoughts have been for naught, because Gideon suddenly supplies a wallet and the appropriate amount of bills in his hand. I hadn't even thought about Gideon retaining any cash. Handing over the colorful bills, Lorelai checks us in and hands us a plain, brass key with a flower adornment.

"You have room number seven, please enjoy your stay at the Aberth Inn."

# CHAPTER 23

Room number seven is the modestly decorated second floor of the farthest rowhouse. All houses have been renovated to connect through an interior balcony that overlooks the office. Surprisingly, the hodgepodge of eras crammed into one space works. Claiming a mint-green, vintage—yet operational—kitchen, a comfortably dated living-room that most definitely had tacky wallpaper at one point, an adjacent bathroom stuck in the modern take of the '50s, and a bedroom worthy of a luxury beach house.

Taking the warded stakes out of our packs, I place one in the four furthest corners of our living arrangement, leaning them against their respective walls. From a mild prickling of energy, I suspect they work even in the formation we've established.

In the living room, the brick fireplace is painted white, a reclaimed wood mantle above it remains as empty as the hearth below it. Fortunately, though an iron basket of dry logs settles beside it and my insides quiver with the thought of the warmth it'll generate for us.

"Go take a shower, I'll get a fire going and then we can see about some food," Gideon offers, and I hesitate only a moment before accepting. I could assist with making the fire, but truly, that is a one-person job. Also, I desperately want that shower. Nodding, I unpack a fresh—and surprisingly clean—set of clothes, and scamper off to the bathroom.

I consider making a joke about asking him to join me, but an unprecedented thrill at the thought causes me to refrain. No longer would it be a light jest with heavily suggestive undertones, not after that kiss. *Those* kisses. The kisses that make my cheeks flame from the memory, the heat and urges that befell not only I, but Gideon as well.

I attempt to keep myself from hurrying, but judging from Gideon's muffled laughter behind me, I believe I've failed. Nonetheless, I do not care, for I luxuriate in the warm notes of his voice. The throaty laugh that he tries to hide. I grin as I shut the door behind me and turn on the most scorching shower I can manage.

Before I get in, I search the drawers for soap and shampoo and as I do I find several sealed purple boxes. I blush as I pick up one of them and set it on the counter. I get in and pretend that the reddening face is from the hot water.

I scrub and lather until the filthy water runs clear and my skin has pinkened from the soapy abrasions. Another indulgence I hadn't expected is a packaged razor. I hadn't brought my dull one from the cabin, but how pointless that would've been now. Once my human guise fell, all the fine hairs upon my body disappeared. In fact, all that's left are my brows, lashes, and silver locks. Even when I'm cleaner than I've felt in my life, and as sleek and soft as I could ever wish for, I remain beneath the waterfall showerhead and bask in the burning ribbons of water.

The town of Aberth is strange. Utterly weird in its presence and stares. There's a niggling thought in my mind, urging to break free to put the last piece of the puzzle together. Or at least the next pieces so I can understand the full picture. Between the colors, the names, the language, the atmosphere…something is underlying, nearly breaking the surface.

Perhaps if I'd had my full memories, I'd have figured it out, but the truth evades me. For now, though, I am safe. For now, in this suite with Gideon, I am safe. That is a truth that resounds in me. The safety may not last, but for now, it is here to stay.

Exiting the shower and the thoughts developed inside it, I dry off with one of the turquoise towels offered on the bar rack. I tuck the purple box into the towel.

Ensconced by a sudden eagerness, I dress hastily, pulling on the near-too-tight jeans and shirt, both while clean still smelling mildly of smoke. Plaiting my wet hair back into one single braid, I leave my cocoon of warmth behind me and find Gideon has a fire roaring in place.

I grin at the sight of him, bedraggled as he is, dirty jacket cast aside, and feel an uneven thump of my heart. I'm caught by a sudden thought as I see him. Truly *see* him.

Dashing character, kind and protective, strong and sensitive, thoughtful and decisive, albeit a bit mysterious. I'm caught by how enthralled I am by him.

A crookedly white smile greets me as I toss the towel to the floor by the bed and make my way over to him, leaning on the floor against the couch before the fire. From his position and the scent of fire and *Gideon*, I'm reminded of eating pizza at the cabin, once again remembering my figurative prison. A pang hits me at the thought and I realize I'm feeling mildly homesick. Homesick for the cabin that the Unseelie Queen devastated. The only home I've ever known.

"They have room service here," Gideon informs me laughing, displaying a folded paper menu. Upon it, I can read a selection of soups and dessert. Beyond that side is unidentified. "I've written down my order, get whatever you like and call them up. I've got it covered." With that, he takes my hand in his and gives it a gentle squeeze, pulling me forward and placing a soft kiss upon my brow. Yet again, I'm reminded of our shared height and I can't help but smile.

"Thank you," I tell him, surprised by how throaty my voice has become.

He smiles, and I notice the darkening and heat in his eyes, it sends a flash of desire through me. But suddenly, he detaches from me and slips into the now vacant bathroom. Without him, coldness invades, and I'm plunged into a small sadness.

Scanning the menu, I'm distracted by the unexpected scandalous thoughts of Gideon. Specifically, Gideon and I, and the fact that only meters from me, he's unclothed. My face heats as I fantasize, though the yearning does not dissipate.

A slight metallic squeal sounds and I select an item on the menu, not bothering to truly decide if I want it when Gideon's shower shuts off. He's taken a significantly shorter one than I. Quickly dialing on the rotary telephone, I call down to place the order, mildly surprised its Lorelai who answers.

I recite our request and I can hear the scratching on Lorelai's end as she writes it down, her voice pleasant and polite as mine wavers with embarrassment. I'd been so busy daydreaming, I'd lost sight of my task. Completing the conversation, Lorelai informs me of the price and the timeframe it should be expected within. I thank her and hang up. Just then, Gideon steps out, toweling off his black hair, haloed by the bathroom light.

"Dinner should be up in about fifteen minutes," I tell him, attempting to keep my eyes upon his and not on his body and the muscles that cling to the white tee shirt he wears.

Sadly though, he pulls on a green sweater overtop. What a pity.

"Great, I'm starving," he says, while flopping on the couch beside me. I, myself, remain on the floor, ultra-aware of his presence. I realize also, aware of his comfort and the difference upon our first meeting to this one. How he'd been hesitant and absolutely uneager to be near me. Now, the proximity is scorching with tension, even despite the fact that I am fae. Something that he's been quite outspoken about fearing and curious over.

I shift sideways as to more easily face him and swallow, trying to come up with something intelligent to say. Or rather, *anything* to say. Unfortunately, longing has made me dumb.

"That was a strange nightclub," Gideon begins, saving me from initiating a conversation. I could cry out from relief.

"You're not wrong," I respond, lightheaded from the swirling emotions, but I gain a bit of clarity. "Did you find it odd that Rachel was upset about my ears?"

Gideon seems to mull it over for a second. "No. I think it would be odd if they *didn't* know about the fae in this town."

He turns onto his side, propping his head up on his hand. "I've heard rumors of small towns and villages coexisting with the Folk, some aware of their presence, some not, yet influenced, nonetheless. This could be one of those, but something not quite, half knowing, half not. There are different situations I suppose. If anyone does know about the existence of faeries though, it's Rachel for sure."

"I agree, should we talk to her tomorrow?"

"I think that's a sound idea, she might have an ear for fae conflict. The Harbinger could have passed through here," Gideon suggests, suddenly tucking a strand of my damp hair behind my ear. I blush at the contact. For a moment he pauses, tracing the peaked edge of my ear, his eyes curious. I heat like an open flame.

What is wrong with my body? All my life I've been so utterly composed, controlled in all my actions and emotions. But now, Gideon has stumbled over and destroyed that wall I'd erected, leaving a crumbling mess where the slightest brush of his fingers sends electricity and heat through my core.

Suddenly, a knock raps on the door and a voice calls out. "Room service!" It's a male voice, one unfamiliar. I glance at the clock hooked on the wall. They're five minutes early. I check with Gideon, debating whether it really is room service, or an intruder.

If they're fae...

We share a deliberating look and Gideon inclines his head to one of the knives set out on the entry table. He then points to me, indicating for me to take it, then follows by tapping on his chest and mimicking the turning of a knob.

I nod and creep over to the weapon, glinting under the small lamp perched beside it. Carefully, I pluck it up, ensuring no scraping sounds with it. I don't sense any faerie presence, but anything is possible. I press myself against the wall, mostly hidden by a jacket hooked upon a peg while Gideon gets into position, eyes flickering to me. I give him a reassuring look and let my eyes stray to the door. Gideon draws in a breath and opens the door as normally as possible.

Revealed on the second-floor landing is a pleasant-faced, middle-aged man, dressed in a white button-down shirt and black slacks. Upon his chest is embroidery that reads *Aberth Inn* and a nametag that reads *Andrew*.

Andrew confirms our dinner with a warm, yet formal smile. Some of my unease lifts, but nevertheless, I remain stoic and still. Gideon smiles in return, relief pouring from his frame. Andrew informs him of the cost and money exchanges hands, including an acceptable tip. Suddenly cheered by Gideon's generosity, Andrew graciously thanks him and hands us the ridiculously large tray of dinner. I can already smell it from beneath the dome and my mouth waters for hot food.

I wonder if the silver dome was a tacky cliché from movies that they adopted for their medley of styles, or if they are wealthy enough to afford such luxury. Regardless, I don't care as Gideon sends him on his way.

Shutting and locking the door behind him, Gideon takes the tray, cheery as a child on Christmas and displays it proudly. I grin, eager to tackle whatever it is we had ordered. As Gideon looks around, his face falls. I don't comprehend at first, but on a quick scan of the room, I realize our predicament.

"No dining table," I announce, confused and twisting my lips.

Gideon's eyes flicker to the coffee table before the couch, but it is a tiny glass thing, and judging by the size of the tray, a balancing act would be quite necessary. I for one, do not want to risk spilling priceless food.

"That bedroom has a king-sized bed, right?" Gideon inquires, a joyful glint in his amber eyes.

I scrutinize him for a moment, unsure what the relevance of a bed is to dinner. "Yes, what does that have to do with anything?"

"I'd say a bed of that size would make quite an adequate table, wouldn't you?"

# CHAPTER

## 24

Stabbing my fork into the last morsel of fudge brownie, I swirl it in the puddle of vanilla ice cream and pop the decadent dessert into my mouth. The rich flavor spreads across my tongue and I shutter my eyes, leaning against the pillows propped against me at the foot of the bed.

The bed beneath is of the utmost comfort, fine cotton sheets and a feather, down duvet dressed in a gray cover. Continuing the gray motif are the floor-length curtains and sofa beneath the windows. Leached beach-wood makes up the structure of the furniture, from the side tables, headboard, dressers, and television stand, all bathed in warm light from glass fixtures.

"I take it the brownie was a good idea?" Gideon teases as I enjoy the last bite. I smile contentedly and fold my hands over my pleasantly full abdomen.

"More than a good idea," I return as I gather the silver tray and set it on the bench below the foot of the bed with the rest of our devoured meal. The tray settles obnoxiously with the clink of silverware and dishes. When I turn around, Gideon is there before me, closer than he'd been already. As close as he'd been when we'd kissed. Not as close as the night beneath the Northern Lights.

I hold my breath, eyes wide and startled.

With devastating slowness, he lifts his hand to my jaw and lightly brushes his thumb against the corner of my mouth. My heart thuds unevenly with the bronze intensity in his gaze. Coming away on his finger is a small smear of fudge. I blush momentarily as he draws away, but I surprise us both by latching onto his wrist and slip his thumb into my mouth, twirling my tongue around the pad of his thumb.

His pulse races erratically against my ring and index finger, a desire simmering in the core depths of his bright eyes. Releasing him gingerly, perhaps lingering ever so, he draws back as if unsure what to do with the hand now.

"I've been thinking about what Callahan said," I begin slowly, fiddling with the hem of my shirt. "I don't want to continue living my life afraid and with '*what if's?*' and regrets. I don't want to leave this earth without at least trying everything that I want in it. I don't want a life lived unfulfilled." I draw his attention to the thin shirt and beneath it my peaked breasts.

Gideon's eyes scorch with burning lust, his lips parting as his jaw slips without his volition. His arousal clear in every line of his body, his cock straining at the constraints of his pants.

I'm tired of fighting fantasy and desire. I want a completion that I yearn for with Gideon. I need these chaste and gentle touches to be deeper and more experimental. I want to know if what I imagine and ache for is requited. That he'll slip inside me and take me over the edge.

"There's something between us, Gideon, I know you feel it too. It might be volatile at times but I think it's because we're scared of its intensity. And…I want you." The truth burns undeniable between us, my stormy gray eyes fiercely intense, his amber gaze glazed with potent yearning. There's no disputing the electricity and connection humming between us. There's no refusing the history endured, and comfort experienced. There's no denying the word I refuse to speak.

"I want you, too," Gideon breathes, coming forward and cupping my face in his strong hands, calloused fingers deft against my jaw as he brings his lips to mine.

His mouth is careful as it glides against mine, applying the most teasing of pressure before he slips his tongue in with mine and that is my undoing. I leap upon him with a ravenous instinct, both of us all teeth and tongue, and caresses and claws. My hands tangle at the nape of his neck, his arms bound around me, pressing us against the other.

"Will you fuck me tonight?" I ask breathlessly, pulling back to look him in the eyes.

"Is that what you want?"

"Yes," I tell him, near growling. "Please."

"Such manners," he teases, trailing a finger down my sternum and letting it glide over my material-clad breast, tantalizingly close to my nipple. "It would be my pleasure. You need not beg."

Exploring, I find my fingers trailing downwards to the hem of his shirt and sweater. With a flourish that startles even myself, I've expertly removed the articles of clothing, revealing him in all his defined glory.

He begins touching me in turn and I throw my head back, relishing in the circles he plays on me, closing ever so around my arousal heavy breasts. "I'll beg if that's what you like. I'll get on my knees."

The answering twitch of his length betrays the excitement my words have elicited. "You have no idea what imagining you on your knees is doing to me right now." His voice is rough; sex-roughened and harsh with need.

"Oh, but why imagine when we have reality?"

Finding my own hem, I lift the edge of my shirt, ignoring my racing heart and furious flush, pulling it overhead. I kneel there, exposed before him, small curves revealed and grotesquely scarred back to the world. His eyes darken in response, his breath coming quick, his own pulse traitorously throbbing in his throat to the rhythm of my own.

"Beautiful," he whispers with devastating tenderness, his fingers tracing my collarbone and gliding down my bare ribs. I close my eyes and shiver, my heart shattering at his acceptance and melting from his now cautiously trailing hands. His fingers brush against the sensitive skin of my ribs before sliding over. My eyes close and I bite my lip.

He runs his thumb across my nipple, squeezing it ever so before truly beginning to play. Such exquisite torment. An ache builds in me, a rush between my legs, a need begging to be sated, yet I indulge in his sure touches and gentle brushes. Excited for the slow build, yet wanting to be taken right away.

"In my experience delayed gratification leads to a more powerful orgasm, and I need to make you come, Evelyn." His words strike a thrill and he replaces his fingers with his mouth, nipping at me and swirling his tongue around my tight bud. I gasp.

"Gideon, I don't know if I've ever…"

He pulls his attentions from my breast. "I don't care if you've been with one person or a thousand. And if you've never slept with anyone, then I'm happy to be your first. Just know all you have to do is say the word and we'll stop."

I shake my head. "I don't want to stop."

Finding my braid, he skillfully unbinds my hair, letting the slightly damp panels stream over my shoulders. He brushes them to one side and lets his fingers flow through the fine strands before returning to his probing attentions.

"You're in control here," he tells me.

Carefully, I take his hands and place them on my hips, tucking his fingers into the waistband of my jeans. His eyes flicker to mine, a question in them. He knows as well as I do that, that is my final layer.

"Then take my pants off" I tell him, my voice throaty and even huskier than I remember.

He helps with the too-tight jeans, flicking open the button and tugging. They roll down as if with practiced ease. Within moments I am kneeling before him, bathed in the glow of his desire, shameless and lustful, dressed only in my wanton yearning.

I indicate his state of dress and seconds later we're a matched set of cool ivory and warm ochre. Naked before me, I can see the strong lines of his body, the carved abdomen and the proud cock straining forward. It is nothing enormous, like the ones described in the erotica novels in the cabin, but he's modestly endowed. The size I could comfortably fit in my mouth with more of his length to spare. His member is thick and I caress it, loving the pulse my touch causes. I stroke him once and he groans. I stroke him again and I watch his abs ripple. Drawing him forward by his manhood in my palm, I kiss him with the breathlessness of my stolen lungs and the beat of my hormonal heart.

"Fuck." He suddenly pulls away. "What about pro—"

"I've thought of it already," I inform him, nipping his jaw, pumping him with my hand. "There's a box of condoms under the towel beside you."

His eyes widen from my ministrations and little secret. While diseases are not an issue for the fae, pregnancy certainly is.

"You clever little minx," he breathes as I push him back against the headboard and kiss him again, tasting of chocolate. Without pause or worry for our surroundings, I find myself climbing atop him. Stradling, I catch his all too familiar gaze before I capture his lips and feel his fingers working between my legs.

He finds my wetness with ease, dipping a finger into my center and running it through the slick folds, finding my clit and swirling. He circles it in tightening moves, working me into a frenzy. I grind against his working hand, eager for the friction. Mouth dipping to my breast, he captures the nipple and suckles and bites, urging my pleasure on. I feel a building ecstasy racing through me, burning like starlight.

"Fuck," I moan, tightening my grip in his hair, burying my mouth against his throat and biting down.

"I want to taste you," Gideon moans against my hot skin, fingers still working at my sensitive apex. His eyes meet mine and they are burning with desire. "I want my tongue between your legs."

I smile. A wicked, devilish little thing as I slowly lean back and part my legs for him. I leave myself fully exposed and bare for him, my wetness shining, my desire aching. His eyes watch my core and slowly, he kisses from my ankle and up my calf, lingering longer with every kiss. He pauses at my thigh, nipping at the tender inside, kissing the small hurt. His nose skims my frustrated center and I cry out with need. Seconds later his mouth is on me. He licks and brushes his tongue languidly across my clit, sucking and biting as I foist my hands in his dark locks and force him down. To be harder. He listens and increases his pleasuring movements as he finds that perfect sweet spot.

"Don't stop, please. I'm so close," I gasp. Feeling his smile on my wetness, he continues and I shatter. My climax comes hard and fast, crashing through me in waves of bliss and Gideon carries me through it, not stopping his oral sorcery until I'm trembling beneath him.

I take a moment to breathe and then sooner than Gideon can react, I pin him down and take his cock into my mouth. He groans and his hands fix in my hair, gently pushing down with my bobbing. I was right, he does fit in my mouth. I can feel him in my throat and I work him, laving up beneath his shaft and twirling my tongue around his head. Lapping up the bead that builds there.

"*Fuck*, Evelyn. You feel so good."

A few moments later and he pulls me mouth from him. I look at him in curiosity, worrying I've done something wrong. He kisses me harshly, our lips giving to the others.

"I need to be inside you."

Without further prompting, he tears open the box and no sooner than I can think he's rolled a condom on himself. A breath later I climb atop him and ease myself down onto his length. A small gasp escapes me at the new sensation, of the heavy fullness at my center. Slowly, I grind my hips forward, eager for friction. I'm still sensitive from my previous orgasm and I find myself building to a second. I ride him hard as he meets my rhythm, his hips slamming into mine. Our moans entwine, and he kisses me and bites me and I keep moving on him. I can feel his climax coming and I grind and bounce faster, finding my second as he finds his first. He moans as he comes, my center tightening on him as I feel him pulse inside me.

I collapse on top of him, trembling with the last vestiges of my climax. He's panting, his sculpted chest rising and falling in rapid movements. Shifting myself off of him, I look at him, take in his lust-sated eyes and parted full lips. He grasps the back of my neck and brings his lips to mine in a crushing kiss.

Pulling away, I get up and clean myself, but it is for naught because fifteen minutes later he's pulled out a second condom and we're back to it. My legs are on his shoulders and when I beg him to go harder and faster he performs as requested.

Like a quartet of strings and tickling of ivories, we find ourselves in a symphony created by our joining, finding a muse in the movements. It doesn't take long before our music comes to its climax, the violins and keys transitioning to cymbals and brass. With a raw moan of his name, I find my release at the same time he lets out a low groan and finds his.

We kiss again, and an hour later we do not bother to dress, but fall asleep tangled in each other's limbs. His fingers contentedly caress the scars on my back, my own comfortable upon his chest, feeling his strong heart beat beneath my palms for me.

# CHAPTER 25

When I wake, I sense something *very* wrong.

It has nothing to do with my luxuriously pleasured—albeit slightly sore—body. It has nothing to do with the peacefully sleeping man beside me where I lie with his arms around me. It has nothing to do with the dawn light breaking through the panels of the curtains.

It has everything to do with the faeries outside the door.

Climbing out from underneath Gideon's safe embrace, I pull on his discarded sweater and my rumpled jeans. From beneath the warmth of the covers, Gideon wakes, casting his bleary eyes about the room, settling on me dressed and watching the panic emanate from my frame.

"What's wrong?" he asks, instantly alert and shucking off the covers.

I turn from him to allow him modesty, but also, to creep from the open bedroom door and to the too-short distance to the front door. My bare feet are cautious against the wooden floor, padding softly to avoid arousing attention from our foes lurking behind too few inches of wood. Luckily, the tent stakes seem to have held them at bay.

"Faeries," I whisper, hardly audible before pausing to count. "Seven of them."

The sounds of fabric sliding and the metal jingling of Gideon's belt sound behind me, the noise is soft enough, but the faeries hear it. A beatific laugh reverberates under the door and across the floor. The voice sends the hairs on the back of my neck bristling.

"I should like to speak to the two of you," the Unseelie Queen declares from behind the violet-painted door.

Purple. Anemones. Silver.

I curse myself out for not putting it together, all signs leading to the Unseelie Court. The trademark silver to contrast the Seelie gold, the amethyst to her counterpart's emerald, the anemones embossed upon her sigil versus the chrysanthemum.

I knew this was too good to be true, but I was so desperate for relief and safety that I hadn't questioned further beyond, nor investigated the queer town.

Aberth does know about the fae. They are allied to the Dark Court's Queen. Rachel or Lorelai ratted us out, that is the only explanation for our quick detection.

The Unseelie Queen has brought her entire entourage. Including the Revenant.

Holding my breath and trusting the stakes will hold and do their job, I take a grip on the knob and lock, turning them in unison. The door creaks with a whine that pierces my ears, and revealed, standing elegantly and utterly out of place on the second-floor landing is the Unseelie Queen flanked by her guards.

Unfathomable hatred spears me in her presence. She nearly killed us, twice. She'd tried to poison us as well as burn us alive. She destroyed my sanctuary, Gideon's family cabin. She smiled while doing it.

She appraises me thoughtfully, her moon-white hair sleek behind her, bedecked in jewels and what I now recognize as spider-silk. Silk imbued with the strength of white sapphire, titanium, and Kevlar.

Cocking her crowned head to the side, the Unseelie Queen presses an obsidian nail to her full mouth and smiles thoughtfully, a malevolent gleam characteristically lighting her black void eyes. "My sources have recently informed me that the two of you have been traveling south for some time. My lovely Rachel has confirmed such tales and has saved herself from Aberth's annual lottery." Her teeth are too bright. Her grin too wide. Face splittingly wide.

I don't linger on her revelation of Rachel and Aberth but stow it away for further mulling. Instead, I incline my chin upwards, locking eyes with the taller faerie.

"We were seeking out the Harbinger. We have not forgotten our bargain." I'm relieved my voice doesn't come out with a waver.

The Unseelie Queen tsks in disappointment. "I believe you were traveling to the Seelie Court, young one. Time's up," she snaps, sclera-less eyes roving to Gideon shirtless behind me. "Clothe yourselves, we leave for my court. Now."

I don't fail to miss how her eyes turn feral at the scratches upon Gideon's back, a wicked light burning in her fathomless eyes. The Revenant seems to notice too because he lets out a broken choking sound. Anger boils in my veins about their knowledge of our night's activities. Such doings were between us and it is only another thing the queen can now use against us.

"I can see you have not been idle," she quips, a haughty twist to her lips.

I slam the door in her face while unfounded waves of wrath threaten to break through from the opposite side. It takes only seconds more for Gideon to have selected the white shirt from last night. I do not offer to change out of his for my own. I will not dress up for the Unseelie Queen. I am a member of the Seelie Court; the Dark Queen does not hold my loyalty.

I realize with a sense of horror that losing Gideon in The Anemone nightclub had not been like the witch in the candy house preparing to eat us. That had only been the bellyache from the excess sweets. The suite was our false sense of security from certain death.

The Unseelie Queen is our witch and entering her court will be our devouring.

The Unseelie Queen takes the lead of our procession, three guards flanking her, three guards flanking Gideon and I. We remain unbound, which I consider a blessing, though with the Revenant marching behind us, I sense a powerful array of emotions boring holes into our backs. Which impends to be a curse itself.

My shoulders are set back, my spine in perfect position as I attempt to not stiffen every time I feel that dark gaze trading off from Gideon to me. For certain I sense fury and confusion, but questioningly, I debate the other emotions of concern and desire. Desire of what? I do not know, but it is there. So is the hatred that belts at Gideon that acts as proverbial whip lashes. It startles me, but I keep my face neutral and cool.

Gideon senses something, unease gracing the set of his shoulders and tight line of his mouth. Unfortunately for him though, he is not as attuned as I, and I will not risk voicing it to inform him. The faeries do not need to know that I am quite so aware.

Wavering in my chest though, is a worry that perhaps the Revenant is so furiously reacting to Gideon is because he's the Harbinger—despite his assurances he's not—and refusing to acknowledge his counterpart. Gideon isn't fae, so there's nothing to prevent him from lying, aside from any guilt he may feel. He is gifted with tenacity for his quest and the highly skilled abilities of both fighting and luring. Not to mention his cleverness, too. The Harbinger would have to be proficient upon all fronts to adequately protect and serve the Seelie Queen. He's jumped at the opportunity to trade our search for the *Ceidwad Cudd*, but had ended it when we'd discovered that I am her, so am I being tricked now? He can so very easily lie to me, what's stopping him?

We see no one as we exit the Aberth Inn, not even Lorelai who should be stationed behind her curved desk. We see no one as we hit the streets of Aberth and I don't wonder why. The Unseelie Queen's presence here is known and it is feared.

Suddenly, I'm struck by realization.

The Welsh translation of the word *aberth* is *sacrifice*.

*Rachel had confirmed such tales and saved herself from Aberth's annual lottery.*

There's an annual sacrifice to the Unseelie Court every year in Aberth. The people fear the queen because she just may personally select them for the lottery. Better to draw no attention and seclude themselves in their homes for a few hours until the danger passes. I almost feel a pang of guilt that I've brought such dangers to their doorsteps, but then again, what choice did I have? I did not know, and in the end, they betrayed me anyhow.

"So, when is the annual sacrifice?" I inquire, attempting nonchalance as we're plunged into the warm, cocooned earth of the Faerie Roads.

I feel surprise bloom around me and try to keep the satisfaction from my face. They'd not thought me so clever. They did not imagine I'd figure out all the clues they dropped in plain sight, for the fae love their trickery as such. To tell you exactly what is happening around you without you realizing. They love to throw it back, feigning innocence. *But I told you all along, you just chose not to see it.*

The queen turns and I'm surprised to find a smile place there upon her otherworldly face. "The lottery is honored every spring equinox at twilight."

I mentally calculate the days passed and my face drains of color. "That's tomorrow," I gasp, awestruck. Gideon had told me the exact date a couple days after his arrival and since then I've kept diligent tabs on the passing of time.

"Correct," the Unseelie Queen answers, her ethereal voice piqued with excitement. "But do not act as if I'm such a monster, I give the residents of Aberth everything they desire. They want for nothing. The only price I ask them to pay is the lottery and they may subvert that requirement by working services for me. They are simple favors as well. They are only to keep the town maintained and functional, such duties you may have seen are Lorelai and Andrew taking care of the inn or Jack who tends the bar of The Anemone."

"And those who don't want to work live in an eternal party," I deadpan, understanding now why nearly everyone was so youthful.

I stutter-step at the initial Unseelie foyer, staring at the two statues. I realize that the two marble statues that I'd noticed upon my first arrival here are depictions of both the Revenant and the Harbinger. Hiding my surprise, I avert my gaze, staring at the starry floor, feeling shame light my cheeks.

I now know for certain that Gideon isn't the Harbinger.

"You are quite an intelligent one, aren't you?" the queen probes as we ascend her gabbro staircase and come upon her glass and crystal throne room. She smiles condescendingly as her guards swarm her, flanking her regal footsteps as she nears her throne with that blasted sigil.

I desperately wish to call her out, for stealing my memories and being the reason for plunging me in this hell-hole. The coin had *her* symbol on it. Somebody orchestrated it. But I refrain. Instead, I tilt my chin up, uncaring of my mussed hair and Gideon's too-large, green sweater on me.

Despite it being the morning, the Unseelie Court remains perpetually frozen at midnight, those eternal stars winking above. I scold myself again. Silver of the stars, violet of the night sky. I should have known.

Courtiers mill about the glass and stone expanse, but halt their progression upon our arrival. Muffled titters begin replacing the choir of laughter and regal tones. I try my best to avoid them, even internalizing my surprise at Tadgh's and Tegwyn's presences. The latter as shining and vicious as ever. Both sets of blue, dual-pupiled and sly, poison-green eyes follow us, awareness and curiosity drawn.

The monarch before me does not take her seat upon her throne, but rather arcs in a semi-circle, dramatically swishing her silver skirts about. There is no question that she be the focal point of the room, but she is ensuring that it remains as such. And how could she not be? Bedecked in amethysts, sapphires, and diamonds, she is a star among rocks. She is above and we are below.

Assessing me like one would appraise the predicted quality of a horse, she tilts her head to the side and an abrupt expression bleeds across her elegant features. Suddenly, she's striding forward as if on a mission and stands before me, much too close for comfort. She fingers my silver locks and I do everything in my power to remain frozen even as my mind screams; *predator, fight, run.*

"I do not remember you being fae. You are unquestionably not one of mine," she breathes, black eyes awestruck. "I am almost certain you were utterly human." She then pinches the tips of my ears and traces my jaw, too reminiscent of the loving touches Gideon bestowed upon me last night.

I hiss at the Unseelie Queen. The sound feral and full of teeth.

The queen smirks and withdraws her hand and slyly turns her eyes to Gideon.

"And *you*—" she inhales deeply, "I hadn't smelled the vampire blood on you before, but now that you aren't covered in the forest it's quite potent. Halfling, are you?"

A choked sound escapes me. My world spirals in an endless abyss. The floor opens up beneath me.

Gideon grumbles an affirmation and I'm thrown, tumbling in my horror. I can't feel my fingers, I can't feel my toes. I can't compose my face. My features have fallen with distress, all color leached from it, jaw dropped, eyes wide.

Shock could have turned my hair white if it weren't already so pale.

Vampires are real.

*I don't know what I'd do if vampires were real, too.*

*Funny.*

*Funny*, he'd said. On the porch when I told him about the book I'd been reading. I'd jokingly voiced my concerns about the existence of vampires. He'd never answered the remark. He'd avoided responding because he *knew*. He avoided commenting about the three vampires—because that's absolutely what they were—we'd encountered—two of which, could have easily killed all of us when the stakes warded against the Unseelies would have done *nothing* to protect us, should they have crossed the threshold. I should have known when the detection felt peculiar. And he avoided it all because *he* is half vampire.

The smear of blood on his lips…

After Callahan died, he'd killed a faerie so silently I hadn't comprehended how. Now I know. He attacked and drank its blood.

How many times have I let him near my throat?

How many times last night had he kissed it and nipped at it?

I don't dare to count the love bites I wear like a collar around my neck.

Revulsion chokes me in its iron grip, tearing my throat and clawing for my lungs. I cannot draw breath. I cannot form words. I cannot move. Memories surge in like a broken dam and I remember more and more.

Faeries.

Vampires.

Halflings.

Witches.

Werewolves—though near extinct.

They're all real.

Gideon is a halfling, born of a vampire father and a human mother. I am a faerie of the Seelie Court, masquerading in twisted truths and near lies as the *Ceidwad Cudd.* We are both not who we thought the other was. How has all this changed so catastrophically in a week?

Somehow, I've missed some of the correspondence between the queen and Gideon because suddenly she shrieks at him. "I want the Harbinger, not complications!"

"I know where the Harbinger is. South is the way to get him," Gideon informs her, all poise, though I know him, and I know the tics that betray him. I see the tightening of his jaw, the contracting of his fingers. He's scared.

Though, by luck, his ploy has drawn the queen's interest. She wheels on me, her brows quirked high. "Is this true?"

Danger thrums through me and I realize the precarious situation we've been placed. I cannot lie. The queen knows that and she's using it to her advantage.

I don't dare glance at Gideon. I don't dare to speak. I muster everything in myself and focus. Faeries can lie on a technicality, *only* if they fully believe what they're saying. It's how misinformation can spread so easily in the Courts. Gideon had plans before, he had knowledge he never shared with me last time we'd visited the Unseelie Court. It wouldn't be a stretch to believe he'd done so again. On the same note, it's not a lie to know that the Harbinger is missing. It's also true that upon meeting Gideon he told me he knew where the Harbinger was, albeit, he only knew he was in this icy territory, but it's enough.

I believe him.

I spend only a moment more convincing myself of this truth before I meet the monarch, eyes locked into hers even when fear skitters down my spine.

"Gideon does not speak falsely. He knows where the Harbinger is."

*I believe him.*

I could deflate from the relief that nearly knocks me off my feet. I feared that I had not had faith in my words, but I suppose deep down I did. He is likely hiding more from me. He'd hid nearly the entirety of his identity without me catching on. What more could he obscure?

The queen inclines her head, folding her hands over her abdomen, suddenly pleased. "You have a final week, Arawn will accompany you." An autumn-haired faerie allows a smile to spread across his lips at this. "Should you fail within the timeline, he shall bring me your heads. Have I made myself clear?"

"Crystal," I intone darkly.

The Unseelie Queen giggles like a young school-girl. "Oh, I don't believe I've made myself quite clear as of yet. Tadgh?"

Shock cripples me even further as the dual-pupiled faerie steps forward. He still bears welted burns from the iron trap we'd laid days before. A queer pang of remorse strikes me, knowing that I'd done that to one of my own, one likely better than I am. If I were to take the defense though, I hadn't known I was fae, but I'm unsure whether that makes it any better, or makes me more selfish for having those thoughts in the first place.

Stepping forward, wrapped in a black linen tunic, Tadgh ducks his dark head of curls to his queen. He shows utter deference to her and a ripple of unease slithers through me, an instinct urging at me to remain vigilant.

"Are you pleased to serve me any way in which I see fit?"

"Yes, My Queen."

"Then I thank you, my child, for your loyalty."

And with that, she swipes her obsidian claws across Tadgh's throat and severs his head from his body.

# CHAPTER 26

I choke and stumble backwards in shock as a wide arc of arterial spray paints the Dark Queen's gown. She wears a sinister glove of it now, like a seamless creation of rubies upon silk. Tadgh's head rolls to a stop only a few steps from my feet, those dual-pupiled blue eyes staring up at the night sky that he shall never again see. Surprise leaves his lips parted for eternity.

She smiles solemnly down at Tadgh, the one faerie who'd begun to change mine and Gideon's opinion about the

Folk. The queen shattered that illusion. She has only further proved that Unseelies are predatory and inhumane.

"I cannot allow weakness in my court, no matter the loyalty of its denizens. He was all too eager to answer your questions without provocation and I can't have loose tongues. Such a pity to see him go though, his brother will be devastated." The queen pouts but turns her head away, as if suddenly bored. Turning to us, her mirth brightens. "In another vein, I would like to extend a formal invitation to the two of you. Your presence will be appreciated at Aberth's Annual Lottery upon our sacred equinox."

"Oh, I don't think that's—" Gideon starts, panic only I can see glimmering in his eyes.

"I *insist*," the queen practically hisses.

We remain silent while the queen smiles and admires the blood leaking down her arm with cruel delight.

"Arawn, please take Evelyn and Gideon back to Aberth, the Town Hall if you please. I do believe they have some catching up to do," she dismisses and titters a laugh, hiding behind her crimson hand. For a faerie who appears to be in her mid-twenties, the action makes her seem young and girlish.

I send a death glare at her back and spin on my heel, showing myself out, both Gideon and Arawn following close behind.

"How could you not tell me you're half *vampire*? What else aren't you telling me?"

Gideon and I are standing in the paved street before the Aberth Inn. Arawn is watching us from the sidewalk, a grin painted on his face with a golden sword whose blade glitters in the morning sun at his hip. His rusty hair is tousled and his whole demeanor holds a wildness that crawls up my spine. His eyes are old, ancient even, and of the darkest brown, so close to his queen's ebony.

"I used to be in a program funded by a society that trained us to become protectors, spies, warriors or assassins. It's an elite unit devoted to protecting or eliminating abnormal or coveted supernaturals," Gideon explains placatingly as if we may begin to draw a crowd. "I was training to become a protector."

"And you dropped out because you weren't good enough?" I demand, fury vibrating in every nerve of my being. He *lied* to me. Deliberately. It was one thing for me not to tell him about my being fae because I *didn't* know, he *did* know his own identity. He kept it from me. But I should have known.

My alarm feels different for each species. The fae is malevolent and demanding, the halfling is a hum, vampires are shriller, witches cause a long echoing beat. I should have bloody known. I should have *realized*.

"No," he breathes, too soft for my wrath as he shakes his head. "I would have had to give up my entire life to pursue it and I realized how much I wasn't willing to do that when my dad—well the man who raised me—nearly died."

"Because your real dad is a vampire."

"Yes."

"Is this the same society that offered your *scholar* dad the job to be an ambassador to the Seelie Court?"

Gideon visibly cringes. "I wasn't entirely honest about that. He's an ambassador to the Arcana Society, hired by the House Council—which is their government—to cover up supernatural mistakes." He takes a deep breath. "They also built the cabin to foster relations between the society and the courts."

Suddenly, I erupt and stomp away from him, my temper blowing wide as I reel around. "I can't believe I trusted you! You lied right to my face! You've lied to me from the very beginning. How do I know that everything out of your mouth this entire time wasn't a lie?"

"Like you wouldn't have done the same," he defends softly, red burning high on his cheeks, shame lighting his amber eyes.

"I have *never* lied to you," I spit viciously. "And I *can't*. Like you said; *faeries can't lie*." I point to my ears as proof of my undeniable claim.

"Lover's quarrel?" Arawn intones from the sidelines, cleaning his nails with an antler embossed dagger.

"Fuck off." I throw him the middle finger.

Arawn laughs, allowing me my childish act of vehemence. It does little good, but it does make me feel somewhat better. It does not, however, dispel the new truth around us.

Suddenly, the residents of Aberth begin exiting their homes and each and every one of them is clad in white. There is little to no variation in shade or color, but the styles differ immensely. A woman streams by me with a basket in arms, dressed in a peasant blouse and leather leggings. Another wears a skin-tight, lace minidress, and then there are more in tee shirts and loose trousers.

I catch the arm of a man passing by, his white suit cleanly pressed. "Excuse me, what's going on here?"

He looks at me startled, taking in my distinctly non-bleached clothes and gapes. "It's the Annual Lottery."

I'm taken back yet I do not loosen my grip. "But that's tomorrow."

His brows knit. "No, it's tonight. Tonight is the spring equinox."

"What?"

He rattles off the March date.

I feel as if my feet have been knocked out from under me. I release the poor soul and whirl on Gideon and Arawn. The latter has humor glimmering in his eyes. Gideon stares back, a puzzled look on his face, but there's a foreboding emotion seething in his eyes.

"What is he going on about?"

Arawn pries himself from the wall and tucks his blade into a sheath at his hip. "I believe my queen was profoundly excited about the equinox and decided to bestow you a gift. You do not have to labor under impatience, for the day has arrived." His fine-boned face is pulled into a mockery of a smile and I set my sights on Gideon.

"She stole a day from us?" I pose it as a question, but it's more of a statement. I know that time can move differently within the courts, but I hadn't been aware of the influence the queens could express over it.

Gideon lifts his face to the sky and studies the sun with frustration. "I believe so. I've heard tell that the queens may shift the passage of time between the Mortal and Faerie lands by several hours," he informs me factually, "but it seems she let time pass quicker at her court and now we've lost twenty-four hours. We have to deal with the lottery today." His voice is dejectedly resigned and I don't admonish him of the fact. I am too.

"Stupid bitch," I mutter. Then I instantly realize my mistake. Arawn's hand tightens on the hilt of the sword and his face contorts into an image of monstrosity. As white brightens on his knuckles, angry, red splotches burn on his cheeks and forehead. I've insulted his queen and he's taken it quite personally.

Just then, I'm saved by a passerby knocking into Arawn, his box of purple anemones upturned and spilling onto the asphalt below. Petals of the hateful hue flutter in a wide arc and the man curses before dropping and scrambling for the salvageable flowers. Arawn is taken off guard well enough to drop focus and lose concentration, releasing the hilt and glaring at the poor young man on the ground.

"Clumsy piece of filth," Arawn spits, pulling back his teeth to reveal pointed incisors. "You've just put yourself on tonight's watchlist."

The young man's blue eyes widen in horror and picking up a final flower he takes off faster than his feet should possibly carry him. He becomes a streak of white against the multi-color and multi-storied buildings, bold against the royal blue of a vintage clothing shop and blinding against the red of a Victorian-esque grocer.

I whirl to Arawn again, unworried about consequences as my fury takes hold. "You put him on a list for tonight's slaughter?" My voice rises an octave and I do nothing to quell it.

He shrugs uncaringly. "It matters little to me, but you should know that it is not a slaughter, as you so distastefully put it. The queen may request the winner of the lottery as many of a thing. The recipient may be awarded a place in our revels, or even a spot in court entertainment. Others may become staff in our kitchens. We use them as we see fit."

"And how you see fit may still be to kill them or torture them," Gideon interjects, disgust painted across every line of his defined features.

Arawn grins, showing off those razor-sharp teeth. "My queen deems them fit for a certain placement, that placement may not be among the living. Though, the living are paid well enough for their services."

"You're sick," I hiss, nausea roiling in my gut. "That's little more than slavery."

The black-eyed faerie hardens his gaze. "I would advise you not to use that word in reference to my queen. She will not take to it too kindly."

I seal my mouth shut, despite the want of giving Arawn a tongue lashing.

*This is so sick.*

I hate this. I hate that sun shines on this odious day. I hate that the sky is as blue as ever. I hate that they wear white when they'll mourn. And I hate even more that there's nothing I can do to stop it.

A young child wanders by, her hand held by her young mother, both of them wearing matching sundresses with embroidered irises. The flowers offer the tiniest splotches of color, enough for me to notice and realize their symbolism. She looks up at me with large, green eyes, full of joy and woefully ignorant as to the fate of one of her fellow townspeople. Waving her chubby little toddler fingers and revealing a gap-toothed grin, I come to a conclusion.

I have to do something to stop this sacrifice.

Arawn laughs at me when I request returning to the inn.

"And gather your weapons? Nice try, girl."

Instead, he leads us to the clothing shop, urging us up the two concrete steps and through the thin, glass door. I manage only a glance through the massive nine-pane window and find myself peering into a sea of white before I'm inside. A tiny bell chimes overhead, much like the one at the inn, though the shop is anything but.

Done up in bold, red paper with a damask print, the walls scream the store owner's favorite color, while the worn hickory floors balance out the overpowering shade. A chandelier glitters overhead, its arms the languorous reach of tentacles, its lazy sprawl reminding me of an octopus.

An Indigenous woman appearing to be in her early twenties steps out from behind the glass counter, dressed in an ivory corset over a short linen sundress. Clapping her hands together and grinning a bright, cherry-red smile, she approaches Gideon and I, her grin faltering at the sight of Arawn.

"What can I help you with today?" the young woman asks warmly, albeit in tense form. She appraises us, noting our lack of white clothing as everyone so far has yet to not do.

"These two require some appropriate clothing for tonight's festivities," Arawn answers, a smug smile to his stupid face.

The woman blinks once and nods, pasting a nervous, yet cheery smile to her pretty face. Her eyes are quite odd; hazel in the center and storm blue outside. They are stunning and peculiar.

Spinning on her high-heels, she clicks over to a rack before the window, to the sea of white I'd glimpsed. Gideon and I follow her while Arawn leans against the counter, admiring the woman's backside. I roll my eyes and continue walking.

The woman—whose silver nametag reads Julia—paws through the options, first surveying the male fashions, succinctly appraising Gideon for fitting and murmurs to herself. In moments, she pulls out a casual pair of white dress pants with cuffed ankles and a crisp button-up, and hands him the selection.

When she turns to me, she looks me up and down. "Style? I can't seem to get a read on you. Definitely not bohemian. Not preppy, either. Edgy?" Her voice is educated and considering, and I realize she takes immense pride in her work.

I can admire that.

"It doesn't matter. Dress the Seelie in white and let's go," Arawn complains from his post, sounding incredibly bored.

Intelligent shock bolsters Julia's peculiar eyes and before I'm certain I saw it, she shakes her long, jet hair to hide it. She turns a corner, out of Arawn's sight and I follow. Squinting beneath beautifully arched brows, she caresses the fabrics, further considering and blatantly defying him.

I can admire that, too.

Seeming to make a decision, Julia unhooks several items from the selection and pawns them off on me. I'm startled by the different textures I feel upon my calloused fingers, knowing the familiar feel of leather and cotton, and the not so familiar texture of velvet. Unspooling the bundle, I find the leather is leggings, the cotton becomes a fitted, open-shouldered top with snug sleeves, but the velvet is what surprises me. A bustier of creamy ivory with hints of golden thorns and ivy woven through where laces of leather cross the sides of it.

I realize with a jolt that all the items contain more cream white, rather than moon white coloring. Leaning more yellow rather than blue. More golden rather than silver.

My eyes fly to her and I understand in that instant the look in her eyes. The defiance. The allegiance.

Sure enough, she pulls her long waves to the side and there, marked upon her neck, is a false mark of the Unseelie. But where the true devotion is, is to the Seelie Court and the matching mark shines on the wrist she exposes to me to prove it. Memory strikes as I watch the gold that glitters there. The fascinating difference between the two marks is that only those loyal to the Seelie Queen can see the golden mark. The silver burns bright for all to see, for mortals and fae, and supernatural alike. Not for gold, gold glows for the faithful. Only those who do not swear fealty to the Unseelie Monarch can ever view the golden mark.

My queen has a spy in this town of Hell.

Curious that the Unseelie Queen took such a risk in this town. Her true silver marks act much the same as my sacred Seelie ones do, but apparently, she decided that wasting resources on her fae marks weren't worthy of the humans. Her mistake, those true tattoos burn should they betray. But who'd expect repressed humans to turn?

I allow my eyes to flicker to it for only a second before meeting her gaze, hardening my look to stone with fidelity, and turn from the Seelie Queen's spy. Gideon and I both make our way to the red velvet curtains of the fitting room, changing into our new attire.

Wordlessly, a pair of boots are slipped beneath my room by a slender, tanned hand with nails painted crimson red. They are essentially relatively tall combat boots. Supple leather, knee-height, with a golden chunk for a heel and soles with golden buckles and laces.

I grin as I put together the ensemble.

When I step out, Gideon is just pulling the curtain aside and I'm startled by how charming he looks in white. The lightness brightens to contrast of his pallor, his rich caramel tone hued with honey, amber eyes that glow orange like a sunset, and wavy dark hair to offset the portrait. Truth be told, he takes my breath away. But he cannot know that, for he has broken my trust. He has deceived me, so he may not discover what I harbor deep in my heart and mind.

I notice also, that Julia has added to Gideon's ensemble. A pair of dress shoes in toffee leather and a matching belt with a golden buckle. It's proudly showed off by the shirt he has tucked into the waist. She hands us two large paper bags of the brightest scarlet and we deposit our discarded clothing into them and remove the burden from the Seelie spy.

"Put the clothes on Caethes's account, she has requested their presence tonight," Arawn tells Julia uninterestedly, scanning a case of silver jewelry.

I pause mid-step and whip my vision to Gideon's, finding his already on me.

*Caethes.*

Caethes has requested our presence.

The memory surges with startling clarity. That Caethes is the Unseelie Queen. What she achieved to become queen. How ruthless her history has painted her. My heart sinks with horror. How are we to stop a tyrant that clawed her way from the darkest depths of slavery to the highest level of monarchy, singlehandedly?

I'm saved from drawing attention to my internal panic attack when a girl steps into the shop, distinctly not dressed for tonight's lottery, still bedecked in club-wear of fishnets and a denim minidress. With a start, I recognize the girl. Mid-size, dark-skinned with bronze tones, teak eyes, and lime-green hair. She's the one who'd tried to pull me into the throng of dancers and separated Gideon and I.

She's also a witch.

# CHAPTER 27

The internal alarm shudders within me, trembling with the innate knowledge before me that this girl is a witch. Just like the distinctive signal I'd ignored upon meeting Gideon that indicated he was a halfling. It was subtle, different from the fae. I'd ignored it then, content to believe it was just the pinging of another human, a different signal to my own.

I won't make that mistake now.

I begin to formulate a plan. It isn't the most conventional of sorts, but it achieves two goals. It is also the long game. Though, it just may save someone from a truly horrible fate tonight.

Drawing in all the fury that has boiled within me from the Unseelie Queen's threats, Gideon's betrayal, Tadhg's unnecessary death, and Arawn's penchant for psychological torment, I fan the flames. As I pour more fuel onto the inferno, I allow the blaze to course through my veins and simmer in my eyes. To show the chaos of my mind.

Without provocation, I launch myself at the witch. "You sneaky little bitch!" I howl, lunging for her shoulders as I wind a hand through her hair. "Please play along," I plead softly in her ear, allowing a desperate tone to seep through. It is so quiet that I fear she doesn't hear me, though luckily, her relaxing shoulders indicate she did.

She throws me off of her and I let her, all the while her eyes flicker to the side. I understand immediately as she throws a punch. The fist was aimed well, and I use it to my advantage, grasping her wrist and twirling her into me.

Locking an elbow around her throat, tight enough to appear constricting—and certainly uncomfortable—but loose enough that she can breathe freely, I lower my lips to her ear and speak quickly. "I know you're a witch, I need your help. Meet me back here in a half hour."

I release her abruptly as she pretends to stomp her heel into my foot. She performs the move proficiently, leading me to believe that she's taken a self-defense course or two, and had she wanted to, she could have shattered the bones of my foot. Fortunately for me, she didn't want, and though it wasn't full force, it still had to look good. But it sure didn't feel good.

I hiss an insult at her, driving home the illusion as I drop to the ground. She grasps my silvery hair in her dark grip and wrenches my head back. I do not resist because I know I could break her hold in half a move if I felt threatened. "Good thing

I'm curious about what you have to say. See you in thirty minutes." And with that, she spits a colorful and expletive-laced insult, before tossing my head back and sauntering off. The bell chimes a final note in her wake.

When I look up at my small crowd, I know without a shadow of a doubt that Gideon and Julia have seen the ruse for what it is. Arawn on the other hand, is tickled pink, pleased by the show and blinded by his Unseelie chaos meter. His eyes are glassy and filled with euphoria, and I internally grin. He was the only one I needed to fool. Gideon's eyes are pleading for answers, but it is hidden deep in the amber depths, just like a prehistoric insect in the fossilized resin. And had I not known him as I do, I'd see the façade of immovable rock in his gaze that Arawn and Julia cannot break past.

Arawn begins ushering us out the door and in his haste, he jostles me and I send my bag flying, contents spilling forth. I mutter a curse and shove my boot aside as I scrounge up my discarded clothing into a mildly torn bag. I don't bother to scowl at him for fear of the expression on my face.

We then leave the shop and I'm startled to discover the street transforming before our eyes. Haunting music floats from the speakers adhered to lampposts. Violins somber, drums depressed, and the voice breathy, ethereal, and anxiety inducing. Christmas lights are strung up between businesses, crisscrossing the street and intersecting with alternating streamers of white and lilac, finished off by silver chains winding through the canopy. The scent of lily of the valley is heady through the air, intermingled with the sugary notes of pastries, and the fried smell from some of the market stands. At the center of the main town square and backing the fork in the road is a newly assembled stage, dressed garishly in the Unseelie tones where people clad in white mill about.

Dawning horror hits me and I come to a realization. The lottery is a sacrifice, yes, but those who survive the ordeal enjoy a festival for the spring equinox and to celebrate not being the poor, unwilling victim of tonight's cost.

It's a party.

It's dark and heinous, and I have a plan.

Arawn leads us past the stage where a large glass ball perches, filled with slips of paper. As we pass, wide and fearful eyes follow our every move as he takes us down a residential street. He's a terrifying figure, I remember, known by his infamous name, originally thought to be the god of death and war, but truly the leader of the Wild Hunt. He confidently dresses in a finely-made tunic of gloomy black and matching leather leggings without a shred of armor to be found.

The Wild Hunt is mostly unknown. The Hunt is elusive and said to draw fae in for eternal servitude and humans for deadly games. The original members were thought to be gods, worshiped by ancient societies. What they are is a sick and twisted band of fae with powers of persuasion lent to them from witch-blood ancestry. Back when magic was wild and potent, flooding bloodlines. Now it is too diluted to make pure members.

Before turning onto another avenue, he indicates a large white building at its end. Built like a gothic mausoleum and tucked behind the shops of the main road, it's imposing. The garden beds lining the long drive are immaculately maintained, purple flowers glaring up at me from their beds and fence spires threaten to stab and pierce my flesh if I come too close. This place is foreboding and unwelcoming at best.

"This is Aberth's council hall, I insist you take leave here until the drawing of tonight's supplicant," Arawn announces with little to no fervor, nearly stewing a hate for his job. He's likely just as bored as we should be.

Gideon and I refrain from responding and follow the Unseelie through the wooden doors and into a circular room with a domed ceiling of glass. Sunlight flitters through, warmth dousing the uninhabited state of things and highlighting the imperfections of the supplied furniture. Scratched arms of a gray sofa, dinged edges of the two armchairs, chipped varnish on the wooden coffee table, sun faded magazines, and dusty vases of silk flowers. The only thing remaining immaculate is the spectacularly large sigil upon the far wall, gleaming to blinding levels, unabashedly displaying the Unseelie Queen's crest for all to take in.

It's the first time I've seen it in color; tipped in violet, antlers light, moon silver, held in a gradient of twilight darkness. Lavender-toned silver embellishments accent it, the entire piece wrought by an artist's hand.

I briefly fantasize about shattering that buck moon, snapping the antlers, and tearing every petal off those wretched anemones.

I refrain, however though, the thought is sweet.

Gideon and I step towards the stiff looking armchairs and take a seat. As I set down my bag from the clothing shop, I sense the distinct lightness as it touches the floor. Allowing a confused expression to crawl across my face, I dig through the bag and swear.

"What?" Arawn growls, turning his back from his queen's emblem.

"I'm missing my boot."

"And?"

"And I'd like to retrieve it."

Arawn laughs, dark humor glinting there. "Now why would I let you do that?"

"Because I swear that I won't run away? I'm fae, I cannot lie to you, so if I swear to do something, it will be upheld."

Arawn's face turns calculating, those dark, fathomless eyes working, flickering between Gideon and I. His assessing seems to come to a decision as a wry smile turns his lips. "Swear it to me."

I gasp slightly in surprise, disguising it as I draw a breath and begin. "I swear that today I will return to this room within the hour and I will not leave the town of Aberth, unless you allow otherwise. I will not contact anyone outside of Aberth."

Arawn searches, looking for loose ends in my statement, ensuring that I cannot leave and that I will return. He nods slightly. "Promise you will not return to the inn either, nor send anyone to retrieve your other belongings."

I smile through a snarl and promise him.

"You will be watched, do not forget, Seelie." He dismisses me with an unreadable look as I glance at Gideon and turn from him and Arawn, and out the door.

I take off through the sea of white and jog through the filling streets back to Julia's shop and past a cornerstone diner. Upon entering, I discover that Julia has turned the sign around to *CLOSED* and perches on the edge of her counter. Her peculiar eyes take me in and she lightly nods across the shop.

There, still dressed in the denim dress with a zipper down the front is the witch. Her boldly done up doe eyes catch sight of me and she makes her way over, confident in her heels. She grins and it is a crazed, maniacal smile that lights up her face and highlights her thin, gold septum ring. She also has the slightest and most endearing gap between her two front teeth. I find that I've taken a fondness to her.

"Come this way, we can talk in private. I'll be back in a bit, Jules," she tells the storeowner warmly and steps through the door. I follow as she rounds the corner of the building and begins scaling the rusting fire escape to the second floor. Confused, I just follow.

Distantly, I make a mental note to recruit Julia for our cause.

"I'm Wisteria Pike, by the way," the witch tells me nonchalantly, humming a tune as she reaches into her purse.

"Evelyn," I respond as I search the area. It's not dangerous by any means, but in a town run by your enemy court, you never can be quite sure.

Jingling accompanies her purse searching and upon finding her keys, she unlocks the buttery-yellow door before us. As soon as the door is open, I'm met with the glow of natural sunlight and an incalculable amount of herbal scents. Pushing through behind her, I find that the apartment is cluttered beyond comprehension.

Plants hang from the ceiling and perch in pots in every nook and cranny. Jars line the tops of cupboards and balance precariously on shelves. Books are scattered about, tomes and fiction, filling bookshelves and teetering in stacks on the floor. Crystals hang in front of the window while a box nearby spills them out like a faucet left on.

Lounging on the indigo couch is a man, perhaps a similar age to the witch and I, with a yellow blanket thrown over his long legs. A pair of black-framed glasses are askew across his straight, refined nose, glasses which highlight his powder-blue eyes.

"Hey Elliot, I brought home a faerie, she wants to talk. Faerie, that's my boyfriend, Elliot. I'm gonna go get changed, then we'll talk." Her voice is succinct, yet pleasant and with a quick wave she slips into the small bathroom nearby. I blink, slightly puzzled but shake the confusion from my mind.

Elliot sits up straighter, running a hand through his carefully styled blond hair and smiles a sweet grin at me. "Well, Faerie—" he pats the couch next to him, "—come take a seat."

Hesitantly, and still guarded I delicately sit on the edge of the couch, surprised to find it freshly cleaned. In fact, most of it, if not all of the apartment is clean despite the clutter.

I introduce myself quickly, extending a hand. Elliot takes it and his hand is smooth and warm, severely unlike my own calloused palm. Suddenly nervous, I make the first idle conversation I can summon. "Have you two been together long?"

"The best three years of his life," Wisteria calls enthusiastically from the bathroom, laughing as she turns on the tap.

"Is, uh, is your girlfriend always so…audacious?" I ask lowly, admiring the confidence that the witch holds in herself but empathy she still exudes. Though I fear that I may inadvertently offend her.

Here, in this quaint apartment, I'm picking up a sense of *something* in this home. Some preternatural awareness that gives me a tiny inkling. I search for it, not knowing what it is that I want to find. Proverbially looking for a ghost, I scan the painted flower pots, the labelled jars, the laptop on the table, wondering if my sixth sense can decipher what I'm feeling. I've always had to make snap judgments on my situations, assessing the details quickly when it comes to life or death. That habit is awakening as more memories resurface.

"Ah, yeah, that's just the way Wisty is. She likes to say things the way they are and she's confident doing it. Some people find her difficult to handle, but they can shove it," he tells me unbothered, leaning back.

"Oh. Well, that's *good*." I stumble over the word. "And I suppose you get to see a different side of her, being her significant other and all," I respond lightly, unsure as to how to make small-talk. I came here to devise a plan, not talk relationship semantics with the witch's boyfriend.

*This was so much easier with Gideon*, I grumble internally, and despite not vocalizing the words, I know they're surly in nature.

"Not really." He shrugs, still smiling as he sticks a marker in the book on his lap and sets it on the table. "She isn't like that."

I cock my head, pickup up on his second use of the way his girlfriend is or isn't like. It's not in the offhand way a lover speaks of a quirk, but rather a deeper statement. Before I can ask what he means, it hits me and I notice what is missing. Tokens of appreciation, romantic gestures, traditionally couple-y photos, cringy love quotes. This home is more akin to two roommates living together, rather than a couple.

Just then, the witch exits the bathroom, face washed, round, wire-rimmed glasses perched low on her nose, and dressed in all white, from her high-waisted, flared pants to her long-sleeved crop top. Her green hair is nowhere to be seen and I realize that it must have been a wig because now dark, spiral curls frame her face.

"All right, so what did you want to talk about?" she asks, planting her hands on her hips.

"We're going to rig the lottery so that it picks you, and then you're going to lie to the Unseelie Queen and tell her that you'll be her spy in the Seelie Court."

# CHAPTER 28

Wisteria barks an incredulous laugh. "Are you joking? You must be joking. Oh my God, you're a faerie, you can't joke. You're serious?"

"I'm dead serious."

"Why? What's in this for me?"

"A chance to get out of this hellhole, I can't imagine you're in Aberth willingly. Not to mention, you've probably known or been friends with someone selected for the lottery."

She sniffs but doesn't disagree, and then her eyes flicker over to her boyfriend. "Only if Elliot gets out too."

Elliot perks up at this, curiosity in his eyes and concern written all over his face.

The boyfriend hadn't been part of my plan, but without him, I have no plan. I need to figure out a way to get Elliot out of Aberth and into the Seelie Court. Though I don't quite know how, I'll manage it.

"I will make it happen."

"So, how do I know that the Seelie Queen won't try to kill me the second I step foot in her court?" Wisteria knits her brows and glares me down.

"Because you'll have irrefutable proof that I sent you."

"What do *you* matter to the Seelie Court? Why will the queen trust me because *you* sent me?"

And so, I lean forward and tell her the proof of my identity, of being the *Ceidwad Cudd,* the sort of evidence she needs before I tell her of my plan. Her eyes widen in shock, but she nods. I then continue. "I need you to use a glamour spell on the ball so that all the papers read your name. From there, I'll convince the Unseelie Queen to send you to the Seelie Court under the guise of you offering your services. When you're there, tell the Light Queen what I told you, admit your heritage, and she'll trust you."

"You think you can convince Caethes to do something she hasn't decided herself?" Wisteria's voice is skeptical.

"I think she can be persuaded, yes. If not, Gideon and I will ensure nothing happens to you and take you directly to the Seelie Queen. You have my word." I'm not sure how I'll get to the Light Queen, but I have sworn and I am oath bound to make it happen.

Wisteria purses her lips. Glancing over to Elliot who throws his hands up innocently. "And Elliot?"

"And Elliot," I confirm.

"Okay, I'm in."

"Before I leave, I need to know your name," I press, folding my hands together, not having left the couch below me.

"I already told you." Her gaze narrows.

"Not your true surname."

Witches do not have simple last names. They have a compound structure consisting of two characteristics, generally aligned with their specific affinity to magical ability. A Blackthorn witch can summon chains of black thorns to weaponize and intimidate. A Goldwine witch conjures physical and magical shields of golden light that act as wards—as well as a proclivity for winemaking. A Frostsinger witch has the ability to lure a victim to hypnotism with their voice and kill with a frozen kiss. And so on, and so forth.

But then there are the exceptions, like the Lockwood witches whose name bears no meaning on their unparalleled warrior status. There are also Prophet Witches that hail from any family and earn their ability through devotion to the goddess.

Wisteria draws in a breath, shuttering her eyes. She opens them and exhales softly. "Greyvale. My name is Wisteria Anne Greyvale."

I grin, extending a hand and standing. "Then we have an alliance."

The mausoleum-esque council hall is just as foreboding as it had been an hour ago, just as daunting, and just as imposing. Mentally, I drag my feet on the black asphalt path, physically, I saunter up, my boot dangling from my fingertips. It had been retrieved from Julia's shop where I'd purposefully dropped it, collected immediately after the meeting with Wisteria.

Julia, unfortunately, was nowhere to be found when I descended the steps from Wisteria's apartment, but perhaps that was good fortune. Although, I decide she could be invaluable once out of here, out of this town of Unseelie making. But for strategy? Another body is not needed for this mission and extra hands can complicate a simple plan. Also, fewer knowing about my idea, the better. Loose tongues are just as dangerous as extra fingers.

Regardless, I leave Julia a note to meet the following morning.

Both Arawn and Gideon's eyes fly up with my entrance, the doors hinge's hair-raisingly loud. Gideon stands to meet me, relief written plain as day across his features and I can't help but have my heart flip-flop at the sincerity in his eyes. My breath catches in my throat and I stutter-step just the slightest. Arawn doesn't notice. Gideon does.

A glimmer of excitement flashes through Gideon's eyes but I avert my gaze before I can dwell on it further—or react at all. I toss Gideon's thieved wallet across the room to him, and look away to meet Arawn. His gaze is trained on me, his jaw jutted outward with a sense of authority and his head tilts as he assesses. His nearly black eyes are narrowed.

"Have you collected your missing item of clothing?" Arawn inquires, his rusty hair slipping over his brow.

I dangle the shoe before him, ignoring the musky odor emanating from it. Between years of continuous use of trekking through the woods, water, mud, and snow—not to mention escaping a house fire—it's bound to reek. "I have. Thank you for allowing me to find it."

"You're welcome. Now go sit next to your lover and be quiet, the lottery begins in a few hours."

With that, I turn and sit, depositing a take-out bag of burgers and fries in Gideon's lap. I don't acknowledge his look of surprise as I lean against the wall and wait.

It's after twilight and tensions are running high. There is a thread of anxiety humming through each and every individual that connects every fearful heart to the next. The crowd before the stage is dressed in white of fabric and dark of mind, each face wearing varying degrees of denial and acceptance.

Gideon and I stand off to the side of the stage, nervous feet planted to the paved road, Arawn flanks us smugly. My eyes scan the area and my belief in our chances of success begin to dwindle. Around us, Aberth residents shuffle, eyes flicker.

Upon every rooftop are fae archers, poised and ready with their polished silver bows, arrows catching the violet light of the festivities. Framing the town square are sword and spear-armed warriors, titanium armor protecting their joints and hearts. Following the Unseelie Queen herself are her six guards, circling her as she ascends the stairs to the stage.

Taking up the forefront and the attention of every being in the square, the queen smiles primly. She's forcing a façade of grimness, of faked solemnity, when in fact there is pleasure burning within those fathomless black eyes. Excitement radiates off of her frame through the silk panels of her deep purple gown, the diamonds of the plunging bodice glimmering like the faux tears in her eyes.

In the crowd, I spot Wisteria and Elliot, side by side both apprehensive and braced. I search again for any familiar faces and find a few at the back. Lorelai and Rachel, both at the rear of the crowd bedecked in loose-fitting, leached fabric and a large silver Unseelie pin. Nearby, I recognize Jack the bartender of The Anemone, and Andrew the waiter from the inn.

The night is deepening with cold and dark, the only light to see by are those designed for tonight's post cull party. There are whispers and titters of tonight's revelry, but no one appears daring enough to fully express their excitement, especially when they may not ever get the chance to attend. This is a sacrifice, after all. I do not forget that a party hovers overhead, I do not forget like these residents do, even if it's to escape their corrupted reality.

Caethes steps from the safety of her guards, raising her arms and the draping sleeves of her gown, welcoming an unwilling subject to their death. Lavender lights shine from below the glass stage, capturing the Unseelie Queen in a bath of ethereal light.

Had I not known better, I'd think she were some goddess of the night and wild things.

"Children of Aberth, you are so very brave, so very loyal, and so very admirable," Caethes begins elegantly, her voice powerful over the depressed crowd. "I thank each and every one of you for your presence here tonight, to honor the spring equinox, and to honor your queen." She grins, her white teeth too white. "Tonight, I would like to bestow a blessing to a fortuitous child. Tonight—" Her gaze beseeches the crowd, her intent predatory as she comes to land upon a victim. "Elliot McCain, shall draw the lottery."

My heart leaps into my throat as Wisteria blanches, next to me Gideon's breath catches, and far from us, Elliot visibly gulps. All the blood drains from Elliot's face as he navigates the labyrinth of the crowd, his shocked blue eyes dead to the world.

I'd managed in breaths to explain to Gideon my plan in the barest of terms, he knows what Elliot is to Wisteria. He knows what a wrench this is.

Caethes plays a wicked game with this lottery. Not only for the fact of an annual sacrifice, but for the drawing. Selecting an Aberth inhabitant is a psychological cruelty untoward any I've witnessed on an innocent gathering by the courts. The queen selects the citizen, and then forces them to draw the name, made worse by the fact that the possibility of drawing their own name is still present. It's also a sick twist if they happen to pull a loved one's name.

The worst part of this, is that Elliot knows he's drawing Wisteria's name.

Winding through the crowd with an expression of drawn acceptance morphing across his face and obscuring the look of raised uncertainty, Elliot trudges forward as the crowd begins to part for him. Caethes extends her lovely fair palm, beckoning the witch's boyfriend forward with obsidian claws. Her lips twitch with distaste as the blond nears. Elliot's eyes flicker around the crowd to find mine, when he does, they're fearful and wide. I nod once, and he climbs the stage.

The queen takes his hand, pulling him forward and sparing not a moment's breath before she leads him over to the glass ball. Beneath that pristine glass, and below the couple hundred names is a glamour spell pulsing in scrawling Latin. With every flicker of the spell only Wisteria and I can see, my heart beats the same rhythm, a tandem dance of nervous energy.

As Elliot dips his hand inside the glass. I draw in a breath that tastes of lilies and baked goods. His fingers swirl over the slips of papers and I hold that breath of floral notes and sugary confections as he shuts his eyes and grasps the paper. The glamour spell throbs once and then fades as his hand is released from the lottery's grasp.

Opening his palm and unfolding the name, Elliot subjects himself to the sacrifice that Wisteria's magic has revealed. He sucks in a breath and too low to hear, but clear enough for me to read, I recognize the name on his lips: *Wisteria Anne Pike*.

The Unseelie Queen grins and malice blooms on her face, joyous for this occasion of sacrifice and thrilled by the prospect of an anguished partner. Her sinister eyes gleam and her smile splits her face as she snatches the paper from the petrified mortal.

"The champion of our spring equinox and the recipient of Aberth's Annual Lottery is our very own Wisteria Anne Pike." The queen's announcement is full of her own bliss and none of the town's horror.

Wisteria had been expecting the blow, but hearing her name sends her doubling over, clutching her abdomen, as she crumbles to her knees. A choked sound slips from her full lips in the silence of the post polled lottery crowd and gasps that follow. Her face lifts to the night air and I see the shock and terror plastered there as her gaze flies to mine. The truth registers within me the same moment I see the blood on Wisteria's hand.

Screams rent the night as black-cloaked figures leap into the crowd, tearing out the strung-up lights and blowing my plan all to hell.

# CHAPTER

## 29

Chaos reigns as the growing number of black-clad figures increases. Panicked screams rip through the night, terrified festival hopefuls upturn food-stands in their quest to flee to safety, and furious faeries blindly shoot arrows into the crowd. More and more lights are yanked from their sockets and the streets turn black, sending us into a pitch-dark night.

The Unseelie Queen lets out a roar of fury as her guards swallow her into the safety of their ranks, thrusting their swords outward in a circle of protection. Her face is hateful and chilling, transforming into a creature of nightmares as she is guided from the stage and stolen by the Faerie Roads.

The shrieks do not cease their cacophony as residents of Aberth become white roses painted red. Arrow wounds bloom upon the pale clothing and blade slashes grow like weeds. The guards of the town close upon the crowd, herding us to the center and into easy prey.

Arawn is nowhere to be found, having took off in the direction of his monarch, disregarding both of us. Thinking quickly, I begin to plot and try to use the chaos to my advantage. Stars pinwheel overhead as I spin in place, searching for avenues of escape and perhaps a convenient fire escape.

Gideon suddenly knocks me to the ground with a shout as an arrow whizzes by my ear. I hit the asphalt, hip first, with my arms crushed beneath Gideon's too warm weight. For a moment we remain suspended there, paralyzed by the terror around us and the connection between us. His arm lies pinned beneath me, his other arm extended above my head, palm to the pavement as our eyes lock.

For a moment, I don't dare breathe, I don't speak, I don't think. I feel. And I feel admiration, devotion, longing, and compassion. Time stilts and turns to the sweetness and consistency of molasses, slow and decadent. Voices and shouts are muted, colors and shades have faded, fright and shock now distant.

"Evelyn," Gideon breathes, earnest and pleading with his eyes above me. His full lips part and desire tears through me. "I'm so sorry." Unfortunately, a more logical part of my brain kicks in as the reminder of his betrayal courses through me.

"*Get off of me,*" I hiss as I shove him away and scramble to find Wisteria.

How foolish of us to have a moment while chaos ensues? How idiotic to imagine a kiss while people are dying? How *truly* stupid are we?

I tear off against the flow of the crowd to the last place I saw Wisteria, praying that she hasn't been trampled. Behind me, Gideon shouts for me to wait, but I ignore him, pushing shoulders and bodily shoving panicked individuals from my way. Near the fringes of the crowd, I begin to see bodies strewn about the street and black-clad fighters battling the faerie guards.

From head to toe the interlopers wear fitted bodysuits of leather and spandex, joints padded by an unknown material and masked by cloak hoods and half masks. A female warrior twirls with the grace of a deadly ballerina, spinning around her fae opponent, curving her lithe frame like a cat and striking with knives like claws. She downs her attacker, a groan slipping from his lips as a long braid slips from her hood and I recognize angular cheekbones and peculiar eyes.

Julia.

Julia slides across the cobblestones, nimble as a figure-skater on ice while she hooks an ankle around a new opponent and comes upon him with a blade to his throat. The two of them briefly squabble as he resists, the blade vibrating with the tension of their met strain when I catch sight of curly hair and dark, mahogany skin.

Wisteria's huddled on a street corner beneath an awning, clutching her bloody belly. Her eyes are frantic behind cracked glasses, her panic reaches for the crowd as she flickers between her wound and the search for her lover.

I sprint over to the witch—thanking her distinct appearance in a sea of white skin and cloth—and skid to a halt upon coming up to my supposed partner-in-crime. Relief brightens her teak eyes before flooding back over to a swell of anxiety.

"Have you seen Elliot?" she asks, alarmed with shaking hands. I wince at the blood staining her slender fingers.

As I stop next to her, taking in the scarlet that ruins her clothing, I don't bother to hesitate before grasping her shoulders. "Wisteria, let me look at your injury," I command, both grip and voice firm.

Glass shatters around us, the sound piercing to my sensitive ears as flames begin licking up downed market carts, roaring its enthusiasm to the cacophony. Smoke plumes into the sky, blanketing the stars and shrouding the moon. Orange fire battles with violet light, the two of them consuming the white of the night and scarlet terror.

My fear of out-of-control fire creeps up my spine, threatening to consume me. A cold sweat breaks out and I have to force all my will into quelling the anxiety attack. Memories of the wildfire and cabin fire flicker through my mind, paralyzing me.

Gideon comes skidding to a halt next to us, a sheen of sweat upon his brow and concern etched across his face. He crouches next to me, shielding my body with his from the riot of the street beyond. I thank him internally, but irritation prevents me from speaking aloud.

"Quickly," I add as her hands shake with cold and shock.

Wisteria nods and pulls down the inch of fabric covering the slice. The wound is a graze, a knife thrown from some height to cut a downward stroke just above her hip. It bleeds with a fervor that is angry in its intensity, but not fatal.

"Use that belt on your pants to apply pressure; you can tie it around your wound."

Wisteria unwinds the loose fabric from her waist and does as she's told. "Keep out of the way of this mess. I'm going to find Elliot. You stay put and Gideon will stay with you." I lay a hand on Gideon's shoulder and take off back towards the stage, weaving through the throng of pandemonium.

More black-clad trespassers descend from buildings, a fleet of them swooping like a murder of crows, taking out Unseelie after Unseelie. They appear to fly through the streets, slipping through the curtain of smoke, only to reappear outside the haze gliding from some height to deliver fatal blows. Their knives are talons, blades hidden within toes and heels of boots, their cloaks wings that carry them through the cloying air saturated with dying violet.

I tear a sleeve from my shirt and use it to cover my face as I wade through the crowd, eyes burning with tears and throat stinging with the restriction of clean oxygen. It takes a well of power that I push to the brink to make it to the stage through streets littered with the bodies of white-clad Aberth residents, silver Unseelie archers, and onyx crows. My sixth sense for supernatural presence hums with intensity, blaring at every faerie and pinging distantly at Gideon and Wisteria on their own frequency.

When I make it to the steps to the stage, I see Elliot huddling behind the discarded lottery table, nursing a clotting head wound. His blond hair is dark with filth, filled with ash, blood and general debris, while his bleary eyes water with smoke-induced tears. As I reach the last step, I drop to my belly when I catch sight of a figure that glitters with diamonds and unholy purple robes.

The Unseelie Queen crosses the stage from the rear. The once impeccable gown is burnt at the hem, climbing up a newly revealed, pure-white calf, and torn at the bust. Her eyes are glazed with battle-lust, her insatiable chaos-meter drinking in the sight of lavender-tinged fire, auburn-edged lights, shattered windows, destroyed carts, and murdered citizens. But in those eyes gazing upon the chaos wreaked by those who purportedly honored her is a fury that strikes me to the bone.

In one seamless motion, Caethes reaches the edge of the stage and brings her arms to her sides. Slowly, folding them into herself, she turns her palms outward to the crowd and *pushes*. A squall of power rushes from her in one tidal wave of rippling air, flattening all those who still fight, extinguishing all flames, dispersing every lingering curl of smoke, and exploding every last fairy-light in the street.

"*Cease this insurrection!*" the Unseelie Queen bellows with a voice as strong as her magic.

I hold my breath as every last individual in the crowd stops on the ground and horror dawns on me. The battle-lust of the riot shouldn't have sent the queen into a frenzy, or an uncontrollable and animalistic miasma, but it should have distracted her, sent her off kilter. Instead, she *harnessed* it. I have never heard tell of any of the fae to be able to complete such a feat.

The Queen of the Unseelie Court can convert chaotic energy into a tangible force.

Which then causes the crowd to realize one of two things. Either; *that* is the power they are allied with, or; *that* is the power they are allied against. And they should be *very* afraid.

Backlit by the moon, Caethes raises her hands, every finger clawed, and every fiber of her being rattling with fury. I flatten myself further against the stairs, ignoring the edge of each step in my hip and sternum, knee and shin.

"You dare tarnish my town?" the queen demands with a voice so full of wrath and hatred that I have to keep my spine from shrinking. I internally thank the over-decorated stage and stair-rails to protect my hiding spot, but even so, every eye is trained upon the vengeful queen. "You dare rebel against your queen? Your queen who has given you every pleasure imaginable in your *insignificant* mortal lives?" Her snarl is wicked and dark, making her face a ruin of unfathomable loathing.

The Unseelie contingency of guards appear from the back of the stage, leaping with grace only possessed by the fae. At their helm is the Revenant, his blood-red hair and ale-gold eyes, evident even at night. The Revenant sports a swelling black-eye and I come to the conclusion that Caethes did not escape like they'd wanted her to, instead, she defied them and returned for this exploitation of her power. Had she used that same power against them?

A slight movement catches the queen's eye and my stomach drops through my feet when she turns to Elliot, who'd been trying to slip from the stage unnoticed. Caethes strides over and with one of those clawed hands she grasps Elliot by his fine blond hair and wrenches him from his hiding spot. Dragging him across the stage, he yelps as she tosses him before her, blood leaking from his scalp as his knees crumble beneath him.

"Perhaps since you all are so eager to defy me, I shall defy you." A chill crawls up my spine as her black eyes glitter malevolently, rage burning in their depths. "Aberth will have its sacrifice, and its sacrifice will have you."

Snarling, the queen strikes a hand forward and plunges her obsidian claws into Elliot's chest, tearing out his still-beating heart. Elliot sputters for a moment, blood pumping from the crater in his chest and spewing from his lips before he drops to the stage, dead.

In one transcendent, disturbing moment, a memory strikes me through.

Caethes, the Unseelie Queen, is petrifyingly known as the *Heart-Eater Queen*.

The queen brandishes Elliot's heart in her hand, gore leaking down her wrist and dripping past her forearm. She grins and without hesitation she bites into Elliot's heart like an apple. She chews decorously before a maniacal energy pours forth and she smiles. With a bloodied grin present and crimson coating her jaw, she looks absolutely monstrous.

Nausea roils in my gut, complete revulsion striking me paralyzed, unending hatred burning in my gaze.

Suddenly, a scream rips apart the night as a bloodied, white figure thrusts her way through the immobile crowd, cracked glasses and wild curls about her. "*Elliot!*" she shrieks, a wail building in her throat. A heart-wrenching sound that buries itself into my stone-cold, faerie heart. "*No! Elliot!*"

In seconds, she has pushed herself to the unoccupied space before the stage as Caethes indifferently kicks Elliot's body from the edge. He lands in a sprawled heap, blue eyes unseeing, empty chest unmoving, bloody mouth agape.

Wisteria falls on top of her deceased boyfriend, wailing unending notes of anguish, rivers of tears pouring from her dark eyes. She grips him with trembling hands and cradles his head in her lap.

"I'm so sorry. I love you. I'm so sorry," she repeats over and over, kissing his brow, cheeks, lips, crying harder with every garbled syllable.

The entire crowd remains frozen, neither faerie nor human daring to move after the terrifying queen's command. The queen herself drinks in the witch's anguish like a fine wine, licking her lover's lifeblood from her lips while squeezing the heart in her hand.

As if something registers within the witch's mind, she brings her tear-tracked and devastated face to the Unseelie

Queen. The queen grins, bits of aorta between her teeth, blood painting every tooth to a ruby.

I watch, disbelieving, while Wisteria's eyes turn as black and as hideous as the queen's. Suddenly, clarity strikes me and with a bellowed curse, I throw myself down the stairs as Wisteria lets loose a soul-shattering scream. As soon as the first note of her screech registers, a soundwave of despair ejects from her like an atomic bomb, and in a mushrooming force it flies from her and throws everyone in a fifty-foot radius from their feet.

# CHAPTER 30

Bits of exploded debris litter the decimated street while the newly deceased sprawl broken from the force of Wisteria's magic. Greyvale magic. The abilities of a rare sort of witch that can temporarily mimic and learn the abilities of another magic wielder, simply by observing; whether it be witch or faerie magic seems to matter little.

Concussed Aberth citizens crawl to the safety of shops and homes, blood streaming from ruptured tympanic membranes and dust-blinded ocular cavities. Wounded faerie warriors disappear through the mysterious Faerie Roads, tugging along more grievously injured comrades. Ravens in their black livery stumble with their clandestine identities remaining masked, taking off in a uniform fashion down an Aberth street.

Caethes draws herself up from her prone position with a crown tine of an antler snapped from the uppermost fork, and shrapnel adorning the otherworldly creature like filaments of scarlet lilies.

With petrification blowing the queen's eyes wide, I discover they had not been as wholly alien as I'd believed, but rather so doe-like, that it had taken their extensive flaring to see the small bit of white sclera surrounding the beetle-black.

In a whirl of tattered skirts, she takes her final leave from the stage, leaping from the edge and slipping back into her court.

The sharp scent of magic burns my nose as I pick myself up from the asphalt I threw myself against, watching bits of ash rain down from obliterated streamers. The Revenant lies nearby me, his body facing me and slowly stirring. He lifts a beringed hand to his bleeding temple, gold eyes hazy. He winces as he flutters his lashes and then he suddenly finds me staring, wounded just as he is. Freezing, he watches me, not breathing. His mouth opens as if he were about to say something. Opening and closing.

"Va—" he starts gravelly, but before he can finish, I snarl at him, reaching for a weapon.

"Come near me and I will kill you."

A hurt look crosses his face, but within moments he is on his feet and fleeing back to the Unseelie Court.

Broken glass crunches beneath my feet, skittering pieces tinkling across stones as I pass Wisteria. Wracking sobs break her back, her spine bowing with every agonized sound. I cannot do anything for her.

Squeezing my eyes shut, I attempt to breathe in air that doesn't burn, battling the tide of emotions thrashing at my dam. My heart lunges into my throat as I notice the vast array of bodies and no sight of Gideon—no sight of anyone living. I crouch beside a dead faerie archer, plucking a dagger from his belt and squeezing it in my dirty fist. Everyone on this side of the otherworld veil has escaped, leaving only the dead, the dying, and myself.

Panic pulls me to the last place I'd seen Gideon, prodding me with my supernatural sixth sense as my heart throbs in tandem with my racing fear. Desperately, my eyes search through the ruin of the town center, pleading for Gideon's safety. I plead to any and every higher power, tripping over my feet and fighting off increasing vertigo. I ignore the berating of the logical half of my brain, I avoid the chastising of the betrayed corner of my heart, I only follow the deepest well of my soul that begs me with everything in its limited power.

Every footfall is the riotous beating of my heart, another pulse of anxiety that hollows out my chest, a final drumbeat in a death march. Hysteria begins burbling up my throat and a cry slips from my dry lips. "*Gideon?*"

A croaking cough answers and relief trills through me, headier than any drug and just as dangerous. Spinning in my white, buckled boots, I find myself facing the mouth of a cobblestone alley where Gideon is locked in Arawn's grasp, a blade to his throat.

My heart freezes as I meet Gideon's fear glazed eyes, the amber light of them bright beneath the single unbroken bulb above them. Gideon's lovely mouth is adorned with a split lip and a purpling bruise decorates his cheekbone. That golden sword from before glimmers in the faerie's grip, pressed to Gideon's throat, with the halfling perilously unarmed. Arawn sneers, shark-black eyes furious, blood leaking from a wound on his forehead.

"*You* did this," Arawn spits venomously.

I brandish the robbed dagger in my grasp, holding steady while anger radiates from Arawn in waves, making his hand shake. "I did not," I respond placatingly, realizing that Gideon's life may lie in my hands.

"You orchestrated this plot, you played a part in it!"

"I did not," I repeat, glacial eyes flickering from a cold abyss to warm syrup and back, treacherously worrying for my—my what? Lover? Friend? I have no idea what we are, what we have become. What is left of us? Did we destroy it? "Have you no honor? To take a warrior unarmed?" I incline my head at Gideon, curling my lip up. "Challenge an opponent who possesses a blade."

"You know *nothing* of my repute. You know *nothing* of my loyalty."

"You're evading my observation. Perhaps, your honor is as infinitesimal as your...*sword*—" I glance meaningfully below his belt, "that you compensate with *that* sword." I indicate the golden weapon, holding back a dark grin.

Gideon's eyes fly wide as Arawn throws him aside, the halfling catching himself on a brick wall. He crumbles beneath his own weight and I realize that blood leaks from a calf wound and his torn pant leg reveals a swollen, violet ankle. He must have fallen on it in the magic explosion.

Worry for Gideon momentarily overtakes my focus, apprehension about his well-being becoming a distraction I cannot afford.

A snarl overcomes Arawn's handsome face, twisting it into a cruel sneer as he advances towards me. "I challenge you, little faerie bitch," he declares, poison dripping from every word. He brandishes the sword overhead and I catch sight of a crest in its pommel, a crescent moon wreathed in ivy and finished with a chrysanthemum.

The Seelie Queen's sigil.

I stare at that sigil and sword much too long before I realize the faerie has stopped advancing on me. He has decided a more delicious and deplorable way to torment us, remembering the depth of the relationship between us from my brief glance of concern. He has decided to violate the challenge and his so-called "honor" so that I'm not to be his prey, but Gideon is yet again.

With a desperate shout, I act with my heart and lunge for Gideon to knock him from the sword's path, realizing far too late that I'm directly in the line of fire. I close my eyes, waiting for the blade to slice through me, to end my existence. I wait for the scorching burn that will cleave me from this earth and from Gideon, from the world I wished to build with him, even though I refused to acknowledge it to myself.

But it doesn't happen.

I feel a sudden pressure, like a bend of wind tossing my hair and ruffling my clothes. The air is charged with static, crackling with energy. And as soon as it comes, it dissipates as if a vacuum sucks it away.

I crash to the alley stone with Gideon pinned beneath me and scrabble to my feet, finding Arawn with his eyes fastened to me, ultimate terror and utter horror plastered there. The sword has been knocked from his grip by an unseen force, lying inches away on the ground and glittering in the rare golden light of the lampposts.

As if time slows, I understand whose sword this is.

"It's you," Arawn utters, struck by some unfathomable emotion with his muscles paralyzed in place.

Dropping the dagger and taking up the sword, I find the balance perfect in my palm and I grin at the righteousness and rightness of the feeling. Before Arawn, leader of the Wild Hunt, can lunge, I whirl and run him through.

The blade strikes true and pierces his heart. Arawn's features shift, his eyes draw downward to find the sword through his chest. Lifting his gaze once more to mine, I stare back unflinchingly while blood spills from his lips. He gurgles.

*"It's you."*

And then he crumples at my feet.

I yank the sword from his chest and it makes a wet sucking noise when it comes away. I frown at his blood turning the golden blade scarlet.

Realization hits me like a cinderblock and I falter in my step. The sword dangles from my fingers as I understand what I've done, what has overcome me, and what I've avoided. I step back, the sword trembling just as terribly as my fingers and I'm suddenly flooded.

A yawning vortex opens within me and memories come pouring forth, crashing over me in a tidal wave. Answers and questions and pictures and words suffocate me beneath their waves, truths and lies, and identities and disguises.

I come apart and reform again, dropping to my knees and plunging Oath-Sworn into the dirt between the stones. Leaning desperately and hopelessly against it, garbed in bloodied white and hints of gold. I bow before it, hands clutching the pommel as if my life depends on it, the sigil digging into my flesh.

The blade that had been quenched in my own blood—bonded to me—has unraveled all the remaining fae trickery.

I remember everything.

*Fuck*...Emrys. *Maelona. Corvina—no, no, oh goddess no.*

I lift my eyes to Gideon who stares at me, dread ripping across his face. Fear skitters through his eyes, the uncomprehending distress so alike to when he'd discovered I'd been fae. That's a pale imitation to the bold horror that roots him to the road of this dysfunctional faerie town.

"I remember."

With silver eyes gleaming with knowledge, my stare is inescapable.

"My name…is Evelyn Corianne Vanora."

My voice is a rasp. My breathing is throaty. My soul is bare.

"You're the Harbinger," Gideon chokes out.

My gaze is ice upon his warmth.

"I am."

# CHAPTER

My world spins and I'm trapped in my memories as I stare at Gideon.

Overcome by the most demanding of snippets, I sink into the time where the vast majority of my life has been spent. It begins with fog before clarity reigns and I'm thrown into my mind's-eye.

The Revenant and I train inside the broken cathedral, shattered stained glass crunches beneath our boots. His blood-red hair is slicked back from his brow, golden wolf eyes intense in focus as sweat beads off his forehead. From afar our mentors shout at us, urging us on in our sparring, vying for battle-lust.

Around us, the damp stone leaches heat from the air and I bathe in the cool against our sweat-slicked skin. The scent of moss and lichen is like home, welcoming me with its darkness and portent depths. Sunlight filters in, shafts of it crossing through the crumbling ceiling, folded arches and leaning pillars divert it from our eyes. Statues line the walls, the seven faces to our seven mentors. Throughout the hundred years we trained together, I'd never come to like any of them.

Hushed moments in secret with breathless gasps and exploring hands. Walls upon backs and nails upon flesh. Lips on necks and fingers on hips. Whispers and growls and hate and need.

Century Training morphs over the years, over and over, I best the Revenant, pinning him to the ground, disarming him, pausing killing blows only a hairsbreadth from soft flesh. Over and over, until he learns and he begins besting me, straddling my hips, tracing my jaw with a blade, fisting his hands in my hair, throwing me to the floor. Over and over, until we cannot compare and we come to an impasse as often as we best.

The Harbinger has only one equal and it is one who has beaten death. The name alone is an omen, a promise of demise. It's why the moniker was chosen.

Century Training melts away and suddenly I find myself facing a brown-eyed beauty, eyes as rich and seductive as Devil's cake, her long hair shimmering from black, to red, to gold in the space of a few heartbeats. A rosy flush is high on her cheeks as she giggles at some terrible joke I make, drunk on both wine and romance. She circles my neck with her slender, warrior's hands, folding them to twirl the locks at my nape.

Maelona.

Lady Maelona.

My lover. A casual affair over the years.

She'd taken others as she saw fit, I never minded. She was my best friend and our dalliances were physical, a means to an end. Her love was limitless, eager to share it with the world. My love was relegated to the loyalty I serve my queen with.

That's not to say I didn't—or rather don't—love her, because I do. In my own way. The way I'm capable.

Maelona pulls me forward, pressing an intoxicated kiss to my lips. A kiss I eagerly return, her lips so soft upon mine, supple and forceful, a perfect reflection of the young woman only half a year older than I. She is a warrior princess, as beautiful as she is skilled, and as soft as she is strong.

Revels spin by, endless revels I spend as Evelyn, or the *Ceidwad Cudd*, or even as the Harbinger, accompanying my queen. Endless nights of dancing plague me, endless carafes of wine intoxicate me, endless games to play in the court to torture me.

Memories of missions stutter across my vision.

A town is dark, an alley lamplit by an orange glow where I fend off a werewolf attack. I flip over the fawn-coated wolf and land with cat-like grace behind it, only to roll back in my spider-silk uniform, and wait for the creature to lunge overhead as I plunge my dagger into its soft underbelly.

As it dies it transforms back into its human form, a man with hair the same tawny color of his pelt. I've split him from abdomen to throat. Eviscerated. Within seconds he bleeds out and I flee the scene.

In a throne room, clad in golden armor, I toss a blonde-haired assassin at the queen's feet. A would-be spy for the Unseelie Court, playing at being the *Ceidwad Cudd* meeting the Harbinger. Unfortunately, for that witch, that title also belongs to me.

I whispered such truths as I relieved her head from her shoulders.

I remember the plane crash.

Another memory threatens to invade but I crush the dark truth from my mind, unable to bear reliving it. Even so, it batters at my consciousness like a feral animal. The most traumatic of thoughts shall do that to one's psyche.

As I claw my way back to the surface of my mind, ignoring another black void as I do, I come alive again blinking away the haze. The town comes into focus, the town of Aberth, the Unseelie Queen's City of Slaughter. Centered in my vision though, is a male.

Gideon Zhao.

Gideon is before me, a handsome halfling of both Malaysian and Chinese ancestry. His amber eyes are his dead giveaway of his supernatural heritage. Something that the Harbinger notices that plain Evelyn never did. It isn't unusual for mixed supernaturals to display peculiar hair or eye colors.

A pity that halflings can't procreate, that jawline is quite desirable.

"We should retrieve our belongings from the inn," I tell Gideon, brushing past him and traversing past Arawn's bleeding corpse. "I believe we left our packs and weapons behind."

Without another word, I weave through the labyrinth of dead bodies and a weeping witch, exiting the town center and heading towards the inn with single-minded purpose and a broad field of awareness. I push down the horror and trauma that threatens to flow over, stifle the urge to vomit. Gideon follows behind, sputtering and calling out my name.

Of course, such negligence of our items was demanded by the Unseelie Queen for entry into her court and not my own preference. Though, I would have practiced sleight of hand and slipped a stake or blade into my boot. But I shall not regret, such done is done and I cannot berate myself further about it. We are alive.

Evelyn without the Harbinger is not the most skilled of characters, but she is much more than your average warrior. There are certain things that the girl without the warrior overlooked. I shall fix those mistakes in due time.

When I enter the inn, Lorelai tentatively raises her head from behind the desk like a mockery of resuming her position as desk clerk. Her cardigan scarcely covers her raven uniform. She looks up startled. Whether her surprise is garnered from my generally being alive, or the prospect that I carry the Harbinger's bloody sword, I'm unsure. Though, likely neither assists the other.

Further beneath the desk, I can hear the sounds of Rachel's breathing and one other, likely Andrew. He is the only other worker of the inn I've seen, not to mention he was with the sisters when the lottery was drawn.

"Hello Lorelai," I announce candidly, balancing my sword—Oath-Sworn—on my shoulder, aware of Gideon on my other side. Impaling the halfling would be a terrible happening. "We are here to check out, we'll gather our things and be on our way."

Lorelai's lips move but no sound comes out while her plain brown eyes widen and her mouth flops open like a fish. Such an unattractive trait, she should shut it. I notice the timid shake of her hands and the throbbing pulse in her throat, it draws attention to the tattoo inked there, the metallic tones catching the overhead light.

Ah, yes. The tattoo. The Unseelie sigil that grants the wearers in this town immunity from the lottery. Such a damaged system. Though I have to give the girl props, she chose a smarter route than her sister. Rachel chooses to live a life of luxury, heedless of responsibility and enjoying drink and vice every night if she so pleases. Lorelai works her keep, it's admirable.

Yet again, they did orchestrate a coup, what with their murder of crows and all, too bad it was such an epic disaster. It goes against one and supports the other.

Ascending the staircase, I plod carefully on every step, practicing silent footfalls and come upon our door. It's closed but not locked. Surprising, considering the queen was likely going to murder us. Pushing through the threshold, I go about the room and gather our packs and tent stakes.

I smile down at the warded iron stakes, thanking myself for my practice of mithridatism. The practice of consuming poison to build immunity. It was torment to suffer through the decades in Century Training of consuming so much iron and gripping the substance until the burns blackened my flesh and peeled it from my bones. Until the scarred palms built up the tolerance that my blood aided. Now I am just as immune as a human or any other supernatural.

The Revenant and I are the only two of the fae in existence to successfully achieve this immunity.

I attempt to force back the deluge of memories. Of clutching the Revenant to me, like a buoy in a storm, as we laid on the ground, wracked with tremors and shivers. Of days of endless nausea and vomiting, each helping the other through their worst spells, assuring with soft words and holding clammy hands. Of nights I thought I would die. Of nights I thought he would die. When we feared we'd lose the other.

Forcibly, I remove my thoughts from the past.

When I move to retrieve the last tent stake from the bedroom, I give pause. The bed is still in disarray from Gideon and I sleeping in it. The sheets tangled from sex. I remain frozen, my vision blurring, my memories clouding. I flash back to our night, recalling the acts and events through a film.

I shake my head to free it from my distracted thoughts and pack up the stake. The other night was an immensely pleasurable experience, a physical necessity that needed to be sated. A means to an end. I shall not linger on any thoughts of the sort any longer.

Returning to the main room, I find Gideon standing by the door, staring at me. His eyes are scrutinizing me and I cock my head to the side.

"How?" he demands, his voice flat. Angry.

I smile condescendingly. "You'll have to be much more distinct than that, darling Gideon." I chuck him good-naturedly under the chin with the flat of the tent stake and stride past him.

Easily gliding down the stairs, I find Lorelai and Rachel cowering behind the desk, the latter wearing a spatter of blood across her face and a shocked expression. The two sisters jerk their heads up in unison at my approach, fear radiating from them.

"Call everyone still alive in this town and tell them to wait here, I'll be back. I have a feeling we may need each other," I tell the two of them nonchalantly, blatantly ignoring my filthy attire and instead taking pride in my battle-worn appearance.

"H-How do we know that she won't come back for us?" Lorelai questions, voice quavering, eyes watery.

"Oh, she will. She just won't be able to get past these," I inform her, twirling my assortment of tent stakes. "You might want to be wary of fire."

With that, I take my leave and cross the threshold with an irate halfling behind me.

"How?" Gideon repeats after finishing the planting of the stakes around Aberth Inn, following me and limping, directionless.

"How what?" I ask him simply as I head for the edge of Aberth and behind the inn, toward the imposing tree line. There's a peacefulness to this side of the town, shrouded by midnight rather than death.

"How'd you become an unparalleled warrior when you're only twenty-three?"

I clap Gideon on the shoulder, pulling him with me out of the town. "Century Training," I answer as we step out of Aberth and onto the Faerie Roads.

When I touched Oath-Sworn, the blood-bathed sword of my own burned away the last vestiges of the amnesia-inducing faerie tonic and my memories resurged. Including the knowledge of how to access the Faerie Roads. To step into the earthen tunnel, one of the fae must think of them as they pass through an in-between while invoking the seed of magic each one possesses. What an in-between's definition is comprised of are the avenues the faerie may use. If one believes that jumping from a stage is an in-between then such a journey is successful. Crossing the border of a town is more realistic, even if such guides are of self-imposed nature and borders created of human constructs.

It's ironic really how simple everything could have been, had I recalled these instructions.

"Once a millennia a doorway opens for both the Seelie- and Unseelie Courts," I begin as I remove my hand from Gideon's shoulder and guide him through the Roads, our only source of light being the bioluminescent mushrooms. "Each court is asked to select a warrior to be trained. Inside that world passes a century, in ours, only a single year will elapse. I was sixteen when I left."

The air in the tunnel is dark and oppressive, thickening with the tension of all the questions that Gideon refuses to pose. Choked with his frustration and blocked by my apathy. I breathe in a steadying breath that smells of rich, upturned soil and smile at the innate sense of nostalgia surging over me. Home. The scent of *home*.

"Also, whatever was between us is over," I tell him, continuing forward.

Gideon can't even muster the energy to be blindsided. He just nods once.

Seven turns later we come upon a vast curtain of gilded ivy, the foliage wrought in gold, but pliable and dense as its natural cousin. I press a hand to the cool leaves, murmuring a Welsh-spoken greeting that speaks of longing. With my touch and words, the ivy slithers back with the barest whisper to allow both Gideon and I passage as we step into the Seelie Court.

# CHAPTER

# 32

The Seelie Court throne room is an expanse that rivals the mountainous landscape of its Unseelie counterpart. Packed earth walls have been polished to an impossible sheen, the rich tones giving the atmosphere a warm touch that ivy crawls across. Both the golden and green variations live here, coexisting and intermingling with the other upon the walls and winding around the tall golden pillars that reach up in arches to a ceiling that is no ceiling at all, but a sky of gold. At the very tops of the pillars, ivy dangles, lazy like a lovestruck fool trailing delicate fingertips though still lake water.

Gold-clad lutenists compose soft, enthralling music, the song the sweetest and most divine sound I've heard. It's the sound of home. Courtiers mill about, tittering laughs and dining on witch-made golden wine and honey-baked apples, dancing and gossiping, twisting the truth and finding thrill in near lying.

At the forefront of the room, upon a raised dais of earth and ascended by gilt stairs is the Seelie throne. A massive structure of three ancient tree trunks, branches bare and reaching heavenward, veined with gold and pulsing with life. With magic. Embossed into the greatest of the three, centered above the queen's head is her glowing sigil. A crescent moon wreathed by ivy and touched with the beauty of a chrysanthemum that holds the moon in its center.

My breath catches in my throat at the sight of my queen. She is regal and breath-taking, her fair skin is flecked with a dusting of gold, her dark chestnut hair wrapped in an elaborate style around her obsidian horns. Topaz and opal dress the dragonesque feature, the horns themselves curving backward as if blown by a strong breeze, her feline eyes the pale gold shade of two mixed gemstones.

At my entrance, the queen cups a delicate hand over her mouth, her pointed incisors revealed ever so slightly. All sounds stop as the queen gasps, all bring their gaze to mine, a contingency of a dozen gold-helmed guards take up arms, flanking their queen. I prickle, identifying the stance of one. Fortuitously, they are my allies, brothers and sisters in arms, for they would never succeed in taking me. Should I try, they would all meet their demise. Though, my identity as the Harbinger remains a mystery to everyone in this room aside from the Seelie Queen herself, her small contingency of immediate guards, and the titanium dressed faerie to her left.

I refuse to let my eyes slide to the Lady Maelona and acknowledge her shock-white hair, changed only by her emotions, and severely impacted by her newfound reaction to my presence. Her high cheekbones are flushed red, her creaseless chocolate eyes comically wide and her generously shaped, blood-red mouth is parted.

That isn't to say that the current company doesn't know me. They know me as Evelyn Vanora, considered Seelie royalty, regardless of blood, and some know of me as the *Ceidwad Cudd* above all. It's humorous to note that they believe the sway of my power and status halt at being the spy between the two courts, when in truth *I am so much more*.

I come to a stop several feet from the edge of the dais steps, Gideon silently trailing after me, his heart racing in the presence of a fae queen. Bowing down on one knee, baring my sword and all to my queen, I kneel and wait.

"My Queen," I breathe, devotion pouring from my voice.

"Evelyn?" Aneira Gwyndolyn implores, hope blooming in her voice.

"Yes," I declare, rising from my crouch, still upholding Oath-Sworn. It's a simple sword, not worth noting, yet it is full of power.

"I don't understand…I—" the queen breaks off, gaze cast about the throne room. "Leave us!" she commands, authority ringing around the room. She turns and pins her guards and Maelona with a look to stay. They do.

Once all the courtiers reluctantly file out of the room, Aneira motions for the remaining guards to close all adjoining doors. They do. She draws in a long, steadying breath and rises, her butter-yellow gown floating about her in diaphanous clouds before coming to a rest against her like a sleek river. She descends the steps, her eyes trained upon mine, her half-dozen guards following.

She comes to a stop at the final stair. "Where are your wings?"

My heart stutters but I refuse to let the waver show, though I do blanch and Gideon's gaze whips to me, horror-struck and realizing. I catch the wheels turning in his intelligent bronze eyes, his face slackening in dismay.

*The scars.*

The memory of my wings is a weight I'm loathe to bear, the loss heart deep and soul-crushing. My wings had been expansive leathery beauties, as much a weapon as a means of freedom. The lack of them upon my back is what I could only define as losing an arm or leg.

"I was betrayed by a halfling bounty hunter, Jacob Dugal. He posed as an informant for the Unseelie Court to my *Ceidwad Cudd* persona. He cleaved them from my person and burned them. He was then able to slip an amulet and tonic into my wounds so that I had no recollection of my history or self. He then attempted to cross borders in what is called a float-plane, crashed our means of aviation, and was then slaughtered by Unseelie fae.

"From that moment on, I was abandoned in the Unseelie wasteland of the northern Yukon and left to die as a hapless human. That was two years ago."

Aneira's façade of coolness wavers, only just enough for me, her personal guard and daughter through kinship, to be able to notice. She inclines her softly pointed chin, displaying the sharp cut of her slightly-squared jaw. "If you truly are Evelyn Vanora, you must swear it by word and prove it by sword."

Such a test is to be expected, there have been attempts of impersonation in the past, some as the Harbinger, or

*Ceidwad Cudd*, others as descendants of the royal bloodline with a claim on the throne—despite succession being through the monarch's choice where blood has no bearing on the crown if they so choose. More than one has been convincing enough at face value, though deeper inspection by word and sword sent each treacherous heart to the land of Lady Fate, their folly paraded for all to see.

"I swear to you, before all those present within the Light Court, to you, Queen Aneira Gwyndolyn of the Seelie Court, that I am Evelyn Corianne Vanora, the Harbinger and *Ceidwad Cudd*." My husky voice is steady, carrying with it the confidence of my declaration.

I'd always found myself blessed by the gravelly tone of my voice, easily able to pass it off as a male tone when I deepened it an octave and muffled it with my full Harbinger armor. My taller height aided that identity as well, being able to pass off as male, yet again.

I spin my sword expertly in my grip, an extravagant show of my prowess. To have my sword in my possession again fills an ache in my chest, softening the blow of the body mutilation I'd endured at the hands of that despicable bounty hunter.

I know that Jacob Dugal may have wielded the blade, but someone ordered him to, someone else had their hand in it. I do not have doubt that it was the Unseelie Queen who attempted to orchestrate my capture and potential death. He'd told me he had an agreement with Caethes, but he lied when he said he was double-crossing her. He was double-crossing me. It is one of my many regrets that I let him discover my identity, I wasn't careful enough when he questioned me into a corner.

Giving the blade a final twist, I catch it with the talent formed by second nature and smirk at my queen, daring a glance at Maelona again.

Her long hair has returned to its natural black, falling in a sheet past her waist, threaded through with glimmering strands of white, her shock lingering still. Her lithe frame is frozen, wrapped in titanium and spider-silk, decked out with a sword and an assortment of blades. Hers and mine are the only ones of the Seelie Court to have imbued iron, due to my imperviousness to it and her intrepidity to it, despite the risk and sickness associated with its proximity.

"You have sworn and proven true, you must now attest without a shadow of a doubt," Aneira continues this formality, a giddiness creeping into her voice. "You must best all seven of my most endowed warriors. To do so, you must not maim or kill."

"I would be honored."

Aneira points to Gideon and beckons him forward with a finger, urging him to come to her. He glances at me, his heart hammering in his eyes, but I nod and he limps to my queen, his demeanor nervous. Hesitating before her, Aneira brings a nail painted like a pearl to his chin, tilting him this way and that. Smiling, she pats him gently and takes his hand, encouraging him to sit upon the steps while she sits beside him.

Caethes would never have gentled a feat, nor sat upon the steps, especially with a non-subject. But Aneira did. She does. Poised as ever, she perches elegantly on the golden stair, Gideon beside her, filthy and bleeding in his white ensemble. He stands out like a sore thumb, like he'd been superimposed into an image that has been blatantly tampered with.

With a singular gesture, Aneira selects her fighters and I grin as they surround me, making note of the two-winged ones, both leather and feather. I watch and assess each of them, recognizing their stances, their energy, their eyes that peek from helms. Deliberately, I keep my eye on the one that will be a particular thorn in my side. I grin, prepared and radiating vigor. The queen lifts her flattened palm and then brings it down.

Start.

Spinning out with a backwards kick planted into a chest-plate, ducking a sword swing and thrusting my blade forward, I cave the armor inward of the faerie directly before me. The damaged armor restricts breathing and the first competitor is out.

"Andras," I shout the first warrior's name.

Adrenaline fuels me with unparalleled stamina, my finesse incomparable and undefeated. My mouth is bared in a feral grin, tongue pressed against the back of my teeth, and drinking in the battle.

Leaping from my planted foot, I spin to my left and swing my sword in an opposite motion, slamming the pommel of the blade into the softly dented helm of my second victim. My arm vibrates with the force of the blow and he drops like a stone. "Elyan."

Throwing myself backward, I avoid a bladed strike by kicking my boot overhead and with a sickening crunch, I shatter the wrist bones of the attacking faerie. He drops his sword with a sharp cry of pain. "Cadoc."

A breath of wind whips my silver hair over my shoulder and I dodge a strike of a fist, the lock of an arm, and the press of a blade all in one fluid motion. I nearly stumble, slightly off-kilter when fighting a winged-one without my own wings that used to balance me. I snarl as I grip the champion as she aims a knife to my ribs, but before she can complete the maneuver, I flip her overhead. "Drysi."

Grappling with the fifth warrior, I use his greater height to leverage as I pull him forward and push off from his torso, lunging only a hairsbreadth away from the sixth. The two collide and take each other out, one taking a sword to the unprotected inner elbow, the other a falling sword strike to the Achilles heel. "Bleddyn. Folant."

The seventh warrior remains unmasked and in three overly stylized moves I've twirled from her eager strikes and overpowered her. Ducking her final attack, I slip within her guard and come upon her chest, my sword pressed between us and the point at the delicate bit of flesh beneath her jaw while the other grips the back of her neck. "Maelona."

I grin and Maelona grins back, her hair flushing rose pink, scarlet red, and golden yellow with her swell of emotions. Overcome, I press my lips to Maelona's red ones. A harsh and brief kiss. The two of us separate and I turn to my queen, my breathing evening. My gray eyes are sure, flashing with pride. "That was two minutes and forty-seven seconds, My Queen."

Gideon has gone white, all color leached from his normally caramel pallor. His jaw is laughably slackened, his eyes foolishly wide, showing whites all around. I realize the absolute on his face. The absolute look of terror. Of betrayal. He's afraid of me. Of my ferocity. Of what he'd once fought. Of what he once fucked.

Aneira is astounded and thrilled. Tears leap to her eyes and a smile that could light up a black-out breaks across her face, showing both of her pointed lateral incisors and canines. "It's truly you."

"It is."

With that, Maelona launches herself into my arms, wrapping me in a chest-crushing embrace, her rich eyes leaking tears that soak the shoulder of my ruined white clothing from Julia's shop. The other girl is tall, yet not as tall as I, and she comes to just shy of my brow when she pulls back and cups my cheeks in her elegant warrior's hands. "It's truly you." Her lilting contralto is warbled, her delicate features pinkened.

Extricating myself from the faerie royalty, I turn to my queen. "I suppose I am required to address the complexity of the halfling," I begin, making my way over to Gideon and my queen. Aneira glances at him beside her, her smile playful, her eyes sinful. "Your Majesty, may I introduce Gideon Zhao, former protector of the Arcana Society."

Gideon remains rooted, stilled by emotional whiplash and from being called to attention. In his fearful eyes I see myself reflected, a shadow of my pale form.

Suddenly, from the deepest recesses of my cold and dark soul, I feel a pang and my heart clenches. Curiously, I pursue it and find a savage despair. Cocking my head, feigning curiosity, I bury my devastation beneath the surface.

"Aneira, if I may? I'd like a moment to compose myself, I am covered in blood and filth. I've also yet to eat a proper meal in some time," I state, gesturing to my completely soiled outfit.

My queen smiles. "Of course, we shall prepare a spread at the witching hour. Take to your chambers to rest and bathe."

I duck my head down in a show of formal respect, allowing a small smile to paint my tightening lips. Gideon frantically meets my gaze, a plea in them, begging for me not to leave him in this foreign environment, this unusual queendom. I consider the idea of ignoring him.

"You are kind, My Queen."

Aneira smiles softly, the smile that hints at a mothering bond. It is the smile she gave me each night after reciting bedtime stories of warrior queens and clever princesses. It is the same smile she sent me as I left for Century Training. It is a smile of pride and faith.

"Please allow Gideon to accompany you to your rooms, I fear the halfling has not yet developed a taste for the Light

Court," the Seelie Queen adds with that enchanting voice. Relief flares in Gideon's eyes, contempt darkens mine.

"But of course." I bow and turn on my heel. Gideon can follow, I shan't need hold his hand like a mother guiding an impotent child.

Smiling and carrying my sword with me, I take a wide adjacent tunnel painted the same gilt that adorns the pillars, the entirety glimmering with the refracted light of my blade. A grand staircase spirals beneath a glass ceiling, each stair a live edge of oak and luminous with gilt magic. At the top an emerald runner meets my booted feet, bisecting the large wing of the private bedchambers.

Gideon is silent and awed behind me, pointedly eyeing my very large, very sharp sword as I traverse the entire length of the twisted hall and reach the end where a set of curving oak and ivy dappled doors stand proud. Slipping through the entrance with Gideon in tow, I lock the heavy wood behind us, the sound echoing in the circular foyer. I stride past him, ignoring every bit of my lavishly decorated private rooms as I march to the bathing room. Gideon begins to say something, but I don't let him finish as I slam the oak door to my bath and slide down the smooth surface, collapsing to the slate floor.

Forcing myself to reach the enormous bathtub, I lean my forehead against the cool stone lip and draw my bearings. Spinning the golden tap and letting scalding water rush from the faucet, I crumble against the dark edge and break.

Silent and tearless sobs wrack my chest, pulling the trauma from the deepest, darkest, most repressed depths of my soul. The damage laid bare; the violation of my butchering revealed for all in such an informal fashion. As if I'd been relaying our recent weather pattern. He destroyed a part of me. Ruined a part of my body. Obliterated a piece of my soul. Violated me.

I mourn my wings. The appendages that carried me through countless battles, protected my queen, and acted as a shield that no one dared act against. Now…I am vulnerable, and I have lost. I lost a battle. I lost a piece of my reputation. What I wouldn't give to have flayed Jacob Dugal alive myself.

Jacob Dugal had betrayed me, acting as an informant on my *Ceidwad Cudd* identity. It was a role I'd been playing since I was thirteen, three years before the Harbinger ever existed. He was relaying information about the Harbinger and tips on a mission I'd been assigned to under the Harbinger identity. Usually when such rumors arise, I put them to rest before they're truly born. But he tricked me, betrayed me and drugged me with more than four times the lethal amount of faebane to thwart my practiced mithridatism and injected me with another triple dose.

I bite my lip as the memories surge. Drugged and hardly lucid images of the forest, bleary and shaky lines of Jacob Dugal's sadistic features, garbled words of his victory, muted anguish as my wings were torn from my back, the stumps carved out by a cold-forged, iron blade.

I suffer through shuddering breaths, each intake clawing my cavernous lungs into the empty pit where depression and fear nestle in to live. I let the double-edged sword press against my heart, letting the anguish and terror wash over me, letting it become an all new weapon in and of itself.

Forcing myself to my feet with steam coiling from the bath, I meet my darkened reflection and command the broken girl to pull herself back together. I switch the antique taps and let the cold water flow over my fingers, letting the chill seep from my fingertips and into my heart. I allow the ice to form, to become a strength unrivalled and indominable so that I can face my queen once again as her fearless warrior, revered as a god.

# CHAPTER 33

I exit the bathing chamber, wrapping a flimsy emerald dressing gown around my still damp body. The silk clings to my moderate curves, flowing down to my ankles and revealing quite a generous amount of thigh from the slit up the side.

In the room, Gideon perches on the edge of my four-poster bed, admiring the white gossamer curtains and coiling golden ivy that adorns the canopy. The bed area itself is obnoxiously centered in the room, sunken below three live-edge stairs. His deft fingers trace the gilt detailing on the sage coverlet as he gazes about the room, the alternating stone and soil walls interspersed with deep green wallpaper, the golden accents, the white curtains upon gemstone-stained glass.

As soon as I enter the vast rooms, Gideon's head shoots up, immediately reddening as he takes in the thin fabric and my long, soaking silver hair. The blush is becoming on his handsome features, that strong jawline and those brilliant eyes. *One can be uninvolved*, I think, *but only a fool would lie, or a blind man deny that degree of beauty.*

Pouring myself half a goblet of the decadent gold wine that I'd had stored upon one of my exposed shelves, I affirm that my wall of ice is firmly in place as I down the drink. "You're more than welcome to use the bathing room," I inform Gideon, swirling the dregs of my wine. "I apologize for not inviting you, but should opportunity arise, I'll consider sending an invitation. No promises."

Gideon snorts as he passes by me, irritation marring his features. "Nice Evelyn, I'm baffled by your wit." Sarcasm drips from his words.

"Oh, and do consider going through that wardrobe—" I indicate a lone oak fixture. "I keep casual male wear in there, you never know when one requires spare garb." I shrug and from his look of dismay, I can tell the words struck a nerve. Whether he fears such clothing is for lovers or myself is a mystery to him and a morsel of delight for me. "Though I don't suppose my court would be overly opposed to your nudity." I chuckle but immediately tamp it down as *something* surges to the surface. Guilt plays havoc on me but I swallow it back, determined to kill the thing inside me that tries so desperately to live.

After selecting a linen button-down and a pair of form-fitting khakis, Gideon storms to the bath and slams the door.

Surviving as a simple human did something to me, changed my perspective. I don't have the utter lack of sympathy any longer. I am tainted by the vulnerability I thought I had. Damaged by my feelings for Gideon, terrified at what it means for him. I heave a sigh, my mask cracking and collect a second goblet of wine. This time I do not skimp and swallow a full glass.

The witching hour meal is wrought with tension. Gideon radiates a curious mixture of fury and desperation, while Maelona puzzles out the atmosphere with an inquisitive and concerned air. Across the table, my queen emanates a palpable energy of joy and I attempt to feed off of it, dousing my depression with her cheerfulness. The four of us try to play a show that does not betray our emotions, some façades more successful than others. Chalices clink with delicate sips and utensils scrape plates laden with fruits and cheese, thinly sliced meats and sugar-heavy pastries.

I shut my eyes against the baked-goods, their sugary scent reminding me of Aberth's slaughter and other memories I wish to repress. Pressing my red lips into a thin line, I hide the discomfiture with a sip of more golden wine, thankful for the faint fuzziness encroaching my consciousness.

Our dining hall is grand, one of the many rooms adjacent to the throne room through an atrium, boasting another non-ceiling and golden pillars. The oak table stretches nearly the length of the room, spotted with crystal vases of greenery and glass flowers. Upon the polished and magic veined walls are stained glass sconces that match the grand chandelier of my bedroom.

For the beginning of the witching hour meal, pleasantries were exchanged, and timid questions were posed, but rather than any probing going deeper, everyone drew into themselves. But now, from the poised wiping of the queen's mouth with a silk napkin, it seems as if that's about to change.

"Evelyn, you must be harboring some curiosity over the state of the mission you'd left upon," Aneira begins, folding perfect white hands on the table. Her words hold no note of condescension, but rather a soothing one.

I shutter my eyes ever so slightly in a display of submission. "Truth be told, I had wondered, but I feared the worst."

Aneira smiles softly. "I know your heart was in the job. You sacrificed much of your romantic prospects for it and I will be forever grateful for your devotion, but furthermore, it became a success. Much thanks are dedicated to your sister."

My fists clench under the table, fingers threatening to tear the fine crimson gown I wear. My heart stutters a beat.

"Maelona, and your sister in your stead, took the place you'd studied and collapsed the organization from within. Unfortunately, while the ring was ruined, the hand that fed it is still at large and the Winter Carnaval remains as clandestine as before."

Maelona blushes prettily—she is proud and should be.

With nails digging into the tiny rubies and garnets under the table, I keep a pleasantly attentive expression on my face. But pleasantly attentive is quite possibly the furthest thing from my racing heart. Although, my disappointment in the mission is not the only thing that cracks in my chest...thoughts of my sister do.

"I am pleased to hear such tremendous results," I tell her fondly, the fake note to my voice luckily ringing true to my ears.

"Excuse me," Gideon interrupts, eyes flickering with concern to mine, "but may I ask what the job and organization was?" Gideon pauses. "Your Majesty."

Aneira preens prettily, her eyes soft. "My dear Evelyn brought to my attention the existence of a supernatural trafficking ring, specializing in illegal trades of the body, utterly lacking consent and willingness of the indentured.

"Evelyn volunteered herself, offering to go as far as needed so that she could destroy the group from within and free the imprisoned people." Gideon's knife screeches across his plate, panic flaring in his eyes. I pointedly ignore him while Aneira quirks a sculpted brow. "It took many years. Many years of study and close calls before we discovered entrance through Unseelie avenues—those unsanctioned by their own queen I may add. Though Evelyn disappeared before we completed the infiltration."

I draw in a deep sigh. Jacob Dugal had been my in for the ring, and that deception was his in on abducting me. Not only had I nearly destroyed the mission by getting kidnapped and dumped, but I left the dangerous job to my sister—who despite her adeptness, was still not the Harbinger. "Aneira, we must speak of my sister."

I dare not say her name for fear of breaking again. I do not tell my queen this, I do not let this be revealed by the pain that threatens my voice and dares to pool in my eyes. My face remains stoic, an emotionless mask that I'd trained with extreme precision for years to achieve during my bout of Century Training. No one at this table is the wiser to the turmoil dancing in my belly.

None it seems, save for Gideon. Every so often his gaze flickers, distress—not for himself—etched there.

"Yes, certainly. Corvina decided to journey north in an effort to ascertain your location. Oh, she'll be so pleased to learn that you've returned home." Aneira's bliss is so sweet, so innocent, and so desperately heart-wrenching.

I fold my hands, staring at the selection of golden rings on my fingers, reigning in the sound of my sister's name. Over and over, it echoes. Over and over, it whispers. Over and over, it kills.

*Corvina.*

Corvina Emmaline Vanora.

"Corvina did find me," I begin, my voice delicate, haunted, my tone deliberate with care.

Gideon's mouth drops open, the wheels turning, his voice hardly a breath. *"Oh, no."*

"She's dead."

Maelona gasps, a hand coming to her mouth, knocking askew the pearl headdress she wears. Her hair is as white as the spider-silk evening gown she wears, leached as white as the opal at her throat.

"What do you mean? I saw her only a fortnight ago…" Maelona demands, anger furrowing her perfect black brows.

I hold my gray eyes to Aneira's gold as I attempt to quash the influx of memories of my sister. The raven hair, the night sky eyes, the dark to my light. She was a part of me, of my soul. My twin, born only moments before me. She died in my arms, staring at the stars, having been happy to find me only to perish in doing so. Her death made even worse by the fact I didn't recognize her, buried her as *The Seelie*, unknown and alone.

*I thought I'd never find you…so grateful.*

She *told* me, she *fucking* told me. I should have known then. I should have noticed the near identical features. I should have seen her cheekbones were slightly higher, or that her nose was a fraction more sloped, or that her thinner brows arched higher. I should have seen past the inverted colors. I should have remembered.

But I didn't.

Succinctly, I relay Corvina's discovery of our cabin, her death, her burial. Folding up my napkin and depositing it on the plate before me, I shove from the table. "I apologize for my abruptness, but I must take my leave. I intend to take a few hours rest before returning to the Unseelie town of Aberth, I have some unfinished business there."

Aneira blinks away the tears that pool from beneath her dark lashes. "Of course, my dear. But may I ask, if not as your queen, but as family, what business do you refer to?" Her voice is thick with pain, laden with the weight of loss that I don't dare share aloud. I shall mourn alone, and no one shall be the wiser to my grief, keeping the pretense of the stone-cold bitch known as Evelyn Vanora.

"I plan to liberate the residents of Aberth and give them the opportunity to end their oppressor. I will give them the opportunity to destroy the Unseelie Queen."

With that, I whirl on my scarlet heel and take my leave.

The slamming oak door is a divine sound to my ears as I kick off my heels and tear off my gown. The red satin lies in a pool at my feet like the blood that seeped from Corvina's heart. Striding away from the horror climbing my throat, I race for my bottle of gold wine, quivering in my short silk slip.

Halfway with the goblet to my lips, the quiet creak of the hinges alerts me, and I spin with a dagger in hand. Gideon enters timidly, surprised at my current state of appearance. I scoff—realizing I neglected my internal alarm—and toss the dagger atop a pile of tomes and swallow a mouthful of the sweet wine.

Padding barefoot across the chamber to my vanity, I alternate between sips of wine and undoing the elaborate updo of my hair, plucking ruby encrusted pins and tossing them before me.

I always had a forced penchant for luxury and my alleged taste in silks and jewels reaffirms such rumored vain qualities. Beauty is a weapon just as much as a sword is. So, despite the fact that I am several times over more comfortable in leggings and a cotton shirt, I must don Evelyn Vanora's disguise of narcissism and boast silks and velvets and jewels and gems.

A vain intellect is commonly underestimated and though I have pride and assurance in my skills, it never hurts to have a second trick up your sleeve. Even so, it does not stop my loathing of finery.

Corvina was always humored by my immediate stripping of luxuries. Time and time again she never failed to laugh at the affair as we shared a goblet of wine for a mission well done. She though, she adored the finer things in life. She delighted in clothing finery and decadent sweets and bittersweet music. She was voracious in her appetite and grand in her ideals.

*Was.*

I take another drink of wine as a pang of loss makes its presence known. The truth begins to settle that for Corvina there is no future, there is no present, there's just…was. Her past. She was a warrior. She was my sister. She was alive.

Gideon sidles up next to me, leaning against the oak and black metal frame of the mirror before me. I cast my eyes at him scathingly. "I don't recall inviting you to my quarters."

"Evelyn, I'm so sorry about Corvina, I—"

"I don't want to talk about it," I deadpan, yanking a particularly stubborn pin from my locks.

What I *wouldn't* give to have Gideon hold me and tell me it'll be okay. To have him kiss my brow and tell me about his dragon and warrior stories. To burn away this façade.

"It's not good to bottle it up, and I know you've been through a hell of a lot, but I'm here for you."

"I said, I don't want to talk about it."

"Please, let me help you."

"*I said I don't want to fucking talk about it!*" I snarl, cracking a palm on my vanity table.

Gideon's brows rise, startled, but he doesn't back away. The snarl still curls my scarlet lips, hardening my eyes to stone as I stare at him through the mirror. Devastation, anguish, and fury cycle through my chest, carving my being into an abyss that I fear I may never crawl out of alive.

"What happened to you?" Gideon asks, pain in his voice.

I refuse to answer, intent upon my undressing. A firm silence that signifies my termination of our conversation accompanying my hollow actions.

Suddenly, a familiarly warm hand is on my shoulder, bringing with it feelings and thoughts I'd tried to abolish. With the cracking of my façade, the ice melts enough and that wild cesspool of an emotional abyss breaks free. Whirling with a speed incomparable to any, I fist my hand in his black locks and yank the hidden blade out from beneath my vanity, pressing it against Gideon's throat.

Gideon's eyes bulge, his hand falling away, terror lacing every line of his features. His lovely lips part, his strong jaw drops agape, those luminous eyes are wide.

"Dare to touch me again and I'll sever every last one of your fingers."

He doesn't speak, whether from inability or fear to do so.

*Like you said, faeries can't lie.*

I hold the sharp edge, pricking the flesh just enough for a bead of blood to slip down my blade. I watch the descent of the drop with a keen curiosity, a sick toying of this man's fright.

Pulling away and releasing my grip on his hair, Gideon stumbles back and presses a hand to his injured throat. Indifferently, I toss a monogrammed handkerchief at him over my shoulder and watch him through the mirror. His expression is aghast, and I smile at the small joy I receive from the distraction of my inner torment.

"If you demand to stay in my chambers, there is a chaise in the sitting area. I've been told it's quite comfortable."

"What? No tempting offer to join you in your bed?" he sneers, his face a furious sight as he cups the fabric against his neck. "Don't need me to hold you this time over Corvina's death? I suppose she meant more to you when she was just a random Seelie and you were a lonely survivor. Because how important could the Harbinger's sister be?"

Fury burns bright hot within me. I turn slowly with methodical calm. I smile at him, sickly sweet and venom on my teeth. "Do not speak of Corvina ever again. I do not owe you answers. Choose to ignore this and bait me, and I might just cut that tongue out of your pretty mouth while you sleep."

Alarm glows in his eyes like twin flames and he turns away.

Returning to my task, I finish unbinding my hair and douse the lights. Slipping beneath the cool sheets of my down bed, I fall into safe oblivion, knowing my training will protect me, should any threat arise. Knowing I am home.

An hour later I rise. Dressed only in my short slip, I climb over Gideon's peacefully sleeping form upon my chaise lounge, carefully hovering atop him. Limned only by the fading starlight of my glass ceiling, I aim the point of my dagger to the very edge of Gideon's full lips.

Coming awake with a wild start, Gideon gasps and I compensate for the movement to avoid slicing his handsome face. Moving the blade before he overcorrects and presses into the sage fabric, I gently return it and trace the lips that lone Evelyn kissed.

Regret and remorse surge within, but I have no choice.

I bend down to his ear like a lover would, still tracing with my knife. My breath is soft and tantalizing, my lips brush against the shell of his ear—something I intimately know drives him wild.

"In case you've forgotten what I'm capable of." I grin like a fiend, dropping my husky voice to a whisper. "*Don't fuck with me.*"

Kissing the racing pulse of his throat, I climb off of him, waving my glinting dagger as I stride backwards. "Dawn is an hour off," I call to him. "Sweet dreams."

I descend the steps and return to my bed alone, content with my threat and sure of the fact that Gideon will not sleep another second this night. He will lie awake fearing the nightmare's return, terrified that the legends of the Harbinger ring true.

He will wonder how the monster replaced the girl he knew.

# CHAPTER 34

Dawn in Aberth illuminates the level of catastrophe wreaked only hours before. Smoke coils linger, scavengers pillage bodies, glass shatters underfoot. Decimation is present, painting the town in shades of white, red, and violet. Even in the pale gray light, where dew sparkles upon fringes of grass and licks across stone, the air is as oppressive as the wasteland it has become.

I have seen this level of ruination in the past, both in history painted to me by my mentors of Century Training, and my own. Riots and rebellion and revolution are no new nor small thing to human and fae nature, but they are uncommon occurrences that fascinate and disturb me.

I remember an insurgent who'd made an attempt on my queen's life when we'd met with a vampire representative. During the middle of a discussion on a potential political alliance, said insurgent erupted with their coup and within moments all likely suitors for the agreement were slaughtered. Aneira and I slipped through the Faerie Roads with our lives.

I hold my chin aloft as I weave through the labyrinth of bodies, careful to sweep my nutmeg brown cloak from pools of blood. Clutching the golden clasp of the Seelie sigil, I skirt the body of an archer as a crow plucks at a gored eye. Loyally at my side is Oath-Sworn, from hilt to pommel done up in golden shades, ostentatious and shining, as bright as those of my fellow Seelies.

Gideon trails behind me, his too kind eyes offering condolences to the deceased. His tightly laced hikers are deft with the grace of the halfling, his long jean clad legs steady as they carry him through the lost battlefield. Courtesy of his supernatural healing abilities—attributed to his vampire father—his injured ankle is fully functioning. I notice the glint of a blade in his boot and another at his hip. Smart, ones like us should never be unarmed.

Maelona elected not to accompany me to the Unseelie town. Faerie royalty tend to have many obligations, evidently, sleeping in until noon being one of the Lady's.

Sniffing the air disdainfully, I'm disturbed to scent burnt sugar and death. Pulling up my cloak, I traverse the worst of the devastation and separate all thoughts but purpose and surveyance of the area. Mentally, I scour all alleys, exits, means of ambush, safe havens, and stragglers.

When it comes to humans caught in the crossfire of fae politics, the opposite court can intervene without reprisal. It's only if a non-human possesses an emissary sigil and is harmed that it can be considered an act of war. And considering Caethes didn't invest in any true tattoos, we're within the lawful perimeters of the fae court agreements.

We arrive at Aberth Inn without incident, crossing the invisible line against the Unseelie, and ascend the steps undamaged beneath my feet. Inside, the floral walls are lined with survivors, more lounging and resting against the warm hardwood. As soon as the brass bell tinkles, Lorelai shoots to her feet, brown eyes wide.

"You came back!"

"I said I would," I reply, removing my cloak and folding it over my arm.

Nostalgia strikes me as I recall cloaks being the signature of my *Ceidwad Cudd* uniform to cover up the existence of my wings. Along with a witch-made glamour and Aneira's own Queen's Glamour, no one knew of the hidden leathery beauties. The way they used to fold and curve to my back, nearly as thin as a tattoo, they defied human design. They were malleable when needed and unyielding at others. Despite the spells and their compressing nature, I was never not too careful, binding my wings to my person and obscuring them further with fine, often hooded cloaks. Though without the glamours, none of that would be possible.

I shake my head from my reverie. "I have a proposition for you all."

Bleary eyes meet mine, Aberth residents coming to. I count ninety-seven, all between the ages of fifteen and forty. No children, no elders. There were no bodies belonging to the younger generation, I'm certain of it. Where is the little girl with irises embroidered at her hem? Scrutinizing the crowd, I return once again to Lorelai.

"Where are the children?"

Lorelai swallows, uneasiness clear in her posture. "Some of the survivors escaped into the forest, nearly all of the older generations took the kids with them."

I spit a stream of obscenities. "They'll all be dead within the day."

Lorelai and Rachel stiffen, trading glances. Beside them, Jack—The Anemone bartender—takes a sigh laden pull from his flask. A few others show more adverse reactions.

Without another word, I turn on my heel, throw down my cloak, and thunder through the door and down the steps. On the decimated streets I whistle sharply and the Seelie guards who'd accompanied us to Aberth sidle up to me. My footfalls hold a single-minded stride, my face locked into a commitment of grim determination.

"We have a rescue mission, children and elders fled into the forest. They are absolutely unaware of what dangers lurk within these woods." My voice is as clipped as my pace and I sense the comfort of my companion's stride turning stressed.

The Seelie guards follow me without question, faithfully toting at my heels because my command is what Aneira has asked of them. If I'd told them to jump from a bridge, they'd do so, regardless of if they were reluctant to. Should they defy me, they defy their queen and every line of their golden Seelie tattoos would burn in treason.

My hammering pulse is the only betrayer of my fear. I realize with a surge of shock that I fear for these children that are alone in the dark woods, with no one who can truly protect them. I fear that they may lose their lives because their elders thought they knew better. I fear what I may find in the Unseelie Hell.

So now, their savior is a monster.

But if it had been Corvina lost and alone as she was, I wouldn't care if a monster was saving her, as long as she was saved. As long as she was *alive*. How must she have felt? Wandering alone and dying, bleeding out in a foreign territory. And then, when a golden light entered her vision in the form of her pale twin, sitting on a random porch with a strange halfling, drinking liquor and speaking of life, it winked out when she didn't recognize her.

In those final moments, when I held her as she faded, I gazed down blankly, unknowing as I held my dying twin. I'd commented distantly on night sky eyes and otherworldly wings, I'd referred to her as "The Seelie" without anything but impersonal touch. Corvina must have been terrified and devastated. She died miserable and anonymous.

I wish someone had saved her. I wish *I* could have saved her. But I can save these children. *They* are someone's sister, or brother, or entire family. *They* are what Corvina was to me.

One of the worst and selfish parts of all this, is that Corvina would have volunteered to save the Aberth residents in a heartbeat. She wouldn't have given it a second thought. But me? Prior to my bout of amnesia, I wouldn't have cared unless it advanced my own interests.

So, I do this, for me, and for Corvina. I do this for the darker twin with a golden heart. And I, the pale monster with a black soul, live when the other is more deserving of the privilege. Of the gift she sought to give me, the gift that was her curse and ultimately her demise.

*I* was her demise.

Behind me, I sense a familiar footfall and alert and I'm surprised at Gideon's presence. There, in a brief flash in his eyes is a look I recognize from my fellow comrades, but it couldn't be. Could it? It is a look of blind loyalty, a sense of surety in a leader. I cannot fathom that look after everything I'd subjected Gideon to. Of seeing me as such a heartless being. Especially since I'd ended things and threatened him awake with a blade to his lips.

*A creature of the night having a nightmare.*

A poor, bitter joke that rings truer than it ever could've in the past. The past, how could it have only been days ago that I was plain Evelyn, human and dull and hostile? Then, a single moment shattered that illusion, the moment when it was revealed that I am fae. And only to obliterate my world further when we discovered I'm truly the Harbinger.

I traverse the Yukon's woods, searching with the sprawling fingers of my sixth sense for any fae presence beyond my current company. I attempt to be selective, searching for the chaotic lining of the Unseelie in my alarm system—another peculiarity about me that I've yet to reveal to Gideon, an ability that even Aneira could not explain.

Greenery passes through my vision, ferns sharpened to a discomfiting degree, moss blurred beyond comprehension, trees stark in contrast from one to the other. Everything is so *green.* So lush, and utterly at odds with the daunting atmosphere of our objective. I spread my hearing far and thin, zeroing in on every crunch underfoot, every snapping twig, every shush of the brush. I push every sense and ability I have to its extremes, having sorely under-utilized them without my Harbinger training. Now, with my memories renewed, my skillset came with it, and knowledge of how to use it.

"Lady Vanora," one of the attending guards—Afan—begins, clearing his throat. He's a faerie who is particularly threatening with a mace and practically harmless at hand-to-hand combat. Too brutish. "If I may, how do you know that we're traveling to the right destination? Are you aware of something we cannot see?"

I whirl on him, surprised he would question me so, but then I realize that he is not one of my regular companions and he is young. He does not know that I am the Harbinger—or the *Ceidwad Cudd*—and that I severely outrank him. He also does not know that to question me is a poor decision. "I have an innate sense of navigation," I tell him firmly, turning once again to the proper direction. "But if you were paying attention to your surroundings, you would notice trampled forest floor beneath you."

I can practically feel his blush burning into my back.

Reigning in my emotions, I center my fear and slight amusement at Afan's expense by clutching the etched pommel of my sword. My Harbinger blade is still beside me and so few and Gideon are the wiser to just whose sword this is. Most simply believe that I'd plucked it from Arawn and decided to would make an excellent trophy. A rumor that I won't dismiss.

Besides, all Seelie blades are gold.

Sweat begins to slide down my spine as I work uphill, weaving between close-knit trees and tangled roots. Despite the horrors I've faced in this Canadian territory, it is a beautiful, breathtaking vista. An untouched paradise of clear lakes and towering cedars. I think back to before I knew I was fae, back when I'd imagined what kind of *human* I could have been. How embarrassingly wrong I was. How naïve it seems now. I clench my eyes shut as more sweat beads and I become even more painfully aware than usual about the distinct lack of weight on my back.

Suddenly, my ability pings, locking in on a victim. I grin ferally and take off into a sprint. "*There*," I hiss. And then I'm gone.

Taking off like a bullet, I fly over rocks and roots, and foliage and brush, sprinting as signals reveal themselves. I chase every alert like an addict after their last fix, a maniacal energy flooding through me. Ten faeries I sense, ten faeries and dozens of hapless victims with speeding heartrates.

I've heard tell of some factions of Unseelies, near rogue groups that govern themselves by an elected leader or stolen titles by intergroup conflict. I wonder if that's what this is. Some prefer to be called nomads, renegades, or anything of that sort, but each of them have enclaves where they host revelries not sanctioned by the true court. Humans are often subjected to torments there, and I've not heard of any survivors. The Winter Carnaval is the most infamous of these parties, and it is equally the cruelest as it is the slipperiest. Few of these rebellious groups endeavored an insurgence in the Seelie Court, such groups were treasonous, and of the utmost hazard to our monarch. Should the group garner support, the Seelie Queen could risk an uprising and an attempt for the throne.

I could not have that happen.

Sliding down a steep incline, I maintain my balance as I glide down on my left side, pillowed by leaves that billow around my wake. At the bottom of the slope, I push myself to an upright position, coming up running to an aggressively flowing river.

At the river that thunders a daunting width of half a dozen men and a depth nearly that deep, are Unseelies leading bound humans through the current. The dark indigo is cold and portentous, fearsome and sinister, but what is most chilling are the two bodies caught in the spiderweb of rocks and moss at the river's edge.

My heart cracks and my thoughts are full of denial as I catch sight of matching white sundresses and hand-embroidered irises. Bobbing there like a water-swollen log is a mother holding her child that clutches her with chubby, toddler fingers despite the death that grips them both. I try to tear my gaze away from the filthy linen that clings to them, at the dead, white gaze, and gray pallor of their skin. It takes a momentous amount of will, but I manage it, fury turning my vision red as I slice my murderous gaze to the fae.

They are lower class, less humanoid and more monstrous. But I do not care for their looks. Their appearance merits nothing as I leap upon a back and tear out a spinal cord with my hands and teeth. Their facial composition matters none as I smash an orbital, everything from the frontal bone to the palatine bone, and exploding an eyeball. Their basic structuring is of little importance when I eviscerate the bowels of another.

It takes three deaths for the remaining seven to realize the danger they've unwittingly stumbled into. Across the river, four humans remain bound with a trembling Unseelie captor, while another ushering two humans could be pissing his pants in fear through the water and no one would be the wiser. I wouldn't be if I couldn't smell it. The five on this side of the bank begin to scatter just as the rest of my Seelie companions arrive, sliding with precision down the hillside, Gideon at their helm.

I grin, crimson dripping from my jaw, and reveling in the petrification that strikes the closest Unseelie as I saunter forward with my blood-soaked front. He isn't long for this world as I plunge my sword through his chest. He dies with scarcely a fight and relief blooms through me. If I should become a darker monster to protect the innocent, so be it. If I should become a demon to protect the memory of the girl with a heart of gold, so be it.

Three of my Seelie companions race for the Unseelies across the bank, wading through the water with impressive speed and finesse. Spinning on my heel, I seek out the remaining prey and find Gideon in all his glory.

Gideon takes on two Unseelies, ripping around them with blinding speed and whipping through their choreographed attacks with lithe skill. Protectors are near unparalleled warriors, their skill is as feared and revered above any other, known for being the closest opponent that I or the Revenant could ever hope for. Unfortunately, for such protectors, their lives are dedicated to their charges and any hopes for marriage or love are dashed by being illegal in their world.

There had been speculations some time ago that I, the Harbinger, was a protector once, though those ideals have no merit. Regardless of the fact that any gendered supernatural can be a protector, such generosities are not extended to the fae nor vampires due to their weaknesses and aversions to iron and sunlight respectively.

For the first time, I see his fangs. They are blade-sharp things, lengthened canines that are unleashed with his anger and I suddenly wonder if they'd appeared before and I've never noticed. He takes an arm of an Unseelie and jerks it upward, popping the joint from its socket and breaking his ulna and radius in the process. The faerie screeches and it's the last sound it makes as Gideon sinks his fangs into its throat and tears out its jugular. Immediately after his second opponent is finished as well.

I eliminate the final two Unseelies with the barest of thoughts and I raise my gaze to the carnage wreaked around us. Ten Unseelie bodies litter the riverside, each in varying degrees of death, some quick and efficient, some brutal and messy. Twenty-five humans huddle terrified around us, all still bound by manacles of chain or tied by rope. All still remain in their sacrificial white, now filthy with blood-splatter and forest filth. White that is just as pale and grimy as their faces.

Continuing my assessment of our bloodbath, my eyes lock on Gideon's finding us both with blood-soaked clothing and scarlet mouths. In that moment there is no divide, we are the same in this world. A pang of nostalgia arrows me, and for a brief, fleeting moment I can forgive him. I believe that we could make it work. Notwithstanding, my blatant threat with my knife, and promising to cut his tongue out, I believe, for a moment, *in us*. But then his bronze eyes darken and I tear my gaze from him and settle on the dead bodies in the river.

As I walk past the captured humans, I find their fear morphing into praise. Humans cry out and thank me as I pass, reaching with their secured hands, tears pouring down their cheeks. Peculiar that faeries have always been reviled, but now, rather than that adverse reaction, I am being worshipped.

Worshipped for being a murderer?

*They would have done worse*, A faint voice in my mind soothes me.

Closing my eyes, I straighten my shoulders and turn around. As I do so, I catch sight of Gideon and there is a queer look there, a look that perhaps considers that I am not quite the monster I've painted myself to be. That perhaps I do have feelings. Strengthened by Gideon's silent support, I call out to my faeries. "Release all the humans and assist them to the Seelie Court. Aneira will offer them shelter and protection."

The captive humans break down in tears as my Seelies travel over to them, easily breaking their chains and releasing their bindings with ease. From there I ignore them and slip into the icy current of the river.

It is cold, but I ignore the accompanying pain, swimming out to the mother and child as the water turns red in my wake. The current is strong, but not a match for a member of the fae. Behind me, I hear a splash and know that Gideon has followed.

Once I reach the tiny, dead family, my throat becomes thick and I attempt to release them from the prison that I can. Death is its own prison, and I am no master over that. I struggle to detach the frozen corpses from the icy fingers of the river, the threat of rigor mortis setting in does not help the fact that they are both soaked to the bone. I want to break down in my frustration, but before I have a chance to, Gideon is there and he senses the defenseless change in me.

He's the most beautiful sight I could picture in that moment. Fierce bronze eyes, water-slicked black hair, and blood-splattered caramel skin and all. He breaks my heart and I feel a brick in my wall crumble. It doesn't matter that I could kill him in half a thought, it doesn't matter that I'd threatened his life, it doesn't matter that he woke this morning with the most dangerous creature in the world perched on his chest.

*He doesn't seem to care.*

He sees through me. No, not *through*. He sees *me*.

"If they don't have family, let's put them properly to rest," he says softly, reaching for my wrist but not touching. Gooseflesh peppers his arm but he doesn't shiver. I can't decide if the reaction is from fear or cold. "We'll bury them, together."

I nod, not trusting my voice and then Gideon and I carry the mother and daughter to shore, all the while worried about where the father might be and if he knows his family is lost.

# CHAPTER 35

After sending the Seelies off to take care of the recently released humans, we discover the two bodies have no kin. Not anymore. The father perished in last night's slaughter. They had no siblings and both sets of parents long dead. Gideon and I set to work and claw out graves with our bare hands and stones. Our nails crack and break, filling with dirt and blood, but we continue. It doesn't take as long as it should, but we are angry, and devastated, and supernatural.

When it's time, Gideon and I gently settle the mother into her grave, her eyes are closed and I silently thank that she doesn't have to see these horrors. But then we come to the child and I pause.

A tiny thing, perhaps three years of age with curly blonde locks she inherited from her mother, and green eyes, flat and bleak with death. I grind my teeth, forcing back a swell of emotion. I've never thought much of children of my own, but I've never wished nor imagined any ill will upon one.

With painful silence, I reach out with a pale, blood-free hand, and close the toddler's eyes, internally grieving for the child. Of a life hardly lived. Of a real, once living, breathing child who waved and smiled at me. A hitch climbs free of my throat and a slight sound escapes me. Gideon's hand comes to rest on my shoulder, and with absolute gentleness he stoops to cradle the child and her head lolls toward him. In that moment, she could just be sleeping, a very deep, very dark slumber.

The rest of the bodies back in Aberth will likely be cremated in a mass funeral pyre, but there's something about these two that I selfishly can't subject them to such forgetting. There's a closure in this burial. For me. For them.

It's painfully clear that in this brutal moment that I am not the same creature who'd woken Gideon before dawn. He knows clearly that there are facets to my personality, dangerous and vulnerable moments. I hate it. It is unnerving. But what is worse, is that he isn't scared now. He should be terrified.

Clenching my fists, I follow him. His mouth is pressed into a thin line and gingerly he lowers her to now be cradled by her mother. Gideon adjusts their arms and now they lie in an eternal embrace.

Gideon wraps his arm about himself, looking at me, his face distraught. "Would you like to say anything for them?"

I realize with surprise I would. I want to give them the eulogy that I couldn't give Corvina. I don't want their deaths to be so unremarkable, without family, without loved ones. I don't want anyone who might've once cared for them thinking they were buried in silence and darkness like my sister was.

"I want to say the proper words, the expected words. I want to know that you're at peace." My husky voice immediately thickens with emotion. "But those words taste like ash in my mouth and the lies won't come. Your life was too short, your potential snuffed from your candle of life before it truly began. You had so much to give, so much to offer, and I am sorry I wasn't there for you. I am sorry that you were alone and scared. The world won't forget you. Won't forget that you were such a golden gift to this world and that for your absence in it, the world is worse for it." My voice cracks and I'm suddenly grateful that it is only Gideon and I here. Only Gideon has learned the most vulnerable parts of me, and that alone is dangerous enough. I come to a conclusion, tears in my eyes and I realize. I draw in a steadying breath and continue, turning my face to the bright, gray sky that is just as oppressive and colorless as my eyes. My eulogy that was partly for Corvina switches to my twin completely.

"You were loved, and will forever be loved…as long as I live and breathe, you are loved. I promise you."

With that I duck my head and this time, I allow a moment of weakness as Gideon wraps an arm around me. I breathe in the moment, comforting in the warmth he brings, before I sigh and disentangle our limbs. Then, together we push the dirt back into the grave, wrapping the mother and child in the earth's blanket.

It's afternoon when we return to the Aberth Inn. None of my Seelies have returned, but lower-level court assistants gather faerie and human bodies, organizing them into piles. A single faerie in gold livery makes notes in a book, marking off names and titles recording all the dead. I make a mental note to review him and his findings and discover the official death total.

Within Aberth Inn, none of the residents have moved. Lorelai and Rachel continue to huddle and Jack continues to nurse his flask. Behind, Andrew stares with hollow eyes and Julia paces with pent up frustration. Faces light up with our arrival, but immediately turn to shock when they catch sight of the bloodstains and distinctly wet clothing. It doesn't help that my hair is unbraided and remains wet and sticking to my skin and sleek against my skull.

Gideon steps forward, a gentleness to his features that I cannot achieve. "We managed to rescue twenty-five of your fellow townspeople, but regardless of that, we cannot begin to express our deepest condolences for your losses. Please keep in mind we will not be forcing you to do anything, however, we do have an offer. All choices here on out will be of your own volition," Gideon tells them, tone like honey, like a warm blanket on a chill night.

Memories at the cabin and the inn trickle into my consciousness. I squander them. I push from my mind every thought that could also remind me of his comforting arm at the riverside grave. Aside from the riverside battle, Gideon has been decisive on keeping his distance from me. Trauma from my ambush once again fresh in his weary eyes and frayed nerves. And that's good. The silly boy should learn not to threaten those that could end him within a heartbeat. Or that's just what he wants me to think.

"I am here, on behalf of the Seelie Queen," I begin, authority ringing in my voice and tensing in my jaw, all traces of fragility washed away. "You all will be welcomed into the Light Court once you resign loyalty to the Unseelie Queen. After, you may choose. Freedom is at your disposal, as is vengeance." Eyes perk up around the room at this prospect. "We will assist you in the destruction of the Unseelie Court. All you must do is follow me."

"And how do we know this is not some faerie trick?" Rachel ripostes, striding to the front of the group, still dressed as a crow without her hood. She looks bedraggled, dirt-streaked cheeks, a tattered hem and torn knees. Her leader is already allied to the Seelies, but that seems to matter little.

Julia visibly berates herself, and I don't wonder if it's about the epic disaster that her coup turned into. It seems her ploy had been to assassinate the monarch and that has clearly failed, not to mention wires crossing between two plans despite the same goal. As is, the road to Hell is paved with good intentions.

"If you're unaware, I have the inability to lie," I inform her fearlessly. "Regardless of what you may believe, I have a stake in this as well. I do not stand for the ethics and traditions of the Unseelie Court—they are barbaric and cruel in a fashion that is beyond my comprehension." While I do enjoy many twisted games, needless slaughter and trafficking are not among them. If Caethes has any hand in the circuit that lead to my capture and my sister's eventual demise, I will ensure she is obliterated for it.

I allow the residents to ponder my offer as I admire the quaint light fixture above me, done up in brass and crystal. A step behind me I sense Gideon vibrating with tension. It isn't overly palpable, but as someone whom was relegated to close quarters with, I feel the familiarity and lack of it in his changes.

"So, do all your plans blow up so enormously?" an angry voice comes forward and I steadily meet the gaze of the absolutely distraught, Wisteria. Her teak eyes are embers, requiring only the barest prodding to erupt, her teeth are set in a lioness's snarl.

I dip my head in acknowledgement, ignoring the urge to fiddle with the ties of my damp, corseted top. "I had not prepared for an attack to subvert our plan."

"Oh, that's your excuse? You weren't *prepared?* Elliot is *dead* because of you," Wisteria hisses, tears pooling in her eyes.

I cock my head to the side and cross the threshold to meet Wisteria. Reaching a hand up, I grip her chin in my grasp none too gently and level her stare. "I am *sorry* that my plan went astray. I am *sorry* about your boyfriend's death. But I will *not* take blame for it. His demise was Caethes's doing, and regardless of my intervention, she would have selected him for the ballot. And above all, Julia and her gang still would have attacked." I bare my teeth. "I understand your anger, it is valid, but do not direct it at me. Use it to fuel you and avenge Elliot."

Wisteria's tears overflow, and I feel her will falter, her strength shatter. Ripping her bronzed-dark jaw from my grasp, a shuddering sob escapes her lips. Rivers flow and weeping grasps her. She slides against the stair banister to the floor and around us Aberth residents pledge themselves to our cause.

Later, I collect my cloak and we all file out and one by one we reach the edge of town. When we pass by the alley where I'd killed Arawn and regained my memories and sword, I discover that the faerie's body has been collected already. Still, a large pool of blood stains the stones scarlet and rust red.

As I slip through the Roads, I find my contingency of fae guards and use them to pull Aberth's residents into the Faerie Roads. My hands are full as I take Gideon and Wisteria, guiding them both back to the throne room. Wisteria still weeps, and Gideon tries in vain to console her. Irritation grinds the nerves along my spine with each sniffle and every tear. At the edge of the throne room, I prod Gideon through and take Wisteria aside.

Gripping her shoulders, I let my eyes penetrate her very essence like a pair of iron stakes. "Elliot's death was a tragedy and you can grieve, but you need to pull yourself together. Now."

She narrows her brows, gasping for breath. "You don't know what it's like."

"Don't assume to know me."

The witch scoffs. "He was the only one who cared. The only one who understood me. Violante knew, but she didn't understand. I'm…I'm different. I don't feel the way others do. I *can't*."

I give pause, letting Wisteria continue, allowing my brain to assemble the pieces of her mystifying speech, drawing from my own conversation with Elliot. There was a distinct air of something, what it was eludes me. What it was is about to be determined. But I wait and gather more intel on the powerful Greyvale witch.

"Who is Violante?"

She smiles grimly. "You weren't wrong when you suggested I knew someone who was taken for the lottery. Violante was my best friend. Three years ago, she was chosen and Caethes did something to her. I saw her only once afterward, she told me she was cursed. She was…different. And I mean, she was always religious, but she *would not* let go of the goddamn cross. Her eyes were red and she moved *so fast.*" She swallows thickly and realization strikes me. "She said not to look for her, that Caethes had cursed her to forever roam the Yukon around Aberth, never allowed back in."

Without a doubt I know that Violante is a vampire, and she had been the vampire I'd saved. The vampire I'd stupidly thought was fae. And the necklace I'd assumed was an Unseelie sigil was a cross. She's being hunted by her own due to Caethes's command. Because she *can.*

"Elliot helped me get through losing her." She swallows. "I loved him, I swear I did," she whispers, a pleading note to her voice that begs me to believe her. "I swear. It just wasn't the way he deserved."

"You fell out of love with him?" I wager a guess.

She laughs, a part hysterical sound. "That's the problem, isn't it? I never fell for him in the first place, I don't think. He was my best friend, the only constant in my life. And I was physically attracted to him, I desired him—in the bedroom. I just…didn't love him. That way."

A niggling thought finds me. "There is a human term for that," I tell her. There are a lot of human terms and I'm certain one fits.

I'd discovered that one can have a lack of love, not the type formed of kinship and family, but rather romantic love. I'd learned that sexual desire and romantic love are not synonymous with the other and that both can coexist together, or one without the other. There's also a human definition for what I am, too—pansexual—it is not a term the fae use, in their eyes, I just *am.*

I'd learned that other conditions or ways people were born can cause humans to struggle to relate, even on basic levels of social cues. The are many levels and many different presentations of it, not one case truly like another.

"Yeah, there is. Aromantic. I used to think I was damaged, that something within me was fundamentally wrong." She barks a laugh. "Hell, maybe there is. What kind of monster doesn't love?"

"You are not a monster, Little Witch," I tell her softly. "Monsters do not weep as you do, they do not feel regret, remorse, or loss. Do not think you are less for the way you feel."

*Take it from a true monster.* I want to add, but I refrain as we return to the group and set about dissolving the Unseelie Court piece by piece.

Each of the one-hundred-twenty-two Aberth citizens swear fealty to Queen Aneira Gwyndolyn, ninety-three of them elect to rise up against Caethes. All earn the Seelie tattoo that ensures their loyalty, burning the wearer should they betray the queen, visible only to those that have pledged allegiance. My own tattoo prickles on the underside of my right foot as I watch Ghislain adorn each of Aberth's citizens with the queen's sigil upon their wrists.

My own tattoo was required to be out of sight, my reputation as the *Ceidwad Cudd* demanded it. I walked the tightrope of loyalty between the two courts, true to the Light, false to the Dark. No one truly knew where my allegiances lay as the *Ceidwad Cudd*. Until now.

The auburn-haired artist whose magic writhes gold beneath his skin completes his final tattoo, a weary light to his spring green eyes. His ability to weave life magic into oaths is secular, only to himself and his twin sister, a girl trapped in Caethes's court.

Aneira strokes Ghislain's long hair, cupping his ochre cheek and thanking him for his services. He bows, pleased to be praised by his queen, and slips away to rest for the afternoon.

"He is quite talented with those hands of his," a voice comments casually by my shoulder. I turn, smirking, having heard and sensed Maelona's presence before she'd announced it.

"You've had your sights set on him from time ago."

"Mm," she agrees, strands of black hair turning crimson with formerly relived lust. "I always wondered if he would finally be the male to turn me from women, but alas, I find myself as devoted to the female form as ever. Mayhap such trysts are in your future." Maelona's hand trails down my arm, lingering on my wrist.

I quirk the corner of my mouth into a smile as I stare ahead, watching fae guards guide Aberth residents to guest quarters. Gideon is not among them. I try not to frown.

Across the room, Aneira is wreathed in the glow of the throne room's eternal daylight, surrounded by seven of her guards, nearly half of them still injured from my challenge. Her wide, painted mouth spreads into a smile as Julia verbally accosts her, war-planning and demanding action. My queen is generous and placating, ruling with a firm hand and level-head. Despite her youthful glow, hardly edging upon a human appearance of thirty years, the millennia in her eyes betrays her age.

Adjusting my sights on Maelona beside me, I watch her devilish eyes glitter with mischief. "Such trysts are not of an immediate concern of mine." Walking from her, edging towards Aneira, I call over my shoulder. "I missed my best friend, Mae. It's good to see you again."

I don't need to chance a look behind to know that the Lady's cheeks are flushed as pink as her locks.

# CHAPTER

Thoughts of a goblet of gold wine and a fine rest guide me towards my chamber hours later. The beginnings of two year's worth of paperwork, consultations, tactics, strategizing, and debriefing plagued me during my meeting with the queen. It came to our attention that it was past time to discuss my sudden reappearance and just how we must pass it off as some have already drawn assumptions between me and the *Ceidwad Cudd*.

Publicly, Evelyn Vanora was assigned a scouting mission with false updates at the fringes of the Seelie territory—ironically enough, it is the entirety of British Columbia and a wide spread beyond it, exactly where I'd been trying to flee to. It is known that Seelies dominate the south of Canada while Unseelies haunt the north. Though, the *Ceidwad Cudd* did not have such a luxury of a cover story and her absence was painfully noted as many years back. We both agreed that I must declare my identity as the *Ceidwad Cudd*, especially if I'm to deflect suspicion as the Harbinger, as well as own the rumors as our own.

Thankfully, my genius of a queen devised a plan for where faeries alternated between each other impersonating the Harbinger. Each had leather wings fashioned as prosthesis— aside from Drysi—and had them glamoured to act real. With the impenetrable Queen's Glamour, no one could see through the ruse, therefore, none was the wiser. That is, until such artifice was exposed when one such imposter was slain several months back and then falsehoods were revealed and rumors abound.

I reach the base of the staircase, but before I ascend, my nerves prickle, the hairs at the back of my neck raising. Whirling, I find Gideon stepping out from behind a pillar. Serious intent is molded against his flushed features, brilliance of color high of his cheeks and in his eyes.

"I think we need to talk," Gideon demands, grabbing my wrist and yanking me down an adjacent hallway. "Threaten to cut off my fingers if you have to."

Halting him, I eye the hallways suspiciously. "Not here," I whisper, lips hardly moving. "The walls have eyes and ears."

Gideon's eyes widen as I drag him to an archway, barely considering half a thought as we step into the Faerie

Roads. The air is warm and dark, rich with soil. Releasing the halfling, I lean against the dirt wall, crossing my arms and ankles.

"You have my attention, darling halfling."

Gideon's face screws up with fury. "What the hell is wrong with you?"

"Not as much as what could be. Though I must admit, I am a slight bit weary from that tremendous failure of a lottery and bloodbath. Thank you for your concern," I tell him mockingly, placing a hand over my heart.

"That," he growls, pointing with an accusing index finger. "That is exactly what I mean. The Evelyn I knew was cocky and had bravado, but she still felt *something*. Now, you don't seem to give a shit. Unless of course, it comes to dead kids."

The emotional dagger hits its mark, but I ignore the blow because he isn't wrong and I can't lie. "Circumstances change." Cocking my head to the side, I consider, going for the low blow that gets all men riled. "Are you sure this isn't about your bruised ego?" I step off from the wall, sauntering forward. "Are you certain you aren't worried that I haven't propositioned you again? That maybe, just maybe, your performance could have been a disappointment?" I lick my teeth, eyes flickering downward, hiding the fact that I have to cast these words as questions. Knowing full well that it wasn't a disappointment. "You must know that I know my way around a sword."

Abruptly, Gideon leaps at me to get up in my face. Surprise hits me and I stumble back. He gets under my skin and he doesn't realize the emotional advantage he wields over me. Heat floods my cheeks in embarrassment, but immediately I capture my footing and push his broad chest with an exorbitant amount of force. He staggers back and returns, wrathful.

"We both know that you're twisting the truth."

Embarrassment further colors my cheeks and I ignore his truth. Even so, I refuse to admit it. Avoidance is one of the lies of the fae.

"I don't understand you, Evelyn."

"I don't think you're meant to."

His voice is deep and angry and it strikes a chord. Excitement burns in my limbs, adrenaline coursing through my blood. The prospect of the two of us engaging in a near choreographed contest sets my heart to hammering, my eyes glazing with delight.

"I don't even know who you are anymore. What happened to the girl I shared a bottle with? The one that wanted to live life without regrets and what could have been?" Gideon's voice is pained.

Laughing, I bare my teeth at him. "She's gone, sweet halfling. I am what remains."

Angrily, Gideon lashes out. I crash against the packed earth wall, causing overhead roots to tremble. Gideon pins me in place, an arm across my throat, his heart stuck in his eyes. Traitorously, my heart races, warmth coils in my belly and his proximity does strange things to my brain. In vain, I attempt to not focus on his lean muscles pressed against my abdomen and chest, his knee trapped between the space of my legs, his thigh pressing against my own.

Bowing forward like I had last night, he murmurs in my ear. "Well, what remains is nothing but a cold-hearted *bitch*."

And I realize.

Leaning forward, I grip his cheek in my free hand and wrench it to the side. Licking up his strong jawline, I pause to lightly nip on his earlobe. "But I'm the cold-hearted bitch that has your heart."

Suddenly I feel the length in his pants harden, his cock twitching with my ministrations. He roughly grinds his thigh between my legs and as he rubs an ache builds and wetness begins at my center. His arm is still at my throat, the other comes to cup my ass, near-painful but exciting. I realize I *like* a hint of pain. I like the threat and fear with it

I gasp and he doesn't miss it.

"Tell me you don't want me," he murmurs, anger still lingering on his tongue.

"No," I growl. Pushing against him, into him, wanting him. Wanting more.

"Tell me to stop."

His cock is hard on my thigh, his chest heaves against mine, his hand groping my ass, his mouth at my ear, his lips on my throat. I'd changed out of my ruined and bloody outfit and the slits on the sides of my cerulean skirt give Gideon incredibly easy access to where I want him.

"No."

The next moment he hauls both of my hands up over my head and manacles them between one of his, my wrists slightly crying out, but the thrill winning overall. His other hand goes to my hip, sliding down my thigh and hitching my knee. Gideon's lips crash upon mine, hard, harsh, demanding and claiming. My tongue meets his in a violent manner, our mouths tasting and fighting and devouring and destroying. Consuming. His free hand has ripped away the scarce bit of lace that served as my underwear. It flits to the ground and I find the tearing of clothing incredibly erotic.

Dipping his fingers in the dripping heat of my core, he moans when he discovers how ready I am for him. He swirls my clit for a few moments with those expert, tantalizing fingers drawing me close to my peak. I rip the buttons off his shirt, pushing it from his shoulders and exposing his beautiful body to me. I want to lick him up and down. A finger slips between my folds, plunging while his thumb swirls. When my cries and moans begin to pick up, my hips bucking against him and for what they want. Without preamble he finds the fly on his jeans, pushing his pants low, freeing his pulsing member and immediately thrusts into me.

I gasp as he fills me, fucking me against the wall of the Faerie Roads. He drops my hands and hitches my other leg on his hip and pumps harder and faster. My head is thrown back, his teeth at my throat, biting and nipping, my nails tearing at his back.

I thought we'd fucked before, but I was wrong. This is fucking. This is animalistic. This is rough. This is a hate fuck.

"Am I disappointing you?" he asks, breathless at my ear, pulling my hair.

"No," I cry out, a climax building.

"Do you find my performance lacking?"

"No!"

"Are you going to come for me?"

"*Yes*!" I shriek as I shatter around him.

The orgasm takes me in waves, exploding within me like stars and light. The pleasure screams through me, leaving me trembling and weak. His own orgasm follows mine and I feel him pulse inside me, spilling heat.

He sets me down and tucks himself away. For a moment we stand in silence, our hair mussed, lips bruised, both of us bearing marks from rough sex.

"Just because we fucked again doesn't mean I care about your feelings," I tell him this brusquely and I ignore that the two don't necessarily mean one or the other.

"I think you're full of shit, I think you're just scared."

I pull back, watching denial take root in his eyes. "Deny it all you want, but may I remind you that I cannot lie."

"Then let me remind *you*," he warns savagely, a rumble in his chest that raises an internal alarm. "That I know the desires of your heart."

Horror lodges me in place, my panic crystalizing as I realize. Remembering our talk on the cabin deck and in the bed. That conversation seems a lifetime ago, dreaming of another time, another world, another reality. Never had I thought such utterances could spell my demise.

*What do you want out of life? Once we get out of here.*

*You mean, what is my heart's desire?*

I shut my eyes against the influx of memory and regret.

*But something that I want? My heart's desire? Just like those faeries, above all I want freedom. I want to know a true home. But more painfully, the real desire of my heart is to get my memory back.*

The words repeat themselves. Over and over.

*The real desire of my heart.*

Over and over.

*Desire. Of. My. Heart.*

Fuck.

For the second time, genuine and uncontrollable fury lashes me.

Potentially three desires.

Potentially three commands.

One for certain.

My blood is poisoned, my nerves severed. My heart and brain attempt to work in tandem, both refusing to cooperate as logic and pragmatism war with the seeds of doubt in my heart.

It shouldn't count. I told him those truths freely when I thought I was human, but now, now they are weapons. It doesn't matter if they're no longer or came true, in that moment they were desires and so the commands still hold weight.

It would be easiest—smart—to kill Gideon. It would be the practical choice to exterminate all chances of him being able to hold the threat over my head, dangling the bait and making me dance. The Harbinger cannot afford such dangers, especially those that could command me against my own queen.

He has to die. I must kill him.

But for some unknown reason, I can't.

Instead, I disentangle our limbs and snarl at him, hatred in my gaze. "Fuck you, Gideon Zhao."

And I leave, selecting the first turn of the Faerie Roads but before I can dismiss him, I hear Gideon's bitter call follow. "May we be as cold as iron, right Evelyn?"

I ignore him despite the stiffening of my spine and slip through my exit to return to the Seelie Court once again.

Fury and fear propel me to her chambers. Within minutes of abandoning Gideon, I'd raced to my suite, knocking back half a bottle or more of gold wine and furiously scrubbed my skin raw in the bath, desperate to remove his touch. Two hours later, I'm intoxicated and knocking upon Maelona's oak door, nerves fraying beneath the cool surface of my always composed expression.

That's the problem isn't it? With being the Harbinger I must wear the uniform eternally, the mask of stoicism, the readiness of my sword. Emotions are a bane to my existence, experienced, yet perpetually hidden from view with not a single living being having noticed the flicker of my constant inner turmoil.

Gideon's wrong. I feel. I feel many things, but many things are not accompanied by pain and in that accord, I am a coward. That is not a word easily admitted, it's a defeat I'm hesitant to accept. It's a word that I cannot yet say aloud, but to myself, I can face it. Conquer it. What I cannot face though is still hurling itself at the dam I've erected and it's only a matter of time before the cracks in its foundation crumble under pressure and drown me in their black waters.

Maelona opens the door, surprise in her chocolatey eyes. She clutches at the throat of her tangerine robe, her scar flecked flesh exposed beneath the coral light of her chambers. Quirking a midnight brow, she steps aside, and I cross the threshold.

"Evelyn—" she begins while shutting the door. But she hasn't a chance to continue as I tug her forward, tangle a hand in her dark locks, and kiss her.

Her response is slow but I'm not. My lips are harsh against hers, pushing her, urging her to her private bedchambers. Capturing the side of her neck with my other hand, I feel her rapid pulse flutter, shock igniting beneath her skin. Gathering her wits about her, she wraps her slender arms around my waist, digging her skillful fingertips into the small of my back.

I need to drive away the taste of Gideon. The scent of him, the feel of him, the memories of his hands all over me, of him inside me. I need Maelona to banish Gideon Zhao from my soul.

Nipping at her lip, a startled gasp escapes her, and I continue my pursuit. Grasping at the silky fabric of her robe, I none too gently clutch the small swell of her hip, curving around to her behind, pulling her closer. She makes a sound almost like a whimper, deep in her throat, her response eager.

But suddenly she freezes.

Pushing me away, I find her scrutinizing me, her hair an array of black, white and red—shock and lust. Her perpetually rose red lips are swollen from my attack, a small bead of blood dotting the full bottom.

"You are not yourself," Maelona states, backing away. Putting distance between us. "You come to me, drunk and reeking regret. Have you washed the scent of male and sex and remorse from your skin?"

I avert my gaze, guilt on my face that I cannot hide, my refusal to answer as much of a resounding yes as if I had said such words aloud. My heart thrums uneasily, unsure and disjointed.

"Ev," she says commandingly. "I'm happy to sleep with you, but not when you're so drunk, and not when it's to forget someone else. We did that once and I vowed never again."

Guilt strikes me. I did seek her once for forgetting, and that time I was also inebriated.

"I feel…*off*. Things, things changed while I was gone. *I* changed," I admit, fiddling with my corset ties. "I—fuck, I need another drink."

"Well, I could have told you as much," Maelona chides, offering me a tumbler of liquor with ice. I pause, staring at the amber liquid, thoughts rampaging.

Amber like Gideon's eyes.

Brandy like the bottle we shared.

Taking the glass, I cup it, wholly unsure of my own perception. I stare down into the liquor, gazing as if it has every answer in the world. As if it could heal the wounds and holes in my heart.

"Searching for the future in your brandy? I thought only Whitecrest witches could do such a thing? Mayhap you'll change that piece of fact." Maelona's tone is light but it edges with a dark air of concern.

I ignore the comment, not because I don't care but because I can't find it in me so summon the energy to be light-hearted. Staring down at my shimmering white dress, the slits in the sides cutting up to the hip, exposing the thigh sheaths that are strapped to my legs and loaded with daggers, all I feel is shame.

"Gideon and I…" I draw in a breath and take a swallow of the liquor. It burns just as I remember, just as potent, just as nostalgic. Recollections of his confidence in his father's health, his dreams of being a writer, our near kiss, my sister's death, our first actual kiss in the woods, the first time we had sex, when held me by the riverside, our latest tryst. "This drink just reminds me of him."

I swallow a mouthful again.

"Come sit," Maelona urges, drawing me deeper into the coral lit room, shades of pink and red and orange bathing the walls into shades of sunset. Her bed is done up in the same vibrant shades. Peach and scarlet sheets match those of the first memories that returned upon Gideon's removal of the amulet.

I must stop returning my thoughts to Gideon.

Perching on the edge of her plush bed, I nurse my brandy, twisting my lips.

"Something happened between you two."

I bark a laugh. What an understatement that is. "Yes, many of a thing."

"No need to feel shame, Ev. You are not the only one to take a lover. In your absence I have taken several, females and even a male—though I truly do not think I will seek out another male lover. In fact, there is a delicious vampire who currently holds my interest. We were not, nor are we, exclusive."

Such statements were true. Maelona and I never treated our escapades seriously. We were friends first, lovers second and one could easily be put on hold for another. We care for each other, but the depth of that care, the degree is not what is required for a monogamous commitment. That fact alone should have been enough to indicate how unfit we are to be a couple. There is also the principle of thoughts of her with another. They do not soil in my belly, they do not make me wish for a pit beneath my feet. But to put Gideon in her place…

I drink.

"I am scared," I whisper to my empty glass. "He saved me, in more ways than I ever realized a person could be saved."

"Do you love him?"

My eyes shoot to hers, slate and mercury upon rich earth, disbelief and fright carving my features into a new mask. Panic writhes in my chest, a parasite of the heart, making itself a new home. Learning its new host.

*I can't.* I want to tell her, but the words refuse to form. The lie will not escape my lips. I cannot utter a falsehood, a consequence of being fae, a curse of my existence.

For these past few days I've been trying to push him away even though my heart bled at every false encounter. I prayed it was enough to keep him from being a target. Being the Harbinger's lover isn't *safe*.

"I don't know," I whisper.

"That isn't no."

"I love you, though," I tell her weakly, my voice ringing hollow.

"And I love you, too. I always have and forever will. But we are not in love. We do not love each other the way that you might love Gideon," she whispers placatingly, cupping my cheek. "At least, not yet."

A shuddering breath wracks my chest and a single tear slips from my eye.

"What if that could change? What if what I feel for him fades and what is between us grows?"

"Then we will discuss it in time, but I am not opposed to the idea." Maelona fiddles with my hair—her love language always was touch. "There is no need to think of these possibilities when we do not know. And it certainly isn't fair to speculate when myself and Gideon aren't the only ones with potential claim on your heart. You know there is one other."

The truth takes hold and latches on with a ferocity that terrifies me. It lodges in my chest, burrowing like the parasite it is, carving a new shape. The enormity of the three paths I could take registers distantly, like a storm on the horizon, brewing and volatile. It would be so much easier to deny Maelona, to kill Gideon, to cut *him* out forever. But I cannot and the threat of love stays my hand.

I am the Harbinger, and I am broken.

Broken by a trivial, insubordinate protector-reject of a halfling. Broken by my best friend. Broken by my equal.

"You can't tell them," I disclose delicately, my voice fragile.

"The truth of your heart will not be spilled from the lips of mine," she declares, a sacred fae saying, an oath that is unbreakable as its magic enforced counterpart. The only difference is that the attempt to reveal will not kill her like the oath cast on the Seelie guards against my Harbinger identity will.

"It would have been easier, had it just been you," I tell her fondly, a sad note to my voice as I lean my head on her shoulder.

"But that is not the way Lady Fate shaped your life. You were meant to become purely Evelyn for a time, and you did. Now, you must trust where she has taken you." She pauses, tapping a crimson nail to her lip. "Perhaps, had you continued your existence, lone as the Harbinger, situations could have been altered. But Lady Fate has drawn her knife."

I don't dare breathe to her about what I know of Lady Fate. What I'd once forced of her. Of the punishment she'd dealt. Not even I fully know what I'd traded.

I smile softly, rising from the bed and traveling to the crystal decanter of brandy.

Without any notice, I gasp and drop my tumbler. The crystal shatters into a million tiny pieces on Maelona's marble floor as I crash to my knees in the carnage. Panic rips me apart and puts me back together, yanking every fiber of my being and smashing it between fists of iron. At the same time, a knock starts on her door.

Maelona crouches beside me, her words unintelligible to my petrified brain. Behind my lids I see gold eyes and amber eyes and death. I see it dancing between the two, taunting and vicious. I know death is coming for them, I know it will be one or the other and I don't know how to stop it. Distantly, Maelona's fear is registering as she searches for blood. She won't find any. Not on me. Not here.

I don't know how I know, but intimately and desperately I know something is horrendously *wrong*.

# CHAPTER 37

Stumbling and crashing against the walls, I race for the throne room and past the servant knocking on Maelona's door. I'm tripping over my feet and missing stairs. Maelona follows, still slower than my panic induced sprint. My world teeters precariously as if I've begun to suffer immense blood loss, the walls ebb and flow like dangerous waves. Waves that mimic the ones that batter against my own damaged internal foundation.

Tearing a curtain of lively green ivy from the wall, I bust into one of the many throne room entrances, finding a wild assortment of people already present. All eyes turn to my fevered expression, anxiety riddled eyes, and labored breathing.

Maelona arrives seconds behind me, barefoot, still clad in her tangerine robe, now loosened and revealing an onyx satin dress recently devoid of the scaled armor that typically adorns it.

Nausea squirms up my throat, burning from my stomach and sending vertigo vibrating through my skull. I waver a step, eyes betraying my sight with double of everything present.

Then, as suddenly as the drunkenness came on, a shroud of black descends and plucks up the tilting axis of my world. I gasp at my fae metabolism, my practiced mithridatism purging the alcohol from my blood in seconds. It has always taken an exorbitant amount of liquor to intoxicate me and even more to stay that way. Adrenaline only burns it away faster.

Blinking at my newfound, perfect sight, and my utter lack of alcohol stupor, I discover a familiar figure and my queen speaking in low, dark tones. Aneira turns, carefully poised concern upon her face. Only I see the true fear under her beautiful, gold dusted façade. Her hand shakes before she presses it to the evergreen velvet of her bodice, clasped with the other. The figure next to my queen turns, lifting the black cloak from his brow with fingers full of rings—silver with gems, a rose gold twist, a gold band, etched iron—and revealing blood-red hair and butterscotch-gold eyes lined with kohl.

"Emrys," I breathe, so shocked I forget to use his formal "lord" title. Refusing to betray the way he catches me off guard. "What are you doing here?"

The Revenant stands before my queen. I know Emrys Gorlassar's presence like my own. I'd recognized him the moment I'd laid eyes on him, even with his cloak obscuring everything else because I'd spent a false century of training side by side with him. Aside from the mentors who alternated between loving us and abusing us, we were the only one the other knew. I know his twitches, his tics, his peculiars, his peeves. I know what he fancies, and what he fears, what he loves, and what he loathes.

The oath tied to keep my identity as the Harbinger secret by the Seelie guards is the same as the one Emrys and I both swore to each other. The oath was sworn in every way and which of the word. There is not a single strand left hanging. Not a simple loophole left allowed. If I dare reveal that Emrys is the Revenant, the attempt would kill me before I could breathe the word.

*And Emrys could never do the same*, I realize. The entire time I wandered ignorant in the Unseelie Court, Emrys stood stock still, watching my blatant idiocy like a frightened child. He could not warn me without betraying our oath, so instead, he watched, pleading on the sidelines. It also explains the anger and jealousy that burned at Gideon.

Despite the fact that we serve queens whom are sworn enemies, and courts that have sieged war staggered through generations, Emrys and I remained…friends. There were moments in our seclusion when we more than that.

"Ah, Lady Vanora," Emrys steps forward, sketching a coy bow. He winks before rising. "I came to deliver a message on behalf of my queen."

"Evelyn," Aneira begins, her full lips tightening, her ale-yellow eyes betraying her turmoil. "I sent messengers to summon for you. I'm afraid to deliver some dark news."

My stomach clenches but I keep my face blank and stoic. Emrys does not miss my utter lack of emotion and smirks. The stupid bastard knows me, too. I study his striking face, irritated by the distant assessment that he is just as handsome as before.

His face is all angles, his high cheekbones are sharp, his jawline near tortured in its severity, with chiseled cheeks doused in shadows. Golden eyes, too bright to be natural gleam beneath heavy, dark lashes, set in wickedly hooded sockets. A devious smirk graces his full mouth, wide like the slash of a blade and covering sharpened fangs just beyond the sight of his teeth-baring smile. Many do not notice the sharp teeth within his mouth, but if one knows to look, they can see the points peeking from the outer corners of his lips. Though, to be close enough, one must either be a lover or his prey.

I turn my attention from my assessing of the Revenant, now facing my queen. "And what news do you bring, My Queen?"

"The ex-protector hopeful you traveled with…" A bleak sensation settles within my belly, Emrys's eyes widen slightly at Gideon's status. "Gideon Zhao has been taken captive by the Unseelie Court. He is now Caethes's prisoner."

My heart plummets, dropping through my feet and shattering on the floor. Horror crawls up my spine, pouring into the cavity my heart once occupied. His being taken is my fault. Had I not left him alone in the Faerie Roads, he would not have been abducted. He would not have been taken prisoner had Caethes not discovered him stranded in the realm of the fae. If not for I, he would not have been stuck in a situation that left him so compromised by a vengeance-seeking faerie queen.

Immediately, the wheels in my mind turn and I begin to calculate.

"What proof does the messenger bring?" I request levelly, my voice untainted by my emotions.

Aneira reaches for an enamel box that a guard holds, handing it over, Aneira opens it and tilts it to my sights. Nestled inside violet velvet is a lock of black hair, matted with blood, and tied with a ribbon the color of rust. Atop the bundle is something circular and amber.

My breath lodges it my throat. I force myself to look and my lungs deflate. It is not an eye as I had thought. It is a small sphere of amber, but the intention to intimidate is clear.

Hyperventilation threatens to grasp me in its hold, reaching for my throat. I squander the anxiety, forcing it into a chest and padlocking it before burying it below my wall of ice. Putting on my mask, I let contempt crawl across my features, and tilt my chin at my queen.

"With your permission, Your Majesty. I would like to have a private word with the Unseelie messenger." My words are distant, resonating hollowly in my head, but ringing with authority beyond.

Aneira bows her head graciously, gathering the members of her court and ushering them to the flowered gardens where the gold sky plays with the true shade of day. Emrys watches her leave, a dark look following her. Maelona touches my shoulder briefly as she passes, eyes softened as she traverses the smooth stone on silent feet. When the last of the entourage slips through the oak doors, I wheel on Emrys.

"What the hell does Caethes want?" I snarl, eyes flashing dangerously with heartbreak and fear.

Emrys does not miss my overreaction, cocking his angular features. He's tall, taller than I, towering half a foot more than my 5'9". I glare at the gap between us. It is easier to menace when one is level or taller than one. It was easier with Gideon being my height, on par with the level of intimidation.

"Now why in the world would the legendary Harbinger react so *savagely* about a halfling's imprisonment?" Emrys taunts, a delightful gleam in his eyes that I recognize as the joy garnered by torment.

"Do not be evasive, Revenant. We may be friends, but I won't hesitate to gut you if need be."

"Touchy, touchy," Emrys chides, cupping my chin, his expression turning soft. "I saw you, in my court." His voice is solemn, and his eyes are filled with devotion. I swallow against the bile burning in my throat. "I saw how lost you were and there was nothing I could do because you utterly neglected to recognize me."

"Magical amnesia, it was an annoyance since amended."

"Yes, it seems so," his thumb strokes my jaw, brushing my bottom lip, and I can't help but want to fall into the familiar touch. Once upon a time he was my whole world, and I was his. And it kills me that I lost it. "I missed you, Vanna." My heart breaks at his use of my nickname, the one only he uses. "So bloody much. I searched for you. I killed for you. For *years*."

It was him. He was the one hunting down the fae. For me.

For a breath, I forget everything and lean into his warm palm, savoring the presence of my equal. I forget—for a moment—about Gideon. "I've missed you too, even when I haven't wanted to. I didn't remember…I'm still missing crucial moments."

Despite regaining all the memories that the faerie tonic blocked from me, the memories Lady Fate stole from me six years ago remain hidden. It's frustrating, the void that stretches from the end of Century Training, the murky battle we'd fought, even hazier is my screaming at Lady Fate, to empty black before I appeared in the Seelie Court. I'd been covered in blood and shrouded in mystery.

"I know, and for six years you've refused to tell me why—" he bites off his words, his other hand coming to rest on my lower back. "I wish we knew what changed."

"Ryss—"

"I know," he repeats and then he shutters his eyes.

I grit my teeth. "You need to move on, my heart is not yours. It is no one's but mine."

Hurt flashes in his eyes. "Funny you say that." His eyes harden, jealousy turning them jaded. "You say your heart is yours, but I saw the way you looked at that halfling."

"How did I look at Gideon?" I spit, brewing fear turning my voice and eyes feral.

"Like you would throw yourself on a blade for him."

My stomach twists. I would. *I did.*

Arawn swung that sword and I spared no thoughts for my own safety; my only thoughts had been to protect Gideon. Lady Fate had deemed that her blade was not the one to fall, but my own, and my own would never dare turn on me.

The Harbinger's sword is sworn to me. Quenched and tempered in my own blood, imbued with fae magic to tie it to my life. The blade shall never cut me, no matter should I wield it or another. Like a living thing, it senses my aura, my life force, my energy and it knows that I am its master.

Unconsciously, my fingers twitch to the golden blade at my hip and Emrys's eyes follow the gesture. They tighten at the corners, a question there, and I watch the wheels turn as he comes to a conclusion.

Emrys tears his beringed hand away from my jaw as if my skin had scalded him. His eyes are scathing. "I convinced Caethes to send me rather than Tadgh's brother, so I could warn you."

"Why would you do that?"

"Because I want you to pick me."

I freeze, taken aback, heart thundering. "How would warning me about Gideon's impending demise garner my favor?"

He leans in close, his breath smelling of lemon-drop candies. "Because I am the better male and offering you an opportunity to save your lover proves it." He grins and it's forced, and I repress a shudder. Emrys referring to Gideon as my lover feels like a twisting blade. "I am nothing if not fair."

Drawing back, his eyes are stony, still bright, but flat like sunshine on a steep cliffside. He avoids my glare by worrying casually at a thread on his sheer sleeve, amused and infuriating. His garments are black and silver, a pair of form fitting leather pants, a tailored blouse that is nearly see-through revealing the cut lines of his abdomen beneath, and shining boots crossed with extravagant buckles.

"You've given me no opportunity."

"I swear that I've given you the ability to save him. Caethes wished to slay him where he stood and send his rotting corpse to your doorstep. I convinced her this game would lead to much more satisfactory results. You may offer yourself in his exchange, or break him free.

"But hurry quick now, she is not pleased that you sacked her town and ruined her equinox. Caethes gives you until the stroke of midnight upon the summer solstice. If you fail, she intends to tear out and devour Gideon's heart."

I know the threat is not false. Caethes is notorious for eating hearts. Something Evelyn was oblivious to, prior to Elliot's unfortunate end, but the Harbinger is all too aware of the Heart-Eater Queen.

Emrys turns on his shiny booted heel, sauntering towards one of the ivy encased exits. A quarter of the way there, he turns with a mischievous gleam to his eye. "He called for you," he tells me conspiratorially, "after he was stabbed in the chest. Do you wonder what he said when he thought he was dying?"

*Yes. All the power in the universe, yes, I wonder.*

Internally, I plead with him to tell me what Gideon said. The irrational part of my brain begs desperately, like how one suffering withdrawals offers and negotiates anything for the drug they crave. My heart races and my blood blanches, my fear turns suffocating and my longing wild.

Emrys is privy to none of this though, I keep my face calm and composed. Despite the roaring in my ears, I let not a thread of the wildness in my soul show. But I cannot lie so I remain silent.

"No?" he asks, quirking a brow. "Pity, I suppose you'll never know."

And with that, he sweeps from the room, striding through the archway and onto the Faerie Roads.

Alone in the throne room, I collapse on the floor, bowing over the earth. As I kneel there, my dam breaks and the floodwaters drown me beneath their icy depths, their savage siren's song playing the tune to the punishment I deserve.

# CHAPTER 38

With single-minded purpose, I take long determined strides to the valley below the court. My booted steps echo unnervingly in the subterranean depths of the Seelie Court, beneath the less traversed lairs where cobwebs mute the gold of pillars and arches, and dust clouds the lively green of ivy. Here, swaths of spider silk flutter on ancient breezes, glimmering without a shred of dullness and reflecting the jewel-toned light of the stained glass sconces. High above these eerie tunnels, moving landscapes of fae history sprawl above, some memories better left forgotten.

An image of the once amicable alliance between the Unseelie and Seelie Courts leaves a bitter taste in my mouth. Gold and silver mingle and melt, twisting together and bursting with sparks of Unseelie violet and Seelie emerald. The artfully depicted scene enchants in a stylized version of stained glass, sparkling on the picturesque moment of the queens holding hands. Holding a united front.

It swirls away into the first of their wars, painting the ceiling in slashes of scarlet and midnight.

This dawn I'd awoken, mildly bewildered to find the chaise lounge vacant, shocked that Gideon truly is gone. Taken. All of it had come rushing back with waves of disappointment and grief, but I shouldered it and dressed before chasing the first of steps to get that cursed halfling back.

Maelona had mentioned a peculiar joke, teasing about Whitecrest witches, all of whom can read the futures of many in pools of water. I may not be able to read futures in a tumbler of brandy, and I don't have any Whitecrest witches at my disposal, but I do have the cryptic Prophet Witches who reside in the bowels of the earth.

The Prophet Witches do not belong to one singular family, their ability to read prophecies stems from the sacrifices they've made to the realm of the living and the dead. They are unsettling and strange, unnatural and sagacious. They also do not belong solely to any one group, the Unseelie Court has their own Prophet Witches as do the Arcana Society and others powerful organizations.

Creeping down the old stone steps, I'm relieved the air is not dank and wet, but rather misted with hints of wisteria and notes of verbena. When I reach the final stair, I'm startled to see not a traditional oak door, but just a golden archway that leads upon a wild meadow.

The vast cavern of the Stone Vale stretches a hundred feet overhead, speckled with glowing veins of magic, giving the illusion of sunlight seeping through. A thunderous waterfall cascades from the arched ceiling, roaring upon the rocks in the pool below. Shrouded in mist, the rippling pool gives an air of mystique, also glowing from the lake floor with more veins of Seelie magic. Ivy climbs from niches in the rock, fingers twining with pink wisteria, coming down to caress gardens of chrysanthemums.

Nearby, a voice floats and it is ominous and breathy, the sort of crooning that chills the core. My hair stands on end as I decipher the words further.

*Draw your blade, Lady Fate,*
*Hum the tune,*
*Mother, maiden, crow,*

Seated upon a mossy rock is a slight girl, singing, who buries her bare toes in the tangled blades of glass. From what I can see, she is young and beautiful. Clothed in panels of sheer spider silk, her fiery hair tumbles unbound down her back, her porcelain skin dewy with waterdrops. Rosy cheeks as pink as her tender and shapely mouth, curve with serenity. While a sloped nose that ends in a perfect point matches a lovely heart-shaped jaw, I'm stopped beyond that. I could imagine her eyes to be as blue as the pools beyond her, but such wonders are left to the imagination.

Bound tightly by a silk blindfold, the onyx material presses polished black stones to her blind eyes to be covered for eternity. The witch makes a sacrifice of mortal sight to the goddess who gifts her with the ability to open her third eye. With the constant pressure of the stones, the witch can see what

Lady Fate determines in the stars of her minds-eye, constellations that sprawl across the fabric of our world.

"My, my, it has taken the fabled Harbinger much time to visit Sybella," the young-woman begins in a throaty voice, turning her unseeing gaze to my approach.

She's easily a handful of years younger than I am.

I creep forward, eyes calculating all means of exits and methods of potential ambush. The way in which I came in is the only entrance or exit to be found. That is mildly concerning. Still, I continue on, the dewy mist permeating my loose cotton shirt and beading on my leggings.

"Sybella," I say tentatively. "Is that what I may call you?"

"What one may be called is immaterial. But if it pleases Evelyn Vanora, then yes, a girl may call the other Sybella."

The obscure and third-person method in which the witch speaks is unusual and irritating. But I need her, and criticizing her way of speaking is not a progressive form of communication.

"I require your help," I tell her reluctantly. I've always been severely independent, unwilling to accept assistance or teamwork unless absolutely necessary or ordered. Commanding forces have never been a burden, sending warriors to the field never gave me pause. But today, today seems to be hellbent on seeing those tides turn.

As if she can see it, Sybella fingers a chrysanthemum petal, gingerly caressing its edges. "Evelyn has come here to steal back her heart; the Harbinger has come for retribution." She cocks her head to the side. "Which is currently present?"

I exhale a heavy sigh, feeling the deliberation warring in my heart and mind, going back and forth in their battle like a pendulum. The war is won quickly. "Evelyn," I breathe.

"Evelyn understands that an individual may only visit a Prophet Witch once is one's existence to receive such clairvoyance, correct?"

I'd come to the witch with such statements and facts firmly understood and accepted, but even so, I hesitate, knowing that I've only spent twenty-three years of my existence and already I seek a prophecy. Eternity and immortality yawns before me, stretching its ever-reaching fingers into the fringes of the future. I've known fae of centuries who've yet to approach the topic of seeking a prophecy.

I nod minutely before quickly realizing that Sybella cannot see me. "Yes, I understand."

The witch smiles and extends a hand. Taking the upheld palm that remains unmarked and smooth, I clasp our hands together and feel a jolt of electricity at our met magic. The energy pulses like strikes of lightning, burning in my bones.

Just as suddenly, the witch releases the magic, simply holding my cold hand.

"Lady Fate does not wish for Evelyn to receive a prophecy today. She believes it is not your time, nor is it the Harbinger's."

Affronted, I release the witch's palm with an electric shock, aghast, staring at her with a poorly concealed revulsion. I hadn't expected anything flowery and poetic and utopian, but I hadn't expected something like a rejection. I step back once, regaining my composure as Sybella cocks her head to the side, almost as if she can truly see me and is assessing the weakness I currently express.

The girl is more than a head shorter than I am, but she remains intimidating in her otherworldliness, more so than even most of the fae. We stand in silence, the sound of the waterfall thundering distantly from the anxiety thrumming through my soul. My eyes flicker around the valley, searching for perhaps a second opinion, or another to leap out and announce the poor joke I've stumbled into.

But that doesn't happen.

"How could she deny me?" My voice is nearly a snarl, frustration about the lack of prophecy grinding my nerves. I would have taken ambiguity of the fortune rather than this nothingness.

Sybella smiles, a soft, almost pitying smile. "Lady Fate knows what mere mortals and immortals as the fae do not. She knows all and knows that it is not Evelyn Vanora's turn. Though she may allow her daughter some assistance to a cause. Listen to Sybella's words in voice and whisper."

I scoff frustration marring my façade. "This is a matter of lives, my friend's and the very fabric of my own!"

"Lady Fate has set the board, collect the pieces and play the game."

"A *game*? My life isn't a game, she has given me *nothing* to play with."

Sybella grins and something malevolent lingers there. My skin crawls and I suppress a shudder of my spine, holding it ramrod straight. The smile is too white, too wide, too savage.

"No, it is *The* Game."

A trill of true fear skitters through me and for the first time upon this meeting, I am all too grateful of the fact that Sybella is blind. I know that I fail to hide the raw emotions flittering across my face, knowing that even as I square my shoulders, and curl my lip, I wouldn't have fooled the prophetess.

"Lady Vanora already possesses several of the nine pieces, it is her job to decipher who they are and how she can utilize them."

"Who they are? The pieces are people?"

"That is not for Sybella to reveal."

"Then what do I do?"

"It is nigh time that Evelyn departs, it is now time for Sybella to pray. Mayhap a visit from her goddess may bestow a gift upon her daughter." She titters a laugh. "Remember," she tells me, stepping forward without opposition to her surroundings and cups my chin, "collect the pieces and play The Game."

Sybella then turns on dainty toes and slips down to the shore of the undulating lake, traversing the waters easily before slipping beneath its golden glowing depths in a final flash of fiery locks. The lingering mist closes in around the spot, obscuring all evidence that the witch had been present.

As I begin my departure I'm accosted at the edge of the stairs. Before the figure can lay a hand on me, I catch her wrist and hold it aloft.

"What do you think you're doing?" My tone is low and dangerous.

"Bambalina wishes to help." It is another Prophet Witch, this one petite also no more than sixteen and blindfolded with a thick fall of onyx hair. Her skin is ochre and dewy, her fingers delicate and tapered. "Lady Fate showed the witches what Evelyn seeks, but she still harbors contempt from a previous encounter."

I loosen my grip on her, shock laying me flat, and Bambalina slips her forearm away.

"Do you know what she took from me? What her price was?" I ask, my voice tinging desperately.

"No. But what it was, cannot condone this treatment. I do not like what the goddess has done and I wish to rectify it. I do not understand you so, why she wants to keep what she stole." She shakes her head clear. "This will not count as your prophecy should you seek another."

I don't say anything when the Prophet Witch slips from their term of speaking, frankly I'm too stunned to. Never to my knowledge has a Prophet Witch defied their goddess. Never have I realized that the goddess hated anyone. *Could* hate anyone. And that she hates *me*.

Bambalina takes my hands and with a hum of magic her mind begins speaking to me through the ether of the Stone Vale.

> *Rooks are crown and scorn,*
> *She is deceit, hers was apart*
> *Knights are murder and mourn,*
> *She is failure, her grief is heart*
> *Bishops are sacrifice and cost,*
> *She is three, his was death*
> *Royals are found and lost,*
> *She is true, his lies are breath*
> *Pawn—*

A vocal cry tears Bambalina's hands from mine and she stumbles away clutching her head. Another shriek rips from her throat as she crumbles to her knees, rocking back and forth.

"Forgive Bambalina, Merciful Mother," she sobs, breath ragged. "Evelyn Vanora's plight was too much for a girl to ignore. Please, Lady Fate, Bambalina is your devoted daughter, she was wrong to question the goddess so."

Bambalina continues crying while I press myself against the staircase wall in horror. Lady Fate attacked the Prophet Witch for helping me. Because of me the young witch is enduring unimaginable pain. Guilt plagues me but at a loss of what to do, I leave.

As I leave the Stone Vale behind, I realize that the first Prophet Witch toed the line of her goddess's rubrics. Sybella did not bestow me with a prophecy, but a sweeter guidance and directions. What the pieces of such a board may be is not within the inclinations of my mind, but what I do know is that *my life* is The Game. And because of Bambalina's defiance I now have clues as to who each piece is.

# CHAPTER

39

The wind whips harshly against my face as I stand atop the uppermost peak of the Golden Hinde, the largest mountain range on Vancouver Island and one claimed by the Seelie Court and their stronghold. It is not only the hub for the Seelie fae, but also all supernaturals, boasting an outpost of Gideon's Arcana Society upon this very island. The outpost itself is not too far off from the mountain itself, but the haven resides in the United Kingdom. The basalt cliff is a popular tourist spot, but that matters none to me. It is evening and hikers have long since retired from the chill permeating the elevated air, regardless of the spring weather.

Drawing in a deep breath, I taste the snow upon the caps and the untouched lake below. The evergreens are lush and populous, hinting with it their heady scent that penetrates even through winter. Above me, stars begin to burn, making their white-fire presence known.

Gingerly, I unpack a pouch. Earlier I'd returned to the site of Callahan's pyre. It felt like dishonor to leave his ashes in a place he feared and hated. Inside the leather sachet is Callahan's ashes. A loneliness accompanies the gesture that I hadn't anticipated. With black-gloved hands, I release the catch and open the contents to the mountains.

"I know this isn't a Santorini sunset, or the Swiss Alps, and it definitely isn't Thailand. But I found you a mountain and the sun is sinking," I say to the empty air as wind catches ashes and spreads them over the landscape. "This is the tallest point of the Seelie Court territory. I hope that in this form you have the opportunity to see all that you wished. I hope that Amari knows how much you loved her." More ashes lift through the air. "This declaration is probably the last thing you want to hear, especially since it was my own kind that spelled your end, but I want you to know that I'll keep your aspirations and hopes alive. Even if you aren't here to do so."

Emotion burns in my throat as I truly comprehend that someone who'd once put their life on the line of their own free will—one not commanded by a queen or captain—is dead. Someone so selfless and good is gone.

I upturn half the pouch and the wind does not hesitate to grasp and carry. Tears begin to sear my eyes. "I wish I wasn't doing this alone, but I've messed up again, Callahan. I'm supposed to be the legendary Harbinger." I choke on a sob.

"But as of late, all I've done for my status is make legendary screw-ups.

"I got you killed. I got Gideon taken. I wasn't enough for Aberth and Wisteria. I wasn't enough for Corvina. Bambalina was even punished. Because of me, people die." I swallow the thickness in my throat. "I'm so truly sorry and I will never forget the impact you made on my life."

Finally, I upend the rest of the contents, emptying the bag in its entirety. Guilt swims in my gut, a matching sadness and desolation that I deserve. I should have to spend my days repenting for my failures, I shouldn't have days when others were more worthy of them. But Lady Fate has not chosen me, she has chosen them. When every last swirl and bit of ash escapes, I cast away the pouch of leather.

For a while I sit, my thighs burning from the excessive training from the entirety of today's afternoon. For a moment, I'm solitary watching the sky darken, taking the moment just to be alone. Its silent and undemanding. For a moment I have no obligations. For a moment I am just a girl grieving. But I cannot live in a bubble and duty beckons. So, I make the long trek back down the cliffside to an in-between and slip through the Faerie Roads.

I don't know whether it's my imagination, but before I leave the Golden Hinde behind, I swear I hear a thank you on the wind.

# CHAPTER 40

Later, in my emerald chambers, I stand before Maelona, Wisteria, and Julia, the three of them assessing and calculating. Each of the women before me are influential in their own mind and vital to the impending ruination of the Unseelie Court.

I too, am calculating, clinically so. Despite the bonds of friendship that I may seek or hold with these powerful allies, my court and my queen are first. Hastily, I dissolve the thought that intrudes that perhaps there may be one thing—one person—who remains first on my priorities.

Drawing my brows together, I deliberate.

Julia, full of passion and ideals, more than eager for a revolution. She is invaluable with her army of ravens—despite the damage that has dawned upon them. I see the fire in her peculiar eyes, the blue-hazel of her irises burning with years of entrapment and manipulation. I see it in the set of her angular frame, the tension that holds her ramrod straight, the same lines that press her bow-shaped lips into a thin slash.

Wisteria, choked to the brim with mourning and regret, she's all too desperate for revenge. She could be dangerous, should the other side obtain her abilities. Swelling in the tears that ridge her eyes are doubts and fear, such emotions that I must absolve her of in order to further our interests. She has drawn into herself, pulled her elegant limbs to her chest, her dark eyes turned to wells of numbness and depression. Every now and then her lip will wobble.

And Maelona. Loyal to the core and near unequaled. Fearless in battle, brave with her iron, and willing to prove her worth. Her ties to the warriors of the Seelie Court and knowledge of the past three years of strategy will aid in the commanding of forces. Despite her composed stature and relaxed mask, her hair betrays her, shimmering a bright, burnished orange with excitement. Threads of gold weave between the brilliant strands, betraying the happiness that ekes out.

Pacing the woven gold rug beneath my booted feet, I consider options before announcing my plans. I take stock of my advantages over the Unseelie Queen, counting them carefully and storing their benefit for later use.

Caethes does not know that I am the Harbinger. She does not know of Gideon's commands over me. She does not know the despoliation depths of odium that fuel the residents of Aberth. She is not aware of the partial prophecy I possess.

Nor does she realize that I hold her precious Revenant's affections in my corner.

She does, however, know about Wisteria's unprecedented ability. Caethes may attempt whatever is in her power to obtain such magic for herself, and that is why for her own safety, she must heal and be protected at all costs.

"Why are we all here?" Julia asks, breaking the silence. My gaze comes to rest on her, her face carved into a facsimile of comfort as she lounges on the chaise with a knee drawn up. It is the same chaise that Gideon had slept on.

A pang of misery strikes me.

I squash it down.

"I had been wondering quite the same," Maelona says.

"Faerie, you told me we'll take down the Unseelie Queen, when is that going to happen?" Wisteria inquires with a certain disdain in her positioning as she shifts away from Julia. I frown briefly. Well, that could be a problem. The root of that issue needs to be investigated before commencing any strategy.

I add that to my ever-lengthening to-do list.

"That isn't why I've gathered you all."

"Oh?" Maelona leans forward, turquoise hair shimmering in peaked curiosity.

I pause before the three, meeting eyes of fudge, teak, and ocean.

With a grin, I begin, announcing the first steps to enacting the actions Sybella and Bambalina granted me. "Tonight, we begin our undermining of the Unseelie Court. Tonight, we start with the announcement that I am the *Ceidwad Cudd*."

The throne room is wild with celebration, the grand oak doors pushed wide open to the garden, revealing golden rays that move in undulating waves through the true night sky. Musicians coax melodies that incite tears and passions in equal measure, eliciting plucking notes of strings and vocals that sensationalize and devastate.

All members of the Seelie Court amble and waltz across the polished floor, faeries and those of other supernatural origin mill about, proudly boasting their loyalties to my queen. Ruby-eyed vampires weave with their elegant grace through the throng, nursing flutes of blood. A few quick-footed werewolves lunge in a predatory dance, one that faeries find enchanting and enthralling. Then there are the witches, lingering at the fringes in their finery with a few Familiars—shadow animals—hovering nearby or perching on shoulders. Witches are the most at risk to our faerie magic, they are too close to human for the protection extended to their lycanthropic and vampiric counterparts. Though, the newly allied humans dot the crowd, Aberth's citizens are inquisitive and safely under the protection of Aneira's rule.

I snag a flute of champagne from a passing waiter, downing it and depositing it upon another's tray. Tonight, I am dressed both of two ways. I dress as Evelyn and the *Ceidwad Cudd*, yet none know of my ulterior side, yet. I grace these halls under a guise of elegance when in truth, I live under duress. It is a maximum stress but concealed beneath a layer of dark makeup—thickly lined eyes and richly painted lips. Furthering my emotional armor are the spiked shoulder pieces and decorative golden chains that sweep from shoulder to elbow with black and gold spider-silk clinging to and enhancing every small curve I possess. Drawn up in a severe tail is my silvery hair, pulled tight and high up upon my crown, highlighting my angular features.

I glide among the party-goers, skirting a witch's Familiar or two, and threading my way to Julia, finding her enthralled in conversation with a winged fae. I show my teeth in a mockery of a smile as I near the raven-haired faerie.

"Drysi, may I borrow Julia for a moment?"

Drysi purses her full, dark lips while her mercury eyes glitter with displeasure. "But of course, Lady Vanora." And with that she sweeps her deep blue skirts, the fabric shimmering around her long, pale legs, her sheet of black hair whipping my side as she goes. I roll my eyes. For someone nearing their tenth decade, she sure acts like a petty teenager. Though, you'd never be able to guess, as she hardly looks a day past twenty-five.

Julia quirks a brow. "I sense some animosity between you two."

"Bad blood," I dismiss. "I wanted to speak to you, about your *group*. What do you call them?"

She peeks a smile from beneath her goblet. "We were just rebels, but I believe the term Crows has stuck. Maelona seems to find it fitting," she tells me, indicating the dress she wears. It is a sleek black gown of feathers, with a plunging neckline, courtesy of Maelona's extravagant closets. "The Lady also believes that I can design better uniforms. Of course, she isn't wrong. I own a clothing boutique for crying out loud, not to mention I've always wanted to be a designer. But that isn't what you wanted to talk about, is it?"

"Are you willing to use them against Caethes? Humans are always an advantage in fae wars, what with your abilities of lying and iron tolerance."

Julia smiles, her smoky eyes darkening with the intent as her ruby lips pull into a true smile, excitement visibly vibrating through her nerves. "Oh, we wouldn't miss it for the world."

"Good," I tell her, plucking two flutes from a golden tray. I pass her the slender crystal. "Then to us and your Crows."

Our glasses clink and we drink. Fuzziness comfortably settles in my limbs, the bubbly hitting as it should, especially with my excessive drinking tastes as of late. With instructions for the following day, I depart from the leader of the Crows.

Nearby, Maelona converses with a vampire, her tone is sultry but her words sharp. A glitter of menace trims her eye, and a cruelty lines her luscious, red mouth. People forget Maelona's prowess. She is a terrifying creature to behold, having led more than one bloodbath and drank her fill of the chaos like an Unseelie would.

"I shouldn't fear for my blood, just as you shouldn't fear for your life during our encounters, no?" Maelona asks, trailing a titanium clawed finger down the vampire's chest, the jewelry catching the light. She visibly quakes and I realize that the Lady may be too much for the poor thing to handle. Pity, vampires are lovely to look at—save for when they hunt and unhinge their jaws. I smile and slide away.

Striding through the crowd with a smirk to my mouth, I hover close to my queen, waiting for her signal. I worry for her despite the fact that she is surrounded by guards, even so, she has been like a mother to me. A mother to Corvina.

Nothing like our birth mother.

Pursing my lips, I push the thoughts from my mind, covering the pain with what would be construed as displeasure. When Aneira finds me, she gives a single nod and I ascend the staircase with ease. As I come up to her, the guards split to allow my passage. She holds my gaze and clasps my shoulder, her eyes are kind, warm and sunny, shining with pride. But she shutters the familial warmth before urging me forward, ahead to the front of the dais. Her six guards who've replaced the Harbinger converge behind me and suddenly I am very much at the forefront.

Voices quiet into whispers, trickles of conversation drying up as I behold the attention of all without uttering a single syllable. In this moment, I am the focus of the ball, I am influential, and beautiful, and utterly unchallenged in my power.

My heels click upon the polished stone and that is the final sound before is speak.

"Tonight, I am here before you all. Before each and every one of you loyally pledged to Queen Aneira Gwyndolyn of the Light Court," I begin the declaration, my throaty voice reverberating throughout the throne room, spiraling out to the open and false ceiling. I ensure they do not forget who and what they owe allegiance to. "I am here to publicly announce a secret I've harbored for many years. Here, I reveal to you that I, Evelyn Corianne Vanora of the Seelie Court, am the *Ceidwad Cudd*."

Gasps and startled exclamations pepper the room, a few snarls break up the shock and many of a sort stumble or reach for another glass of champagne or gold wine. Near the edges of the witches, Wisteria stands apart, a distant beacon among all the gold. She is grinning with an undying thirst, still having hadn't changed out of her hooded sweater that boasts a cult-like symbol, but is more likely a band logo, and leggings combo—surprising, since I met her as such a party-girl. Maelona leans against a pillar at the back of the room, a tilted crown of icicles upon her brow. She winks, toasting her indigo goblet that is an identical shade to her gown. In the center Julia puts on her façade, playing her part, bedecked in the feathers of her leadership namesake.

I push on, past the exclamations that are undoubtedly coming, of accusations against me for betraying the Seelie Court, what with my being a spy, but I do not let them evoke it into existence.

"I had been taken captive and abandoned in the Unseelie Lands. Left to *rot* without my memories. Forced to bear a glamour. There, I learned about the Unseelie Court and their machinations. There, I met the Unseelie Queen, and there, she took what is rightfully ours." My gaze sharpens, my arctic eyes cutting through every soul, sharp as ice. "She stole a halfling emissary of the Seelie Court and had a hand in the Harbinger's disappearance."

My lips pull back from my teeth in a feral snarl, revealing too white teeth.

Intrigue through the court heightens, curious listeners leaning in to catch my every last breath. Low level guards fanned throughout the room straighten at attention, they too are eager. The air vibrates with nervous energy, filled with the scent of wine-soaked breath and too-close bodies.

"Tonight, on behalf of Queen Aneira Gwyndolyn, I am here to formally declare that we are at war with the Unseelie Queen."

# CHAPTER 41

After the cacophony of cheers disturbed the tension of the throne room, I took my leave, smiling that I've gifted the Seelies with the opportunity of a fair bloodbath. Faerie wars are messy, dirty, and underhanded under polite pretenses.

I am not sad for the impending war. The Unseelie Queen initiated the first act by kidnapping Gideon and sending her evidence of political betrayal as a gift. It was undeniable proof. Gideon formally allied himself with my court after Ghislain tattooed our sigil upon his wrist with the emissary addition of an "E" atop the circle surrounding the ivy, moon, and flower. It was only chance that the Seelie Court had a single opening for non-fae emissaries, only allowing seven at a time. Quite the unfortunate occurrence to the Unseelies that they cannot see a sigil they are not loyal to.

It makes it easy for the Courts to declare war crimes.

One lovely tidbit of faerie law is that non-fae emissaries are illegal to touch by the other court, kidnapping or murder of one is grounds for war. Humans exempt. Gideon, unknowing of himself, is an emissary—a favor I'd asked of Ghislain for the halfling's own protection, and the faerie obliged. I was certain Gideon would not accept my help, not after I obliterated whatever was between us, so I had to be clever and save him the ways I am capable of—through distance, of course. By my request, in theory, Gideon is—or rather was—untouchable unless the Dark Court decided to incite war. Mistakenly, they did.

In my chambers, I perch at the edge of my chaise lounge, tugging an onyx heel from my newly aching feet. On my arch is hardly a scar, the glass from the cabin fire having cut as deep as I'd originally thought, but courtesy of my fae nature, it's completely healed. I'd lost some of the resilience to such footwear during my entrapment in the Yukon. Useless and ridiculous design they are, though handy for puncturing eyeballs if need warrants it.

"*You knew,*" an enraged voice booms from the window.

I turn, a smirk painted upon my deep, red lips. There, Emrys stands before the open stained-glass pane, another sheer black shirt billowing against the furious figure—this one with lace silhouettes of peonies and azaleas. His golden eyes are fierce and angry, his severe jaw clamped, nostrils flaring. Beside him, his hands are claws as he steps toward me.

"You knew that your stupid halfling was a member of Aneira's court and that taking him would lead to my side starting a war. On a *technicality*."

I shrug. I hadn't meant for my leaving Gideon on the Faerie Roads to be used as an instrument to this war, but I had to turn disaster into our advantage. All my allies were all too willing to help.

"Would that have stopped you from taking him?" I ask nonchalantly, pulling the other stiletto from my foot.

"Of course, it would have!" he explodes.

"Pity."

"You're infuriating."

"At least it gave you an excuse to sneak into my chambers."

And suddenly Emrys races forward. In the blink of an eye, he is before me, and I react, stepping forward and locking his arm behind him. He wriggles out of it and before I can take him in the next move, he's shoving me down against the chaise lounge. My spine slams into the cushions, his hands pinning me down. The legs scrape across the polished floor, tracking black streaks three inches long.

I laugh, pressing my high-heeled shoe to his throat, stiletto nearly brushing his smooth skin. I flick a pearl and a blade whips out, the tip puncturing the soft underside of his jaw. A small bead of blood slips from his throat, the trail painting a line the same shade as his hair.

Not entirely useless, after all.

"You'd do well to remember that you are forbidden from killing me in my own court, the same that I am prohibited to kill you in yours," I tell him, voice sultry as I watch the blood leak slowly from the new wound.

"Ah, yes, our Century Training law. Seems it's difficult to keep up with all your identities, *Harbinger*. Or shall I call you the *Ceidwad Cudd?*" he snarls, not leaving his hovering position as he traps me against my lounge, his long legs tangled in the silk slits of my gown. His dark ruby hair is tousled and hanging about his face, cutting bloody lines on his cheekbones.

I knew him through all my identities. I'd seen him in passing as the *Ceidwad Cudd,* as I collected secrets and made allies in the Unseelie Court while determining enemies in the Seelie Court. I'd recognized him when we'd been thrust into Century Training. I've known him ever since. I knew him before. I know him now.

Not of my own volition, wetness pools between my legs, heat aching in the center of me. I can feel my muscles tensing, blood rushing through my body as arousal surges. The powerful grip of his hands on my shoulders pushing me into the cushion strikes a thrilling chord within me. So much want burns through me, a desperate, aching need.

*What a compromising position one could find us in.*

"Regardless, we are at an impasse."

"I gave you hope for your halfling, and you threw it back at me."

"No, you wrote him a death sentence and gave me the letter."

His eyes soften in sadness, a vulnerability I can only read due to spending a false hundred years with him. He lifts a hand from one of my bruising shoulders, bringing a long, slender finger down the length of my jaw. I stiffen, inhaling sharply with a twitch in my jaw. A second finger joins the first, his knuckles skimming my cheek. Memories unfold and I recoil inwardly in surprise. "Why him?" he asks, desolation bleeding in the tone. "What about me?"

I unfurl a lip from my teeth and bare those pearly whites at him. "*Leave.* Before I decide to put this stiletto through your jugular."

"Vanna," he begs softly, that nickname my undoing. His burning eyes searing me with matched arousal. I feel a distinct, familiar hardness pressing into me. It is fire through me, his touch, his very presence. His fingertips grip my jaw, turning it to the side as he dips his lips to my throat, trailing his breath along the column. "Tell me you don't feel this between us." His sharp teeth nip me and he soothes the small hurt with a press of his mouth and my eyes roll back in my head, a flick of pleasure coiling in my core. "Please just answer me once."

Hazy with a rush of ecstasy, the stiletto tumbles from my grasp, falling away from his throat while I allow him his perusal of mine. He trails his lips lower, dragging sultry kisses down my chest and between my breasts. His breath smells of lemon and whiskey, his skin of vetiver and leather. Caught in the moment, my hand finds the small of his back, digging my fingers into the muscles I once knew so well. My fingertips slip beneath his shirt and trace his ridged abdomen, slipping higher until I find his smooth chest.

He moans low in his throat and a memory spills into my thoughts. Remembering that husky sound so many years ago as he pressed me against stones and fisted his hands in my hair. I remember the want, the need.

"What do you want to ask me, Emrys?" I ask breathy, luxuriating in the familiarity of this male. Moments flashing beneath my lids, stolen memories eager to return. This feels so right, but why does something feel missing?

I slide my fingers across his chest, grazing his nipple, nails scratching until I stop on the scar over his heart.

"Why did you stop loving me the day I died for you?"

The moment is shattered like an ax to ice. I freeze, shoving Emrys off of me.

"I've told you before," I snarl, angry and embarrassed. Loathing myself. "I never loved you."

If you could see a person's heart in their eyes, then I could always see Emrys's beat in his golden depths. It's how I know in that moment that I shattered it. That my words plunged a blade into his soul and twisted. The agony that fills his gaze strikes anguish through my entire being and for a breath I feel so utterly empty. Turned into a husk. And I realize that it is my fault, and that is exactly what I've done to him.

He leaps off of me with cat-like grace, disgust warring with sadness over his cruelly lovely features. "I could kill him." His voice is cold. Detached.

I pull myself up, a leg dangling off the edge of the chair, my other planted on the cushion. I channel every ounce of self-hatred and use it as a shield, slipping on a mask, and donning it like armor. "You could've before, but not now. Not since you swore to me earlier. The bargain stays and you leave."

"I think you've made a mistake."

"And I think you're wrong."

"There's no need to birth this war between us two. We could join forces, we could destroy and remake this world if we wanted to."

"Not when Caethes designed a town of annual sacrifice. I will not be associated with a night of annihilation and murder." I grit my teeth. "Not when it was her fault that I was butchered and abandoned in a wasteland."

"Vanna," he whispers pleadingly. "I just found you, I can't lose you again."

"Good bye, Emrys."

"Please, Vanna…you are my reason for living." Tears burn in his eyes.

"Then die."

Emrys inhales sharply, mouth thinning and devastation written across every line of his body. With that, he turns on a polished-booted heel and leaps through the open window, knocking a white vase to the floor. It shatters, glass gliding across the floor.

The moment he leaves I drop to the floor and sob.

I am a cruel, horrible monster.

How can Emrys say I loved him, yet he cannot lie?

My heart must be stone because how can I destroy a male whose heart bleeds for me so clearly? His every adoration painted across his face and dripping from every word. How could I abandon a lover in the Faerie Roads with no hope of getting out? I was so petty and angry that I wanted him to hurt and fear like I did. How can I keep Maelona on a hook, giving and taking without promises of a future? Trysts and moments and secrets and truths.

I am a mess. I am confused. And I have no idea what I want.

The sobs wrack my chest, carving out my soul. Black runs from my face, the tears sliding down my cheeks like poison. I hate myself. I hate every fucking moment I hurt everyone around me. I am a disease and my contagion is killing.

I am not whole and I curse Lady Fate for it all. Emrys believes I loved him, yet I cannot remember any moment I spoke the words. I know he fucking died for me and *I can't remember it*. I know she took something. I know I traded something for his life and I curse this broken memory.

Reaching for a bottle of gold wine, I find a neck and drink. The bottle is empty. With a furious yell I throw it at the wall where it smashes to pieces. I watch the wet shards flicker in the light and for a moment I can't find breath. What if I'm like that bottle? Irrevocably irreparable. The air I manage is wheezy, it is tight and strangling.

I wait a few heartbeats, counting down from my panic, moving to the window for fresh air. Minutes later I'm returned and I manage to close the window and move to my bedside drawer. Within the drawer is the box from Emrys, all the evidence I needed to initiate this war. A last piece of Gideon that I'd lifted from one of Aneira's guards—they must really be trained better if they cannot detect a pickpocket of that magnitude.

Clutching the box, I carry it like it's the most fragile thing in the universe. Dropping onto the chaise lounge, I open the clasp once again to find the jet-black lock of Gideon's silky hair and the amber stone that nearly identically matches the irises of his eyes. Those beautiful eyes. Dropping my brow to the box, curling over it as if I could protect him—as if I could have if I'd not been so negligent—and make an oath, dropping every whispered word like a prayer at the altar.

"I will find you. I will bring you back. I swear it."

I'm utterly alone. I haven't felt so alone and empty in so long, not since Gideon came tearing into my life like a hurricane. His absence is painfully evident. Emrys's departure a new wound in my heart. I truly am ruined. I am not the Harbinger of legend…not anymore.

I am what remains. Broken and fragile.

After a short time, I tuck the box beneath the chaise lounge, up inside the lining that I'd ripped specifically for the purpose of hiding precious goods. Once I finish, I sigh, wiping away the ruined makeup before going over to clean up the broken glass left by Emrys's departure and my despair. Staring down at the water and liquor-soaked shards that gibe me, I realize that Lady Fate is calling out my impending doom.

Sybella's song.

Bambalina's prophecy.

Had Emrys and I not both reiterated identical statements? Of what is lost and found? Of death and murder?

My heart races as I realize that Sybella nearly defied her mother goddess too, that she truly did deliver a sliver of prophecy. If I own already several of the pieces, are those pieces spelled in her song? It is not a song I'd ever heard before.

*Draw your blade, Lady Fate,*
*Hum the tune,*
*Mother, maiden, crow,*

Could those three characters be connected to Bambalina's prophecy?

*Rooks are crown and scorn,*
*She is deceit, hers was apart*
*Knights are murder and mourn,*
*She is failure, her grief is heart*
*Bishops are sacrifice and cost,*
*She is three, his was death*
*Royals are found and lost,*
*She is true, his lies are breath*
*Pawn—*

I count and realize that there are nine characters mentioned in Bambalina's prophecy. There are two of each piece but several pawns, which means that there is only one pawn, or only one pawn is important. *Crow* and *murder* and *failure* can only mean Julia, so it stands to reason the girl is a knight. That leaves eight more to decipher. Are the royals referring to the queens? If so, what does crown mean?

My mind begins twisting itself into knots when a niggling truth strikes me. Sybella's words.

*My life is The Game.*

I draw myself up, leaving the glass behind and gather a pair of boots and sheath my sword. As I leave my chamber behind, I know that the clock is ticking and Lady Fate's knife is poised at the ready.

# EPILOGUE

The moment I step outside my chambers, my mental alarm pings. Only around the corner from my home is a faerie lingering, lying in wait on the emerald runner. I pluck a blade from my boot and with practiced nonchalance, I round the oak-walled bend and brandish the blade.

My eyes alight on the intruder and rare surprise floods through me. Mercury eyes widen ever so, but the tell is hidden as the faerie leans against the wall, careful not to pin her wings, as she folds her arms.

"Drysi, what are you doing here?" I demand, tension thrumming between us. My lip curls without my own volition and my nostrils flare, betraying the potent emotion. The bad blood is surging and boiling in my veins, narrowing to a focal point. Red is all I can see.

"Going somewhere?" she quips, ignoring my poor concealment, and eyeing the thigh high slit in my black and gold gown that reveals the thigh sheath and tall boots done up with wicked buckles. They're knee high and thick soled, worthy of face-stomping nature.

"That isn't any of your concern."

"Can't a mother worry for her daughter?"

"You are *not* my mother in any way that matters, Aneira is. You lost that privilege twenty-three years ago." My voice is a snarl and to any lesser fae it would have terrified. Unfortunately for me, Drysi does not scare easily. Reluctantly, that is one thing I'm happy to have inherited from the other faerie.

"I carried you—"

"Just because you birthed me doesn't mean you deserve the title. If you were a true mother, you wouldn't have abandoned me."

Upon the birth of her twins, Drysi left, naming us and dumping both Corvina and I at Aneira's feet. She ran off, allegedly hunting down a coven of witches without an explanation to be made, and was never seen again until the year I left for Century Training. I met her only three months before I departed and I had no interest in the woman who never cared enough for me. In my false century I spent decades brewing with resentment, using such fury to power me through lessons. Only Emrys was the wiser to the loathing that fueled me.

"Did you even notice that your other daughter is *dead*?" I throw the words, hissing them like insults.

Corvina always tried harder, wanting to be loved by Drysi. But she was too busy. It was sad too, watching the girl that was so much an echo of the elder. Drysi has the same jet-black hair that Corvina did, falling in a sleek sheet the same way mine stubbornly falls. Her eyes are the same arctic silver as my own, feline as both her twins. My lips are fuller though, Corvina's cheekbones higher, our features lightly softened from whatever genetics our father gave us. He was a man we'd never met, never likely to, nor has Drysi mentioned.

"Did you hear me? Corvina is *dead*."

There is only silence. Drysi's lips thin into a pursed line, her eyes glassy, her jaw clenched tight. She didn't know. She didn't realize. That's how absent of a mother she was. How absent she is. I hope guilt and regret plague her. I hope she mourns and punishes herself every day.

"How?" she finally manages, her voice rough.

"She was murdered by Unseelies."

She's quiet, her eyes downcast at the magnificent gown she wears. Corvina would have loved it. Grand and bedecked with diamonds that seem to have fallen like raindrops. "I didn't know."

"That's kind of the point of abandonment," I tell her brusquely.

"I'm here now."

I laugh. The sound humorless and blunt. "So, what does that mean? You can't resurrect her."

"I want to help."

I stare at her. Silence stretches between us, our matching glacial eyes frozen in a deadlock, the mercury hardening with our stare. I begin to calculate, weighing my odds. She's a talented warrior, not as adept as myself nor Maelona, but still ferocious in her own right. I don't have to like her as family, but in a battle, she is someone I'd trust at my side. Drysi has a long bloody history, and despite appearing frozen in her twenties, she's that five times over. If she can assist in the takedown of Caethes, who am I to stop simply on private grounds of personal grudges?

"Why?" I ask, authority in my tone. If this is to ever be considered, she shall not forget that I am her superior.

"Because you have a noble cause," she answers simply, her thick, black lashes bowing as she tilts her head in submission.

I try not to be disappointed. She isn't driven by some twisted maternal instinct. Nor a latent one either. Just for her queen. Our queen. It's a start, knowing that despite all odds I'd still hoped, still harbored a small spark that maybe, just maybe…But that's just foolish and I shall not make the same mistake. Letting none of this inner turmoil show, I bare my teeth. It is not a smile.

"Let me make this clear, you are not here in any capacity as my mother. I do not forgive you but I value you as a warrior and I will treat you as such. Understood?"

"Yes."

"Don't hold me back," I say as I stride past her. The elder faerie follows me, gathering a few items for herself and then to the Faerie Roads and Yukon beyond.

The Yukon is doused into blackness. The trees around us are so painfully familiar, as equally a prison as they were my salvation. Twisted nostalgia strikes me, reminding me of everything done the past two years. Reminding me of my human side that I was forced to stare through until Gideon intervened.

We've transported to a swath of evergreens, whose canopy obscures what sliver of moonlight that should have been visible. I sigh and produce Oath-Sworn from my hip, whispering a single word to the sword.

"*Golau.*" The golden blade erupts with a pillar of golden light, the magic of the Seelies, the same magic that bound my blood to the sword. It sends every pine needle in stark illumination, tossing blinding light against the curtain of dark. Wielding the blade above my head, I begin to search the area around us, Drysi at my side.

"You informed me we were here to find something. What such object do you seek?" Drysi asks, twirling a wickedly curved scythe between her fingers.

"Not something," I tell her, assessing. "Someone."

I close my eyes, prodding at my internal alarm and extending it outward with eager fingers. I spread the sixth-sense far and wide, praying for the hit that will aid me in my endeavor against the Unseelie Court. A headache begins to throb at my temples with the mental strain, but still I push.

There. At the fringes of my ability I sense the vampire. Grinning, I set off, Drysi following obediently behind. We easily leap over rocks and roots, skirting brush and thorns, leaping a trickle of a stream and come up upon a young woman.

Violante whirls at our presence, hissing a startled sound. Blood rushes to her eyes, boldening the shade and swelling in the veins around her eyes. She looks just the same as before, dark brown hair that is ever so slightly hued by purple, scarlet eyes that glow orange under the golden gaze of Oath-Sworn, and fangs that lengthen into sharpened points. She wears a tattered blouse that might've been white at one point, and a pair of blue-jeans, ill-fitting upon her slight frame. Still, she remains barefoot.

"We meet again," I tell the young vampire. She's frozen at sixteen, exactly the age that Wisteria was when she lost her best friend.

"Please, I don't want to hurt you," she begs, clutching her cross, the broken chain dangling from her fist.

"You won't hurt us, Violante. We've come to rescue you from this place."

"How do you know my name?"

"We have a friend in common."

"I can't," she whimpers, a faint accent on her tongue. "I'm cursed here, they'll hunt me down and then catch me. They'll kill Wisty."

Internally I cringe at the name Violante uses. Wisty is what Elliot called his girlfriend. Elliot, who will never again see the woman he loved. A flare of blame attempts to settle through me, but I throw it from my shoulders. I do not need that shame.

"No, she won't. We'll protect you and we have Wisteria already."

Violante pauses, her fangs slowly disappearing back into her mouth, the blood draining away. "Wisty is safe?"

"Yes," I tell her, stepping forward, Oath-Sworn still overhead, its weight a burden on my muscles. I must train more.

Tossing an object toward Violante, she locks in on the bag of blood before her, not able to resist the allure. Tearing into the blood bag, she drinks greedily, not spilling a drop. Within seconds, the bag is drained and the girl's teeth are stained red.

Violante averts her gaze, color burning high in her cheeks. "She used me—Caethes, I mean—for years. Once I'd been picked from the lottery, I became her scout. I had to tell her of everyone stuck here, to keep track. I couldn't leave my cave in the summers and she threatened more frequent hunts in the winters. I reported to her about all the lost souls." Her eyes flicker to mine. "Including you. Two years ago, you were in one of my caves."

I blanch and my heart freezes.

I'd watched the sheets of rain fall, frazzled by nerves and drugged by adrenaline. Through a haze of pain and exhaustion I'd stared out beyond the mouth of the cave, swearing I'd seen ruby eyes. I'd sworn it was a trick of the light because when I blinked the eyes were gone.

But I was right. I did see ruby eyes. I saw Violante's eyes.

"Is there anyone left out here now?" Drysi interjects, her sleek hair now braided back and pulled into a crown around her skull.

Violante bites her lip. "Not that I have seen."

"Okay, good. Let's go, we'll keep you safe. Caethes will never touch you again."

She nods, lip quivering, and gathers her feet beneath her as she sets out with us.

I draw in a breath, both Drysi and Violante behind me, unknowing of all the mixed eagerness vibrating beneath my skin. Of recruiting Violante away from Caethes during the inception of this war. Of earning Wisteria's trust in order to follow Bambalina's prophecy and Sybella's song.

Here, under the veil of midnight and canopy of evergreens, I begin collecting the final pieces of the board.

THE
END

# PRONUNCIATION GUIDE

## CHARACTERS

Evelyn: EVAH-LINN
Gideon: GID-EE-UN
Maelona: MAE-LOW-NA
Aneira: AH-NAY-YA
Caethes: KI-THES
Violante: VEE-OH-LAN-TAY

Emrys: EM-RISS
Tegwyn: TEGG-WIN
Tadhg: TAIG
Róisín: RO-SHEEN
Arawn: AIR-RAWN

## OTHER

*Ceidwad Cudd*: KAI-YD-WAH COO
Aberth: AH-BEH-TH

# ACKNOWLEDGEMENTS

Writing this book was a journey and I can't believe I'm finally saying these words and this book is in your hands.

Thank you to my husband, Michael, I truly could not have done this without you. You encouraged me to self-publish years before it happened, ready to do whatever it took to make this dream a reality. I love you.

A huge round of thank you's to Rebecca F. Kenney, you were the first to ever read this mess of a book several drafts ago and I'll never forget you calling me "The Queen of Plot Twists". Thank you for basically holding my hand through this process and helping me with every annoying question I asked, I really appreciate it.

(2025 ADDITION: Thank you eternally to Bookish Averil for these GORGEOUS covers. I'm absolutely in love with them and you brought my characters to life.)

To Ali, (aka Whore for Mor), thank you for the endless enthusiasm—especially about a certain love interest—and catching all of my truly embarrassing grammatical and spelling errors. Also, the ruthless editing was needed. I treasured every text and shamelessly used it for self-promo, thanks.

Thank you to Catherine Labadie, ('cause no one supports you like an internet friend you've never met), for hyping me up every step of the way, sharing and liking every book related post I made, for sending me memes and sharing motherhood struggles. (This isn't the book we discussed, but just know certain scenes wouldn't exist without you.) Ily bby.
To my brother, Brandon, who thinks I'm going to get rich from this, I love the faith—however misguided—you have in me.
My parents, thank you for everything and for buying this book, but dad, please don't read it.
Vivienne, you didn't do anything but you are everything. I love you.
Thank you to every person who shared any promotional material for This Broken Memory, for taking an interest and for pre-ordering or ordering it, and urging me on to do this.
And finally, thank YOU, Dear Reader, for reading this book. Thank you for supporting this passion of mine. I hope you love Evelyn, Gideon, Maelona, Emrys, and Wisteria as much as I do and hope you decide to find out what happens in book two and how everything is going to change.

Kayla McGrath has been writing since the age of thirteen out of spite, having read a book with a love triangle that didn't go her way. After that, it became a passion. If she's not writing, then she's reading, or drinking endless cups of chai. Kayla lives on Vancouver Island with her husband, daughter, and two boxers.

This Broken Memory is her debut book.

You can find her on TikTok (@kaylamcgrath_), and on Instagram (@kaylamcgrathbooks).

**COLD AS IRON**
This Broken Memory
These Ruined Dreams
Our Shattered Fates

**A DEATHLESS EMPIRE**
A Deathless Empire
AUQ {Coming 2026!}

**INFERNAL CURSES**
The Nightmare Curse
The Hallow Curse

**LOVE AND OTHER TROPES**
Love & Other Tropes (Emmett & Illiana)
Romance Thy Enemy (Mina & Graham)
JTW (Nate & Sloane) {Coming 2026!}